SAMANTHA MOON
FOREVER

SAMANTHA MOON
FOREVER

BOXED SET

J.R. RAIN

Samantha Moon Forever

Published by J.R. Rain

Copyright © 2014 by J.R. Rain

All rights reserved.

ISBN-10: 1512043710

ISBN-13: 9781512043716

ACCLAIM FOR THE NOVELS OF J.R. RAIN:

"Be prepared to lose sleep!"
—**James Rollins**, international bestselling author of *The Altar of Eden*

"I love this!"
—**Piers Anthony**, international bestselling author of *A Spell for Chameleon*

"J.R. Rain delivers a blend of action and wit that always entertains. Quick with the one-liners, but his characters are fully fleshed out (even the undead ones) and you'll come back again and again."
—**Scott Nicholson**, bestselling author of *Chronic Fear*

"*Dark Horse* is the best book I've read in a long time!"
—**Gemma Halliday**, bestselling author of *Spying in High Heels*

"*Moon Dance* is absolutely brilliant!"
—**Lisa Tenzin-Dolma**, author of *Understanding the Planetary Myths*

"Powerful stuff!"
—**Aiden James**, bestselling author of *Plague of Coins*

"*Moon Dance* is a must read. If you like Janet Evanovich's Stephanie Plum, bounty hunter, be prepared to love J.R. Rain's Samantha Moon, vampire private investigator."
—**Eve Paludan**, author of *Witchy Business*

OTHER BOOKS BY J.R. RAIN

STANDALONE NOVELS
The Lost Ark
Elvis Has *Not* Left the Building
The Body Departed
Silent Echo
Winter Wind

SHORT STORY SINGLES
The Bleeder

VAMPIRE FOR HIRE
Moon Dance
Vampire Moon
American Vampire
Moon Child
Christmas Moon
Vampire Dawn
Vampire Games
Moon Island
Moon River
Vampire Sun
Moon Dragon

SAMANTHA MOON SHORT STORIES
Teeth
Vampire Nights

Vampires Blues
Vampire Dreams
Halloween Moon
Vampire Gold
Blue Moon
Dark Side of the Moon

JIM KNIGHTHORSE SERIES
Dark Horse
The Mummy Case
Hail Mary
Clean Slate
Night Run

JIM KNIGHTHORSE SHORT STORIES
Easy Rider

THE WITCHES TRILOGY
The Witch and the Gentleman
The Witch and the Englishman
The Witch and the Huntsman

THE SPINOZA TRILOGY
The Vampire With the Dragon Tattoo
The Vampire Who Played Dead
The Vampire in the Iron Mask

THE AVALON DUOLOGY
The Grail Quest
The Grail Knight

SHORT STORY COLLECTIONS
The Bleeder and Other Stories
The Santa Call and Other Stories
Vampire Rain and Other Stories

THE VAMPIRE DIARIES
Bound By Blood

SCREENPLAYS
Dark Quests

Co-Authored Books

COLLABORATIONS
Cursed! (with Scott Nicholson)
Ghost College (with Scott Nicholson)
The Vampire Club (with Scott Nicholson)
Dragon Assassin (with Piers Anthony)
Dolfin Tayle (with Piers Anthony)
Jack and the Giants (with Piers Anthony)
Judas Silver (with Elizabeth Basque)
Lost Eden (with Elizabeth Basque)
Deal With the Devil (with Elizabeth Basque)

NICK CAINE ADVENTURES
with Aiden James
Temple of the Jaguar
Treasure of the Deep
Pyramid of the Gods

THE ALADDIN TRILOGY
with Piers Anthony
Aladdin Relighted
Aladdin Sins Bad
Aladdin and the Flying Dutchman

THE WALKING PLAGUE TRILOGY
with Elizabeth Basque
Zombie Patrol
Zombie Rage
Zombie Mountain

MOON RIVER

VAMPIRE FOR HIRE #8

DEDICATION

To the Source.

ACKNOWLEDGMENTS

And a very special thank you to my Street Team!
Terri Chapman, Sunshine Hiatt, Joline Novy, Erin Kathleen
Finigan, Sheree Beans, Dinah deSouzaGuedes VanHoose,
Lynne Lawson, Susan A. Gadbois, Yvonne Roga, D'Aulan
Collins, Patricia Boehringer, Evonna Hartshorn, Heather
Beyer, Angela Jermusek, Dana Bokelman, Lisa Downing, Jeanie
Mueller, Lisa Hollingsworth, Jackie Neubauer, Pat Zunino,
Marie Mock, Sherry R. Bagley, Elizabeth Green, Cassie Wilson,
Erin Adams, Leah Kilgore, Jodi Brooks, Flora Samuelson,
Melissa Grubbs, Tracy M. Golden and Candy Waggener.

MOON RIVER

"There is something within me.
Something alive. Of that, I am sure."
—*Diary of the Undead*

CHAPTER ONE

I would miss Judge Judy today, which was always a damn shame. Judge Judy should be required viewing for anyone without a backbone. Tough woman. Fair woman. Scary woman.

My kind of woman.

Instead, I found myself being escorted by a young cop with perhaps the third- or fourth-cutest buns I'd ever seen. I ranked his buns right behind Rand's, the UPS driver who'd turned out to be a vampire hunter. Officer Cute Buns led me down a hall that ended up being far too short. I had just barely started ogling him when he turned to me, smiled and motioned for me to enter.

I did so, smiling in return, and I think I might have—just might have—had me some smiling sex.

Whatever that was.

Waiting inside was, of course, Detective Sherbet. I knew he would be waiting for me because he'd called and asked me to come down and meet with him. I also knew he was inside because I could smell the bag of donuts from the hallway.

Who I wasn't expecting was the tall guy sitting opposite the detective. He was tall and dark-haired and sporting shoulders nearly as wide as Kingsley's. Nearly.

"Detective," I said to Sherbet, who made no attempt to stand. Rude. Then again, the old detective had been gaining a little bit of weight these days, and he was veritably poured into that chair.

1

I heard that, he thought, telepathically catching my thoughts. The detective, among a small handful of others in my life, could read my thoughts...and I, theirs. *I might have put on a little holiday weight.*

It's the summer, Detective. And there's no 'might have' about it. I'm a trained observer.

Well, the Fourth of July is a big deal in the Sherbet household.

I grinned. He didn't, although he did look down at his growing belly.

"I didn't bring you in here to judge me," said the detective.

"Excuse me?" said the other gentleman, who had been looking at me, but now snapped his head around to glance over at Sherbet.

Sherbet, unfortunately, still hadn't quite gotten the hang of telepathic communication with someone like me. The old guy would occasionally blurt his thoughts, rather than think them. *Rookie.*

"Nothing," said Sherbet. He motioned to the partially masticated pink donut with rainbow sprinkles. "Samantha Moon likes to give me a hard time about my donuts."

"I didn't say anything, Detective," I said, shrugging innocently.

"You didn't have to...now, let's cut the crap. Samantha, this is Detective Sanchez from the Los Angeles Police Department."

He stood like a true gentleman, reached over and shook my hand with a firm but soft grip. His grip told me a lot: confident, warm, comfortable with himself. Most important: human.

I'd had my hand in my jeans pocket where I had been holding a hand warmer. Yes, a *hand warmer.* They sold them at the local market...and they did wonders for creatures like me. If I knew a handshake was imminent, I could pop one of these open, grip it in my pocket...and shake hands with confidence.

Sherbet asked me to have a seat, and I did, next to Sanchez.

"Boy," I said. "Two big, bad homicide detectives and just little ol' me. I feel honored."

"Cut the crap, Sam," said Sherbet. "We're going to need you on this one."

Sanchez listened to this exchange and smiled. An easy smile. Friendly. But there was a strength to his jaw, and the way his forearms rippled as he moved slightly. He sported a thick, gold wedding ring. He said, "You were a federal agent, Ms. Moon?"

"Call me Samantha. And yes. For a few years."

"You're too young to retire. Sorry if I'm prying. Call it occupational spillover. Sometimes, I can't stop asking questions."

I nodded. I understood completely. I said, "I developed a… condition."

"A condition that kept you from working as a federal agent?"

"No. A condition that kept me out of the sun. It's called xeroderma pigmentosum and it's a bitch."

"I'm sorry to hear that. And here we dragged you out into the sun. My apologies." Sanchez's concern was real as he leaned forward and looked from me to Sherbet. "I hadn't known. I would have met you at your home, or anywhere that you were more comfortable."

I smiled at his sweetness. "It's okay, Detective. I've learned to adapt."

Truth was, six months ago, I'd adapted quite nicely, as I had then sported a medallion that enabled me to step out into the light of day. That the medallion had been buried under my skin was another story—or that a body-hopping demon had torn it from me…was, in the least, a horror story for another day, too.

Lots of stories, I thought.

Focus, Sam, came the detective's thoughts.

I nodded to him as Sanchez said, "As long as you're okay."

"Oh, I'm fine, thank you," I said. "So, how can I help you, gentlemen?"

Detective Sherbet looked at me for a long moment. Then he looked at Sanchez, who was looking down at his hands.

"Either someone starts talking about the case, or I'm going to start knocking heads," I said.

That seemed to break the ice. Sanchez chuckled. Sherbet might have grinned. Finally, the handsome LAPD homicide detective said, "We think we have a serial killer on our hands."

There was, of course, no reason why two experienced homicide detectives would be talking to me, a lowly private eye, about a serial killer. Homicide detectives, in general, didn't look favorably upon us. We were seen as a nuisance, amateurish. There was, of course, only one reason why I had been called in. *Something wicked this way comes.*

I had been called in on such a case last year. Sherbet and I eventually caught the bastards behind what had turned out to be a blood ring. Right, a *blood ring*. For vampires. Sherbet, of course, no longer had any memory of my involvement in the case, thanks to Detective Hanner, a fellow creature of the night who had been overseeing—and concealing—the bloody enterprise for many years. Thanks to her otherworldly ability to remove and replace memories, most of the department—and anyone involved in the case, for that matter—believed that only one man had been behind the killings. The fact that the bodies had been drained of all blood had never made it into police reports or autopsy reports. Any connections to vampires had been removed from documentation. Sherbet himself was remembering more and more of the case, thanks to my help. But much was forgotten and would, undoubtedly, remain forgotten.

Now, I looked at Sherbet and thought: *How much did you tell him about me?*

Sherbet held my gaze then finally looked away. *Everything, Sam. Everything.*

CHAPTER TWO

"**S**am, he agreed to have his memory removed. About you, about vampires. Everything."

Sanchez nodded, although he kept staring at me. "Whatever it takes to catch the bastard killing these people. That is, of course, if you really are a, you know…"

"A vampire," I said.

"Yeah, that." And now, Sanchez looked a little uncomfortable.

He should look uncomfortable. Either he was surrounded by a lot of craziness, or he was sitting next to something that, had I lost my grip on it, would like nothing more than to drink from his writhing body.

Jesus, Sam, came Sherbet's thoughts. *Dial it down a little. You're scaring even me.*

I'm pissed, Detective.

Don't be pissed, Sam. Sanchez is a friend of mine. A good detective. No, a great detective. He's dealing with something he doesn't understand. You can see how willing he is to find the killer. He'll do whatever it takes.

Still, I fumed. My life was difficult enough as it was, without the world knowing *what* I was. I drummed my longish, pointed nails along the wooden arm of the guest chair.

"So, it's true, then," said Sanchez, watching me carefully. God, I hated to be watched carefully.

"Maybe," I said.

"I told him everything, Sam," said Sherbet. "No need to be evasive."

I sighed. "Fine," I said. "I'm a blood-sucking creature of the night. Hide your kids and all that." I raised my clawed fingers half-heartedly like the vampire in the silent movie, *Nosferatu.* "Rawr."

Sanchez laughed lightly, hesitantly, undoubtedly not sure what to make of all of this. He never took his eyes off me. Hell, if I were him, I wouldn't take my eyes off me, either. It wasn't often that someone met a freak like me.

"You're not a freak," said Sherbet, picking up my thoughts like a freak himself.

"Like hell I'm not," I said.

"Am I missing something here?" asked Sanchez.

"Sorry," said Sherbet. "Sam and I can sort of, ah…"

"Sort of what?"

"Read each other's minds," said Sherbet, and he suddenly looked like he wished he was having any other conversation but this one.

"You're kidding."

"Trust me. I wish I was."

Sanchez thought about that—or tried to—then looked back at me. "I've never met a vampire before."

"That you know of."

"Do they all look like you?"

"Short, cute, spunky?"

Sanchez grinned. "Something like that."

"We look like you, Detective, until you look a little deeper."

"Your skin is pale," he said. "Your nails…they're pointed."

"Very good, Detective. Anything else?"

"Your eyes. They are…never mind."

"They're what?" I needed to know this. I'd seen vampire eyes—Hanner's eyes. And they were wild and not very human.

"You don't blink very much," said Sanchez, but I knew he was holding back. He wanted to say more.

"My eyes look cold," I said. "Don't they?"

He held my gaze, studying me, looking deeply into me. "Yes."

"Like a killer's eyes?"

"Yes," he said.

"Like I'm not all there?"

"Yes," he said again. He held my gaze. He didn't shy away.

I sighed. When had the change in my eyes happened? I didn't know. Maybe it had happened the instant I had turned. Then again, I wouldn't know since I hadn't seen my eyes in more than seven years.

They don't look that creepy, Sam, thought Sherbet.

Thanks, Detective. But maybe you're just used to them.

Or maybe we're all nuts.

Have they changed to you, Detective? I mean, recently?

I haven't noticed—

Detective...

He sighed, look at me again, looked deep into my eyes, and thought, *Yes, Sam. They've changed recently. Darker, perhaps.*

Evil?

I wouldn't go that far.

"You guys are doing it again, aren't you?" asked Sanchez. "That whole teleport thing."

"Telepathy," I said, winking. "Get it straight."

He gave me a crooked smile. A handsome smile.

A married *smile,* added Sherbet. *His wife is a bit nuts. She would take you on, vampire or not. And she just might win.*

I almost grinned. Yes, someone wanted the world to know that Detective Sanchez was married. I was guessing the psycho wife. After all, he sported a thick, gold band that could have been seen from the Russian Space Station.

Sanchez said, "So, you're really a vampire?"

"That's what it says on the tombstone over my grave."

"You're joking."

"Let's hope."

Sanchez might have smiled. Mostly, he kept his considerable stare on me. I was noticing more and more how he was making the small office even smaller. Either that, or Sherbet was bigger than I thought.

Hey, Sherbet thought.

I grinned, and said to Sanchez, "Tell me about your case."

He said, "Better I show you."

CHAPTER THREE

We were driving.

While we drove, I looked through Detective Sanchez's police file. In particular, I studied photos of the bodies. Two women. Both with grisly wounds to their necks. Not so much bitten as *torn*.

"Who found the bodies?" I asked.

"Hikers."

"The same hikers?"

"No. Two different hikers. Two different days. But the bodies were left on the same trail."

"Or killed on the same trail."

"That, too," said Sanchez.

We were winding our way through heavy traffic along the I-5. It was past seven p.m. and the sun had set and I was feeling damn good.

Sanchez glanced at me. "You look a little different."

I was intrigued. "Different how?"

He studied me for a heartbeat longer, then looked forward again like a good boy—or a good cop—keeping his eyes on the road. "I dunno. You have more color in your face. You seem…"

"Peppier?"

"Cops don't say words like *peppier.*"

"Sure they don't."

We drove some more. I continued studying the photos of the two dead women. I searched for a psychic hit but found none. What kind of a psychic hit, I didn't know. Hell, I would have taken anything: a face, a name, a distorted image. However, nothing came to me.

"You know a friend of mine," said Sanchez, as he pulled off onto Los Feliz Boulevard—along with about half of Southern California.

"Oh?"

"Well, he's not so much a friend but a great admirer of mine."

I groaned. "Knighthorse."

"How did you know?"

"Because you two are the cockiest sons-of-bitches I've ever met."

Sanchez chuckled. "Does he know about your...secret?"

"No," I said. "Which raises a concer..."

Sanchez, perhaps even catching a whiff of my own thoughts, nodded. "I know what you're going to say: what's to stop me from telling Knighthorse—or anyone else for that matter—your secret? That is, before you erase my memory."

"Right," I said. "For all I know, you could have texted your wife that you're on a ride-along with a vampire."

He chuckled. "Ride-along. Funny. But, no, I haven't texted anyone. Is *texted* even a word?"

"My kids use it, so that's good enough for me."

Sanchez grinned, but then turned somber. "Truth is, I'm damn nervous about having my memory erased. I mean...how much of it will you erase?"

"I can be fairly exact," I said.

In fact, I had been practicing the technique for the past few months with Allison, or, as I called her, my guinea pig. She didn't mind being called my guinea pig, and she also didn't mind helping me practice my various vampiric talents. Mostly, she didn't mind me feeding on her. In fact, she encouraged it.

Strange girl, yes, but there was a reason for her madness—the more I fed on her, the more her psychic skills developed. The more they developed, the stronger she got. The stronger she got, the more of a pill she became.

Sanchez shot me a look. "How does it work?"

"I'm not entirely sure, but I think it's based on autosuggestion."

"Like hypnotic suggestion?"

"Right."

"Are you kind of new to all of this?" he asked.

"Being a vampire?"

"Yes."

"New enough. Turns out, there's more to it than running around graveyards at night."

"Do vampires do that?"

"I don't know," I said. "But that's what I always thought. In my 'before' life."

Sanchez laughed a little and made a right into Griffith Park, thus bypassing what looked like hours of traffic ahead on Los Feliz Boulevard.

"I read somewhere that Los Feliz Boulevard is the busiest street in Los Angeles," he said, seemingly out-of-the-blue.

But it wasn't out-of-the-blue. Little did Detective Handsome realize that he was already picking up on my thoughts. I must have been feeling pretty comfortable with him. Comfortable enough that our connection was growing stronger. Granted, getting comfortable—or cozy—with Sanchez wasn't an entirely an unpleasant thought. His psycho wife, however, *was* an unpleasant thought.

As he pulled into a parking space along the perimeter of the quiet park, he looked at me curiously. "Did you just call my wife a psycho?"

"No, I *thought* it. And I'm sorry."

"No worries. She *is* kind of psycho...wait, you what?"

"I *thought* it," I said. "As in, you just read my mind, Detective."

"No..."

"Oh, yes."

"I *heard* you."

"You heard my thoughts, Detective. In your head."

"This isn't happening."

"I've said that a thousand times, Detective, but yet, it still happens. And it's happening now. To both of us."

"Shit."

"You can say that again."

11

"I'm a detective. I don't read minds. I read…" he stumbled for words. The handsome cop looked truly perplexed. He reached up and removed his glasses, rubbed his eyes, pinched the bridge of his nose. "I read police reports, study crime scenes, deal with real facts, real people."

I reached over and pinched his shoulder. "That's for insinuating I'm not a real person." And, yes, I wanted to pinch something *else*, but I didn't want Mrs. Psycho Wife showing up on my doorstep.

"She's not that bad," said Sanchez, and then started nodding. "Yes, I'm aware that you didn't actually say anything, that your words just appeared in my thoughts. I…think I can tell the difference now. The words are softer, whispery."

"Like a ghost," I said.

He snapped his head around. "A what?"

"You scared of ghosts, Detective?"

"Who isn't?"

"Well, you're safe. I'm just your garden-variety bloodsucker."

He kept looking at me. Sweat had appeared on his brow. Some of it had collected at his temple and was about to trickle down. And, as I thought these words, he reached up and wiped the sweat away.

"Yes," he said, "I heard that, too. Does this happen with everyone you meet?"

"No. But this is certainly the fastest."

"What does it mean?"

"Maybe we were married in a past life."

"Are you being serious?" he asked.

"I don't know. I don't think so. But it might explain what's happening."

"And what is happening?"

I gave him my biggest grin. "Congratulations. You've just mind-linked with a creature of the night. Your life, I suspect, will never be the same again."

"Until you wipe my memory clean."

"We'll talk about that later," I said.

12

He nodded and rubbed that spot between his eyes. His oversized ring caught some ambient lamplight and flashed brilliantly. He got control of himself, took in some air.

"Can we talk about something else now?" he asked.

"Like murder?"

He exhaled. "Like murder. After all, this is where the bodies were found. Come on."

Chapter Four

We followed a narrow trail.

Dusk was a special time for me. The disquiet of the day was forgotten. That I could ever feel less than I did now was inconceivable. Now, at this hour, at this time of day, I felt like I could conquer anything and anyone. Literally. I was bursting at the seams. I wanted to climb the highest cliff or tree or whatever the hell was out here. The Griffith Observatory was nearby, with its massive dome that was visible for miles all around. It could see into the universe and all its secrets. *Not my secrets,* I thought. Yes, the observatory would work. Give the astronomers something to really look at.

Mostly, I loved that quiet moment just before I leaped, just before I was about to cascade out into the night, just before I was about to turn into something much greater than I am.

I felt the animal within me wanting out. Nothing that I couldn't control, no. More of a polite request. A mild urging. Was the animal me? Maybe, maybe not. Whatever it was, I briefly inhabited it as this body of mine slipped away. To where, I didn't know. And from where the creature came, I didn't know that either.

Another world, I'd heard. Summoned from *elsewhere.*

Sanchez, who had been leading the way along the trail, looked back at me. "I'm hoping like hell that you just made all of that up."

Oops. I probably should have closed off my thoughts. I didn't want to overwhelm the poor guy. Better to break him in slowly. This was, I suspected, only the beginning of the freaky crap he was about to face.

14

Then again, maybe a part of me wanted the detective to see a little more, to know a little more about me. Why, I didn't know. I felt a connection to the man. A professional connection, yes. Maybe even a brotherly connection. Or, maybe I wanted him to know what he was in for. What he had signed up for, so to speak.

Or maybe I had a crush on the man and had simply forgotten to shield my thoughts.

Maybe.

So, I did so now, shielding them with an imaginary wall that wasn't so imaginary. It really worked.

"Yes," I said, as I kept pace behind him. "Just a flight of fancy."

"It didn't seem fancy. It seemed real. I saw it. Or I saw you become something...huge."

"Well, we all dream of being something a little more than we are, right?"

"That was a lot more. That was actually quite fucking cool."

Soon, we were following a narrow trail that wound up into the park. Although the trail was dimming rapidly as the sky darkened, Detective Sanchez picked his way over the trail like a true expert. Myself, I wasn't much of an expert. Although I had spent the early part of the summer hiking through trails on a remote and private island up in Washington State, I hadn't sniffed a trail since then. And, if it hadn't been for my enhanced reflexes and my own version of night vision, I was fairly certain I would have hit the dirt a few times. After all, if there was a tree root, I seemed to find it. Who knew vampires could be so clumsy?

We continued along, picking our way quickly, brushing past only slightly overgrown bushes and plants. For the most part, the trail was well-maintained. Beyond, through the trees, I could hear the steady hum of L.A. traffic. It was an angry hum.

Finally, after about twenty minutes of this, as the dusk was beginning to turn into night, Detective Sanchez fished a small flashlight from his pocket and clicked it on. He shined the beam just off the trail, to a flattened clearing that I suspected had been trampled to death by police activity.

And sitting next to the clearing, shimmering in and out of existence, was a ghost.

A young woman who was watching us.

CHAPTER FIVE

To my eyes, ghosts appeared as concentrated light energy. How and why I could now see into the spirit world was still a mystery to me; although, truth be known, it's probably one of the least mysterious things in my new life.

Well, *relatively* new life.

I'd been a vampire now for over seven years, long enough that I almost—almost—forgot what it was like to be mortal. To be normal. To sleep normally, to eat normally, to exist normally.

Then again, what was normal?

Certainly not me, I thought, as I approached the ghost sitting there on the boulder.

She wasn't fully formed. In fact, she was exactly half there. As in, I could see one of her arms, but not really the second. One of her legs hung below her as she sat on the rock...and the other, not so much. The staticy light particles that composed her ethereal body crackled with bright intensity, which signaled to me that she was a new spirit. Then again, what did I know? I was still fairly new to all of this.

Still, I'd seen my share of ghosts. Hell, I saw them every day. But rarely, if ever, did I talk to them. Most didn't seem capable of communicating. Most, I suspected, didn't even realize they were ghosts. And those that did, had, quite frankly, seemed to have forgotten how to speak. Mostly, I ignored ghosts, because my life was freaky enough as it was.

But I didn't ignore her.

17

I approached her carefully, nervous that she might disappear into the ether-sphere, as ghosts are wont to do. But she didn't. She jerked her head up as I approached, and that made me wonder... could ghosts actually hear? Surely, they could. Or did she catch my movement? Perhaps they sensed sound waves, or vibrations.

So much I didn't know.

I recalled a little boy ghost who'd come to my front door last year, a lost boy who had been murdered by a sicko who'd lived just down my street. Yes, the boy had definitely heard me and responded to my words.

Ghosts are weird, I thought, as I got closer. *Then again, talk about the pot calling the kettle black.*

"You're all weird," said Sanchez behind me. "And is there really a ghost here?"

"Yes, now shush. Don't scare her way. Stay right there."

I glanced back as he stopped in his tracks, holding up his hands. "Far be it from a homicide investigator to get in the way of a murder investigation."

Shh, I thought to him, and added a mental wink. I liked him. Too bad he was married.

"I heard that."

Oops.

As Sanchez chuckled lightly behind me, I continued along the dirt path, and soon approached the young lady who'd watched me the entire way. She wavered in and out of existence. What prompted a ghost to appear or disappear was beyond me, but I very much wanted to talk to her. I approached carefully, non-threateningly.

I knew there was a difference between ghosts and spirits. Ghosts were still tied to this world. Spirits came and went as they pleased. All looked the same to my eye...except spirits tended to be more fully formed and didn't appear lost or confused or frightened.

This girl was all three.

Also, ghosts tended to take on the look they had at the time of their death...and as I approached the young lady, I could see the gaping wound in the side of her neck.

18

Vampires, I thought.

Or something mimicking a vampire. Or someone who wanted us to believe it had been a blood-sucker. Vampires, I knew, didn't have to go for the jugular. The jugular was messy. Blood pumped uncontrollably from the jugular. It splashed on clothes and shoes and just made for a helluva cleanup. Much easier to drink from a controlled cut, on the arm or wrist, with no biting involved.

The damage to her neck was too obvious, too vampire-y.

Someone wants us to believe it's a vampire, I thought.

But why? came Sanchez's voice.

You're still in my head?

I guess, he thought back. *Your words just keep appearing, and I keep answering like an idiot.*

You're not an idiot, but I'm going to close you out now. No offense.

Believe me, none taken.

I laughed and put up mental wall, thus sealing Sanchez out. The wall only stayed in place for so long. I'd noted that after a few hours, it tended to fade away, How all of this worked, I didn't know, but I'd learned to work with it, rather than against it. *Swim downstream, not upstream,* as the saying went.

I'd long ago learned how to continuously tune out others. Generally, when I was with Detective Sherbet or my friend, Allison, I mostly pushed aside their own thoughts. Yes, I heard them, but they existed as small background noise that I could tune into, if I chose to. Mostly, I chose not to.

Only with Fang—and sometimes, here and there with Allison— did I pick up long-distance thoughts. Meaning, they didn't have to be nearby. But with Fang's ascension to immortality, well, he was forever cut off from me, just as all immortals were cut off from me.

Hey, I didn't make the rules. I just did my best to live within them.

So, with my mental wall up, and with Sanchez's own internal chattering reduced to low background noise, I approached the dead girl and stood before her.

Chapter Six

"**Y**es, I can see you," I said. "And I know you can see me."

She didn't say anything. I had actually conversed with a ghost only a few times. And only then, I'd simply received *impressions* from them.

This girl wavered in and out of existence. I suspected I might lose her, and so I said quickly, "I want to help you."

I was getting a very strong impression that she was terrified, even in death. Terrified by what had happened to her, and by what was happening now.

"It's going to be okay," I said. "No one can hurt you now...or ever again."

Whether or not she heard me, I didn't know. She continued staring at me, sitting there on the rock, her knees pulled up to her chest, head slightly tilted, revealing the ghastly wound that that somehow looked even more awful in death, a wound composed of tens of thousands of glowing light particles. The wound, I saw, was deep. Someone had literally torn open her neck. Yes, she would have bled to death quickly.

"I'm sorry someone hurt you," I said.

She hugged her knees tighter. Her feet were mostly not there. Sometimes they wavered into existence, but mostly, her legs stopped at the ankles. She had been wearing Asics running shoes.

She'd been attacked in the park, while running.

As that thought occurred to me, I caught a psychic hit of her running up a trail. I turned...that trail there, which led off down the hillside and through a tangle of gnarly little trees. Yes, she'd been running up there when something powerful had overwhelmed her...knocking her down, pouncing on her.

And then pain. So much pain.

And that was it.

Her next memory was of sitting beside her dead, broken body.

That had a familiar ring to it. I, too, had been attacked in a different park, while running. Of course, I hadn't been left to die, to bleed out, as I'm sure this girl had. I had been given vampire blood...no doubt by my attacker himself.

Of course, I would never know the truth, since my attacker—a very old and powerful vampire—was now dead at the hands of a vampire hunter named Rand. I'd recently had the pleasure of working with Rand and his merry band of vampire-hunting misfits, in a faraway land in a remote mountaintop castle. Lord help any vampire who crossed paths with those badasses.

Anyway, her plight was familiar to me, even if the end result was far different.

This could have been me, I thought. *Dead and lost and wondering what the hell had happened to me.*

Truth was, had I been killed that night, I probably would have never known what had happened to me. I had been hit hard and ravaged and it all had been a blur...and I had awakened the next morning in a hospital, lucky to be alive.

Lucky to be able to see my kids.

This girl wasn't so lucky.

Then again, I had a certain fallen angel named Ishmael who had, no doubt, something to do with keeping me alive. Which led to another question: how had Ishmael managed to convince the old vampire to attack me—and to keep me alive? To feed me his blood?

I didn't know...but suddenly, I wanted to find out.

But this girl hadn't been part of a fallen angel's nefarious plan to find love, to break his immortal bond with the living by turning a mortal *im*mortal, thus freeing him from servitude.

A twisted, reckless way to go about love.

21

If it was love.

I suspected it was closer to an obsession. Anyway, luckily, the fallen angel, Ishmael, had mostly kept his distance. For now.

"Do you remember who attacked you?" I asked the girl. "What did they look like?"

She didn't move, but the light filament around her, the thousands and thousands of light filaments, shook and scattered and reformed. She was sobbing.

Her attack had been violent, sudden. I knew this. She might not have seen her attacker. I hadn't seen my attacker.

Or, if I had, I couldn't remember.

But maybe someday I could remember.

And if I could remember the night I was attacked...maybe a lot of what happened to me would make sense.

Maybe.

As she wept, her etheric body shuddering, I saw something else: a bulge at the back of her neck. The bulge was undoubtedly caused by a protruding bone. Of course, in her current state...it was only a *memory* of a protruding bone. Not actual bone.

I went back to the edge of the clearing, where Sanchez was watching me. He had been intently scanning the surrounding area, ever the homicide cop.

"Had her neck been broken?" I asked.

"Did the ghost tell you that?" he asked. "And did I just ask you if a ghost told you something?"

"You did, and, no, you're not losing your mind. At least, not at the moment. We'll see how you hold up when this is all over."

"And what's *this?*"

I thought about that. The night was chilly, but nothing my immortal flesh couldn't handle. The detective, on the other hand, kept both hands in his jeans pockets in an effort to look both cool and keep warm. Guys.

I said, "Someone wanted to make sure this attack was obvious."

"Obvious that it was a vampire attack?"

"You catch on quick," I said.

"So, is there some sort of vampire war that the rest of us mere mortals aren't aware of?"

"You've been watching too much *True Blood*, detective. Vampires live discreetly, kill discreetly. The ones I know enjoy their anonymity and try like hell to exist in the real world."

"So, why would someone want us to think this was a vampire attack?"

"A good question, Detective, but one I don't know the answer to. At least, not yet. And the girl—"

"You mean ghost."

"Yes, the ghost doesn't know anything. She didn't see who attacked her."

Sanchez shivered a little. "Kind of creepy to think that these woods are full of vampires and ghosts."

"And nervous cops with guns."

"Touché ," he said. "And you promise to wipe my memory clean of all of this later?"

"If you want."

"I very much want."

CHAPTER SEVEN

We were at Zov's Bistro.

Yes, the same Zov's Bistro where I often saw one of my favorite thriller writers. I loved his books, but I didn't love his fake hair. He was here now, eating with his wife, and looking very serious while he did so. That was okay. I liked my thriller writers looking serious.

"Do you read his books?" I asked Allison as we were seated.

"Whose books?"

"His books." I pointed at the little man, and told Allison his name.

"Never heard of him."

I stared at her. "Do you even like to read, Allison?"

"I read magazines."

"Books, Allison. Do you read books?"

"Not really. They're kinda, you know, boring—wait, I did just read a book."

As she said the words, I saw the book in my mind's eyes. Yes, Allison and I were deeply connected. Too connected. "You read a book on *witchcraft?*"

"On Wicca," she said, lowering her voice. And this might have been the first time I'd ever heard Allison lower her voice. "There's a difference."

"Enlighten me."

She was about to when the waitress came by and took our drink orders. White wine for me, red for Allison. I would have preferred a

24

margarita, or something fun and foofy. Sadly, my body barely tolerated the white wine.

Zov's Bistro was a quaint, upscale restaurant with reasonable prices in exchange for uncommonly good food. At least, that's what I was told, since I hadn't eaten regular food in seven years. No, I came here for the ambiance...and sometimes a raw steak. Raw steaks didn't always do it for me. The blood that pooled around the steak had been warmed and seasoned and so wasn't pure enough. Anything impure—i.e., not blood—was liable to get a violent reaction from me. And by violent, yes, I mean projectile vomiting.

The local writer, I noted, was staring at me. I remembered back in the days when he was bald. He looked good bald. He looked serious and kind of sexy. Like a literary Burt Reynolds. The fake hair looked disturbing. And it wasn't just a little fake. It was a massive pile of it. Thick and proud and weird. In a way, I admired him for it. After all, if you're gonna get transplants—and not fool anyone in the process—then, by God, you might as well go all in.

"You seem way too fixated on the poor man's hair. I think it looks nice," said Allison, picking up on my thoughts. Generally, I didn't close my thoughts off to Allison. Lately, I'd been thinking of her more and more as a sister.

"I'm glad you think so," said Allison, "because there is a good chance that, in a past life or two, we very well could have been sisters."

"You're losing me."

"It goes back to the book on Wicca...and someone else."

I saw the old lady in Allison's mind. And it wasn't just any old lady...

"Since when do you see ghosts?" I asked.

"Since last week."

She told me about it. Allison had been hired by a man to help him find his daughter's killer. She had done so, and strangeness ensued. "But I'll tell you about him another time," she added.

However, I had already caught her thoughts regarding him. I shook my head at the wonder of it all, and said, "Fine. Tell me about the old lady."

"She's one of us," said Allison.

"What the devil does that mean?"

Allison gave me another image, this time, of the old lady looking not so old. She was younger now, our age, mid-thirties—although I would forever look in my late twenties. At this younger, more youthful age, the woman looked frustratingly familiar.

Allison was nodding. "See, you recognized her, too."

Our drinks came and Allison dove into hers. Literally. Head first. When she pulled away, wine sparkled on her lips. Lips that were smiling contently. The girl liked to drink.

"What's going on, Allison?"

"We're soul mates, Sam. We've always been soul mates, and so is Millicent. There are three of us. Bound together throughout time and space."

"I just met you last year," I said, sipping my wine. I had to sip it. If I drank it too fast, I'd get stomach pains. Who knew vampires would have such sensitive stomachs? Granted, it could be the thing that lived within me who had the sensitive stomach. The thing that I kept alive with each consumption of blood. Knowing that I was simultaneously keeping something wicked and hideous alive, while at the same time keeping myself alive, was something that, to this day, I hadn't quite wrapped my head around.

"Yes, we just met," said Allison, "but we were *supposed* to meet. It was destiny."

"You were the fiancé of a murder victim," I said. "Destiny arranged for your fiancé to die so that we could meet?"

Allison looked down immediately into her wine. The strangeness of her fiancé's murder did nothing to diminish her loss, and I reached out and took her hand and apologized from my heart. "Sorry, that was harsh."

"It's okay, Sam. And I can't begin to understand how the world works, or how the Universe works, or even how God works. For all I know, they're all one and the same. But, somehow, someway, we came together, but this time, as friends."

"And we were sisters before?"

"Often," said Allison, perking up a little. The wine might have had something to do with that. Hers, I noted, was nearly half gone. "And sometimes, brothers. But we'll call that a failed experiment."

I laughed. "I prefer being a girl, thank you very much."

Allison giggled. "Likewise."

"And the old woman—"

"Young woman," Allison corrected. "Millicent."

"Yes, Millicent. She is also a soul mate?"

"Yes."

"But, she is in spirit, passed on?"

Allison shrugged. "She was a soul mate who got here a little earlier this time, perhaps to pave the way for us..."

I caught the thought that she didn't voice. I said, "Or perhaps to guide you in spirit."

"*Us* in spirit, Sam. You are deeply connected to her, too."

"This is weird," I said.

The waitress came by and took our orders. I wasn't in the mood for raw steak. I told the waitress I was just here for the wine. She smiled weakly at that. Allison, of course, ordered enough for two people.

When the waitress left, I said, "Two baked potatoes?"

"They're earth energy," said my friend, who tilted back the rest of her wine.

"You lost me again."

"Earth energy, Sam. They're grown within Mother Earth, and she has infused them with her love and energy."

"Love and energy?"

"Yes."

"Do you know how crazy this sounds?" I asked.

"Says the vampire."

"Fine," I said, taking another sip of wine. "Tell me about the book on Wicca."

"Millie gave it to me."

"The old lady?"

"The young lady. Yes, her."

"And she gave it to you why?" I asked.

"Because, Samantha Moon, you're not the only freaky one in our little duo. I'm a witch, you see."

Chapter Eight

"A witch?" I said.

"That's right. I said witch."

"Since when?"

"Since forever, Sammie. It looks like I've been one throughout the ages. And since you and I have been sister soul mates, so to speak, I suspect you were one, too. Along with Millie."

"Trust me, I'm no witch."

"Well, not now, silly. You can't be both a witch and a vam—"

"Shh," I said. Allison always had a bad habit of talking louder and louder, especially when the booze was flowing. "Maybe we should keep our voices down, huh?"

"Oops, sorry. I'm just, you know, super excited."

But her excitement was short-lived. A moment later, she turned her head and buried her hands in her face and I was left staring at her in confusion.

That is, until I saw the image of a thirty-something man in a schoolroom…and then the image of that same young man lying dead from multiple wounds over his face and neck. All of this, I knew, was from the perspective of Allison.

Something very bad had happened to her—and something worse had happened to the man lying dead at her feet. What exactly had happened, I didn't know.

But first things first. I rushed around the table and knelt next to her and hugged her tight and as I did so, she wept silently into my shoulder.

29

———

A few minutes later, after the waitress had asked if everything was okay and all eyes were on us, I stepped away from Allison and went back to my seat.

I didn't care that all eyes were on us. I cared about my friend and that something very bad had happened to her, and as we looked at each other across the table, as our wine glasses sat forgotten and the water glasses collected condensation, I saw all that she had been dealing with this past week...and, in particular, what had happened just the night before.

When she was done, and I had seen further and deeper into her than I had ever seen before, I reached across the table and took her hands and told her over and over again that it was not her fault.

A man, after all, was dead because of her newfound skills.

Skills that were, to say the least, jaw-droppingly powerful.

"You see, Sam," she said, speaking for the first time in many minutes, "I'm a freak like you, after all."

"Maybe freakier."

She laughed lightly. "I doubt that."

"It wasn't your fault, Allie. He tried to kill you."

She broke our contact and reached for her wine glass, but didn't pick it up.

"And you should have called me," I said.

"I know. I just...I just didn't think things would get so out of hand."

"He was a child killer...and desperate. Anything could have happened. You got lucky." *And,* I added telepathically, *you're not immortal. He could have killed you.*

Allison nodded again and wiped her eyes and finally did lift her glass of wine. When she set it down again, it was quite empty.

We talked more about her newfound skills, about Millie and about Peter Laurie. We talked about his little girl and her art work.

"I promised I would help find good homes for his daughter's artwork."

"I would be honored," I said. "Put me in for two."

Allison laughed, and we shared a quiet moment, holding hands again across the table. The waitress soon brought Allison's dinner, which looked heavenly. It was also, I noted, vegetarian.

"Since when did you become an herbivore?" I asked.

"Since discovering that abstaining from meat helps me tune into Mother Earth."

"Mother Earth?" I said.

"Yes, Wicca is an earth-based religion that draws power from the energy of the Earth itself."

"Of course," I said. "Who doesn't know that?"

"Don't you dare laugh, Samantha Moon, who just so happens to draw her own power from blood—"

"Shhh," I hushed. "You talk too loud."

"I talk the way I talk. You're just going to have to deal with it."

I rolled my eyes. "So, is this the new you?"

"The new and empowered me," said Allison.

"Fine. Then tell the new and empowered you that we have some important secrets that we don't need the world knowing."

"Fine," she said, and happily dug into her salad.

It had, of course, been a long, long time since I'd had anything like a salad. My mouth watered, which was a useless leftover trait from my human days. Still, the salad, with all its bright veggies and leafy greens, looked incredible...and crispy. The crispy part was proven to be true as Allison bit into each forkful. She crunched her food in a way that made me long for cucumbers, tomatoes, and lettuce dressed in a nice balsamic vinaigrette.

I sighed and looked away, and my thoughts turned to my own problems.

"Do you want to talk about it?" asked Allison, between bites. She had also, somehow, managed to order another glass of wine without my knowledge. Maybe she had a telepathic link with the bartender. Wouldn't surprise me.

31

"Rude," said Allison, picking up my stray thought.

"Sorry," I said. "I'm just cranky."

"I would be, too, if I couldn't eat. So, let's get back to what else is making you cranky."

I nodded. She had, of course, picked up on my brooding thoughts...and what I knew I had to do.

"You're going to break up with him," she said.

By *him*, she was referring to my boyfriend of the past four months. Russell Baker was a professional boxer and about the sexiest thing I'd ever come across. He was also, of course, the man who had killed Allison's fiancé. Or, at least, that's what we had initially figured.

Turned out, the case had been far stranger than originally thought, and Allison never held a grudge against him, and as well, she shouldn't.

"Yes," I said. "I'm breaking up with him."

"Why?"

I thought about it again with a heavy heart...then told her why.

CHAPTER NINE

We were jogging Tri-City Park.

The park connected three cities: Fullerton, Brea and Placentia, cities that didn't mean anything to anyone outside of Orange County. Truth was, I wasn't sure which city the park was actually in. I liked to think that with each one-third loop around the park I was entering a new town. I was easily amused.

My jogging partner was Russell Baker. He was a professional boxer and, I guess you could say, my kind-of boyfriend. We'd been dating now for six months, and we seemed to be committed enough, although no one had said much of anything about anything. Meaning, we'd never discussed our situation. We just sort of *flowed*.

I saw Russell about twice a week, which was enough for me. Maybe I wasn't ready for more, I don't know. Or maybe Russell and I didn't have enough chemistry. We were always comfortable, relaxed, friendly…and yes, passionate, too. But the passion didn't extend much further than the bedroom.

The evening was warm. It was early summer. School had just gotten out. I would have my kids for the next three months. A good thing on the one hand: I could sleep in. My kids knew my super-secret identity, and kept it brilliantly, including secrets of their own.

That my kids had to go around keeping so many secrets was something of a burden for me. I hated knowing that I had inconvenienced them. Lord knew I tried to keep it all from them…I just couldn't. Not consistently.

Granted, it hadn't all been bad. Truth be known, our combined freakiness—my immortality, my son's super-strength, and my daughter's ability to read all minds—had brought us closer. It was a sort of *us versus them,* and it was nice.

For now.

We'd see how this all played out.

As we jogged, Russell and I chatted amicably, easily, neither of us out of breath. My shield was up with him, as usual. It was always up. Otherwise, he would probe, unknowingly, deep into my psyche. He would have been surprised as hell by what he found in there.

No, Russell did not know my super-secret identity. I had purchased a lifetime supply of hand warmers, which I kept in my pockets at all times, so that when he and I held hands, there was some semblance of warmth. Granted, there wasn't much warmth when we were body to body, but I didn't think Russell had noticed how cold my flesh might have felt in those intimate moments.

Afterward, I rarely lay naked next to him. I would jump up, pretend to use the bathroom, then get dressed and lay next to him again.

It was weird. He knew it was weird, but never said anything about it.

For us to work, for us to make it to another level, I would have to trust him with my Big Secret. And I would have to trust him without controlling his mind, which I swore to myself that I would never do.

He knew about my inability to go into sunlight, and he knew I wasn't much of an eater. I also suspected that he knew I was keeping something important from him.

Boy, was I.

Hardest of all was that Anthony had fallen in love with Russell. And why wouldn't he? Russell was a professional fighter...and we had gone to his last two big fights. One in Los Angeles, and one in Vegas. Anthony was Russell's biggest fan.

Not to mention, I had spent the last six months shielding my thoughts from him, which got exhausting. Russell and I had developed an almost immediate psychic link, much like I had with

Detective Sanchez. Except, with Russell, I could never fully *go there* with him.

I wasn't sure why. I think, perhaps, out of a need to have a *real* relationship. To be as normal as possible. Except, being normal was proving exhausting and almost impossible. I spent half my time lying to the poor guy. Yes, lying came easily to private investigators. We lied to get what we wanted—we pretended to be other people, other occupations, whatever it took to close a case.

I'd found that once the lies had started with Russell, I just couldn't take them back...and I didn't want to be known as a liar. I didn't want him to think he couldn't trust me.

But, nevertheless, I was indeed fibbing to him. I was a fibber. The whole damn relationship was built on fibs.

"You're quiet this evening, Sammie. Are you okay?" Russell asked. His voice was silky smooth. His movements were silky smooth, and they were in the bedroom, too. The man had full control over his body...and what a body it was.

Sadly, he also thought that we were closer in age than we really were.

He thought I was mortal.

I lied about the food I ate.

The drinks I drank.

I lied about my friends.

About my kids.

About the real reason for my divorce.

I lied about everything to him.

Yes, I probably should have come clean about it all...but once the lies started, I couldn't take them back. And I didn't want him to know what a monster I really was. He adored me. I knew he did. His interest was genuine, real.

He didn't deserve me or my lies.

As we jogged, I turned to him. "No, I'm not okay," I said. "We need to talk."

Chapter Ten

We stood together on a little bridge.

The bridge spanned a stream that flowed into the bigger pond...or maybe it was the other way around. Maybe the pond flowed into the stream. Hard to say since the water was mostly stagnant and smelled. Beneath the dark surface, I could see glowing torpedo-shaped fish swimming idly. I could see other forms glowing, too. Water spiders and flying insects. Most life gave off a sort of bioluminescence, at least to my eyes. I could see anything living at night. And sometimes things not living, too.

I see all, I thought.

I was, I suspected, the ultimate hunter.

Anyway, Russell and I were both leaning against the wooden railing. The park was mostly empty at this hour, as it should be. No one but vampires and professional boxers should be out jogging in a city park at night.

There was, however, a man who strolled casually off on the far edge of the lake, hands behind his back, whistling softly to himself. To my eyes, in the dark, he looked very bright, his aura shining a radiant blue. I knew of such auras, although I rarely saw them. *Blue* meant that he was deeply spiritual, and the brighter the blue, the more spiritual. His was a brilliant sapphire blue that extended far beyond his body. Who he was, I didn't know, but I suspected he was a true master. As such, he had nothing to fear from the dark. Indeed, all good things were attracted to such masters, and they, in turn, radiated good things. I wondered what he would make of me.

I sensed Russell's rising anxiety. He knew that nothing good was going to come from the talk. I could almost hear his heart beating, too. Lord knew it certainly wasn't my own lackadaisical heart, which tended to beat once every ten seconds or so, if that.

I'm so very, very weird.

At the far side of the lake, the bright blue light stopped. Within the blue light, I saw the man turn and face me, his hands still behind his back.

As I stood there on the ridge debating what I needed to do, I sensed a warm tingling come over me. Almost never does the word *warm* ever apply to me, and so I perked up at the rare sensation.

Russell hadn't moved, and there was no wind. There was, in fact, no obvious source of the warmth, which now surrounded me gently, as if with loving arms. The hair on my neck and arms stood on end, too, but not because I was cold, but because something alive and warm was moving around me.

It's him, I thought, looking again at the figure at the far side of the lake, a figure who was still facing us, hands still behind his back.

I knew that no one but a fellow creature of the night should be able to see us. In fact, I doubted that Russell even knew there was a man watching us.

But he wasn't a creature of the night.

He was, I suspected, just the opposite.

Something holy, something filled with light, something that repelled creatures like me.

But he wasn't repelling me now.

No, he was reaching out to me. It was, in fact, *his* warmth surrounding me.

"So, what did you want to talk about, Sam?" said Russell. He didn't turn his handsome face toward me. He continued looking out over the bridge, out toward the black lake. The lake wasn't so black to me. It was alive and well, and shining with more light than I would ever have dreamed possible.

"Release him, child," I heard a voice say. A voice, I was certain, that had come upon the wind.

For a moment, I thought it had been Russell who had spoken to me...but no, the voice had come from over the lake, drifting to me on warm currents.

Drifting to me from *him.*

Was that you? I thought, looking out toward the man who was still watching us.

I didn't get a response, but I still felt the warm current moving over the water, enveloping me completely. As I reveled in it...after all, it was so rare that I felt warm these days, the full impact of the words hit me: "Release him, child."

Release who? I thought. But I didn't get an answer.

I looked again at Russell, who was now watching me. I could see the concern in his eyes. He knew what was coming.

"Sam," he said. "I know what you're going to say, but please don't say it. Please. I'm happy. We're happy. Don't say the words, okay?"

When I looked back over the water, the figure had continued on, moving slowly. His blue aura shined brighter than ever.

Release him...release Russell?

"Russell, I haven't been entirely honest with you—"

"Samantha, I don't care. I don't care if you're a mass murderer. I can't lose you."

I blinked, processing. "You don't care if I'm a murderer?"

"No, Sam. I need you. I love you."

We had, of course, never talked about love, although I sensed that we had been getting closer.

Release him, child...

As Russell stared down at me, as he took my hand and held it tightly, I suddenly realized why he didn't care if my hands were cold, or that my body was cold, or why I never ate. Russell didn't care if I was cold, or different...or even a mass murderer.

I suddenly knew what the words meant, words spoken to me on the wind by a blue-aura master.

Russell, I suspected, was bonded to me.

Chapter Eleven

"**W**hat, exactly, does *bonded* mean?" asked Allison over the phone.

It was later and I was heading home. Unfortunately, I had been unable to release Russell Baker as the voice had asked. I hadn't intended to *release* him…I had intended to *break up* with him, as normal people do.

But you're not normal, Sam…and you never will be again.

Truth was, I had been too stunned by the revelation that another human being was bonded to me, to think clearly. I had made up some lame excuse of wanting to talk about him and the dangers of fighting…and Russell had said he would give up fighting for me.

Give up fighting.

For me.

My head was still spinning.

Yes, I had intended to break up with Russell Baker, although he'd done nothing wrong—and I had done *everything* wrong. I had lied to him from day one…but, I now knew, he would forgive me for the lies. He would have forgiven me for anything.

I saw the look in his eyes, heard it in his voice.

Bonded.

"You never noticed it before?" Allison was asking.

"No," I said. "I just thought he was, you know, *into* me. I just thought he was agreeable. Sweet."

"And the more he agreed to, the worst you felt."

39

"I always felt bad," I said. "I mean, he has no idea who I really am."

"So tell him, Sam."

I opened my mouth and closed it again. The road before me was empty as I drove through the night along the hilly Bastanchury Road, heading home. Yes, I'd considered telling Russell a hundred times about my super-secret identity, and a hundred different times I had talked myself out of it. His life was normal. His life was pure, uncomplicated. Sure, he'd chosen a rough route as a professional fighter. But it was still *normal.* The moment I had opened my mouth about who and what I was, his sweet, simple, uncomplicated life would be thrown upside down.

"Well, your uncomplicated life was thrown upside down," said Allison, following my train of thoughts.

"Yes," I said, "and the one person who could have stepped in to keep it that way, didn't."

"Ishmael," said Allison, referring to my one-time guardian angel who had, in fact, set me up. Yes, Allison knew my entire story inside and out. Hell, she knew me inside and out.

"Yes," I said. "And I hate him for it. And I'll hate him forever."

Even as I spoke those words, something flashed across the sky through my windshield...something that could have been an errant headlight, an advertising spotlight...or something else. A fallen angel, perhaps.

"What the hell was that?" said Allison.

"You saw it?" I asked. Then I remembered her psychic specialty was remote viewing. Undoubtedly, she was right by my side as we were talking, in a metaphysical sense, of course.

"Yeah, and that was weird."

"Welcome to my life."

"*Our* lives, Sam. We're kind of in this together."

I took a deep breath, held it longer than humanly possible, and then came to a stop at a red light near St. Jude Hospital. "I don't want to be the one responsible for introducing him to a world of vampires and werewolves...and witches."

"He's already in it, Sam. He just doesn't know it yet."

"Maybe it's better to keep it that way. Ignorance is bliss, and all that."

I continued through the green light, and then made a left turn into a housing tract.

"I can't tell you, Sam, if it's right or wrong to tell him. But I think he has a right to know who you are and the real reason you are breaking up with him."

"Maybe," I said.

"But you're not convinced?"

"Not yet," I said.

"So, what's the deal about this bonding thing?" Allison asked again.

"I honestly don't know," I said.

"But you're going to find out?"

"Yes," I said.

We hung up and I thought about Russell and bonding and the streak of light in the sky and the blue aura master and shook my head…

I think I was still shaking my head when I finally pulled up to my house.

CHAPTER TWELVE

"**A**nthony has a girlfriend, Mom."

I was in the kitchen, making dinner. Not quite as normal as it might sound. On a platter next to me were precisely fifteen grilled hot dogs. All for Anthony. And, yes, I had grilled them with my George Foreman. That's the way Anthony liked them, and it was easier than arguing with him. And, true to form, he wanted nothing on them. No buns, no ketchup, no mustard, no relish…nothing. Just fifteen Ballpark Franks, grilled, piled high.

Simmering on the stove next to me was Tammy's latest obsession. Chicken in yellow curry sauce. She'd gotten it into her head that she loved Indian food. Apparently, she'd had the stuff over at a friend's house, and now that's all she ever talked about…Indian food. And now, my kitchen smelled like, well, curry and garlic, with a beefy hot dog chaser.

The trouble was this: the hot dogs smelled heavenly…and so did the damn curry, although I never remembered liking Indian food before. It all smelled good. Heavenly, in fact.

At this point in my pitiful existence—anything, and I mean *anything*—would be a wondrous change to the every-other-day blood shots I took from sealed plastic bags that I popped open and gulped out of necessity.

Of course, I thought, *it didn't have to be that way, did it?*

No, it didn't. There was one more medallion out there, one more mystical talisman that had been created ages ago to help lessen the side effects of those afflicted with vampirism.

42

The diamond medallion.

Another such medallion was presently absorbed within my son. Yes, *absorbed*. Sounded weird, I knew, but my son had taken an alchemical potion that had contained the dissolved medallion. Somehow, the magicks within the medallion still flowed through my boy. Where and how, I didn't know. But one thing I did know was this...

I was a freakin' horrible mother.

I stopped stirring with this last thought and stared down into the simmering chicken and curry. No, I thought...not a bad mom. A desperate mom. I saved him, didn't I? My son was alive to this day, wasn't he?

He was, of course. In fact, he was in the living room even now, watching *SpongeBob Squarepants* on Netflix. How the kid could watch those cartoons over and over was beyond me. But watch them he did, and often, all while laughing and giggling and slapping the floor hard enough to shake the whole damn house. In fact, these days, the house seemed to be shaking harder and harder.

No surprise there. The kid had shot up an inch over the last four months...all while filling out, too. He was only ten, but he now had the body of a high school football player.

Yes, I was a very, very bad mother.

I did this to myself often. I rarely, if ever, forgave myself. But I needed to forgive myself for doing what I did to my son—

For saving his life—

For turning him into a monster—

I paused, took a deep breath, collected myself, and then continued stirring the chicken and curry. Yes, my son had had some unforeseen side effects. But, I supposed, the side effects could have been a lot worse.

He could have been a true monster.

Of the blood-sucking variety.

And then a horrible thought occurred to me...one that I refused to entertain for longer than a few seconds before I beat it back into my subconscious...but here it was:

What if, someday, he did become a bloodsucker?

What guarantee did I have that he wouldn't just keep getting stronger...but also more monstrous?

I didn't, of course. There were no guarantees in my world. A world that my son—and now my daughter—were now a part of.

No guarantees, yes, but there were answers...and I knew just where to go to find them.

The Librarian, I thought.

For now, though, I heaped a pile of steaming rice on a plate, covered it with chicken and curry, then stuck my head in the living room and told Anthony his hot dogs were ready. He nodded without looking at me and stood smoothly and effortlessly, all muscle and long limbs. I next headed down the hall and told Tammy her dinner was ready, too. She said she would come in a minute.

Anthony grabbed his hot dogs first, but I wouldn't let him leave without telling me thank you. He mumbled something utterly incomprehensible. It could have been a thank you. He also could have been having a seizure. I gave him the hot dogs anyway.

"Wait," I said. "What's this about a new girlfriend?"

He blushed mightily, which might have been cute. That is, of course, if we had been talking about anything other than a girlfriend. "She's just a friend, Mom. A friend who happens to be a girl."

Except he kept on blushing, his ears practically on fire, as he escaped back into the living room.

Next came Tammy. As with Anthony, I made her say thank you before I gave her the food. Except, of course, she stared at me with defiance for exactly two minutes before hunger finally got the better of her.

"Fine!" she said, louder than was necessary. "Thank you! But it's your *job* to make us food, you know."

"Oh?"

"Yes."

"And what's your job?" I asked.

She grinned at me before exiting the kitchen with her plate of food. "To eat it. Oh, and Tisha is *not* a friend. Trust me on this one,

Mom. I've seen them smooching." She made a kissing gesture that, quite honestly, I never wanted to see again.

A moment later, I heard her door slam shut, and I was left alone in the kitchen, with no food, and no real thanks.

Sigh.

Chapter Thirteen

"**S**o, why do you oversee such a creepy library?" I asked Archibald Maximus, the young librarian with the ancient name.

As usual, Maximus was been nowhere to be found when I had first entered the Occult Reading Room at Cal State Fullerton. I had rung the little bell on the counter and, after a moment or two, out walked the young man wearing nondescript slacks and a black long-sleeved shirt. He was handsome in a nerdy way.

"Someone has to," he answered. He stood on one side of the counter, his hands resting lightly on the counter itself.

"What does that mean?" I asked.

"It means that the knowledge in these books is not just for everyone."

"Who then?"

"Those ready for such knowledge."

"And you decide who's ready?"

Archibald leaned back against the wall behind him and folded his arms over his chest Archibald didn't have a lot of muscle tone. He had an average shape, perhaps even on the slender side. When he was done looking at me, and, probably, thinking about how to answer my question, he said, "I, and others like me, decide who may have access to such Reading Rooms. As for this particular collection, yes, I am the final gatekeeper."

"And what if someone demanded to have a book?"

"That someone would have a hard time finding me."

"What do you mean?" I asked.

"Look behind you, Sam."

I did, just as a student walked past, a young girl looking forward, oblivious to us. It was rare enough to see any students on this floor as it was, let alone catching one just as she passed by. Still, one thing seemed apparent.

"She didn't seem to notice us," I said.

"And she wouldn't, Sam."

"I don't understand. Are we invisible?"

"Not quite," said the Librarian, and he cracked a rare smile. A nice smile, and one that suggested he had seen a lot...perhaps far more than I would ever realize. "To those who have not earned the right to use this room—or, more accurately, who are not ready for this room, it is, shall I say, not on their radar."

"You mean they can't see it?"

"In a way. They would have to be drawn to it by a very strong reason, but, even then, they would have no interest in it, and would continue on. It is similar to those who hear a great truth. If the listener is not ready for the truth, it will fall upon deaf ears."

"But how was I ready to meet you?" I asked. "I mean, I'm no one."

The Librarian looked at me with compassion. "I've been aware of you for some time, Samantha Moon. Indeed, it was only a matter of time before we met."

"Geez. Who the heck are you?" I asked. Except I knew the answer to that. Archibald Maximus was, I knew, a great alchemist who had mastered life and death, albeit through alchemical means, rather than the alternative. The alternative being, of course, creatures like me.

"I'm not much different than you, Sam," he said with a smile.

"Do you have a highly evolved demonic entity living within you, waiting and plotting to take over your life?"

"Okay," he said. "Maybe we are a little different."

He smiled. I wanted to smile, but couldn't. Archibald was an immortal, and thus, his thoughts were closed from me, but, like the angel Ishmael, he seemed to have access to my own innermost thoughts…or perhaps he was an expert at body language, after all this time on Earth.

"But fear not, Samantha, for you are stronger than it."

"I don't feel stronger. I feel helpless."

"You are far from helpless, child," he said, and even though he looked years younger than me, his term of endearment touched me and I wanted to hug him tight and have him tell me everything was going to be okay. Whoever he was.

"Everything will be okay," he said. "If you allow it."

"Fine," I said, wiping my eyes. "And where's my hug?"

He came around the counter unhesitatingly, with open arms, and I slipped inside them easily and he hugged me tight and I felt his surprising strength and even his love—not a romantic love, and not necessarily a love just for me. His love seemed to radiate out, in a wide arc, encompassing, perhaps, the whole of mankind.

"Who are you?" I said again, into his shoulder.

He patted my own shoulder sweetly, as a father would. I wasn't sure anyone had patted my shoulder in a long time. The gesture was so comforting that I didn't want to let him go. It was, perhaps, the first time in many years that I truly felt safe.

"I am a friend," he said into my ear.

Finally, I pulled away shyly, wiping my tears. "Thank you."

He gave me such a warm smile that I nearly hugged him again. Finally, he said, "I assume, Sam, that you came here to talk."

I nodded, taking a deep breath, getting a hold of myself. "No, I came for the hug."

He laughed.

"Okay, and maybe one or two questions."

He waited calmly. As he waited, I heard the familiar whisperings from deeper in the small reading room, a room that was crammed with every imaginable book on the occult and arcane, books on life and death and hidden histories, books on secret societies and black magic. Some books, I knew, opened doorways into other worlds, or worlds that were layered just over our own, worlds that sometimes crossed our path and interconnected. The whisperings, I suspected, were from these entities seeking entry into our world...and, I suspected, seeking willing hosts.

Like the creature within me.

She was a female, I'd come to discover. The sister to a powerful body-hopping demon that I had somehow managed to banish from an accursed family.

Now, from deeper in the Occult Reading Room, which, really, was just a few rows packed floor to ceiling with mostly oversized, darkish books, I heard something slowly, calmly, disturbingly calling out my name.

"Sssister," it said in a dry, raspy voice that seemed to be many voices speaking as one, voices that could have just as easily been my imagination. "Sssister Sssamantha...come to us...waiting... waiting..."

"Ignore them, Samantha. They have no power over you."

"But *she* does," I said, tapping my chest.

"No. Not if you don't let her."

"But she already does," I said. "I can't eat normally, or go in the sun, or breathe or die or..."

He placed a hand on my shoulder. "I never said you had an *ideal* situation, Samantha. But she has not won, nor will she."

I nodded and wanted to cry. His touch did something to me...so comforting, so warm, so gentle...but I kept it together.

"I have two questions..." I finally said.

He waited, and this time I plunged forward, ignoring the beseeching whisperings from deeper in the room.

"Will my son...?"

Except I actually couldn't plunge forward. Not with Archibald Maximus looking at me so kindly, and not with the emotions that raged through me...from fear to fragile hope.

"Your son's condition was unexpected," said Archibald, perhaps tapping into my thoughts. "But, remember, your son did consume the ruby medallion. He will neither revert back into vampirism, nor can he be turned into a vampire."

"But is he immortal?"

"Immortality must stand the test of time."

"Is that a joke?"

"Not really, Sam. What it means, I do not know, and, I suspect, no one knows what will become of your son. But one thing is certain: he will never need to drink blood, nor will he ever shy away from the sun. The curse of vampirism has been lifted."

"But what is he?" I asked.

The Librarian's gentle blue eyes twinkled. He looked so much older than his smooth, handsome, nerdy face implied. "I suspect something very special, Sam. Now, I believe you have a second question about Russell?"

"Yes, how—never mind."

"Thoughts are vibrations, Sam," he said, answering anyway. "I don't so much read your mind, as read your vibrations."

"Of course," I said. "Doesn't everyone?"

"Everyone could, if they knew how."

"Then teach me."

"You are far better at it then you realize."

"Fat lot of good that does me." I gave him a small grin. I liked the Librarian, whoever he was. "Okay, here goes: can another human being be bonded to me?"

"In short, yes."

"Without them knowing it?"

"They know it, Sam. They allowed it. But, perhaps, they did not understand the full extent of the connection...and neither did you."

"Full extent of the connection?" I said, phrasing it as a question, mostly because I hadn't a clue what I was talking about.

"It means, he's devoted to you completely, and if coitus was involved, then the connection might be even deeper."

"Oh, don't get all puritanical on me now," I said. "You know very well we had sex."

"I might be many things," said Archibald, nodding slowly. "But one of them is not crude."

"Fine, whatever...just tell me what to do."

"You don't enjoy his devotion?"

"No…not like this. Not against his will."

"His will has allowed it."

"It's not right," I said.

"Good," said Archibald, and I suspect his last few questions had been a test of some sort. "Then you must release him, Sam."

"And how do I do that?"

"There's no correct way, I'm afraid."

"I don't understand."

"The connection between two people is deeply personal and intimate. You will need to find your own way through this."

"Great," I said. "Who makes this stuff up, anyway?"

Maximus grinned and leaned against the counter. "Oh, just us nerds."

CHAPTER FOURTEEN

I recognized the girl.

Granted, this time she was lying on a slab of cold steel in the Los Angeles County Coroner's office. With me were Detective Sanchez and Dr. Mueller. The detective and I stood to one side of the mostly-covered body, while the medical examiner stood on the other.

Dr. Mueller wore a white lab coat that was mostly clean. There was a very faint splatter near his lapel. It was a fresh splatter...and it made my stomach growl.

Such a monster.

With that thought, Sanchez glanced over at me, alarm in his eyes. Our communication was open, as we had intended it. Sanchez and I had determined beforehand that a private, inner dialogue between ourselves wouldn't be a bad idea.

Don't worry, I thought to him now, *I can control myself.*

You had me worried there.

Trust me, drinking from stiffs in the morgue isn't my idea of fine dining.

That's disturbing on many levels.

Welcome to my world.

Sanchez didn't respond, but the look of *extreme concern* in his eyes said it all. Yes, I was a freak...so freaky that an armed LAPD homicide cop was nervous.

Not nervous, he countered. *Just...alarmed.*

Bullshit.

Okay, fine. You scare the shit out of me. In fact, I haven't been the same since we last met. I've been a nervous wreck and...

He paused, but I picked up his stray thought.

And you've been reading up about vampires? I asked.

Well, yes. Wouldn't you if you were in my shoes? I have to know more. I'm...so intrigued...and scared...but mostly intrigued. It's just so bizarre. I don't want you to remove my memory, Sam. I'll keep your secret. Just like Sherbet does. I need to know what I'm up against out here.

I looked at Dr. Mueller, who was staring at us from over his bifocals and waiting with, what I gathered, was extreme patience. I suspected that when you worked with corpses all day, you developed eternal patience.

Can we maybe talk about this later? I said to Sanchez.

Yes, of course. Sorry.

Meanwhile, during our conversation, Sanchez and I had been idly scanning the body. My line of work didn't call for me viewing a lot of corpses. Neither did my job back when I was a federal agent for the Department of Housing and Urban Development, or the Office of the Inspector General. Back then, I mostly cracked down on fraud and waste and abuse in the various HUD programs. No, not very glamorous, but there were a lot of jerk-offs out there who were more than willing to scam the poor out of their life savings. Mortgage fraud and low-income housing went hand-in-hand, and I was proud to say that I had helped take my share of scumbags off the street.

So, with that said...no, not a lot of bodies in my chosen field. But I had also been recruited to help on other cases. The federal government did that sometimes. Grabbed agents from various departments to work bigger, more complicated cases. Or more important cases.

Yes, I had seen my fair share of examining rooms and corpses.

These days, death meant little to me.

I knew that was the result of the vampire in me, the killer in me, the predator in me...or *her* in me. She was trying to steal my humanity, my sympathy, to make me more like her, and less like the rest of the world.

Like the good Librarian had said, she didn't have power over me.

Go away, I thought, wondering how much of me she could hear. *Go far fucking away.*

No, I had never heard her before, nor had I seen her or experienced her in any way, other than my enhanced powers and cursed affliction, all courtesy of her.

However, I had seen firsthand the evil that bubbled up to the surface when Kingsley had transformed into his hybrid form. Not to mention, just a few months ago, I had conversed and fought with perhaps the most powerful entity of all.

Her brother, in fact.

As I thought these thoughts, and as the good doctor waited for us patiently, I was very aware that Sanchez was staring at me again.

Not so cool anymore, is it? I asked.

Detective Sanchez said nothing, just glanced at me some more, then we both turned our full attention to the victim under the blanket. The stench of cleaning agents was strong in the air, scented ammonia and bleach being the predominant odors. Mostly, though, I detected another smell. The decay of rotting flesh. The victim wasn't in advanced decay, and so her stench wasn't very strong, but I could smell it clearly. Perhaps most disturbingly, it didn't bother me. Not at all. Perhaps most disturbingly, I thought I liked it.

Something is seriously wrong with me.

"Jesus," whispered Sanchez next to me, clearly picking up on my thoughts.

Scratch that last, I communicated silently to him. *I'm dealing with something here...something in me. Something I may or may not explain to you.*

He nodded, although he looked shaken, and not because we were standing over a body.

"Did you witness the autopsy?" I asked Sanchez aloud.

He nodded. "I did."

If the autopsy had bothered him, he didn't outwardly show it. Still, I sensed the mild revulsion ripple through him, and as it did so, I caught a brief glimpse of memory as he'd watched them use a bone saw around her scalp and lift out her brain.

He shuddered again. I didn't shudder. I was intrigued.

Lord help me.

I looked at the medical examiner, who was watching me with an eternal calm that might have made Half Dome in Yosemite envious. I said to him, "And what were your conclusions, Doctor?"

"She bled to death."

"May I see the wound in her neck?" I asked. There was a chance—a very small chance—that I might have asked this question a bit too eagerly. Sanchez glanced over at me again. I was making the poor guy nervous. Hell, I was making *me* nervous.

The doctor nodded and reached down and pulled back the sheet. The woman's face—a face I recognized from two nights ago, although that woman had been in a very different form—in spirit—was stapled back in place below her jawline. Her pretty face had been peeled back during the autopsy to expose the skull. Now, her face had been positioned mostly back into place, although it was slightly askew. I glanced at where some of the curled, unattached skin hung loose.

Fascinating.

Except, of course, I knew that I wasn't fascinated. *She* was fascinated...the thing that lived within me.

Freaky bitch.

The pathologist had us step around to his side of the examining table, which would have been the right side of the woman's neck. Yes, there was the gaping wound. I could see bruising and red, raw, hanging flesh. I noted the arched openings. Bite wounds.

"Looks human," I said.

"We believe so. We recovered human saliva along the opening, as well. The carotid artery was bitten clean through. She lost, precisely, half of her blood. Enough to bleed to death."

"One problem," said Sanchez, hovering somewhere above me. "We only found evidence of about a quarter of her blood."

"So, she bled elsewhere," I said, playing devil's advocate. Or, perhaps, the devil in me was just playing advocate.

Sanchez shook his head. "There's evidence that the attack took place on the trail, where she was also found. We didn't see any evidence that she was moved. We believe she bled to death where she was attacked."

"Except we're missing a quarter of her blood."

"Yes."

I glanced at the pathologist. "Are we being recorded?"

"No, the cameras are turned off. They're only turned on if someone wishes to view an autopsy from an adjacent room."

"From the safety of a TV monitor."

He didn't smile. Death was serious business. "Something like that. The smells can be a bit overwhelming at times."

That I was enjoying the smells, I kept to myself...and to Sanchez, who glanced at me again. I stepped closer to the medical examiner.

Can you hear me, doctor? I thought.

He cocked his head slightly, then nodded.

I'd learned last year that vampires can control others. To what extent, I didn't know. Truthfully, I didn't want to know. But something within me—the devil within me, I suspected—enjoyed controlling others. Needed to control others.

But I needed to now.

And I was enjoying every moment of it.

Good, I thought. *You are to destroy any evidence that links her death to a human. Your official report will state she died of an animal attack. We'll call it a rabid coyote. Understood?*

The good doctor stared at me from over his bifocals, then nodded.

Delete all computerized files and destroy all written reports. Additionally, erase the cameras.

The doctor nodded again, and soon, Detective Sanchez and I stepped out of the laboratory and into the air-conditioned hallway.

To say that Sanchez was looking at me warily would be an understatement. "What happened in there?"

"We have to keep this on the down-low. You can appreciate that."

"No, I mean…all that creepy shit. You really enjoy death that much?"

"No," I said, answering truthfully. "She does."

"And who's she?"

"Another place, another time."

Chapter Fifteen

We were sitting in Sanchez's squad car in one of Griffith Park's many entrances. I noted we were parked in a handicap spot.

Sanchez picked up on my observation, and said, "I'll move if it's needed."

"Good to know," I said.

We were one of a dozen or so other cars. A family of four was currently gathering blankets and an old-fashioned picnic basket. Their two young kids were kicking rocks at each other while the dad was texting, oblivious. The mother, of course, was doing everything, stowing the gear away and telling the kids to knock it off.

Typical. Moms are the true heroes of the world.

I want to wring the dad's neck and tell him to pitch in. To get off his goddamn phone and do something.

Then again, I was in a foul mood. Who wouldn't be? After all, for the first time since becoming a vampire—or whatever it was that I was—I'd really felt the influence of the thing living within me. Her desires were merging into my desires…and I didn't like it. I hated it, in fact.

And it scared the shit out of me.

Worse, I knew that she liked that it scared me…that she craved my fear, in fact. She fed off it. I suspected my fear made her stronger, braver, more audacious.

"Are you catching any of this?" I asked Sanchez.

"All of it, and I'm sorry. I mean, I don't know what the hell happened to you—or is happening to you—but it sounds pretty shitty."

58

"You have no idea."

"And this *thing* inside of you. Does it possess you?"

I looked at the handsome detective who filled the driver's seat completely. His hands were hooked over the lower half of the steering wheel. Big hands, squarish nails. The nails looked thick and healthy. All of him looked thick and healthy. Finally, I shook my head. "It's complicated."

"Try me, Sam. I'm a big boy."

I thought of burdening the detective with who I was, and what was happening to me. Why burden him and not Russell? What was the difference? I thought about that as the detective and I sat together in the dark car, at the base of a park where two innocent women had been slaughtered by a vampire, or a wannabe vampire.

The difference, I knew, was simple: Russell had never asked for any of this. The detective had a job to do, and part of his job included finding answers to two homicides. The answers just happened to be supernatural in nature.

Russell deserved answers, too. Since his girlfriend happened to be supernatural in nature, too.

"I know of Russell Baker," said the detective, picking up my thoughts.

"You follow boxing?"

"I do. He's a champion in the making." Sanchez studied me some more. "And I see he's bound to you in some way."

I chuckled. "You're getting pretty good at this mindreading thing."

"What can I say, I'm a natural. So what does it mean, bound to you?"

"I don't know yet, Detective. I'm still figuring that part out."

"Sorry, I ask a lot of questions."

"You're a homicide cop. It comes with the territory. And if I were you, I would be asking a lot of questions, too."

"If you were me, would you be afraid?"

"Are you afraid of me, Detective?"

"Back there, in the autopsy lab…yeah, I was a little."

"It's not me, Detective. It's her."

"Which comes back to my question: are you possessed, Sam?"

I almost laughed. "Now that's a question I bet you don't ask every day."

He smiled and waited. I felt suddenly sad and empty and lost. His eyes held compassion, but also wariness. That a grown man...that such a huge hunk of a grown man with a gun and his training and his muscles, would be wary of me, just made me realize all over again just how much of a monster I'd become.

"Not a monster, Sam. I just don't understand what's going on with you. Tell me about the thing within you."

"She's a highly evolved dark master."

"What does that mean?"

"Think of a highly evolved master—like Christ or Buddha. But she would be the opposite."

"She is evil."

"Perhaps," I said. "Although I'm not sure what evil means, exactly. I do know that she enjoys death. She enjoys taking life. She feeds on the fear of others. She enjoys creating fear. She enjoys, for instance, that you are wary of me. She wants me to exploit that. I can feel it within me. She hungers to control, to feed, to consume."

"Sounds evil to me."

"She does not see it that way. She sees it as a balancing of the light. A necessity."

"A necessary evil?"

"I think so, yes."

"Do you communicate with her?"

"No. Not yet. But she is getting bolder. I can feel her inside me more and more. I sense her impressions now. They filter up from wherever she resides."

"Sweet Jesus."

"The name alone makes her recoil."

"Interesting," said Sanchez.

"Very," I said.

"So, she doesn't possess you?"

"No. I am still me. But she influences me heavily."

"She is the source of your current powers?"

I nodded. "Or as some would have me believe, the source of my immortal condition."

"Why is she here? Why does she do what she does?"

"It is her entry into this world."

"Through you?"

"And others like me."

Sanchez blinked. "I just received an image of a hulking creature. Is that a…"

"A werewolf, Detective."

"You have got to be kidding me."

"I'm afraid not. Would you like for me to erase your memory now?"

"No. Not yet. Perhaps never. I need to know this stuff."

"Why?"

"I have a job to do, for one."

"You need to know what you're up against, and all that?"

"Yes. But also…"

His voice trailed off, and I caught where he was going with this. "No, Detective. I can't let you."

"I want to help you, Sam."

I shook my head. "No. You don't know what you're talking about."

"Maybe I don't, but I know one thing, Sam: you need help. A lot of help. I may not be this big, hairy Kingsley fellow, but I have resources at my disposal, and I'm pretty good with a gun."

I chuckled…and as I did so, he sat back a little.

"Wait…Kingsley Fulcrum, the defense attorney…is a werewolf?"

"Does it surprise you?"

"He is a big-son-of-bitch."

"And hairy," I added.

"There is a lot of weird going on," said Sanchez, whistling lightly.

"I would say welcome to my world…"

"But it's my world, too," he said. "Now."

I didn't say anything about that, and as we sat here together, I focused on something that had been troubling me since I'd first met the LAPD detective in Sherbet's office.

"Tell me again why you first approached Sherbet?"

Sanchez looked at me, blinked, and as he did so, I noted something very curious in his memory. It was blank. He said, "You guys dealt with a similar incident. It seemed obvious to approach Detective Sherbet."

Except, of course, I knew that the official records had been stricken of any connection that had anything to do with vampires. Officially, the murders taking place under the Fullerton Theater were the result of a serial killer. Unofficially, the murders were the result of a blood ring—mortals who supplied human blood to vampires. Any of that evidence had been destroyed and memories erased by another vampire named Hanner.

Sanchez, who had been following my train of thought, shook his head. "No, I remember reading something in the newspaper."

"Details of the crimes were not reported in the paper. Try again."

"I...I thought I had read it in the paper."

"The details of the crimes were covered up, Detective. Anyone and everyone associated with the Fullerton Blood Ring have been dealt with."

"What do you mean dealt with?"

"Memories altered."

"So, then, how did I know to call Sherbet?"

"That's the million-dollar question, Detective."

CHAPTER SIXTEEN

anchez left me there at the park.

He didn't like it, but I told him it was part of my process. He had asked what process that was and I told him I hadn't a clue. He liked that even less, but he also sensed I wanted to be alone with my thoughts. And then, finally, I gave him a small glimpse of the creature that I would soon become.

"Holy shit," he said.

"That about sums it up," I said as I stood outside the driver's side door of his squad car. "Go home to your family, Detective, and forget about vampires and ghosts and giant flying bats."

"I couldn't if I tried."

"I could help you."

"No, please."

He gave me a lingering look, then looked out over the dark park, shook his head, then drove off, his tires crunching over the gravel parking lot.

I set off along the same trail, the same trail where a young lady had been killed recently, where she had bled to death. Where a quarter of her blood had gone missing.

Enough to feed a hungry vampire.

Perhaps even two.

———

The park was mostly empty.

Sometimes, I heard the rustling of smaller animals and the rarer mid-sized animal. Raccoons and skunks, mostly. Griffith Park was famous for its observatory and zoo and Greek Theatre, all of which have been featured in movies and TV shows ranging from *Rebel Without a Cause* to *Three's Company.*

Yes, we were directly above Hollywood, and Hollywood loved to film in its own back yard. Griffith Park was, quite literally, Hollywood's back yard.

I passed the crime scene again, and was pleased to see that the young lady's spirit was gone, although I saw residual energy, energy that would never go away. A murder scarred the land, perhaps forever. And what I saw, as I moved past that same boulder where I'd seen the ghost of the young woman sitting, was a chaotic collection of light that formed and reformed, swirling and dispersing, over and over again. Perhaps throughout all eternity. Playing out the scene of her murder, at least at an energetic level, forever.

The world might forget this young jogger, but the earth never would. Perhaps this was its way of remembering the dead. Or not, I don't know. I was just a mom. Albeit a freaky mom.

I stepped into the frenzied energy, and, as I did so, I caught a faint feeling of fear, of pain, of confusion...and of excitement. The excitement was not from the victim. It was from the killer.

I paused on the trail, turning slightly, feeling the mass of energy around me. Psychics can tap into such energy, read it like a book. I was not a real psychic. Refer back to my mom comment. But I am real freaky, and sometimes I get psychic hits with the best of them. The hair along my arms and back of my neck prickled. I kept turning slowly, tuning in, locking in.

I knew the girl had no memory of what had happened to her. Her last memories were, in fact, a crazy mess of pain and fear and dying. Whatever had hit her, she couldn't see it, or never had a chance to see it.

My inner alarm system remained quiet. Whatever had been out here a few nights ago wasn't around now. Perhaps it was time to take another look around. So, I closed my eyes and reached out around me, expanding my inner sight as far as it would go.

I saw nothing human, although I saw plenty of glowing life forms, ranging from mice to a young deer. That I suddenly imagined myself pursuing the deer and feasting upon it might have had more to do with my recent viewing of the *Twilight* movies, than any bloodlust.

Still, I idly wondered what the deer's blood would taste like. Probably warm and delicious. I rarely, if ever, feasted on a living animal, and wasn't about to start tonight—Oh yes, I'd almost forgotten that time I had gone to a castle in Switzerland on a business trip and was accommodated, but I hadn't killed for my supper...someone had done it for me.

Try it, came a sudden thought. A very distant, faint, small thought at the far reaches of awareness. It sounded like my own thoughts, admittedly. Like something that had originated within me, but I knew, somehow, that it wasn't mine. It was too firm. Too controlling. Too evil.

It was her.

The entity that lived within me. I was sure of it, and it was, I was certain, the first time she had ever directly communicated with me.

I snapped back into my body, as a cold shiver came over me. The image of the grazing deer disappeared in a literal blink. I rubbed my arms and then my temples and wished like hell I hadn't just heard those two words. I wished like hell she would stay far away, or stay buried. I did not want to have to listen to her, too.

Indeed, hearing her now, her words rising up from the depths of my subconscious, hit too close to home.

Now she was pissing me off.

More importantly, though, hearing a second set of thoughts in my head, thoughts that sounded far too similar to my own, felt a bit like I was going insane.

As I stood there in the woods, feeling the scattered energy of a heinous murder around me, seeing animals I shouldn't see, hearing sounds I shouldn't hear, and hungering for something no sane person should ever hunger for, I knew I was fighting a demon of another kind.

My own personal demon.

No, I wasn't talking about her, the entity buried within me.

Ever since I first woke up in the hospital bed seven years ago, back when I first felt the changes coming over me, back when I first knew that I would never be normal again, I also wondered something else.

I wondered if I had gone insane.

At what point I had gone insane, I didn't know. Maybe I'd had enough of my kids fighting. Maybe I'd had enough of Anthony's skid marks. Or of Danny's cheating. Or of life itself. Maybe I had checked out long ago, mentally, that is. Maybe my mind was long, long gone.

And hearing a second voice in my head seemed to confirm that. Seemed to confirm my worst fears.

I didn't want to go insane. I didn't want to lose my mind.

I took a few deep, shuddering, worthless breaths…breaths that served no purpose other than to calm me down. Except the first few didn't do anything for me, but the next batch did. Finally, finally, I felt myself calming down. I reminded myself that I'd been hearing voices in my head for over a year now, ever since I'd first heard Fang's whispered thoughts.

This was no different, right?

But it *was* different. It was very different. Fang's thoughts sounded like Fang. I heard his inflections, his tone, his distinct voice inside my head.

These thoughts…

Well, these thoughts sounded like me. Just like me. As if they were my own.

Except, of course, they weren't.

Deep breaths, Sam.

Breathe, breathe.

Good.

Very good.

I turned in a full circle, hands on hips, breathing and calming down and saying anything I could think of to not lose it right here in the woods above Hollywood.

As I did so, as I calmed my mind, as I did my best to get something out of my head that might never leave my head—Lord help me—I found myself particularly tuned into the chaotic energy around me.

Most curious, I was tuned in holistically, from seemingly everywhere at once.

I forgot about the voice in my head, the demon within me. I forgot that just moments earlier, I'd nearly gone into a full panic attack.

Instead, I saw the scene play out before me.

Not like a movie, exactly, but close. Perhaps a badly edited movie that jumped forward and backward in time, with a wildly swinging camera.

I saw her murder.

All of it.

———

She is running alone. I see this in real-time, as if it's happening now.

Panting, careful of her footing, looking at her wristwatch, looking up into the sky, clearly aware that it is getting late, clearly aware that she might be in a vulnerable position.

I see the shadow keeping pace behind her, too.

It is a smallish shadow. A lithe figure. Dressed all in black and wearing a hoodie. Tendrils of blond hair peek out, flap about.

She is moving far too quickly for human eyes to follow her, detect her. Except that a human's eyes aren't following her or detecting her. These are Nature's eyes. The land's eyes. Moving fast or slow, supernatural or not, it was obvious to me, as I stood there on the trail, tuned into the scene, that nothing escaped the eyes of Mother Nature herself.

The scene continued playing out before me:

67

The jogger is fleet of foot, stepping smoothly over roots and rocks, brushing past overgrown shrubs and through high grass. She pumps her arms rhythmically, breathing evenly through pursed lips.

She is unaware of the creature following, a creature that pauses every so often but keeps to the shadows.

A creature who undoubtedly assumed she was going undetected, unaware that her every movement was being forever recorded into the land, seared into the soil.

The female jogger hears something, and pauses, cocking her head to one side, and that's when her stalker attacks.

It's not pretty. It's violent and hard to watch, even for me. Especially for me. The force of the attack drives the girl to the ground. Something dark and shadowy and evil seems to be clinging to her. Not quite clinging...*attached*. The girl fights at first, but mostly, she screams, and soon she's not screaming anymore, but jerking violently, all while the little shadow stays on top of her, clinging like a hungry parasite.

It's over quickly.

I listen to the wet sounds of feeding and chewing and soon the little creature stands...and wipes the blood from her mouth.

This is the first time I get a clear look at the face inside the hoodie, a face that's illuminated by millions of particles of light.

I recognize her immediately.

I am most curious, however, at the identity of the person who's approaching from the shadows. Shadows that are alive with light, at least to my eyes.

A tall man is standing there, watching her, head cocked to one side.

I know him well, too.

Chapter Seventeen

I was flying.

These days, I'd learned to pack my clothing into my pants themselves, tying off the whole shebang at the ankles like a makeshift duffle bag, all of which now dangled from one of my longish talons.

That I had a longish talon was still something I wasn't entirely used to, and if there was any upside to having something dark and evil living within me, this was it:

Flying.

Okay, kicking ass wasn't bad, either. I was stronger than most men—many men combined, in fact. Truth was, I wasn't entirely sure just how strong I was. I suspected I could channel—or perhaps funnel—whatever amount of strength I needed for any given situation.

And, if someone put a gun to my head (a gun with silver bullets, of course), I would admit that being psychic and reading minds had its upside. So did having an inner warning system, which had alerted me many countless times to potential trouble...and saved my ass countless times, too.

As I flew over Griffith Park, beating my wings slowly, languidly, feeling the rush of wind on my face—or the creature's face I had temporarily become, I suddenly realized *why* I had such gifts. Why I was so powerful. Why I could fly and read minds and do all the crazy things I do.

These weren't gifts. No.

These were tools.

Tools to keep *her* alive. To keep her host healthy and viable. To keep me from dying off too quickly. So that she could grow stronger. So that she could plot and scheme.

Bitch.

Beneath me, the park gave way to the glowing dome of the Griffith Observatory, then over the Greek Theatre, then finally down along bustling Hollywood Boulevard. Yes, even from up here, I could see the Hollywood Walk of Fame, and its many brass stars embedded in the sidewalks. If I looked hard enough, I could even make out a name or two. In fact, I might have just seen Cher's.

Lucky me, I thought. Raptor-like vision and yet, as the creature, I could read.

Had anyone bothered to look up, they wouldn't see much. Just a shadow passing beneath the smattering of stars, briefly blotting out the celestial lights. Perhaps a stray strobe light might fall across me. This was, after all, Hollywood. But mostly, I was high enough and dark enough to go unnoticed, which I did, looking down at the mortals who went about their lives, idolizing stars, dreaming of stars, never guessing that something now flew among the stars themselves, directly overhead.

I banked to starboard and headed for the LAPD station, where I'd left my car earlier today.

As I flew, I turned my thoughts toward the person I had seen feasting on the young woman...and to the person I had seen step out of the shadows.

I had put off thinking about it.

I didn't want to believe it.

But I had seen him clearly. He was wearing his own hoodie, and his eyes glowed softly from within the dark depths. Not all vampires could see the flame just behind the iris. I could. Again, lucky me.

Fang's eyes had been glowing softly with twin flames of fire as he watched from the tree line. He did more than watch, of course. He soon came over and knelt next to the dead jogger, and when he lowered his face to her neck, I snapped out of the reverie.

But not before I'd seen Detective Hanner smile broadly, her lips coated with fresh blood. Another bitch.

I continued along, banking again and headed toward downtown.

Once there, I circled high above the police station, wondering if I would show up on any radar, but doubting it. I found an alley not too far away, and dropped down into it.

Yes, there was a bum sleeping in it. No, he didn't wake up, even when a hulking, winged creature settled in next to him, a creature that I now knew was summoned briefly from an alternate world.

So weird, I thought, as I focused on the naked woman in my thoughts...the woman who was the real me.

She stepped forward, and I gasped, and the sensation that came over me was not entirely unpleasant. No, I didn't go through a physical transformation. My bones didn't break or elongate, and I didn't twist and writhe in pain, all of which, I was sure, made for good TV or movies.

I'd come to understand the process of transformation as the slipping into and out of existence, slipping into and out of this world and another.

And, naked as the day I was born, as I unwrapped my clothing, I suddenly wondered where, exactly, I disappeared to. Where did this body go?

If I summoned the winged creature from another place and time, did I, perhaps, switch places with it? I doubted it, but now I suddenly wanted to know.

Where did I go?

I would tackle that question another time.

For now, I had Fang on my mind, and in my heart. Seeing him again, even as he approached a murdered woman, even as he gazed down upon her dead body with hunger in his glowing eyes, brought back a very intense feeling within me.

I remembered just how much I'd loved him.

Lord help me, I loved him still.

Chapter Eighteen

We were in bed together.

It had been a fun night. A sweet night. We had held hands and laughed and kissed. I needed this final, sweet memory, knowing what I was about to do, the heart that I was about to break.

I didn't know much about anything, but I knew that I couldn't live with myself knowing that another human being was supernaturally bound to me.

I don't want another bound to me.

I want them to love me, for me.

Russell was on his side, his warm hand flat on my stomach. Being a bloodsucker had done wonders for my body, but I was still a little curvy, yet still had a small stomach. I liked my stomach. Washboards were overrated and not very fun. Russell had a washboard stomach. In fact, he might have just been the hardest human being I'd ever touched. Yes, hard looked good, but wasn't very fun to snuggle next to.

Russell and I were still dressed. He had tried to undress me numerous times, and numerous times, I'd resisted. He didn't complain. He didn't get all whiny the way guys got when they didn't get sex. Instead, he lay next to me contentedly. I sensed a smile on his handsome face.

Sadly, it wasn't a natural smile.

It was a goofy smile that seemed oddly plastered on his face. It was a smile that reminded me of the body-hopping demon of a few months ago…but not evil. Russell's smile was goofy. Like a man hopped up on love.

But maybe that was too much to ask for. Maybe I didn't deserve love. Maybe it was selfish of me to love another, to bring them into my train-wreck of a life.

Yes, came a distant thought.

A thought, I was certain, that wasn't my own. It was her. Except it sounded so much like me. It could have easily originated in my own thoughts. It could have been my own. But it wasn't. This single word had been faint, distant, and slightly random.

It wasn't going to be easy to distinguish her thoughts from my own, but I had to. If I wanted to stay sane. If I wanted to keep myself from going crazy.

She was changing the rules.

Never before had she made a direct appearance into my thoughts. Yes, her influence could be seen outwardly, by changing the chemistry of my body, the natural and supernatural state of my body.

But internally, she had stayed away.

Until now.

She was getting bolder, more brazen, more challenging. She had said "yes" just when I figured that I shouldn't love again. I didn't have to wonder why for long. Of course, she wanted me to feel lonely, to feel unloved, to feel less than what I was. And I knew the reason why. Low self-esteem, low self-worth were key components to her master plan. Most key was the absence of love. All of which made it easier to move in, to take over, to push me aside, or, perhaps, to remove me completely.

Love, I suspected, was the key.

However, I heard nothing further from her—thank God—and instead, turned my attention to Russell next to me, who was gazing at me even now with his big, round, puppy eyes. I could feel the love radiating from him.

No, not real love, I reminded myself. A *semblance* of love. Infatuation, perhaps. It was, in fact, a spell of some sort.

Very clever, I thought, directing my words to the thing that lived within me. *And shitty, too. Give me a feeling of love, a sense of love, a hint of love, and I confuse it for the real thing.*

When, in fact, it wasn't.

No, I was *controlling* Russell. I was *using* him for love. What he really felt for me, I didn't know. But it wasn't real love.

Controlling others fed her. A lack of *real* love fed her. Low self-esteem and depression fed her.

All of which, I knew, would help her to eventually take control of me.

I'd seen what such a demon can do. I had watched her brother control an entire family.

I couldn't let that happen to me, ever.

Most important, I had to remove her.

Forever.

And it started with letting Russell go.

To sever his tie with me.

Except, of course, I hadn't a clue how to do it, and the Librarian had been no help.

No, he had been helpful.

He had said that I needed to find my own way through it, that the connection between two people is deeply personal and intimate.

I thought about that as I turned to my side and reached for Russell's hand. I opened my mouth to speak...and hadn't a clue what I would say...

CHAPTER NINETEEN

"Hi," I said.

"Hi, baby," he said, and squeezed my hand lovingly and with so much emotion that his grip literally shook.

Lord, help me, I thought.

"Are you okay?" he asked, and the exaggerated look of concern in his eyes was almost comical.

That's not him, I thought. The Russell Baker I knew was strong, confident, controlled.

The expression on his face suggested that his whole life, his whole existence, all of his happiness, hinged on my happiness. In fact, on my answer.

Lord, help me, I thought again.

"I love you, Russell," I started.

"I love you, too, baby, more than you know."

He tried to release his hand—except that I knew where that hand was going: to the first boob it could find.

Sex connected us beyond what was normal, what was healthy.

So, I held his hand firm and he relaxed it. He continued gazing at me with those big, beautiful, brown eyes. His muscles flexed and undulated just under his skin, like slumbering vipers. God, he was so sexy.

Not anymore, I thought.

Release him.

I considered telling him the truth, and then erasing his mind later. Yes, I could do that, but that wasn't fair to him, or his subconscious.

I suspected that even if I did erase his mind that his subconscious would remember…and haunt him forever. Maybe not. Maybe he truly would forget. But I doubted it. His heart would remember. Somewhere, deep inside he would remember.

Was it fair to just break up with him, with no explanation?

No. He has to know, I thought.

It was the only way.

No lying. No hiding. Unfortunately for Russell Baker, I had been unaware of my ability to control him. Now I knew, and as I thought those words, tears came to my eyes.

The tears were for my heart.

And for Russell's heart.

Yes, I loved him. Yes, I thought there was a chance it was going somewhere.

But I will never control him, and would never allow myself to control him. Or anyone. The bitch within me had effectively cut me off from loving another human, another mortal.

I had tried to keep Russell from the truth of who I was, but now the truth, I knew, would set him free. I swallowed and looked away as the tears continued to come to my eyes, knowing what I was about to, what I had to do.

Lord, help me, I knew what I had to do.

CHAPTER TWENTY

It was after.

I'd spent the last two hours pouring my heart out to Russell, telling him everything, from my attack seven years ago, to my hunger for blood, to my supernatural abilities, to the love spell he was under.

At first, he had laughed lightly, holding my hand and wanting to change the subject. He tried to even have sex again. Then he tried to change the subject again. Then he asked me to stop. Then he asked why I was telling him all of this. Then he asked if I was crazy. Then he grew angry. He stormed out of the bedroom, only to return, rubbing his temples and pacing randomly.

He wanted to know why I was telling him all of this, why I was doing this to him, why I was pushing him away with my crazy talk. We had something good, he kept saying. Something beautiful and pure and real.

I got up from the bed and took his hand and led him through my house and into the garage. I had planned ahead for the night. The kids were with Mary Lou, and Russell and I had the house to ourselves. He liked that idea. He thought that meant a night of sex.

He thought wrong. Sex was the problem. Sex was binding him to me against his will. I suspected sex had this effect on many people, although perhaps not as strongly.

Once in the garage, I showed him the old refrigerator in the far corner. Dusty and dirty and forgotten—and also padlocked.

"What's this?" he had asked.

I said nothing, only fetched the key from under the old coffee can filled with random nuts and bolts, a can hidden behind a tool box on a shelf under the workbench Danny had made years ago. A workbench that never saw any work, since Danny had decided that chasing whores and neglecting his family was the best way to spend his free time.

I unlocked the refrigerator and pulled the door open. Inside was my latest shipment from the butcher in Norco. It was a simple cardboard box pre-filled with sealed packets of blood. The butchery had thought the blood was for laboratory experiments. At least, that's what Danny and I told them way back when, back when Danny had tried to be there for me. That lasted only a few years.

Danny had thought it was a good idea for the butchery to think the blood was for scientific purposes. I agreed. We used his name, and added a "Dr." in front of it. So now, all the packets and boxes are labeled: "Dr. Daniel Moon." A name I got to see every time I had the displeasure of drinking from one of these filthy packets.

"What's this?" Russell had asked.

"Dinner," I said. "Although these days, I have a human source."

Russell had been bending down, holding one of the malleable packets, which oozed between his long fingers. He looked up at me, the light of the refrigerator highlighting his scarred but handsome features. "What do you mean, a *human source?*"

I was leaning a shoulder against the refrigerator, arms crossed. I figured that if I was going to tell him the truth, then there was no holding back. "Allison Lopez."

"Your friend?"

"Yes."

"The psychic?"

"And, apparently, witch," I said.

He looked at me, then looked at the packet of blood some more. "This is blood," he said. "I should know. I see enough of it in my profession."

I nodded, waited.

"You really drink this stuff?"

"I do."

"Prove it."

I held out my hand and he slapped the packet down in it. I used my naturally pointed nail to deftly slice through the plastic, as I'd done hundreds of times before. I held the clear packet up to him, which swirled with fragments of bone and hair and meat, and said, "Bottoms up."

I drained the packet quickly, fought the initial gag reflex I always felt when drinking the butchery-supplied blood, then showed him the empty packet.

"Holy shit," he said.

"That's about what it tastes like, too."

"But that doesn't prove anything, does it? Just that you, you know, like to drink..."

"Animal blood?" I said. "You think I enjoy this? That I have some twisted fetish?"

"I...I don't know."

I gripped his tee shirt and slammed him against the garage wall. He didn't have far to travel, maybe just a foot or two. Still, he hit the wall hard, which was fine. He could handle it. He was a big boy, a tough guy. Not to mention, the overgrown love bug needed some sense knocked into him.

Except he kept looking at me with that big, goofy, loving grin.

Granted, I *liked* the big, goofy, loving grin. It wasn't a bad thing to have a lover look at you this way. Except, in context, the look wasn't appropriate. If anything, Russell should have been nervous, or even afraid.

I'd just shown him a refrigerator of blood.

I'd told him my greatest secret.

He should have been running for the hills. Or curled up in a big, muscular fetal position.

Not looking at me lovingly.

I lifted him off his feet, his shirt now ruined. "Stop looking at me like that, goddammit!"

Except he didn't stop looking at me like that. In fact, he looked down at me with even more love than ever. "I don't care what you are, Sam. I don't care if you're the devil himself. I love you. I will always love you."

"You should care, dammit."

And I didn't just drop him, but threw him as well. He went spinning and stumbling, slamming against my minivan, and ultimately skidding along on his bony ass. He was wearing sleek basketball shorts, and so he went skidding a half dozen feet.

"Why are you doing this, Sam?" he said, as I bore down on him, stalking him, hunting him. I had a sudden image of me pinning Russell down to the dirty concrete floor of my garage, burying my face in his neck, as I had seen Hanner do with the jogger.

I shook my head and fought off the image.

But it came again and again.

It was her, of course.

Tempting me.

She wanted nothing more than for me to pounce upon Russell, to feed from him, perhaps destroy him. She wanted nothing more than my own humanity to be destroyed in the process, to be abolished and removed. My humanity, I knew, was her greatest obstacle to coming forward. As long as I remained who I was, she would stay in the shadows. Must stay in the shadows.

But that didn't solve my present problem.

Russell, of course, being my present problem. A man who had become bonded with me, so much so that, even as I stalked him, he looked up at me with pure bliss. Pure love.

How did one erase the effects of a potent love spell? Or, perhaps more aptly put, a love curse?

I didn't know, but whatever I was doing, it wasn't working. I seemed to only be hurting him more. Confusing him more.

My instinct was to break him. To physically remove the love from him, to beat it out of him. To hurt him so much that he would never love me again. I knew this wasn't the monster in me. This wasn't *her*.

This was me.

80

But it wasn't right, and so I stopped before him, standing above him, my fists clenched as he looked up at me with hurt and confusion and, yes, more love than ever. Russell was a tough guy. He could withstand an onslaught, even from me. I would possibly permanently hurt him before I saw any change in him. He would take the punishment, and go on loving me afterward.

I stared down at him as he stared up at me. His shirt was torn. His knees were dirty from his tumble over the concrete of my garage. His big, beautiful, brown eyes were full of tears held in a sort of holding pattern. One good blink would send them cascading down his face.

That's when I felt my own tears running down my face.

All he knew was love, of course. He didn't understand what was happening. I wasn't getting through to him. Not on a conscious level. I needed to go deeper.

Whatever that meant, I knew I had to go deeper, break through the spell, to the real Russell beneath.

I dropped to the concrete next to him, sat cross-legged before him, and took both his hands…

Chapter Twenty-one

"I'm sorry," I said, squeezing hands.

"It's okay, baby. We all have our bad nights."

"Did I hurt you?"

"*You* hurt *me?*" He laughed.

None of this was right. We shouldn't be sitting in a filthy garage—which, by the way, I needed to rally the troops and get cleaned this weekend. The troops being, of course, Tammy and Anthony. Anyway, we shouldn't be sitting here in the garage. We should have been in bed, making love. Holding each other, falling deeper in love. And Russell was so easy to love, too. Russell was easy to be with…but now I know why. Everything was too easy. He was too amenable. There was no fight in him. At least, none left. Our relationship, I realized, wasn't real. It was built on the supernatural. The unnatural.

"Did you forget the part where I told you that I'm a vampire? That I drink blood? That you should want no part of me?"

He pulled me into him and tried to kiss me. I pulled back. He shrugged and kept on smiling. "Baby, I want every part of you."

"And don't you see how cheesy that sounds?"

"Baby, when it's love, there is no such thing as cheesy."

Okay, this had to stop, even if it was just to put a stop to the nauseating sweet nothings. I had to go deeper. I had to reach the real Russell.

"Will you do something for me, Russell?" I asked, still holding his hands.

"Anything for you, baby. You know that."

"I want you to close your eyes."

He did so instantly, without question, without hesitation. Had I been prone to, I could abuse his devotion to me, his bond to me. I could use him and abuse him and have him do my bidding, and that was exactly what *she* wanted me to do...the using and abusing would steal away more of my humanity, break me down further.

Such a bitch, I thought, and closed my own eyes.

I expanded my awareness out and around him. I wasn't going to control Russell's thoughts, not like I had done with the martial arts trainer last year, or the medical examiner recently. No, I was doing something different with Russell, something I had never done before, something that I wasn't sure could even be done.

I was looking for the real him.

Hi, Russell, I thought.

He jerked and opened his eyes. I didn't have to open my eyes to know this. Our psychic connection was strong, although I kept my own wall up, keeping him out of my own thoughts, as I had always done with him, never wanting to reveal to him my true nature, or just how freaky I really was.

I had wanted to build a real relationship.

Little did I know that I was controlling him more and more. In effect, I was inadvertently doing to him what the bitch wanted to do to me.

I couldn't do that. Not to Russell, not to anyone.

"Is that you?" asked Russell. "In my head?"

I nodded and thought: *Yes. Now close your eyes, Russell. And keep them closed and focus on my words.*

"Okay," he whispered.

His hands, I noted, were shaking. A part of him was scared. That part of him was not allowed to surface, hidden beneath the spell, no doubt frightened and lost and confused as hell.

I literally felt myself slip into the flow of his thoughts. They were not jumbled, as many thoughts were. Indeed, poor Russell's thoughts were a steady stream of love flowing toward me. I had to admit, that felt nice. What girl wouldn't want her man to think such thoughts?

But they weren't natural.

I dipped into these loving thoughts, reveled in them briefly, and pushed forward...and downward.

I'd never slipped this deeply into anyone's thoughts. Never thought I had to nor would want to. In fact, I had doubted I could. But sex did wonders, connecting two people deeply...perhaps deeper than they realized. Certainly deeper than I had realized.

After my attack, Danny and I had never had sex again. Maybe that had been a good thing. After all, he would have been bound to me like a lovesick puppy. Then again, he probably wouldn't have cheated on me, either, and my family would have remained intact.

But that would have been controlling, and I wouldn't have learned his true scumbag nature.

Russell wasn't a scumbag. At least, I'd never seen evidence to the contrary. Then again, within a few weeks, we had gotten intimate, and, perhaps, the spell had begun then. So, again, I wasn't seeing the real Russell. Perhaps I never had.

No, I had seen the real Russell in those first few weeks: strong, jovial, confident, driven, and sexy as hell.

Down I went through Russell's thoughts, deeper and deeper. And the deeper I got, the more chaotic they got, too. Gone was his undying love for me. Here were thoughts about boxing, working out, the death of Caesar Marquez. There were thoughts about me, too—wondering what he felt about me, wondering if we really had something here, wondering why I always felt cold, wondering why I never ate, wondering why I was so pale, wondering why he couldn't see a section of my face when we had walked past a mirror, wondering why I was so strong, wondering why I only slept during the day. These were his normal thoughts, and they were thoughts from many, many months ago.

Russell was in a sort of holding pattern, I knew. Which made sense. He hadn't fought for three months now, and he rarely worked out.

He had been, of course, focused on me, while the rest of his life was forgotten.

Yes, I had to stop this. Now. Despite the heaviness in my heart. Then again, perhaps what I felt for him wasn't real, either. His sweetness, kindness, and attention was all a sham. It was all spurred on by a spell.

No, he *was* sweet. I'd always remember the quiet, confident boxer who first came into my office and hired me last year.

I went deeper still, slipping beyond phobias and fears and secret sexual desires. I paused briefly at one, raised my eyebrows, and then continued down deeper into his subconscious.

How, exactly, I did this, I didn't know.

But I saw it almost as a physical journey, flying down through the various layers of his consciousness. I knew I was sitting in the garage, in dirt and oil and filth, holding his hands, eyes closed, but I was on a surprising journey through another person's consciousness.

But I still hadn't reached the *real* Russell Baker.

I passed through some of his oldest memories, and down into his early childhood. I watched him both picking fights and being picked on. Those who picked on him soon found themselves in a lot trouble. I almost laughed as I watched him single-handedly beat up two bullies.

Down I went. Deeper and deeper.

Early childhood memories. A loving mother. An asshole father. The father beat him, but Russell always fought back.

Deeper and earlier, and soon I saw something rather amazing. Burning brightly in his deepest memories was a furious ball of white light. Hovering there in his thoughts.

Waiting for me.

Two words appeared in my mind: *Hi, Sam.*

Russell? I thought.

But, of course.

85

Chapter Twenty-two

smiled, although I kept my physical eyes closed.

Yes, this sounded like the real Russell. Confident, humorous, care-free. Not obedient, agreeable and, well, love-struck.

I did fall in love with you, Sam, but something funny happened on the way to the Forum...

You fell under my spell.

I sensed him chuckling. *Something like that.*

So, who am I speaking to, exactly?

It's me, Sam. The Russell you met and remember, I'm just sort of...buried down here. Watching myself from a distance, watching myself act like a love-starved schoolboy. That's some spell.

The ultimate pussy-whipped spell, I thought, and blushed, although I didn't think Russell could see me blush. I was still talking to his ego. The part of him that was him. Not his higher self or spirit.

He laughed lightly in my head. I was still looking at a very bright spot...what this was, I wasn't sure. Perhaps his focused energy. Or perhaps this is what the mind looked like at its deepest, most unreachable spot.

Unreachable by most, Sam. Not you, apparently.

So, you believe me now? I asked. *That I am, you know...*

A vampire?

Yes, I thought.

You have a hard time saying it, don't you, Sam?

Yes, I thought. *I do.*

Why is that?

86

Because it's crazy. I can only handle so much crazy.

You're in denial, Sam.

Oh, yeah? And what do you know of vampires?

Not much, but it's pretty obvious you are one.

That obvious, huh?

I knew something was up by our third or fourth date.

What gave me away?

Your skin, mostly. You were always so cold.

But I used hand warmers!

Russell laughed, the sound reaching me distantly. *True, but the rest of you was always so cold. Your cheeks, your lips, your shoulders. And I mean cold. Ice cold. Dead cold.*

Ouch, I thought.

There are no secrets here, Sam. We're both an open book. At least, I am. I can see that your mind is still closed.

You know more than I give you credit, I thought.

We all know more than we give ourselves credit for. The problem is, there's too much surface shit that gets in the way, too many clouds obscuring our thoughts, filling us with worry and doubt and fear. It stops us from tapping deeper within ourselves.

Good to know, I thought. *But I have a hard time believing you could ever be afraid.*

You would be surprised, Sam. For instance, I'm afraid now.

I caught his meaning. *You are afraid that you might never come back.*

Yes, Sam.

How do I release you? I asked.

You're doing it now.

And how, exactly, am I doing that?

By reaching out to me, connecting to me, bringing me out of the funk I was in.

You call this a funk?

It's the funkiest of funk, Sam. Limbo, actually. A dull state where days and weeks and months slip past, and I can only watch from a distance, watching as I act like a love-struck fool.

But you love me, too.

I do, Sam.

I'm sorry I did this to you, I thought.

It wasn't your fault, Sam. I believe you didn't know what would happen.

I wanted to bury my face in my hands, to hide the tears that had started to come, but I needed to hold tightly to Russell, to keep the connection.

Had I known, I thought, *I never would have let things get as far as they had.*

I know, Sam. I also know that you have total control over me. I am, quite literally, at your mercy. You could do with me as you wish. I would do anything for you. Or, rather, the cursed part of me would do anything for you.

The love-struck schoolboy?

Yeah, him.

I don't want to control you, Russell.

I know you don't, Sam.

But you need to know that there's a part of me that I struggle with, a part of me that does want to control you. To use you, to make you do...

Your bidding? he asked lightly, laughing.

Yeah, that.

We all have our inner monsters, Sam. Yours is just a little more obvious.

I had given Russell a glimpse inside of me, of what I dealt with, and he had obviously sensed the demon within, the demon waiting to come out.

I'm sorry you have to deal with this, Sam.

Thank you.

But there's one thing I do know above all else.

The tears were really flowing now. I felt them running unhindered down my face, into my sweatshirt.

I know that you will beat her, Sam. You will beat the shit out of her, too.

That's just the boxer in you, I thought, and nearly laughed.

Maybe, he thought. *But I also know this. There comes a time when we all have to stand up for what we believe. There's a time for love, and a time for war. And your time for love is not now, Sam. Your time for war is now. Get her, Sam. Remove her and beat her back to wherever she came from.*

And what of love? I thought, weeping silently.

Not now, he thought. *And not with me, Sam. Not ever.*

I buried my face in my hands, letting go of his own.

Release me, Sam, I heard him say from somewhere deep in my thoughts, his voice fading, now barely discernible. *Release me...release me...*

Chapter Twenty-three

Russell was gone.

I felt empty and alone and unlovable, almost suicidal. Almost. I would never leave my kids or my sister or Allison or any of my friends. No, not over lost love. But as I sat there at my kitchen table, my head in my hands and a cup of lukewarm tap water in front of me, I felt as if something very precious had been stolen from me.

Stolen by *her*.

The ability to love and be loved romantically.

I fought more tears, then decided not to fight them and let them flow and shook my head and cursed her and God and the Librarian and myself. I cursed the vampire who had first attacked me. I cursed Fang because I was pissed off that he left me. I cursed Kingsley for cheating on me, and cursed my ex-husband for abandoning me when I needed him the most. I cursed the stupid glass of water in front of me and the filthy blood in my freezer in the garage. I cursed my unattached garage because who buys a house with an unattached garage? My cheap ex-husband, that was who. So, I cursed him some more. And cursing him felt the best of all, and so I did that for a few more minutes until I couldn't curse anymore and couldn't see through the tears. I picked up the glass of water and threw it across the kitchen, so hard that it shattered into a million pieces and put a hole in a cupboard. I cursed the million pieces.

And then I was done cursing. I just sat there and wept, my mind empty. And later, when I was done weeping, I thought of one person. The person I missed most of all. Not Kingsley or Russell and certainly not Danny.

I thought of Fang.

I missed him so much that I thought I would scream.

And then I did scream.

Loudly.

So loudly that a dog down the street started yowling along with me.

Chapter Twenty-four

After I had cleaned up the glass, I made a mental note to call a handyman. I might have been able to fly to the moon and back, but I sure as hell couldn't fix something like this.

As I sat back at the kitchen table, I got a text from Anthony. It was a close-up picture of his nose. Actually, it was a picture of the *inside* of his nostrils. It was kind of blurry. Under the picture were the words: *Miss you, mama!*

I wrote: *Miss you, too, now go to bed.*

Boo, he wrote. Then added: *"ger"*

Yes, booger. Go to bed. Tell your sister I love her.

Better yet, I would. I texted her cell phone directly, telling her I loved her and missed them. Her response was immediate: *Anthony's annoying me.*

That's all you have to say? I wrote back.

Well you know I love you, mom! Do I always have to tell you????

Yes.

Fine!! I love you! Better?!!?

Yes, so much better.

Gawd!!

I told her to go to bed, too, to which I didn't receive a reply back. I sighed and turned my ringer off for a few minutes and got up from the table, found a pad of paper and a pen in my messy utility drawer, and sat back down.

I took in a lot of air, held it for a few minutes then expelled it slowly. I did this again and again, clearing my thoughts, ignoring my troubled heart. I continued doing this until I felt my hand jerk slightly. Followed by my whole arm, the pen began to move across the blank page as if on its own.

Three words appeared on the page before me: *Good evening, Samantha.*

"Is this Sephora?" I asked aloud.

My hand jerked some more. *Yes, Samantha.*

"It's been a while since we last spoke."

Yes.

"Does that bother you?"

I am here for you, Samantha, as I will be until time immemorial.

"You have nothing better to do?" I asked. It was meant as a flippant joke, but it came across as sort of rude to my own ears. "Sorry," I added. "Didn't mean that it way."

My hand jerked, coming alive with small impulses of electricity. I watched in mild amazement all over again as my hand wrote seemingly independent of me.

You are the better thing for me to do, Samantha.

"Now, that was a sweet thing to say," I said. In fact, those words were exactly what I wanted to hear. I nearly broke down at their kindness, even though I wasn't sure who or what Sephora was. But I powered through, fighting back the tears…after all, I had cried enough for the night.

A kind word goes further than you think, my hand wrote on its own volition.

"I've heard that," I said. "The Ripple Effect."

Kindness is kindness, Samantha. It's not a theory or an effect or a movement. It just is.

I thought about that, and I thought about the bitch living inside of me, the demoness, as I thought of her.

"And what of her?" I said, knowing that Sephora knew my innermost thoughts, suspecting she was as close as I got to a guardian angel these days, since my own guardian angel abandoned his post nearly two years ago. "Do I show her kindness, too?" I added. "Perhaps let her take me over for all eternity, while I watch from the shadows, a prisoner in my own body?"

It is a grim picture you paint, Samantha.

"It's a grim reality," I said. "And, for the love of God, please don't tell me to choose a new reality."

I won't, Sam, especially since you summoned in the love of God.

"Is that a joke?"

An observation. Love is a powerful tool. In fact, it's your only tool.

"To beat her?" I asked.

To help her, Sam.

I blinked in the darkness, which wasn't really darkness. All around me, like sunlight sparkling on ocean waves, glittered flashes of radiance. As always, within the radiance, I could see anything and everything.

I blinked again, and said, "Help her how?"

To move on, Sam.

"Move on to where?"

There was a long pause and my hand remained motionless, finally I felt the tiny electrical impulses and watched as my hand spelled out a single word: *Home.*

And just as the word appeared, I heard a small shriek in the back of my mind, deep beneath my many layers of consciousness. It was *her.* And following that faint shriek, I saw an image of a bright soul being absorbed by a much brighter light.

"She's showing me an image," I said, not liking this at all, not liking that she could leak images to me now. Yes, she was growing bolder and more powerful. I swallowed and said, "At least, I think it's her. She's showing me a soul—hers perhaps—being absorbed by a much bigger soul...or by something eternally big. God, perhaps."

Yes, Sam, my hand wrote, *she will be returned to the Creator.*

"I don't understand what that means."

This question was followed by silence. In particular, my hand remained motionless.

I added, "You don't know what that means, either."

No one does, Sam. Not exactly.

"Is it a bad thing?"

Never. It's a loving thing. A loving process.

94

"At least, you think it is."

She will be returned to the Creator…who created you and me out of love.

"I see lots of people around me who are not very loving."

You see lots of people who are growing, Sam. Evolving.

"Meanwhile, they hurt others, terrify others, and wreak havoc upon the world."

These lost souls are not as abundant as you are led to believe, Sam. Remember this: there is more good than bad.

"But there is bad."

There is also confusion, anger, hate and misery, all of which can drive good people to do bad things, temporarily.

"So they are not really bad. They are bad in the moment."

Bad is relative, Sam.

My head was hurting, which was saying something since my head almost never hurt. And, like the true freak I was, the pain in my head went away almost instantly. I said, "What's bad to one person…"

Is justice to another, or fair to another, or right to another.

"But there is evil in the world?"

There is only light and dark, Samantha.

"Then who or what is in me?"

There was a long pause before my hand twitched and twitched, and the words it spelled out left me sick for the rest of the night… and it wasn't the kind of sickness that my immortality could heal.

Perhaps the darkest of them all.

Chapter Twenty-five

I was alone in bed.

Dawn was coming. I knew this because I could feel it coming in every fiber of my being. It wasn't a good feeling. In fact, it made me nervous, agitated. Now I knew the reality behind the feeling. Sunlight made *her* nervous and agitated. The demoness within.

And Fang wanted this? I thought. *Fang sought this?*

I shook my head and clawed at my covers, restless as hell, agitated as hell. My kids were still with my sister, as they often were during the summer. She took them willingly enough, knowing my penchant for working the late shift. I think she also wanted to give them a normal home, even if for a few hours a night. She hadn't said so in so many words, and, truthfully, I didn't blame her. In fact, I was okay with it. A few times a week with her was okay by me, especially during the summer.

Yes, I had missed a golden opportunity to dig deeper into the murdered jogger case tonight, but I had needed my time with Russell. It had to be done, and now was the time.

And now, of course, he was gone.

Would I ever see him again?

A part of me thought no. A part of me thought my handsome, young, sexy boxer with the bad-boy tattoos was forever gone.

I loved him, yes. But our love had never had time to mature. Too soon, it was stunted and distorted by the curse. I had not gotten to know the *real* Russell, and now, I never would.

Yeah, I moped around most of the night, depressed, pissed, agitated, slightly sick to my stomach. The blood packet I had downed had too many impurities in it. Enough to make me slightly sick.

But now, the need for sleep was coming hard. I was presently in stage two of three, of what I thought of as my before-sleep countdown. Stage two meant that I damn well better be near a bed, and in a dark room. I suppose a casket would work, too, but how weird was that?

"Too weird for me," I whispered into my pillow.

The entity within me was silent, as she usually was. What provoked her into contacting me recently, I didn't know. And whether or not she was truly getting stronger, I didn't know that either.

But I suspected she was, and I thought I knew why.

Her strength had been building over the years, but not because of time itself. I added to her strength each time I lost a little more of myself. Sephora had hinted at it.

No matter what, at all costs, I had to retain who I was and not let the vampire in me consume me completely. If so, she would win. If so, I might not ever return.

I did not want to spend an eternity on the sidelines, watching the thing within me ruin and destroy lives.

With that thought, as the rising sun approached on the distant horizon, not quite dawn but only minutes away, as I slipped from phase two into phase three, I thought of Detective Hanner, my one-time vampire friend.

How far gone was she? I knew Hanner had killed without remorse or discrimination. She had personally run a blood ring, overseen by psychotic killers. And I had watch her kill the lady jogger.

As Fang stood by and watched...

And then joined her.

Yes, Hanner was very far gone, although, I suspected, not entirely consumed by the darkness within her. And, with sudden clarity, I suspected I knew why.

"She made an agreement with it," I said sleepily to myself.

I nodded into my pillow.

Yes, that was it, of course. She had made an agreement with the entity early on. By allowing it to surface, to briefly possess her body, to live in this world sooner rather than later. By doing so, it, in return, gave Hanner access to her own body.

Kind of it, I thought.

Well, I wasn't making a deal with the bitch within me. She wasn't going to surface. Not now, or ever.

"You can go to hell," I mumbled aloud, barely coherent.

And, just before sleep hit me, I knew what I had to do.

I had to find Hanner…and Fang.

Chapter Twenty-six

I was in my minivan.

Driving along the winding Bastanchury Road through the back hills of Yorba Linda, on my way to see an honest-to-God werewolf and a butler who may or may not have been Frankenstein—yeah, no shit—when my cell phone rang.

Restricted. I.D.

It was either Detective Sherbet or Detective Sanchez, so I played it safe. "Hi, Detective," I said.

"How did you know it was me?" asked Sanchez.

"Lucky guess," I said.

Our connection wasn't so strong that he could read my thoughts long distance, which was a good thing, because he might have known I wasn't quite so awesome. *Can't have that.*

"We have another body, Sam."

My smug grin faltered. "Where?"

"Same place, same trail. Griffith Park."

"Who?"

"A park ranger this time, which means this is about to get ugly fast."

"Griffith Park has park rangers?"

"Apparently so. Look, rangers are cops in their own right, and there's going to be a lot of questions about this one. A lot of people are going to want answers."

99

He was right, of course. Park rangers were cops, too, and when one of their own went down, well, whole departments—hell, whole agencies—kicked into gear.

"Officially, it's going down as a cougar attack."

"Good," I said. "Leave it at that. Fight for that. Don't let anyone suggest otherwise."

"Sam, the wound is identical to the jogger. We can't hide this for long."

"You won't need to," I said.

There was a pause. I swear to God, I thought I might have even heard his heart beating through the phone. Maybe our connection was stronger than I'd thought. "What do you know, Sam?" he asked.

I shielded my thoughts of Fang. "I can't tell you. Not yet."

"Do you know who did this?" asked Sanchez.

"I do."

"Tell me, goddammit. I will personally hunt these fuckers down—"

"And that's the problem, Detective. I don't know where they are or what's going on, or why they're killing the way they're killing."

"They?"

"There's two of them."

"Are they like you?" asked Sanchez.

"They are just like me," I said.

"What's your plan?"

"I'm going to find them," I said. "And stop them."

"How?" he asked.

I aimed my car into Kingsley's long-ass driveway. "Any way I can."

Chapter Twenty-seven

Franklin the butler answered the door.

As usual, he gazed down at me from high above his long nose. That his ears were two different sizes—and two different color tones—was something I was almost getting used to. Almost. That the ears were not quite level was another matter.

"Master Kingsley is…indisposed," said Franklin.

"Indisposed, as in, with a woman?"

"*Indisposed,*" Franklin intoned irritably, his enunciation impeccable, with a slight British accent. And something else, too. French perhaps.

I was surprised to discover that I felt mildly jealous at hearing these words. I brushed past the big butler, touching him for the first time, my hand on his shoulder. As I did so, I couldn't help but notice the fact that he was hard as a rock…and just as immovable. Good thing there was just enough Samantha Moon space between him and the door frame.

"Well," I said from the foyer, as Franklin turned slowly and scowled at me. "Then I shall wait in the sitting room until Kingsley is *un*-indisposed."

———

Footsteps.

Two sets of them. One barefoot, one heeled. The barefoot ones sounded like two slabs of beef slapping against the tiled floor. The heeled ones sounded a little too cute and spunky for me. The foot-steps wound down the spiral stairs, then through the hallway, then over to the front door. At the door, there were whispered words spoken. I couldn't quite make them out—didn't want to make them out. Still, my hearing was kind of awesome, if not superhuman. So I did catch a too-sweet "See you soon" followed by sounds of lip smacking. *Eww.* Finally, mercifully, the door opened and the sounds of clicking heels faded away, cut short by the shutting door.

More sounds of bare feet slapping, and a moment later, Kingsley stood at the entrance to the sitting room.

"This couldn't wait?" he asked.

"I waited," I said sweetly.

"Franklin came to the bedroom at a, um, crucial time."

"Gee, I'm sorry," I said, equally sweetly. I might have batted my eyelashes once or twice. "Did I throw off your rhythm?"

He growled from deep within his throat and swept into the room, his silk robe fluttering open, briefly flashing me. I nearly wretched...knowing where that *thing* had just been. He smiled slyly at my reaction and sat across from me, exposing himself once again as he crossed his tree-trunk-like legs.

"Did you at least shower?" I asked.

"I didn't have a chance, Sam. You see, Franklin came to my door and said that you were here waiting. That it was important. You think I would waste precious time showering when something is so important?"

"I've been waiting twenty minutes."

"I asked if you thought I would waste precious time showering, not finishing."

"You're a pig."

"I am, but you knew that when you first met me."

It was true. Kingsley had been an infamous womanizer back when he'd hired me two years ago. I'd made an honest man out of him; that is, until my fallen angel had decided to show me Kingsley's true colors...and baited my then-boyfriend. Kingsley had fallen for the bait, and screwed his way out of our relationship. He had been trying to win me back ever since.

He laughed lightly, got up again—this time, mercifully keeping his robe closed—and went over to the bar in the far corner of the room and poured himself a finger or three of Scotch. He next reached into the wine cooler and removed what I could only imagine was a fine bottle of white wine—a chardonnay, no doubt. He poured a healthy amount, re-corked it and returned the bottle to the fridge—knowing I generally only drank one glass.

"Ferrari-Carano," said Kingsley, coming over to me and handing me the cool glass. "Your favorite."

It was, although a fat lot of good it did me, since I hadn't been buzzed in seven years. At least, not buzzed on alcohol.

"Thank you," I said, "and thank you for flashing me for a third time."

"Third time's a charm," he said, making himself comfortable on the couch across from me.

"More like three strikes and you're out," I mumbled.

"I heard that, Sam. My hearing's a little better than yours."

"That's right, because you're part dog."

"Sam…"

"Or, should I say, *all* dog?"

"Sam, I've apologized for what I've done."

"Then apologize again, dammit."

He looked at me from over his amber-filled glass. His bare foot waggled nervously, like a dog's tail. His shaggy hair hung disheveled around his shoulder. He gave me a sincere look. It was the same look, I was willing to bet, that he'd given jurors in courts of law. Still, he was trying, and I appreciated his effort.

"Sam," he said, "I'm truly sorry that I did what I did. It was stupid mistake."

"Damn right it was stupid."

"I was stupid."

"Damn right, you were stupid."

"Now, other than getting on me for the hundredth time about my stupidity, why did you come here tonight?"

I wanted to still be mad at him, but how did I stay mad at a werewolf who wiggled his foot like a puppy dog who needed attention? I couldn't, and let it go for now, and I told him about my new case. He listened quietly, drinking idly, nodding sometimes and making wolfish grunting noises. Okay, maybe not wolfish. That might have been my imagination.

When I was wrapping up, I added, "You know Hanner, Kingsley. And you knew her well before I did. Hell, she supplied you blood for me…or for your other vampire guests. I need to find her."

"I don't know much about her, Sam. In fact, I would hazard to guess that you know far more about her at this point than I do."

"How did you two first meet?" I asked. I was holding my wine, but it was mostly forgotten. Little things like my throat getting dry or my voice getting hoarse from too much talking never, ever happened to me these days. Minor irritants like that healed instantly. And my body, apparently, didn't need much water. I knew water helped remove dangerous toxins from normal people. Except, of course, I had no more fear of dangerous toxins of any sort. I knew water cushioned joints and helped carry nutrients to cells and helped regulate body temperature.

What, exactly, was cushioning my cells, I didn't know. And whether or not my cells needed any nutrients, I didn't know that either, but one thing I did know was this: blood did the universal trick. It had everything I needed, and then some. I'd gone days without drinking water and hadn't missed a beat. And, no, I didn't use the bathroom, either.

Like I said, I'm a freak.

Yes, I operated by different physical rules, although the emotions had mostly stayed intact. I could still feel hurt and jealousy and rage. Losing control of myself was just what *she* wanted. I had to stay in control. Stay human.

"We met at a paranormal convention," Kingsley was saying. "At the North Pole with Santa Claus."

"Jerk," I said.

He chuckled lightly. "Sam, I'm involved in a sort of network of the undead, you could say. Or, in my case, supernaturals."

"You are not undead?"

"Not quite, Sam. I can live for a very long time, but werewolves are not ageless."

Kingsley had explained once the reason for his great size. He had not started out so big. Over the years, and with each cycle of the moon, his body adopted the werewolf's form more and more. The bigger he got, the closer he got to the beast within, the easier it was for him to transform with each full moon. A change that was not very pleasant.

I nodded. "If werewolves were immortal…"

"We would be big as cars," he finished.

I recalled the hulking beast standing in my hotel room two years ago. Yes, Kingsley was huge in his changeling form. Truth was, he was not that far off from his alter ego's size.

"How old are you again?" I asked.

"I'm close to eighty, Sam."

"And you don't look a day over forty-five."

"I was thinking forty, but whatever," he said. "And I know what you're thinking…"

I looked at him for a long moment, and fought a strong need to reach for his big hand. "What am I thinking?"

"You're wondering how I could possibly be so good looking. It's not easy, let me tell you. The hair care products alone cost me a fortune."

I laughed, and as I did so, I realized there would be a day when Kingsley wasn't here for me either, and that thought brought anguish to my heart and tears to my eyes.

"Hey, kiddo," he said, reaching over and gently lifting my jaw. "I'm not going anywhere for a long time."

"How long?"

"A long, long time."

I nodded and briefly hid my face in my hands. I guess I cared about Kingsley more than I realized. No, I had always cared about

105

him. Our timing hadn't been right. Not initially, when I was dealing with a cheating spouse. And just when my heart was healing, just when I was coming around to really loving Kingsley...he'd cheated on me, too.

I let it go, and fought back tears, and said, "I need to find Hanner."

Kingsley blinked with the sudden shift in conversation. He said, "I was under the impression that she was still gone."

"She's back."

Kingsley had, of course, known about Hanner turning Fang. "I was unaware of that."

"How plugged into this supernatural network are you?" I asked.

"I'm as plugged in as I need to be, or want to be."

"I need to find her," I said. "And Fang."

"I'll see what I can find out," I said.

"They're killing out of L.A." I hesitated to say *training*, although that was what I suspected the killings were.

Kingsley nodded, held my gaze. "Have you considered why they're leaving bodies in the park, Sam?"

"I have."

"Any thoughts?"

"Not many, other than it's obvious they want people to know a vampire is around."

"People?" asked Kingsley. "Or just you?"

"Me?"

"Yes," he said. "You."

"What do you mean?"

"Their actions have flushed you out, in a way."

"But why?"

"I don't know, Sam."

I next told Kingsley about Sanchez's memory gap.

"I think we know the reason for the memory gap, Sam," said Kingsley. "Someone wanted him to contact you."

"But he contacted Sherbet first."

"Which would be protocol, and less obvious," said Kingsley. "Contact Sherbet first, who would obviously turn around and contact you. So, who would know to contact Sherbet first?"

"Hanner," I said.

"And Hanner, according to you, is particularly adept at altering memories."

I looked at Kingsley grimly. "We need to find her, and we need to see what the hell is going on."

Kingsley looked at me with a lot of concern in his big, brown eyes. "And stop the killings, too, right?"

I blinked, realizing I'd overlooked that crucial reasoning. "Yes," I said, mildly alarmed at my oversight, "that, too."

CHAPTER TWENTY-EIGHT

I was seated outside of Detective Rachel Hanner's home in the Fullerton Hills.

It was late and the hills were mostly quiet and I was smoking again. The occasional car drove by, winding up and out of sight, or winding down and out of sight. The homes up here were far too big, and far too beautiful for a lowly private eye. Or even for a homicide detective. Yet, this is where Hanner lived...and lived well.

Detective Sanchez had called me on the way out and asked how the investigation was coming along. I hadn't told Sanchez too much of what I knew. And I certainly hadn't revealed Fang or Hanner's identity. So, I debated about how much to tell him, and finally told him that I was following a very strong lead. He had asked how strong. I said I was going to the vampire's lair. He asked if I really said *lair*, and I said I had and that I would fill him in later.

And lair it was, although it looked less like a lair and more like an opulent home. That a homicide detective lived up here—in the priciest part of Fullerton, no doubt with the attorneys and doctors and Starbucks franchisees, should have been an indicator that something was amiss. Undoubtedly, Hanner had been many things throughout her long life, and had amassed tremendous wealth.

Or not. Who knows. Maybe she had killed the owner of the house and assumed her identity. Truth was, I didn't know much about Hanner.

Yes, we had sat together on her deck, drinking blood. Yes, she had been kind to me early on. She alone had cleaned up two of my

108

messes, back when I had taken on two powerful vampires. One a Texan and the other, perhaps the oldest vampire of all, or one of the oldest. In both cases, witnesses at both scenes had to have their memories cleaned or replaced. Yes, she had been there for me.

As I smoked, hating the taste but enjoying the focus it gave my mind, I knew that it didn't have to be this way with Hanner. She would have been my best friend, if a killing machine like Hanner could have a best friend. I'd never forget the hungry look in her eyes. The feral, wild look of a predator. Yes, she was very far gone. Her humanity often took a backseat to the darkness within.

The *thing* within.

But I had gone against the program, so to speak. I had bucked the system. As far as I knew, there was not a council of vampires. There was not an official hierarchy or a vampire leader, although I suspected some groups of vampires had banded together here and there. Yes, I thought Hanner was hoping she and I could band together, too, form our own sub-group. I had been on board as far as being her friend, or hanging out with her and learning from her. I had enjoyed our pleasant evenings together...

As a friend, Hanner was creepy at best. As an enemy, she was frightening. I thought she now fell into the latter category.

Now, she was forming a new union with a new vampire.

Fang.

And perhaps setting up another blood ring.

Or worse.

What was worse, I didn't know. But the two of them were up to something. It had been many months since Fang had left with Hanner. I had been given the idea that it was far away, somewhere remote.

But what if it wasn't far away?

What if it had been in my own back yard, so to speak?

What if Hanner and Fang had been in Los Angeles this whole time?

Maybe, I thought, and inhaled deeply on the cancer stick. Then again, they might as well have been a world away if I couldn't find them.

109

Truth was, I would have let them be.

I would have let them run off together, to be the best goddamn vampires they could be.

That is, if they hadn't left the bodies in Griffith Park.

That is, if they hadn't compelled Detective Sanchez to come calling for Sherbet, and, in turn, me.

They were bringing me into something.

What, exactly, I didn't know.

But I was going to find out.

Chapter Twenty-nine

I snubbed out my cigarette in the minivan's ashtray, reminding myself later to clean it out before the kids got home. Yes, I no longer hid the fact that I was a vampire from my kids, but I still hid the fact that I smoked.

I drummed my fingers on the steering wheel.

It was past midnight, and I felt strong and alert.

Of course, any vampire would be strong and alert. Hanner, for instance, was older than me by many decades, perhaps centuries. A concept that still boggled the mind and, as always, made me seriously question my sanity.

The moon was in its half state. It appeared and disappeared behind the taller trees that ran along this upscale neighborhood. A few cars came by. I was parked behind a bend, between two massive homes. Fullerton Hills might not be Beverly Hills, but these homes were damn nice in my book.

I drummed my fingers some more on the steering wheel, and decided to use what skills I did possess.

I closed my eyes and cast my thoughts out, wondering if I was close enough to Hanner's house to get a good look inside and outside. Turned out I was close enough, although at the far edge of my abilities.

Still, I could see that there were two people inside. A lithe figure who seemed to be moving slowly around the house, and another, broader figure.

Hanner and Fang? No, that wasn't right. Fang was taller than that, and not so broad-shouldered. The woman could have been Hanner, but I wasn't sure. Technically, she was on the run from no one. This was her house. Why shouldn't she be here?

I thought about that.

Hanner had made it personal by going after Fang. Yes, she had fulfilled his wish, but had gone behind my back to do so.

Worse, she was turning my friend into a killer.

Yes, Fang was a big boy, capable of making his own decisions. He had chosen this path. He had wanted to be a vampire from the time his damn canine teeth grew in too long, a fluke of nature that had led to a severe disorder, which led, in turn, to him killing his girlfriend. That murder had made national headlines. His ultimate escape from prison was big news, too. That he was never caught seemed mostly forgotten these days.

I had taken something precious from her—and from many vampires, no doubt. A steady supply of blood.

So, she had taken something from me.

I wasn't a gunslinger, but I knew Hanner and I had a score to settle. It may not go down at high noon in the middle of Main Street, but it was going to go down somewhere, probably at midnight, and probably somewhere a lot more discreet than Main Street.

She knew I had her in my sights. She knew I wanted to take her down, and if I knew Hanner, who was proving to be one hell of a calculating bitch, she was going to come after me first.

I thought about that as I continued drumming my longish, freakish fingernails on the steering wheel.

Finally, I pulled out my cell phone and made a call. Allison picked up on the second ring.

"*Hola*, sweet cheeks," she said. She sounded out of breath.

"What are you doing?"

"Lunges," she said, breathing hard. "I happen to like my own sweet cheeks, thank you very much."

"Are we done talking about our asses?"

"Fine, Grumpy Cat. Where are you? Wait. You're outside a house. A big house. On a hill. I don't know this house."

"Detective Hanner's house," I said.

"Is she back in town?"

"No," I said.

I gave her a peek into my own thoughts. Okay, more than a peek. I gave her access to everything I'd been dealing with for these past few days. And, unlike audible communication, the telepathic kind went quickly. Within a few minutes, she was fully caught up on my situation.

"I agree with you, Sam," said Allison. "I think it's a setup, too."

"Setting me up for what?" I asked.

Allison glugged some water. I could imagine her throwing back her head and drinking intensely. Allison did everything intensely. But, again, I had to use my imagination. Unlike her, my remote viewing only went so far. Allison could see across miles; hell, continents. Me? I could only see a few hundred yards.

"I don't know, Sam," she said when she was done drinking. "But it can't be good. They're willing to kill innocent people to set this trap for you."

"You really think it's a trap?"

"You've been a thorn in Hanner's side for some time now. You could probably turn Fang against her, too. Fang, if I'm understanding you right, seems sort of indebted to her, but I don't understand why he seems so indebted."

I knew what she meant. He seemed unusually loyal.

Allison picked up on my concern. "Can he be compelled by her, Sam?"

"As far as I know, vampires can't control other vampires. I can't read another vampire's mind. Or Kingsley's mind. Or, I suspect, anyone or anything supernatural."

"Either way, Sam, she fears you. You've proven to be stronger than her, and seem to have more powers."

"I've proven to be a bigger freak, you mean."

"No, Sam. That's not what I mean. But think of it this way: she wasn't able to recruit you, so she's probably going to do the next best thing."

I read her mind easily enough. "I thought of that, too," I said.

"Let me help you, Sam."

"No."

"I have powers now. A lot of power. I'm stronger than you know—"

"No," I said, cutting her off. "Out of the question. I'm dealing with Hanner."

"I can help you, Sam—"

"No. End of discussion."

"Why do you get to dictate when the discussion is over?"

"Because I'm the boss. You still work for me, remember?"

It was true. A few months ago, before heading out to the world's creepiest island, I had deputized Allison, so to speak. She was, officially, a private eye in training.

"Fine," she said, throwing a small tantrum. "But you can't just walk into a trap, Sam."

I looked at the dark house before me. "You think the house is a trap?"

"It can't be good, Sam. None of this is good."

"I have to stop her, Allison. And…"

"And bring Fang home?" she said.

"Maybe."

"And what if he doesn't want to come back, Sam? What if he's too far gone?"

I didn't have an answer to that. Instead, I said goodbye and, with her still protesting in my ear, I hung up.

And stepped out of my minivan.

114

Chapter Thirty

As I approached Hanner's home, I cast my thoughts out again. More reconnaissance. Yes, there was a woman upstairs, in the kitchen, moving slowly. Almost as if she were drugged. There was a broad-shouldered man sitting at the kitchen table, unmoving.

"Creepy," I whispered.

I was about to return to my body when something told me to keep searching. For what, I did not know, but I'd learned to trust this *something*, this inner guidance system, so to speak.

So, I continued scanning the house, slipping in and out of rooms and hallways and bedrooms. I came across a door and pushed through it, and ended up going down a narrow flight of stairs. The stairs dead-ended into another door, which I mentally pushed through.

Basements were uncommon in California, but not unheard of, especially if someone was a psychopath or a vampire running a secret blood ring. Or both.

The room beyond was small and composed entirely of brick. My guess would be very thick bricks. Sound-proof bricks. There was a drain in the center. Most important, there was a young woman in the room, shackled to the wall, her arms above her head, whimpering uncontrollably. Like something out of a medieval dungeon. She looked like anything but a willing donor.

Jesus.

I snapped back into my body. I considered all my options, from calling Sherbet to breaking the girl out of the basement prison.

In the end, I decided on one course of action.

One obvious course.

I continued up the driveway and up the front steps. There, I gathered myself, and was about to break off the doorknob, when the door opened, and the broad-shouldered man smiled at me.

"Samantha Moon," he said, stepping aside and gesturing toward the interior of the house. "We've been expecting you."

Chapter Thirty-One

My inner alarm remained silent.

Except this seemed like a damn good time for my inner alarm to be going crazy, but it wasn't. Not a peep. I opened my mouth to speak, to ask who, exactly, had been waiting for me, and who, exactly he was.

Instead, I studied the man before me. Thick, broad-shouldered, handsome. He wore a frozen smile. Not quite the demonic smile I'd seen recently at the Washington island, but pretty damn close.

"You've been expecting me?" I thought of my conversation with Sanchez. Had she compelled him to report to her, as well? I think probably, which is why he'd called at such a strange time. To follow up. To see where I was in my investigation. And report his findings.

"Yes, Ms. Moon. Won't you please come in? We have some things we need to discuss."

"Some things?"

"Yes."

"What things?"

He smiled even bigger, and now it did look demonic. "Inside, Ms. Moon, if you don't mind."

"And if I do mind?"

He said nothing, only smiled and cocked his head a little, and it occurred to me that he didn't have an answer for that question.

Or, I thought, *he wasn't given an answer.*

I hadn't come across many instances, if any, of another vampire compelling a mortal, but I thought I was seeing one now. Trusting my inner alarm, I nodded and stepped past him. He turned and watched me as I went, and shut the door behind me.

I knew Hanner's home well enough. It was a big home, with the bottom floor dug into the hillside. The upper deck overlooked the rare Orange County woods and the many larger homes beyond, one of which I'd ventured into, meeting, perhaps, the creepiest man on planet earth. A man who had bargained with years from my son's life.

But just as quickly as the old man entered my thoughts, he left again. After all, the smell of blood was thick upon the air.

My stomach growled, and I salivated like the ghoul that I was.

I ignored my stomach, too, and followed the broad-shouldered man through Hanner's home, following a path from the front door to the dining area, a path I had taken a handful of times before this.

The house was dark, except for a single light in the kitchen. Back in the day, back when Hanner and I had been pals, I'd rarely ventured through the house. In fact, she had almost always made it a point to lead me from the kitchen to her balcony with its majestic view of the woodsy canyon.

I hadn't known about the basement.

No, not a basement, I thought, as I followed the man into the kitchen, *a dungeon—a torture dungeon.*

I shuddered. And as I did so, I saw three figures waiting for me in the kitchen. Two were living, and one was very much dead.

The living figure was the woman I had seen in my surveillance of the house. She was sitting alone at the far end of a long dining room table. Before her was a cloth napkin. There was something clearly under the napkin, something small and lumpy. The cloth napkin was stained crimson. The woman, who was maybe in her early thirties, was smiling, too. That same serene and creepy smile.

The ghost behind her was of a woman, but decidedly younger, perhaps in her early twenties. The ghost was particularly bright and well-defined, which meant she'd died recently. At least, that was what my experience told me. Anyway, her ethereal, energetic body crackled with living shards of light, light so bright that I was stunned these two couldn't see her. Then again, maybe they could and were ignoring her, but I doubted it. I had only to remember my pre-freak days, back when I couldn't see such spirits, either. Those were good days.

It was obvious that her neck had been cut open with something sharp. Her staticy body was so well-defined that I could actually see ghostly hints of tendons and muscle inside of her exposed neck. Whoever she was, she'd been drained and killed, right here in Hanner's house.

The man, oblivious to the spirit, went over and stood by the side of the seated woman. They both smiled at me, both cocking their heads, both compelled to act against their wills.

"How do you two know Detective Hanner?" I asked them.

The man spoke. "We are her private source." He sounded excited, like this was an honor, a privilege, and something as great as being chosen for the next manned mission to the moon.

"You live here?" I asked.

"Yes," he answered, sounding, if possible, even more excited. "We both do."

I noticed their wedding rings. "Are you two married?"

"Yes," said the woman. As she spoke, she kept her head tilted to the side. "We met Detective Hanner on our honeymoon."

"How long ago?"

The man and woman continued staring at me, continued smiling and tilting their heads. "Over three years now," said the man.

"You've lived here for three years?"

They both looked at me, blinked, and smiled. "Oh, yes," they said in unison.

I shook my head and took in some air and continued smelling the strong scent of the red stuff. Blood, that is. Everywhere. In particular, something bloody under the napkin before the woman.

Hanner had met the young couple. Compelled them to follow her home while they had been on their honeymoon, no less. Probably the couple had met a certain specification for Hanner. I suspected they neither had family nor many friends. Few would look for them. And those who did would easily be turned away by a simple phone call that would reassure anyone concerned that they were okay. Hanner, in effect, had kidnapped them.

"Who's in the basement?" I asked.

"A bleeder," said the man.

"A bleeder?"

"Yes."

"What's a bleeder?"

"We bleed her for others, Samantha Moon. In fact, we have recently bled her for you. Would you care for a drink? It's chilling in the refrigerator now."

I should have shuddered. I should have recoiled in horror. I should have called Sherbet to come out and shut this craziness down.

Instead, I found myself about to nod. My ears rang a bit. And my thoughts were fuzzy.

In fact, I started to nod, then shook my head vigorously. As I did so, I backed up—but not at the reality of an innocent woman who was being bled in the basement below. But at the horror of my very, very strong bloodlust.

Yesss, came a single word from the depths of my mind. *Yesss, yesss, yesss, yesss....*

Fresh blood. Procured unwillingly. Taken against another's will was *her* ultimate craving. Such blood, I knew, would feed not me...but *her.*

"No," I heard myself say, as the hissing continued, a long, slow leak just inside my eardrum. "No, thank you."

"Are you sure, Samantha Moon? It was tapped for you and you alone. It will be wasted otherwise."

*Well, in that case...*I wanted to say, but I didn't.

Tapped, he had said. Like tapping a maple tree. This should have sounded horrific to me. But it didn't. No, it sounded intriguing. It sounded...interesting. *Tell me more about this tapping business,* I wanted to say.

But I didn't.

I rubbed my head, pressed my fingers hard into my temples. She was in here somewhere. Where she was, exactly, I didn't know. But she was getting bolder, stronger.

No…she was getting desperate.

She wants out.

She wants her freedom.

Her freedom meant my imprisonment, of course.

I took in a lot of air and held it and willed her out of my mind, and the hissing, finally, faded slowly away. I expelled the air and looked at the compelled couple.

"No, thank you," I said again.

Behind them, the ghost faded in and out of existence. Once or twice, she looked at me, but she was lost. Lost even before death, I suspected. A runaway, I sensed. Lost and forgotten, even in life and death. How many other such spirits were here, I didn't know, but I suspected more.

"Why don't you go home?" I said to the couple.

"We are home, Samantha Moon," said the woman.

"We are *very* happy here," said the man.

I doubted that. I doubted they even knew what they were saying. I suspected that Hanner's compulsion was so extensive that she controlled them either from afar, or gave them pre-recorded responses, so to speak.

"Why were you waiting for me?" I asked.

"Because our mistress said you would come."

I looked at them again. Had they been recently fed upon? Hard to know, since vampire wounds inflicted on mortals—those living, that is—healed almost instantly, as was my experience with Allison. But I was suddenly sure of one thing.

"She was here recently," I said.

They said nothing.

"Tell me, goddammit."

They continued smiling, heads tilted to one side. They both blinked together.

From below, I heard the chained woman crying up through the floorboards. The bleeder, as they had called her. Bleeders, I suspected, didn't last long in the house of horrors.

When Hanner had been here, I didn't know, and how she knew I would come calling, I didn't know that either.

121

No, I thought. She would have known. Everything she had done, thus far, had been orchestrated to lead me here. But why?

I looked again at the bloody tissue before them.

"What's under the napkin?" I asked, although I suddenly didn't want to know.

The woman nodded slightly and straightened her head for the first time. She rested the flat of her palms on the table. She held my gaze. "Mistress has a message for you, Samantha Moon."

I swallowed and stepped forward. Curious and repulsed at the same time, horrified yet intrigued.

What's wrong with me? I thought.

"Mistress wanted you to see this."

And with that, the woman lifted the napkin. Underneath was a severed finger...a pinkie finger with a ring still attached to it. I knew the ring. It was Danny's pimp ring, as I called it. An ugly garnet ring, too big for any man to wear with a straight face. He loved that ring.

Had I any color in my face, I suspected it would have drained about now.

"What the hell did she do with Danny?"

"We don't know," said the man. "But he is the first."

"The first what, goddammit?"

The finger had been neatly severed, with the use of a knife, no doubt. Blood crusted around the open end. I could see the dozens of dark hairs lying flat across one side, beneath the main knuckle.

"Master wanted you to know that she will systematically kill your entire family until you meet her."

"I'm here now," I said, unable to take my eyes off the pale finger. *Oh, Jesus, Danny...*

"Not here, Samantha Moon."

"Then where?"

"She will tell you."

"Where is she?"

"Mistress is busy at the moment."

I nearly leaped across the table. Nearly strangled them both. But I couldn't. They were just the messengers, after all.

122

For the first time in a long time, I felt sick to my stomach. "Busy doing what?"

They both looked at me for a heartbeat or two, and for the briefest of moments, I sensed a small wave of compassion coming from them. But then, that compassion was gone as quickly as it had appeared.

"She is seeking another."

"Another *what*, goddammit?"

But they didn't answer. They only smiled and looked at me and stood together at the far end of the table, heads cocked to one side. As if listening to someone or something I couldn't hear.

Chapter Thirty-two

I was back in my minivan.

Had my body been any less than it was, I would have been hyper-ventilating. My hands were shaking as I did my best to dial my sister's home number without crushing the phone into pieces.

Now I waited in the dark while the phone rang, the light of the half-moon above coming through the big windshield.

"C'mon," I said. "c'mon."

Mercifully, thankfully, the call was answered after three rings. It was Jordan, Mary Lou's husband, a man, I suspected, who knew my secret, although Mary Lou claimed to have never told him.

"Hi, Sam," he said pleasantly enough, although I always detected a hint of reservation in his voice.

"Hi, Jordy," I said, forcing myself to stay calm. "Can I speak to Mary Lou?"

"She went out to get some tacos. You can try her cell."

I said I would and then asked, as calmly as I could, about my kids.

"They're here, playing something called 'Go, Go, Racer Go.' Damn game nearly gave me an epileptic seizure."

I'd been holding my breath after my question, and expelled it now, perhaps a little too loudly.

"Is everything okay, Sam?"

"Yes."

He paused. "Are you sure?"

"Yes," I said. "I'm going to try Mary Lou now."

"Good, and ask her where the hell she is." He laughed lightly. "She left an hour ago."

I nearly hung up on him. I said I would and was soon dialing her number in such a rush that I screwed it up twice, dialing Kingsley both times by mistake. I hung up on him both times.

I got it right on my third attempt and it rang once.

"Hello, Samantha," said a familiar and cold voice. A female voice that instantly shot dread through me.

The voice, of course, belonged to Hanner.

CHAPTER THIRTY-THREE

"Where's my sister?"

"She's here, Samantha."

"If you've hurt her—"

"I have not hurt her, Sam. Not yet. Now, Danny on the other hand, is a different story. Speaking of hands…"

"What have you done with him?"

"I remembered your stories, Sam. I remembered how he hurt you and cheated on you and tried to destroy you. Danny is fair game."

My stomach dropped. Danny was a bastard…but he didn't deserve this. He was the father of my kids. A worthless father, yes, but their father, nonetheless.

"Is he dead?" I asked.

"Not yet, Samantha. But he will be. Along with your sister." She paused ever so slightly. "And you, too, of course."

I detected a strange note in her voice. Her answers were monotone, automatic. I also detected a slight hiss. "I'm not speaking to Detective Hanner, am I?"

"You are perceptive, Sssamantha Moon." The hiss was stronger now, more pronounced.

"If you kill me," I said, "then you kill *her*, too."

I was, of course, referring to the demon within me.

"Not quite, Sssamantha. Our sssister has decided that you are too problematic, too difficult. She wishes to move into a new host. We have the perfect host with us. She looks remarkably like you, Sssamantha. But, we suspect, she will be much more manageable."

I ran my fingers through my thick hair. "I must die for her to leave me?"

"You are a fassst learner, Missss Moon."

"Who are you, godammit? Why are you doing this?"

"Yes, we are damned, very damned. Which is exactly *why* we are doing this."

"What do you want with me?" I asked.

"We want you to die, Samantha Moon. And our host, here, your one-time friend Detective Hanner, is just the one to do it."

"What have you done with my sister?"

"She's here with us, Sam. Sitting quietly in the front seat like a good girl. Like a good future host. We suspect she will be much, much more manageable."

"If you fucking touch her..."

"We will do much more than touch her, Samantha. But first, of course, you must die."

I took in a lot of air. I couldn't get a read on Hanner, as she was immortal. And I couldn't get a read on my sister, either, as she was my blood relative. Dammit. I couldn't even get a read on Danny, as he and I had never connected deeply enough to develop that bond, which told me a lot about my ex-husband.

"What do you want me to do?" I asked.

"We want you to meet us, Sssamantha. We have a good place in mind for you to die."

Then, the demon told me where to go, although this time she sounded very much like Hanner.

And then the line went dead.

Chapter Thirty-four

I was at Allison's apartment in Beverly Hills.

It was all I could do not to call Kingsley again. In fact, I had nearly done so as I drove to Allison's house in a blind rush. Yes, I nearly flew there, too. But the truth was, I wanted the hour drive from Orange County to Beverly Hills to think this through. And I knew I needed the van to bring Mary Lou home and take Danny to...a hospital.

That drive hadn't helped much.

The thinking soon turned to panic, and I didn't accomplish anything other than nearly killing a half dozen other drivers as I whipped around them recklessly, aiming my screaming minivan to Beverly Hills, and to Allison's place.

Now she was sitting at a table with a rolled-up napkin in front of her. A rolled-up napkin with bloodstains. Allison looked sick. She should have looked sick. There was, after all, a severed finger in front of her.

"This can't be happening, Sam."

I was pacing in front of her. I was alternately wringing my hands and shaking them, trying to come to terms with the fact that a rogue vampire possessed by a hellish demon currently had my sister...and Danny.

Danny. How the devil had *he* gotten in on this?

I didn't know, but I had his finger and ring in a rolled-up napkin to prove it. And I'd had Hanner answering my sister's cell phone to prove she had Mary Lou, too.

"Yes," I said to Allison, who had, undoubtedly, been following my hectic train of thought. "This is happening."

"But I don't understand, Sam. Why drag you out to...where is it? I'm seeing a tunnel system in your thoughts?"

"It's a cavern," I said, "beneath the Los Angeles River."

"Where's that?"

"Not far from here," I said. I had to Google Map it, too, being an Orange County girl myself. "It flows between Griffith Park and Glendale."

"You mean that big ditch."

"That big ditch was once a natural river, and had only within the past seventy-five years been controlled and cemented."

"And did you say *beneath* the river?"

"Yes."

"What, exactly, is beneath the river?"

"An old cave network and something that, I think, is a cavern, from the way Hanner described it."

"A cavern? Under the river?"

"Under it or close to it, which is why I need you now."

Allison, who was tuned into my mind and following my thoughts almost as fast as I could think them, said, "Oh, gross."

"It's the only way, Allison. I can't lock onto my sister or Fang or even Danny. And even if I could, my range only goes so far."

Her range was, of course, potentially global. In fact, there didn't seem to be any limit to Allison's ability to see distantly. Remote viewing, as it was called in psychic circles.

Earlier, after getting directions to the underground caverns beneath the Los Angeles River, I'd dashed back in the house, where I had found the newlyweds sitting and standing in the same position I had left them in, and snatched the finger and the napkin.

Now, it was sitting in front of Allison, who'd been staring down at it for the past ten minutes.

"Please, Allison. I need your help."

The color had drained from her face instantly when she's caught on what was inside the napkin. She'd been pale ever since. I was fairly certain she'd yet to look away from the wrapped package sitting before her. Finally, she nodded. "He went through a lot of pain, Sam."

"I can imagine."

"But..." she trailed off, but I caught her psychic hit just as it occurred to her.

"Jesus," I said.

"Yes, Sam. He's involved with this somehow. Entangled. Not completely innocent."

I shook my head and swore and cursed my ex-husband all over again. My stupid, stupid ex-husband. So stupid that he had lost a finger.

"He was trying to exact revenge," said Allison.

"Did you just say *exact revenge?*"

"Yes. I know it sounds cheesy, but that's the feeling I get. He was trying to get back at you, somehow. To stop you somehow. To control you somehow."

"And he teamed up with Hanner."

"Or she teamed up with him," said Allison.

"He made a deal with the devil," I said. "Literally."

Allison nodded and we both looked down at the wrapped finger. Yes, Danny had paid a heavy price for his stupidity—and his hate for me, but I didn't have time to think about that now. I had to see what I was up against. I had to see—through Allison's remote viewing—what the hell was going on.

"It's time, Allison," I said.

We both knew what that meant. She nodded, then slowly reached forward and began unrolling the greasy napkin. As she did so, she calmly got up, walked over to the nearby bathroom, and wretched for a half minute. She came back, wiping her mouth, gave me a weak smile, and then sat before the still-rolled up napkin.

She undid it completely...and, after taking a deep breath and visibly fighting the rising vomit at the back of her throat, took hold of the severed finger in both her hands.

Chapter Thirty-five

"I see him," said Allison.

I saw him, too, but I waited for her to make sense of what she was seeing, for her to focus, to hone in, to get a feel for the place. To, quite literally, slip inside.

More details came through.

In her thoughts, I saw Danny in a chair. No, a desk. Perhaps a high school desk, as he seemed to fit in it well enough. Both arms were lying across the flat surface of the desk. Both arms were secured with duct tape. Both hands hung over the lip of the desk. Blood dripped steadily from the gaping maw where his right pinkie had been. The wound itself looked badly infected...and old. How long Danny had been down there, I didn't know. I realized I hadn't heard from him in about a week. Nothing unusual about that. He saw the kids every other week. And sometimes, he even missed those dates. I'd gone as long as two or three weeks without hearing from the sleazy bastard.

Danny looked like hell, and my heart went out to him, despite everything. I forgot that he had turned on me...and that his current situation was, apparently, a direct result of him trying to hurt me.

As I watched him sobbing and shaking, I saw the chains around his bare ankles. The skin was bloody and raw and mostly peeled away. Dried blood pooled around his bare feet. For once, in a long time, the sight of blood did not trigger a hunger in me. The sight of Danny and his wounds, instead, triggered a deep sadness...

And anger.

Although I could see what Allison could see, she got a far better picture than I ever could: "I see a big room. Rock walls. Yes, a cavern. It appears natural, although some of it could have been chiseled. Danny is in the room, crying softly to himself. I can feel his fear, his pain, his self-hatred. He hates that he put himself into this mess, hates you even more for introducing him to this dark world. A part of him, a very small part of him, understands that this wasn't your fault, that your attack seven years ago was unprovoked, that you, in fact, never asked for this. That small part of him is overshadowed by his fear and hatred for you, Sam. He feels abandoned and humiliated and angry."

"Is he alone?" I asked.

"Hold on…"

And now, Allison's perspective widened further as she searched the room. She might as well have been an actual bat, swooping around the room. Her remote viewing ability was uncanny. Then again, I didn't know much about any of this. Maybe her abilities were normal for one who allowed a vampire to feed from her. Maybe the newlyweds in Hanner's home had such abilities, too.

Or not. I knew Allison had started out as psychic, and that my feeding upon her only made her more psychic. And, of course, she had been a witch down through the ages. And so had I.

But not in this life. No. And if my immortality held up, perhaps never again.

As Allison swooped mentally through the room, I followed her thoughts as best as I could, her path, as if I was swooping right there with her. It was thrilling and bizarre, but I didn't think much of any of that. This was, after all, a recon mission. Meaning, we were here to gather information—anything that would help me save Mary Lou and, yes, Danny, and help get us all out alive.

"There," I said. I directed her thoughts toward a dark opening in the far wall.

Allison oriented on that and we swooped down through the cavern and into the opening and into yet another cavern, this one smaller, and this one occupied by more people.

I saw them through Allison's perception. Unfortunately, this cavern was mostly dark...and Allison could not see through the dark. Or, perhaps, her distance sight could not see through the dark. But there were a few touches on the wall, and enough to see a handful of people I didn't recognize.

The cavern, I saw, was something out of *The Lost Boys*...filled with old and new furniture, haphazardly arranged, tapestries and paintings on the walls, statues and trinkets. Most of it looked old, and some of it even looked valuable. Mostly, the room looked like a big hangout.

"It's a sort of safe house," said Allison. I knew she could read deeper into what she was seeing than I could; feel deeper, too. "It's where vampires go when on the run, or when they are new."

"A training facility," I said.

"Something like that. But it's also more. There are old vampires who dominate here. Powerful vampires. They kill here, too. They plot and plan and kill and train."

"A sort of supernatural headquarters," I said.

"Yes," said Allison faintly. She was scanning the room, searching for what we had yet to find.

"Can you hear anything?" I asked.

Allison shook her head. "I can only see...and feel."

"Do you see my sister?"

"Not yet, Sam."

I was still seeing what Allison saw, as she swooped through the room. "Can they see you?" I asked.

I sensed Allison almost smile...then again, it was hard to smile when you were holding a severed finger. "No, Sam. They are unaware of our snooping."

"You're a good sidekick to have around," I said.

"Partner," she said.

"We'll see," I said.

"There!" said Allison suddenly. I saw it, too. Three figures emerged into the room. Detective Hanner, my sister and Fang.

My sister was blindfolded, and plastic ties held her hands together. She was sobbing and stumbling as Hanner pulled her along.

They were met by someone I had seen before.

Someone I had fought before.

Someone—or something—that had nearly killed me, if not for Kingsley's help.

It was, quite possibly, the oldest vampire in the world. The same vampire who had kidnapped a boy he had thought was my son, a vampire I had fought under the Mission Inn Dome.

It was Dominique.

"Okay," I said, reaching out and touching Allison's arm. "I've seen enough."

Chapter Thirty-six

I was pacing.

The finger was back in the napkin and on ice in Allison's freezer, although she didn't seem too thrilled about that.

"Because there's a severed finger with my green peas, Sam. You wouldn't be too thrilled either," she said defensively.

But I wasn't paying her much attention. My thoughts were focused on the caverns beneath the Los Angeles River. Most importantly, on how to get my sister and my rat bastard of an ex-husband out alive.

"And Fang," said Allison suddenly.

I paused and looked at her. "What?"

"It's there in your thoughts, Sam, although you haven't acknowledged it. You also want to get Fang out. To save him."

"I…" But I didn't know what to say. So, I closed my mouth.

"He's one of them, Sam. A kidnapper and a killer."

I didn't know what to say to that, either, except that I didn't share Allison's convictions. I knew Fang, perhaps better than anyone. He was not a psychopathic killer.

As I thought those words, I picked up Allison's thought: *Once a killer, Sam, always a killer.*

I shook my head and ran my hands through my hair and thought about what I had to do. They took my sister. They took my ex-husband. *My God, they cut off his finger.* They were going to kill him, I was sure of it. They were going to kill me, too. The evil bitch inside me was getting impatient, growing weary of my resistance. Well, fuck her. And fuck them, too.

Poor Mary Lou. She hadn't asked for any of this. She had been heading out to get, what, tacos for the family? And that piece of shit Hanner had been waiting for her? Waiting because Sanchez had reported my activities to her. Sanchez was a good cop who had been compelled to do a traitorous thing. My guess was that he wouldn't remember calling her.

"It's a trap, Samantha," said Allison. "It's been a trap all along."

I didn't say anything, but kept pacing. I knew that, of course.

"Sam, when I was in those caverns, I sensed something else, something that I think you might not have picked up on, something that occurred when Fang, Hanner and your sister appeared."

I stopped in front of my friend, who, only now, was getting some of the color back to her cheeks since dealing with the finger. "What?" I asked.

"They're getting rid of you for another reason."

"What reason?"

She swallowed, looked at me. "I mean, they are going to *try* to get rid of you."

"I know what you meant, dammit. What's the other reason?"

"It's Fang," she said. "They sense great potential in him. Great potential to kill. I felt it from Hanner and the other vampire."

"You can read other vampires?"

"Only immortals can't read each other, Sam. I'm not immortal and I'm growing stronger, thanks to you."

"You're doing a lot more than remote viewing," I pointed out.

"I think of it as remote sensing." She shrugged. "It's a growing ability."

Like me, Allison's abilities seemed to be progressing rapidly. Unlike me, her abilities were tied to my drinking of her blood.

"Not just blood," she corrected. "Blood isn't the only source of my power. I'm developing my abilities in other ways now."

"Witchcraft," I said.

"Of course," she said.

"Fine," I said. "What about the other vampires? What else is going on?"

"Like I said, Sam. They sense great potential in him."

"Potential to do what?"

"To kill, to supply and perhaps someday to lead. Mostly, they sense in him a willingness to go along with the program."

"To give himself up to them," I said. Or, put another way, to allow himself to be controlled, possessed and perhaps taken over by the evil within him, too.

"Yes, Sam, except for one problem, which is where you come in."

I stopped pacing and stood before her. I was surprised to discover that my heart had suddenly started beating faster than normal. Hell, faster than it had in some time.

"What are you getting at?" I asked.

"His love for you," said Allison. "It's posing a problem, a hindrance."

My heart continued pounding, and knowing that Fang still felt something for me—anything for me—was a gift I wasn't entirely prepared for. I would have felt excitement—and hope—if not for the fact that he and the others had my sister.

"They need you dead, Sam, so that they can properly cultivate him for greater things."

"I have to leave," I said, grabbing my keys and opening the front door.

"I'm coming with you."

"No, you're not."

"Sam, you need me."

"No, I don't—"

I hadn't quite finished my sentence when the front door suddenly slammed shut again. I jumped, startled. I was about to ask what the holy hell had happened when I turned and saw Allison holding out her right hand, her eyelids half closed.

"Jesus. Was that you?" I asked.

"Like I told you, Sam, my powers are growing." She lowered her hand and opened her eyes.

"Well, it's a nice trick, dear," I said, opening the door again, "but I'm still not bringing—"

She turned, raising her hand. The comfy overstuffed chair and a half, where I had sat many times before, lifted off the floor and hurled through the apartment. Pillows and Allison's purse, which had all been on the chair, went flying in different directions. Unfortunately, the chair was heading for the sliding glass door, which led to her patio and a nice third-story view of the other Beverly Hills apartments. I braced for the coming crash when the chair—sweet Jesus—stopped in mid-air. Stopped just before the glass door. The chair rotated slowly...and settled carefully onto the floor.

"Holy hell," I said.

"Now, can I come with you, Sam?" she asked, opening her eyes and lowering her arm.

"Sweet mama," I said.

"I second that," said a deep voice behind me. A voice I recognized.

I turned to find Kingsley standing in the doorway, filling it completely, wearing jeans and a black tee shirt and hair down to his shoulders. Good cologne wafted from him as if the stuff flowed from his veins.

Allison said, "Oh, did I forget to mention that I called Kingsley, too?"

CHAPTER THIRTY-SEVEN

We were in my minivan.

It wasn't exactly the Batmobile, or something cooked up by *Iron Man*'s Richard Stark. It was just an older minivan—the same minivan I used to pick my kids up from school, to buy groceries and to run errands. Just last week, I'd backed into a pole at my kids' school, putting a good-sized dent in the bumper that was going to cost me more money to fix than I wanted to spend.

And here we were, charging through the night. Three freaks to battle a cavern full of freaks.

Yeah, my life is weird.

"You shouldn't have called him," I said to Allison for the tenth time.

"Hey," said Kingsley, "you say that enough times and I might start getting offended."

"Well, she shouldn't have called you."

"Yeah, you mentioned that. Except I'm not going to let you walk alone into a vampire nest."

"Is that a politically correct thing to say?" asked Allison from the backseat.

"You keep quiet," I said to her, aiming the minivan down Sunset Boulevard. I kept the car at well over the speed limit, not giving a damn about a ticket. Hell, I would compel the fucking cop to forget what he saw and to crave a pink donut instead.

And, yes, I thought of Sherbet, and, yes, I wished he was here, too. Same with my other detective friends: Knighthorse, Spinoza and Aaron King, who may or may not be Elvis.

No, I thought, shaking my head again. *I can't put them—or anyone—in jeopardy.*

"You also can't do this alone," said Allison, reading my mind.

"Huh?" said Kingsley. "Oh, I see. You two are doing your mind-reading thing."

I was fairly certain the minivan was listing to his side. I swear to God, Kingsley was bigger than the last time I'd seen him. Kingsley would, in fact, keep growing, minutely, with each transformation.

So weird, I thought.

Earlier, I'd made a number of my own calls. First up, I had called Mary Lou's husband. I had told him I was with Mary Lou and something important had come up that we couldn't talk about. I suggested very strongly that he should stay indoors and make dinner there. He agreed. A little too quickly.

Yes, I had used some of my own compulsion on him. No, I didn't have any clue that it would actually go through the call. But it had.

Next, I called both Anthony and Tammy in turn. Yes, they each had their own cell phones. And, yes, they each cost me an arm and a leg. But, dammit, I loved knowing I could get a hold of my kids at any time of the day. And, yes, they had strict orders to keep their cell phones with them at all times—and on. Anyway, I told them each to watch out for each other. Tammy, my telepathic daughter—yes, a family of freaks—picked up a stray thought of mine that her aunt was in trouble. I told her to keep that information to herself and that I was doing all I could to help her aunt.

Finally, as I had been heading out to Allison's, I called Sherbet— and kept my mind closed in the process. I hadn't wanted him to know where we were, or what we were up to. But I had asked him to keep an eye on my sister's house. He had told me he would do it himself, with one of his officers. He had asked if everything was okay. I had told him no, everything was *not* okay. He said he wanted to help, and I had told him no. He didn't like it and insisted and I told him no again. He still didn't like it, but finally gave in, and told me to stay safe. I told him I would do my best, and, before we hung up, I told him to send a car out to Hanner's. He asked why and I told him he wouldn't believe me if I told him. He said try him, so I do, telling him about the newlyweds and the bleeder. Sherbet then said that I was right, he didn't believe me, but he would send someone out right away.

As I drove, Allison caught Kingsley up on the layout of the caverns, as she had seen them remotely.

Kingsley shook his shaggy, blockish head. "Your powers have grown considerably since the last time I saw you."

Which had, of course, been at Skull Island months, ago. Back then, Allison was just coming into her own, just exploring her increased powers.

"You could say I've had an epiphany," she said from the backseat, sticking her head between us.

"What kind of epiphany?" he asked.

"I'm a witch."

Kingsley glanced down at her, somehow managing to see through all his thick hair. "Witches scare the shit out of me."

That was news to me. Truth was, I didn't think anything scared the big oaf. "Why?" I asked.

"They're unpredictable...and seem to have nature on their side. And after the demonstration I just saw at your house...well, remind me to stay on your good side."

Allison beamed, but as she did so, I sensed her self-doubt. Yes, this was all new to her. Yes, she could perform some incredible tricks, but, no, she did not feel worthy of her newfound—and growing—powers.

Truth was, I didn't know much about any of this stuff, either, let alone what a witch could and couldn't do.

Not true, Samantha, came Allison's thought, as she picked up on my own. *You were once a witch, too. We both were.*

Along with Millicent, I added, referring to the spirit that had first broken the news to Allison of her supernatural pedigree.

Yes, Millicent. And we were both supposed to be witches again, except you've taken a slightly different path.

A bloodsucking path, I thought grimly.

141

Well, we're together again, said Allison, *and that's all that matters.*

"Are you two quite done?" asked Kingsley.

"What do you mean?" I asked.

"Your telepathy crap…it's kind of rude."

"How did you know we were doing telepathy?" I asked, genuinely intrigued.

"Because the two of you get all quiet at the exact same time, which is rare enough as it is. Were you two talking about me?"

"Maybe," I said, and, despite the seriousness of our current situation, and despite knowing my sister was at the hands of forces that would love nothing more than to rip her life away from her, I giggled. So did Allison.

"C'mon. What were you two talking about?"

"Your hair," said Allison, lying and giggling some more.

"What about my hair?" asked Kingsley defensively. For some reason, the big gorilla was always defensive about his thick locks.

"We think you need a haircut," said Allison.

"We do?" I asked her.

"Yes, we do," she said.

"Okay," I said, laughing some more. "We do."

"Well, I can't cut it," said Kingsley.

This was news to me. Despite having dated the big goof for a while, I hadn't known this fact.

"Why not?" we both asked at once.

"It just grows right back, within days, and sometimes within hours. And, even worse, it always grows back a little longer."

I think Kingsley was trying to get our sympathy, but he got the exact opposite reaction. Allison and I burst out laughing. I wasn't expecting to laugh. I was pissed and ready to take on every fucking vampire in Los Angeles if I had to. But now, I found myself laughing, nearly uncontrollably. The van swerved. Kingsley gripped the dashboard, and I laughed even harder. Truth was, I think I needed to laugh. And hearing Allison's snorting in the backseat made me totally lose it.

"Are you two quite done?" growled Kingsley, shaking his head.

"When he cuts his hair," said Allison, sitting forward between us, gasping and wiping her eyes, her voice barely above a squeak, "it just keep growing out even longer...within days...hours...that's the funniest thing I've ever heard."

I wasn't sure if it was the funniest thing I'd ever heard, but it was definitely a tension breaker for me. And as I gasped and fought for my own breath, Kingsley mumbled, "I don't know why I open up to you two."

"And now we know why you don't ask for a free haircut, either," squealed Allison.

I reached back and put a hand on my friend's forearm. "Let's leave him alone," I said. "We don't want to piss him—or his hair—off."

Allison giggled some more, while Kingsley shot me a grumpy look. "It's really not funny," he said.

"No," I said, struggling to keep a straight face. "Excessive hair growth is never funny."

Allison literally snorted in the back seat, which made Kingsley finally crack a smile. "You two are clowns," he said. "I think we should get serious."

"Yes, serious," Allison and I said together. We stopped laughing almost on cue, even though Allison might have snorted once more for good measure.

I turned left from Sunset and headed up Los Feliz Boulevard, following my recently added navigational device. No, this old van did not come with navigation, but this one worked easily enough... that is, if it would quit falling from its mount, which it did now as I made my left turn. I caught it and returned it to its spot before I had completed the turn.

"If you two are done making fun of my affliction, maybe we should discuss a game plan."

I turned left into one of the Griffith Park entrances, stopped the van and killed the engine.

"Good idea," I said. "Oh, and we're here."

CHAPTER THIRTY-EIGHT

We sat in the minivan.

Technically, the park was closed, but there was nothing to keep us out either. The park was, after all, an entire hillside…a chain of hillsides, in fact.

"She told me to come alone," I said.

"And what did you say?" asked Kingsley.

"I told her to go fuck herself."

"That's my girl," said Kingsley. "So, where is this place?"

"The river—which is now an aqueduct—flows not too far from here. It's popular with bikers and joggers."

"And vampires," said Allison.

"And how do we get to their underground lair?" asked Kingsley

I nearly asked the big guy to quit calling it a *lair*, except that's exactly what it was. A breeding ground for the undead. A nest, perhaps.

"There's a cave opening close to here," I said. "She described it to me."

In fact, as I spoke those words, I told the gang to hold on while I closed my eyes and cast my thoughts out. Unlike Allison, who needed something personal, I needed no such aid. At any point, in any place, I could close my eyes and cast my mind out, scanning my immediate surroundings within a few hundred feet. And, yes, that net seemed to be growing wider these days, but not by much. Still a couple of hundred feet, give or take.

144

My sweeping, all-seeing internal eye didn't have any problems with the dark either. The night was bright and alive and I could have just as easily been a dark demigod looking down at his realm.

Or the world's weirdest mom trying to save her sister.

Either way, I confirmed that the park was empty of anything human. It was also empty of most things animal, except for a few stray cats and a squirrel that seemed to be dancing the jig on a nearby tree branch. I next searched for the landmark Hanner had described: a red post off to the side of the main river path. *There, found it.* Next, I mentally hung a left and continued on to a pile of boulders—and found them exactly where Hanner had said they would be. I also found the small opening into the rocks—an opening that might pose a problem for Kingsley, and slipped inside it, but not very far. I had reached the limits of my abilities. One thing was certain, though, the cave entrance was not guarded.

A moment later, I returned to my body, waited a moment to get reoriented, and then reported my findings. Mostly, I reported them for Kingsley's benefit, as I knew Allison had internally followed my traveling, swooping mind.

"I'll fit," said Kingsley.

"How can you be so sure?"

He tapped his thick skull. "Mind over matter."

"Fine," I said, "so what's the game plan?"

"Get your sister," said Kingsley, "and get the hell out of there."

"What about Danny?" I asked.

Kingsley turned and looked at me, and as he did so, his eyes flared amber. Not the flame I sometimes saw in other vampires' eyes. No, this was the glint of something wild, feral, untamed. Something animalistic.

"Well, I can't just leave him there," I said.

"He's part of this, Sam. You told me so yourself. That they turned on him is his own fault."

"He's my kids' father…"

"He made his own bed, Samantha," said Kingsley.

As he said those words, I wondered about that. I wondered if Danny had, indeed, made his bed, or if someone had made it for him, so to speak. Well, I would learn the truth soon enough. One thing was certain, there was no way in hell he had willingly allowed his finger to be cut off.

I didn't mention Fang, although Allison was well aware of my plans to save him, too. Kingsley already didn't like Fang much, and vice versa. Both saw the other as a threat, and if Kingsley was already having a problem with me helping my ex, well, I knew for damn sure he would put his overgrown paw down in regard to Fang.

He doesn't like Fang, came Allison's thoughts.

You can read his mind, too? I asked, surprised.

Not really. Kingsley is a master at shielding his thoughts, but I can read his body language and some latent feelings he's had. If you are going to save Fang, and possibly even your ex, you can count him out.

And what about you? I asked her.

Oh, you can always count me in, silly.

Fang has the diamond medallion, I thought, referring to the one artifact that could return me to a mostly-normal life.

I know, Sam. Is that the only reason why you want to save him?

I didn't have to think long about the answer. *No,* I thought back to her, *I'm pretty sure I love him.*

That's what I thought, Sam.

"Are you two done?" asked Kingsley.

"We're done," I said.

"Good," he said, "because I have an idea about how we can save your sister...and maybe even your lying, cheating ex-hubby, too."

CHAPTER THIRTY-NINE

The trail from the parking lot soon wound along the Los Angeles River.

No, not a traditional river, but it had been once, before man, concrete and zoning commissions debased, muzzled and graffitied it. As we followed a dirt path that led along the flowing water, which sparkled to my eyes, but probably not so much to Allison's—Kingsley was a different story—I scanned ahead, verifying that we were not being followed or stepping into a trap. We were okay on both fronts.

So far.

Crickets chirped endlessly, seemingly coming from everywhere at once. A small hum filled the air, too; mosquitoes were alive and well along the banks of the tamed river. Beyond, the drone of traffic along the I-5. Many people didn't realize just how hilly Los Angeles was. We were surrounded by such hills now, each dotted with bright lights from bigger homes.

A friend of mine, Spinoza, had his office near here, in Echo Park. So did another friend of mine, who bore an uncanny resemblance to Elvis Presley, despite the obvious facial reconstruction.

We probably could have used both their help now. But they were mortals with guns. These were vampires with teeth. Vamps with teeth trumped guns.

I had another friend out here, too, a private eye who had recently passed from lung cancer complicated by AIDS. I'd met him long ago while working with the federal government. We'd both been involved with a missing girl case, a case on which many government agencies and local police and private eyes had found themselves working. We never did find the girl, but I had met James Coleman. His good friend, a stoic Nigerian named Numi, had been kind enough to send me an email about his passing. I would miss James. He had been a troubled guy, but a great investigator.

I took my thoughts off James and put them onto my poor sister, who didn't deserve any of this. God, she was going to be so pissed off at me. And, yes, I was already assuming that we would save her, that she was going to get out of this alive, and that I was going to have to spend the next five years apologizing for getting her involved in this mess.

Nothing wrong with thinking positive, Sam, came Allison's words.

I nodded as we continued along. I led the way, periodically pausing and scouting ahead, occasionally pushing aside an errant tree branch or stepping over thicker bushes crowding the trail.

Soon, I found the red post in the ground, mostly hidden by thick creosote, huckleberry and something that could have been an overgrown fern. The path beyond was mostly nonexistent.

"Here?" asked Kingsley, his eyes shining like twin suns. God, we were such freaks, all of us.

"This is it," I said, and led the way. Behind me, despite his best efforts to stay quiet, he crashed through the forest like an oversized bear drunk on fermented blueberries.

The trail narrowed further, and I forced myself through the thickets and brambles, snagging my jeans and light jacket. I heard Allison behind me struggling a bit, and behind her, cursing under his voice, was Kingsley. We were a motley, ragtag bunch, an unlikely trio to take down a coven of vampires, or whatever they were called.

Covens are for witches, Sam, came Allison's words. *And Kingsley looks like he could take down a whole forest.*

Are you always in my head? I asked, finally spying the clump of boulders through the pines and spruces ahead.

These days, yes. We're very connected, Sam.

Lucky you, I thought, and sent her a mental wink.

And just like that, the tangle of branches and leaves and thorns and roots gave way to an open space, and a big pile of rocks.

"Here we are," I said. "The entrance."

Chapter Forty

The opening was smaller than Kingsley had hoped.

"This could pose a problem," he said, which, of course, is exactly what I had said.

Kingsley, who'd scampered up onto the rocks with surprising agility, looking more like a hulking, hairy mountain goat than anything else, peered down into the dark hole that was surrounded by piles of boulders. That anyone consistently used this hole as an entry point to anything was beyond me. That my own flesh and blood sister had recently been forced down into this hole was unfathomable.

Poor Mary Lou.

Once again, I wished desperately that I could reach out to her in some way, but my sister and I were not in telepathic contact with each other, and neither were Danny or Fang; at least, in Fang's case, not anymore.

What have you done, Fang?

The opening was not obvious, even if a hiker had managed to work his way to this spot, which I suspected few had, and those who had might not live long enough to talk about it. Indeed, the boulders were surprisingly free of graffiti, which was a rarity anywhere in Los Angeles.

The three of us had climbed onto them and were presently looking down into a small opening. I could have been Alice looking down into the rabbit's hole. Except there were no rabbits down there, nor even a hallucinogenic Wonderland. No, nothing but murderous vampires.

And my sister. And Danny. And Fang.

Lord help us all.

Anyway, I could see through the darkness to a dirt floor below. I could also see imprints of shoes. Fresh imprints, too. Women's running shoes included. If I had to guess, those were Mary Lou's running shoes.

Seeing them now, and knowing she was close by, sent a fresh wave of panic through me.

I reported what I saw to the others, knowing that the entrance would lead down into a natural tunnel system.

"Tight squeeze," said Allison, "even for us girls."

She was right. How a grown man, no, a werewolf man, could expect to drop down into the hole, I didn't know.

"Yes, this is a very big problem," he said again.

"No," said Allison, "you are the big problem."

Believe it or not, I might have detected some flirtation in Allison's voice. Yes, she'd always had a crush on the big oaf. Anyway, Kingsley grunted at that, then reached down into the hole, grabbed hold of the edge of one of the flatter rocks, and did something that surprised even me. He pulled the sucker out. The huge rock—which was a borderline boulder—flipped out and tumbled down the pile, landing with a heavy thud in the dirt below.

We all looked down into the now-much-bigger hole.

"It's not a problem anymore," he said a little smugly.

Allison literally melted. "That was very impressive."

Kingsley looked at her, his eyes glowing wildly, blinked, and then shrugged. He might have just realized my best friend was smitten with him. "Yeah, well, I'm a bit of a monster."

"Well, it was just so...very impressive."

Cool your jets, I shot to her telepathically, and to Kingsley, I said, "It was also loud as hell...so much for the element of surprise."

"I thought we agreed that we *weren't* going to surprise anyone," said Kingsley, slightly annoyed at my reprimand.

"Well, not anymore," I said, and shot Lady Goo-Goo Eyes another hard stare, and then I leaped down into the tunnel entrance. "Come on," I said up to them, stepping aside, and soon my friends, one after the other, landed next to me.

Chapter Forty-one

We were all in.

Although Kingsley and I could see just fine, Allison, despite her newfound witchy gifts and her ability to remote view, could not see in the dark. Which is why, presently, she was using the flashlight app on her Galaxy Note.

Kingsley, I couldn't help but notice, filled the narrow tunnel completely. In fact, he had to turn his massive shoulders slightly to stand reasonably comfortably. Even still, he hunched forward a little and looked, in general, miserable. Like a caged beast, perhaps.

The walls of the tunnels were mostly natural, but the ceiling, I saw, had clearly been carved out by someone. When this had been done, I wouldn't know, and, since none of us were archaeologists, we probably would never know. In fact, I wasn't even entirely sure vampires had hacked their way through this tunnel system. It could have been hobos or even a WWII bunker, for all I knew.

Of course, the only thing that mattered was who—or what—was using the caverns now.

And that would be vampires, and according to Allison, there were at least three of them.

Under the glow of Allison's cell phone app, I closed my eyes a final time and cast my thoughts out, down through the narrow tunnel, sweeping around a procession of ghosts—a host of lost spirits haunting the tunnels themselves…and into the caverns beyond, which were well within my range.

Once in the caverns, I noted the many torches flickering along the rock walls. No, vampires didn't need light, but light wasn't a bad thing, either. Perhaps these vamps wanted some additional light, perhaps the light was even for their human guests. I didn't know, and I didn't really care.

Next, I saw the first chamber. The room was decorated with a ragtag collection of furniture: old lounge chairs, garish couches and stools. Actually, the furniture looked like something from an old nightclub, which it very well might have been. How, exactly, the furniture had made it down here, I hadn't a clue, although I suspected there might be another entrance somewhere. I didn't know.

Anyway, on a purple camelback couch with an exaggerated hump sat a very old man who wasn't a man at all. He was a vampire, in fact, and I recognized him from Allison's own scan of the cavern. Of course, I recognized him from elsewhere, too. He was a vampire with a death wish. A vampire who, quite frankly, didn't want to be a vampire anymore, and had been willing to kidnap a boy—a boy he'd thought was my son—to force me to give him the ruby medallion, which would have reversed his vampirism, thus rendering him mortal. His plan hadn't worked, and now here he was, sitting casually on the couch, looking like an old creep at a nightclub, wearing black slacks and a white dress shirt, legs crossed. He appeared to be waiting for someone. Who that someone was, I could only guess.

I expanded my awareness out and into the next room, where I saw my ex-husband still secured to the desk. But this time, he wasn't alone. This time, Detective Hanner of the Fullerton Police Department was standing next to him, her hand on his head...and there was my sister, sitting in a straight-back chair, guarded by, of all people, Fang, who stood next to her.

Her arms were tied behind her back, her head was covered by a burlap sack. Her chest shuddered with each sob. Bile rose in my throat at her terror. *My sister!*

Hanner was holding a long blade away from her body, a blade that Danny kept his widened eyes on closely. My ex-husband, who had once been a loving and caring father, who had actually once even been a good husband before life—and the afterlife—had become too much for him, was scared shitless. I knew Danny and I knew that look. It was a look he'd given me many times after my turning.

Hanner's head was bowed slightly as she held the knife in one hand, the other still resting on Danny's head. And then, it occurred to me what she was doing.

She was scouting ahead, too. Or, rather, she was performing a sort of reverse surveillance. As Danny continued watching her, as blood dripped from his right hand, and as my sister continued weeping nearby, Hanner slowly raised her head and looked up…

And seemingly, directly at me.

She lifted her hand from Danny's head and waggled her finger at me slowly. She was admonishing me, and I suspected I knew why. If she could see me as I could see her, she had seen Kingsley and Allison with me, as well. I hadn't come alone, as I had been instructed.

And then she did the unthinkable.

She gave me a soulless smile—and plunged the knife deep into Danny's chest.

Chapter Forty-two

I screamed and shot back into my body.

I was about to hurl myself down the hallway, as fast as I could, and into the caverns. In fact, it was only the hulking Kingsley in front of me who literally blocked my path that kept me from doing so.

"What happened?" Kingsley said, as I fought to get past him.

Allison answered for me, as all I could see was white-hot fury.

"Hanner stabbed Danny," I heard her say. "I saw it, too."

I was beyond thought or control. "I have to get to him. I have to get to him *now!*"

"We will, Sam."

"Kingsley, it's a trap," said Allison. "There are others waiting for her. I saw them. In particular, the old vampire."

"I'll take care of him," said Kingsley. "We do, after all, have some unfinished business." He was, of course, referring of their epic battle last year under the dome, when the old vampire had bested him and escaped. Kingsley looked grimly from me to Allison. "You remember the plan?" he asked her.

"I'll take care of the hunters," said my friend, who suddenly didn't seem very confident. She swallowed and I would have admired her bravery if I hadn't known the clock was ticking on my ex-husband.

This wasn't happening. I hadn't just seen my ex-husband get stabbed in the chest. I hadn't seen my sister with a bag over her head.

This wasn't happening, this wasn't happening.

No, no, no.

Kingsley gave me a final look, his handsome face full of determination and pity, and what happened next should have surprised me. Hell, it should have fascinated me. But it didn't.

Before our very eyes, Kingsley transformed.

Back in the minivan, he had told us he would do this. This had been, in fact, his plan. The old vampire was too strong for him in his human form. But the fight would be even in his changeling form. His werewolf form. I had spoken against this, reminding him that he lost all control of himself during transformation, and what Kingsley said next surprised and thrilled me at the time. "No, Sam. I lose control when the moon is full. Not so much when I *choose* to transform."

This had, of course, been news to me.

And now his transformation couldn't happen fast enough. Kingsley tore off his shirt and hunched forward, away from us. I had a sense that he didn't want us to see his face. He jerked and contorted and howled in what I assumed was agony. Allison slipped behind me, and I didn't blame her. The man she had a crush on was metamorphosing before our eyes.

The change took only seconds, perhaps twenty seconds in all. All the while, I thought of Danny with a knife in his chest.

Nothing you can do about it, if you're dead, I thought, which might have been my only rational thought during these moments. Yes, I knew we were walking into a trap. But they weren't expecting a full-fledged werewolf to make an appearance, a werewolf who would take on their oldest and strongest vampire.

Now Kingsley dropped to his knees and arched his back and what I saw there surprised even me. Hair had sprouted almost instantly. Short, silver-brown, thick hair.

No, *fur.*

Yes, I had seen what Kingsley turned into each full moon. A true wolfman, hulking, bipedal, frightening. What was emerging now was something different. It was, in fact, an actual wolf.

Within moments, a massive, four-legged wolf was now standing before us in the tunnel, looking haggard and pissed off, his mane hair erect, his tail held high in aggressive position. It turned once, looked back at us with Kingsley's same amber eyes, then it was off and running, faster than even I could run, which was pretty damn fast.

I was torn between running behind it and keeping Allison safe. Yes, I knew my friend had recently come into some powerful new skills—and could quite possibly take care of herself—but I couldn't take that chance. Ultimately, I held back with Allison, not wanting to leave my friend behind in the tunnels. The wolf that was Kingsley charged ahead and was soon out of sight.

CHAPTER FORTY-THREE

I paused just outside the cavern entrance.

While I waited for Allison to catch up, I listened to the horrific sounds echoing from within the big, underground room. I was tempted to dash into the cavern, but I didn't. That was what they wanted. I was sure of it. For me to act recklessly, dangerously.

For me to die.

I held back, despite my natural instinct to rush forward and help. Kingsley had his hands full—or teeth full—in there. But he was a big boy. Or a big doggie. Instead, I closed my eyes and cast my thoughts forward a final time, into the cavern, and saw two people waiting not too far away. Whether they were vampires or not, I didn't know—but one thing was for certain.

Each was holding a crossbow notched with a silver-tipped arrow.

Allison, breathing hard next to me, communicated with me silently: *I see them, Sam. Let me take care of them. Go get Danny and your sister.*

What do you mean?

Allison took point, stepping around me and into the cavern, holding her hands up before her.

———

She continued into the cavern in full witch mode, hands raised, palms out, like a battle was about to go down.

Her back was to me. I nearly ran to her, but waited, knowing what she was doing. She was clearing the way for me. I was expecting the worst. I was expecting a silver-tipped arrow to blossom in her chest.

But that didn't happen.

Instead, as the vicious fighting sounds of the werewolf and the vampire grew even louder and fiercer, Allison stood at the cavern entrance, unscathed, hands still up. Her hands, I saw, were shaking.

"Now, Sam!" she said, turning her head slightly toward me. Her arms were shaking even harder.

I was instantly in the cavern—and saw the two men guards now pinned against the rock walls, their crossbows crushed at their feet, their faces and hands physically forced into the stone wall behind them. They couldn't fight or struggle, or perhaps even breathe. They stood there, immobile, frozen, while Allison slowly walked forward, her hands still up and shaking even harder.

"Hurry, Sam!"

I was about to dash forward, into the adjoining cavern, when I saw a sight I wouldn't soon forget: Kingsley, in wolf form, was engaged in mortal combat with the vampire, the very old and very powerful vampire. As I watched, Kingsley went for the vampire's throat, hurling his long, muscular body through the air, only to absorb a devastating blow by the vampire that sent the wolf reeling, flipping head over tail, to crash into a nearby wall. The vampire, I saw, was covered with deep wounds, skin flapping at his scalp and neck. Yes, Kingsley had done some damage.

In the next room, I heard my sister scream.

I moved faster than I ever had in my entire existence.

CHAPTER FORTY-FOUR

I knew Hanner was waiting for me.

In fact, she might have organized the others—the old vampire presently ensnared with Kingsley, and the two hunters waiting just inside the entrance—just to occupy my friends.

Yes, Hanner wanted me.

And only me.

Well, she was going to get me.

I doubted she would be waiting on the other side with a crossbow, nor would Fang. That didn't seem like her style. So, I took my chances and plunged through the opening, and into the second cavern.

Yes, there was my sister.

Fang stood next to her, too, holding a long knife...a knife that was presently pressed against her fabric-covered throat, no doubt the reason why my sister had screamed in the first place.

Detective Rachel Hanner bent down next to my seated ex-husband, Danny, her ear pressed to his bloody lips, making a show of listening to him.

Hanner leaned in a little closer, and almost lovingly caressed the handle of the dagger that protruded from the center of his chest. I was too dumbfounded by the scene to act. I just stood there, absorbing the craziness, absorbing the fact that my life had so radically spun out of control that my jerk of an ex-husband was sitting with a dagger in his chest, and that my sister had a bag over her head, with another dagger pressed against her throat, held there by my one-time best friend, Fang.

I took another step into the room, and my sister screamed again, as Fang pressed the blade harder against her throat. I stopped. Hanner straightened and gave me a small smile, although her eyes did anything but smile.

"He keeps calling for you, Sam. I wonder why?" She moved around him as I saw Danny's body jerk a little. His eyelids fluttered. Blood bubbled up around the blade handle, which meant she had punctured a lung, but not his heart. At least, I didn't think she had. "Now, why would he be calling your name when he, in fact, called me?"

"Why would he call you?" I asked, and took another step into the room.

"Sam?" screamed Mary Lou, "Oh, my God, Sam, what's happening?"

"It's going to be okay, Mary Lou," I said. "I'm going to get you out of here."

"It's very much *not* going to be okay, Samantha," said Hanner, now facing me. "Just ask your ex-husband. Oh, and there might have been a small chance that I came across your husband at his sleazy little strip club a few months ago, and told him to call me when his little vampire problem got out of hand."

Danny jerked his head; a small sound escaped from his bloody lips.

"There he goes again," said Hanner, shaking her pretty head, but not taking her eyes off me, eyes that burned with an inner flame. "Calling your name like you give a damn."

"I do give a damn," I said.

"And that's your problem, Samantha," said Hanner. "You give too much of a damn over these humans."

"You're not Hanner," I said, stepping forward again, and this time, Fang didn't press the knife any harder against my sister's throat. I noted that Fang looked nothing like the man I had once known. Fang and I had never had a physical relationship, and the truth was, we hadn't seen too much of each other outside of the bar where he'd worked, Hero's. Still, the man—or thing—in front of me, holding a knife to my sister's throat, looked dead and lost.

"No," said the female detective in front of me. She spoke in a slow, calculating, slightly lilting way, an accent I could not detect. "Hanner has taken, to use a modern idiom, a back seat. But rest assured, she's watching with interest from the shadows where she belongs. Where all of you belong."

"He needs help," I said. "Let him go. Let my sister go. You want me. I'm here."

"Oh, we want you all, Samantha Moon."

I looked at Fang, and decided to address him by his real name, "Aaron," I said. "What have you done? What have they done to you?"

"He can't talk, Sam," said Hanner.

I snapped my head around and looked at her. "Why the hell not?"

"He's been compelled not to, as you might have guessed. Just as he's being compelled to hold the knife to your sister. Just as he's being compelled to watch you die."

"Compelled by whom?" I asked, but knew the answer immediately. "Dominique."

"But of course, Samantha Moon. Only the most powerful vampires can compel another vampire. And Aaron here, or Eli, or Fang, as he still prefers to be called, has been such a good little boy. And quite the killer, too. Truly vicious. You should see him in action. He makes Mommy so very proud."

"You're sick."

"We're all sick, Sam."

"No," I said. "You're different. You're evil."

"We are mavericks, Samantha, nothing more, nothing less."

"What the hell does that mean?"

"It means we have seen how the world works, how the Universe works, and we have decided there is a better way."

"What way?"

"*Our* way, Samantha Moon. But to do that, you see, we need our sister to be free. You have bottled her up, so to speak, for far too long."

"You want to give her a new host."

"Yesss," Hanner hissed, although it was not Hanner who spoke to me. She looked over at my sister. "Yesss, and we found another, Sssamantha Moon. And she carries, of course, your bloodline."

"What about my bloodline?" I asked.

"You don't know, do you?"

"Know what?"

"Never mind that, Samantha. You'll be dead soon."

Hanner reached behind her back and pulled out an old-fashioned .38 revolver. "Not just any gun, Sam. This one happens to be equipped with silver bullets."

I almost sprang on her, believing wrongly that I could move faster than she could pull the trigger, except she was a fairly old vampire herself, and I would be dead before I took a step.

The fire in her eyes flared brightly.

I turned my shoulders as a shot rang out. Pain blasted my shoulder as the sound of the gunshot split the air. Mary Lou screamed. Even Danny made a noise. Most interesting was the noise I heard in the next chamber, the sound of something growling and the bellow of something dying.

But that all seemed very far away from me now.

"You are fast, Samantha Moon," said Hanner, approaching me, holding the gun out. "I've never known how you could anticipate another vampire. Then again, maybe it's something in your blood. Maybe it's something that's in your sister's blood, too. Something we can dig out, understand, and perhaps use."

I stumbled away from her, holding my shoulder, as her eyes flared again. The next shot shattered my elbow and I felt my right arm drop limp. I cried out for the first time in a long time. Mostly from the burning, the unending, goddamn burning.

She stepped around me, still holding the gun before her. She was smiling, but her eyes were dead...when I saw the slight change. The deadness was replaced with something close to compassion.

"I'm sorry, Sam," she said, the lilt in her voice gone. "I'm sorry it had to be this way. I liked you. I really did. I thought we could be friends. I thought we could be friends forever. But you wouldn't play by the rules. By *their* rules. Just know that I didn't want this for you."

She paused, and the deadness returned, replaced by the spark of fire just behind her pupils.

"Enough," said the accented voice.

She raised the gun, aimed it at my chest, and that was the last thing she ever did in this world.

The silver tip of Fang's knife blade appeared through her chest.

The bloodied silver tip.

Chapter Forty-five

I was all alone with Danny.

"Allison has gone for help for you," I said. His head was on my lap as we sat together on the dirt and rock floor. My arm was messed up, but already healing. I kept it at my side. I could literally feel my bones moving, finding their way, forming and reforming.

"Who's Allison?" he asked. "Never mind."

I almost smiled. Indeed, a fat lot of good it did him to learn the name of one of my friends, especially if his condition didn't improve.

"I don't feel so good, Sam."

"I know you don't, you idiot."

With Fang's help, we had done our best to staunch Danny's bleeding.

Fang...he'd been released from his compulsion the instant that Kingsley had killed the old vampire. And when I'd said killed, I meant he could have been killed many dozens of times over. The old man was now nothing but chunks of bloody meat scattered around the cavern. Kingsley had stated that the old man had finally given up, and had just stood there when Kingsley had come for him. He was now certain the old man had wanted nothing more than to finally die. Kingsley had very much given him his wish.

And thus, he'd released Fang from his compulsion.

Instantly, Fang had sprung into action to save me.

Kingsley was now wearing my sweater around his waist, which now looked more like a loincloth. Truth was, with his scratched chest

166

and thick shoulders and wild hair, he looked more like Conan the Barbarian than Orange County's most prominent defense attorney.

I shook my head at the absurdity of it all and returned my attention to my mortally wounded ex-husband.

"Why did you do it, you big idiot?" I asked.

Danny coughed and as he did so, more blood appeared around his bandage and from the corners of his mouth. "I hated you, Sam. You always seemed to get the better of me."

"I wasn't trying to get the better of you, you big friggin' moron."

"Do you mind not calling a dying man names, Sam?"

"You're not dying."

"You, better than anyone, could see that."

He was right, of course. I could see the aura around his body had darkened considerably in the last fifteen minutes, fifteen crazy minutes during which all of us were doing our best to make sense of what had just happened.

When Allison had finally released the two hunters, they'd dashed off, leaving behind their ruined crossbows and silver-tipped bolts. She was certain they had been compelled by Hanner. For as soon as she'd died, her control over them had vanished, as well. Yes, Hanner, my-one time drinking companion, was dead. The demon within her wasn't dead, of course. No, I had seen the black shadow pour from her dying mouth, to disappear into the ether, to one day find a new host.

Now Allison was off seeking help for Danny, and keeping in telepathic contact with me, too. At the moment, she had just made it to the parking lot, but she didn't have cell reception there either. I had given her my keys. She was just now getting into the minivan.

"I made so many mistakes, Sam," Danny said.

"I know."

He coughed. "Jesus, you didn't have to agree so fast."

"Well, you were a jerk and a moron and—"

"No name calling, remember? I know I screwed up."

"Royally," I said.

"I was afraid, Sam. Afraid of you. Afraid for my life. I mean, I had no idea that such things existed."

"I'm not a *thing*, Danny. I was your wife. That was always your problem. You made me into a monster. I wasn't a monster, and you know it. I was fighting it and winning, and you abandoned me, abandoned us."

As I spoke, I couldn't help but notice his aura had darkened some more, and a deep, rich blackness was creeping through what had once had some color.

He coughed harder than before. He kept on coughing, and as he did so, the darkness kept spreading.

"Ah, Danny. I'm sorry this happened to you."

"I asked for it, Sam. And don't you dare save me. Don't you dare make me like you. Please."

"I won't, Danny."

He coughed harder than ever, and then lay back, wheezing. "I didn't know what I was doing, Sam. Hanner promised me she would help me get the kids back."

"You don't want the kids, Danny. They would only get in the way of your new…playboy lifestyle."

"That's where you're wrong, Sam. I love them more than you know."

His eyes closed and the darkness surrounded him completely.

"I know you love them, Danny," I said.

He didn't respond, of course.

My stupid idiot of an ex-husband had just died in my arms.

CHAPTER FORTY-SIX

It was weeks later.

I was in my office, working, doing anything I could to get my mind off Danny's death. We had left him in the cavern, along with the remains of the old vampire and Hanner. Kingsley had sealed the entrance with more rocks and destroyed another entrance we had found at the back of the caverns.

For all intents and purposes, the cavern had ceased to exist, and was now, in fact, a tomb, adding to its legions of dead three more lost souls.

There was no hiding Danny's death from my kids, especially when I had a mind-reading daughter. So, I had told them what had happened. I told them that their dad had died trying to be with them, that their dad had made friends with the wrong people, and that their dad had died telling me how much he loved them, his last words, in fact.

It had been a hell of a shitty week.

Yes, I had asked my kids to keep one more whopping big secret. I asked them not to let the world know that their dad had died. Yes, I was a horrible mother, but the world at large needed to think that Danny had disappeared, perhaps with a stripper prospect, or perhaps because of some dirty business dealings. These explanations weren't far from the truth. Hanner and Fang had disappeared months earlier, back when Fang had first turned. Hell, Fang didn't technically exist, anyway, having been on the run since his escape from the insane asylum two decades earlier.

I had all of this on my mind in the weeks that followed, weeks during which I threw myself into my work, and threw myself into anything to avoid thinking about my lying, cheating ex-husband, my ex-husband who I suddenly missed with all my heart, my ex-husband who I forgave and would forever forgive.

Sanchez had also come by with questions of his own. I told him what I knew. I even told him about the caverns under the Los Angeles River. I told him that he had been compelled to act as a sort of puppet for Hanner.

I told him all of this, then took his hand and looked him deeply in the eyes, and then compelled him to forget it all. I told him to go home to his psycho wife and to forget anything about vampires. I told him to close his related cases and to write all three off as animal attacks. I told him I thought he was very handsome, but asked him to forget that I'd said that, too.

It was with these heavy thoughts, as I was leaning down and filing papers away in my office, when I heard a whisper of clothing and the swish of pant legs.

I looked up to find Fang standing in my doorway.

Chapter Forty-seven

"I'm sorry about your ex-husband," he said.

The truth was, I had been pissed at Fang, too. His desire to be a vampire—his own personal compulsion—had led to circumstances and events that had led, in turn, to Danny's murder.

But I knew that wasn't fair, either. Fang had just wanted to be a vampire, to be immortal, to live the life of characters in books and movies, but he had not fully comprehended the horror of the reality of such an existence.

The reality was, of course, that something very dark and sinister now called Fang's body home.

"Thank you," I said. "Danny was a good man who made bad choices."

Fang was seated in one of my three client chairs. Yes, I was ever the optimist. His long legs were crossed, and the drape of his jeans hung neatly. He was wearing leather boots that looked expensive. I suspected that Hanner had dressed and splurged on him these past few months. He was, after all, supposed to be her golden boy. As in, the perfect vampire and perfect killer. I didn't want to know what Fang had done, or how many he had killed these past few months.

I could see the fire just behind his pupils, the fire that hadn't been there when I'd first met him for drinks last year, back when he had finally revealed his super-secret identity, and I'd realized the extent to which I had been stalked. Back then, he had been a bit starstruck, awed to be in the presence of a real vampire. He had been excited and goofy and funny and charming.

Now, he was none of that.

Now, he was controlled, reserved, cautious and careful. He watched me closely, rarely taking his brooding eyes off of me. His mannerisms were nonexistent; instead, he kept his hands folded on one knee, hands that had once poured us drinks at Hero's, where I had first met him, back when Mary Lou and I had thought he was just another cute bartender, back when my marriage had been shaky, at best. Now, those hands had been compelled to hold a silver blade to my sister's neck.

"You miss him," said Fang.

"Danny was my first love. He was the father of my children. He died in my arms." I looked away. "And he was never given a proper funeral. Yes, I miss the big idiot."

Fang looked down for the first time. He adjusted the drape of his jeans then returned his hands to his knee. "I'm sorry that I played a part in his death, Sam."

I nodded and wiped my eyes and looked back at him. It was, of course, hard to tell how sorry he was, with no inflection or emotion in his voice.

"I miss you, Sam," he said. "I know now may not be the time to say it, and, for all I know, you're still dating that muscle-bound boxer or even Kingsley or someone else, but I want you to know that I miss you every day. I missed you even when I was compelled to do bad things. I missed you while I silently screamed inside my head. I miss you every day, every hour, every minute. I never stop thinking about you."

"Did you kill, Fang?"

"Yes. Many."

"Were you compelled to kill?"

"Sometimes."

"And, what about the other times?"

He looked away. "No."

I bit my lip and fought the tears that threatened to come. "I think you should leave."

He nodded once and stood smoothly on long legs. He crossed the room and paused at my office door.

"I'm sorry I failed you, Sam."

He looked at me for a long moment and something hit me, something deep in my heart. I suddenly remembered the love I felt for him, the deep longing to have him back in my life.

As he turned to leave, I said, "Wait, Fang."

He looked back. "Yes, Moon Dance?"

I hadn't heard him say my old username in so long that I nearly lost it right there. Instead, I kept it together and said, "I miss you, too."

He smiled and I saw the tears in his eyes.

"More than you know."

The End

VAMPIRE SUN

VAMPIRE FOR HIRE #9

DEDICATION

To Sandra again…and again.

VAMPIRE SUN

"We watch you from the shadows, sometimes from within your very homes. We watch you live your mundane, dreary lives… and we wonder why you don't crave more, hunger for more. Live more. But never fear, we shall do it for you. Oh, yes, we will."
—*Diary of the Undead*

CHAPTER ONE

I was watching Judge Judy...and wishing I was her.

I didn't wish I was very many people—in fact, very few—but she was one of the few. No, I didn't want to be on TV (that was, if I could even show up on TV, which I didn't think I could without copious amounts of makeup), nor did I want to deal with the steady stream of derelicts who filled her courtroom.

I wanted to be confident like her. Fearless like her. Smart like her. Hell, I wanted to *talk* like her, too.

I checked the time on my cell phone. It would probably have been easier to check the time on my watch, had I owned a watch. The last one I'd owned had gotten destroyed on a case. Now, I had my eye out for a shock-resistant, werewolf-resistant and demon-resistant watch. Maybe Timex made one.

My client was late, which I hated. But that gave me more time with Judge Judy, whom I loved. It also gave me more time to finish sewing up Anthony's boxer shorts. These were the third pair of shorts I had mended today. I'd seen enough skid marks to last a lifetime. Hell, this last pair looked like an aerial shot of a drag strip starting gate.

But, new boxer shorts cost money, and sewing the old ones was mostly free. And so, like the good mother I was, I powered through Anthony's homage to Jackson Pollack, and sewed the gaping tear in the crotch area. I sewed quickly, deftly, never even poking my finger. The vampire in me heightened all my physical senses, even during the day, but more so at night. Now, something as mundane as sewing was almost fun. I still got a kick out of what I could do. I was learning to appreciate who I was, or what I was.

I didn't have much choice, of course.

I either appreciated my current condition, or I went mad. I hadn't entirely ruled out the latter. I was only ninety-eight percent sure that I wasn't in a padded cell somewhere, wearing a straitjacket, rocking absently, and drooling—looking, on second thought, a lot like Anthony when he played some of his video games.

As I finished sewing the shorts, I heard a car door slam in my driveway. Synchronicity at its best.

I quickly snipped off the thread with my weirdly sharp fingernails—nails that could never, ever be filed down, damn them—and hurriedly tossed the shorts in Anthony's room, just as the doorbell rang. More good timing, as Judge Judy had just pronounced her latest verdict, a verdict I couldn't have agreed with more.

I smiled, turned off the TV, and headed for the door.

I'd like to meet Judge Judy someday.

Chapter Two

My client's name was Henry Gleason.

He didn't look like a Henry Gleason. To me, a Henry Gleason should be a big, chubby guy with a cherubic face who gesticulated a lot, and made "to the moon" comments.

This Henry didn't gesticulate. He sat dourly in front of me. His aura was dour, too. Yes, I can see auras. I'm a freak like that. His aura suggested that someone had run over his cat.

"How can I help you, Mr. Gleason?"

I sensed, right off the bat, that there was something drastically wrong. Not even *sort of wrong*, but *chaotically wrong*. His aura was literally spitting fire, snapping around him like solar flares, or so many dragons breathing fire. I kept seeing the image of a small, pleasant-looking woman. These days, I got psychic hits with the best of them. I could also catch fleeting thoughts…words and images. But only those who were tuned into me could catch my own thoughts. This man, this stranger who was about to become anything but a stranger, was not privy to my thoughts. He also wasn't privy to what I was. Or, rather, what I *really* was.

Judging by his mental condition—or lack thereof, as he appeared to have hit some sort of rock bottom—I doubted he would care what I was. Mr. Gleason needed help, and he would have taken it from the devil himself. Little did Henry Gleason know how close he really was to that.

"My wife is missing," he began…and that was about as far as he got for the next few minutes. He broke down completely, and his

183

aura snapped and flared and shrank in on him. That Henry was a total mess, I had no doubt. Ever the good hostess, I pushed a box of Kleenex his way, although he didn't see it at first.

I waited as he struggled to get hold of himself. I got this sometimes: clients who came into my office and lost it. Generally, it was because a loved one was cheating on them. I didn't always take the cheating spouse cases. The truth was, I wouldn't take *any* of them if I didn't have to. However, I had something called a mortgage to deal with. And a car note and bills and two kids.

And food...oh, God, the food. Who knew twelve-year-old girls could eat so much? Anthony I was prepared for. But not Tammy.

Anyway, I mostly took the jobs that came my way. Mostly. Some cases, I turned down. Some prospective clients, however, I never heard from again. It sometimes turned out that they just needed a shoulder to cry on, but then, they didn't hire me. So, the sympathy seekers who came to my home office and cried and got it out of their systems, well, I never saw them again.

I didn't make a dime off them, either.

You win some, you lose some.

But Henry Gleason wasn't airing his marriage's dirty laundry. He wasn't walking me through, step by step, his wife's sordid affairs or the intricacies of her deception. No, he was weeping for one of two reasons: he truly missed his wife, or he was putting on a show.

I would know soon enough which it was.

No, I didn't know all. I wasn't God. In fact, I was about as far from God as one could get. But these days, I could tell if someone was lying to me. It wasn't very hard for me to learn their secrets. What exactly was going on here, I didn't know. But one thing was obvious: Henry Gleason wasn't putting on a show. His pain was real.

So, I waited. As I waited, I sent him a mental nudge to reach for the box of tissues which, after pausing briefly and cocking his head slightly, he did. He hadn't known I had given him a mental nudge. It was probably better that he didn't.

He blew his nose, gathered himself, and said, "I'm a total and complete mess. I'm sorry."

"I hadn't noticed."

He tried to smile, failed miserably, and gave up. I noted his shaking hands, and his darting eyes that never seemed to settle on anything longer than a few seconds, if that.

I decided to kick things off.

"What happened to your wife, Henry?" I asked.

"I don't know. How did you know?"

"Never mind that," I said, and gave him another mental nudge to drop it. I asked, "Did you hurt her?"

He looked at me sharply. "No. Never."

I used my demon-given gifts to dip into his thoughts, and slip just inside his aura. Yes, I was cheating. Then again, the sun was also stolen from me, along with Oreos and cheesecakes, fettuccine alfredo and mango margaritas. Or mangoritas, which just so happened to be Allison's favorite drink these days. So, if the demon inside me— the thing that fueled this supernatural body of mine—could actually give me something back, could actually add value to my life, rather than steal from it, then I would take it gladly. *Lord knows enough had been taken from me.*

"Cry me a river, Mom," as Anthony would tell me these days. Kids, they grew up so fast.

Anyway, the ability to read thoughts was a decent trade-off for having to give up dinner at The Cheesecake Factory, not to mention, the ability to quickly discern truth from lies was invaluable to my profession. Now, I no longer had to guess if someone was jerking my chain or not.

Now, as I psychically slipped inside his personal space, without him knowing it, of course, I dipped into his thoughts, which turned out not to be an entirely good idea. The guy was borderline losing it. No, correction, he *had* lost it. Weeks ago. He'd lost it when his wife had seemingly disappeared at a Starbucks just outside of Orange County, which I had pieced together from his own chaotic memories.

No, not quite chaotic. His mind, I quickly realized, was continuously looping the crime scene. Over and over, even for the few minutes I was inside his mind, he relived his last moments with her.

Sit back, I commanded, *relax.*

Henry Gleason looked at me, blinked, and then sat back in my client chair. His thoughts calmed a little, and I was able to piece together what I saw. It wasn't a pretty picture.

"Tell me what happened, Henry," I said, and as he spoke, I relived the scene in his thoughts.

———

Henry is waiting impatiently, drumming his fingers on the steering wheel...

His wife has gone inside the Starbucks to grab them some iced mochas. Henry doesn't even like iced mochas. His wife doesn't either. What the fuck is an iced mocha, anyway? And why had she insisted they stop here, dammit? Lucy is acting weird today, he thinks. So weird.

He waits in the heat. His window is down. Hot wind blows through the open window. He checks the time on his cell phone.

I hear him say, "C'mon, babe, where are you?"

More drumming. More hot wind.

He turns around, scans through the back window of a truck toward the busy Starbucks. Nothing. No wife. No damn mochas.

More drumming.

Finally, he gets out and pads across the shimmering asphalt. I can feel the heat. I can also feel the panic rising in him. I know from his thoughts that he has waited about fifteen minutes for her. He thinks she's in the bathroom. Maybe she's sick. If that bitch is in there talking to someone—especially some guy—he was going to go off on her. *Off.* Maybe even slap her around a little. Maybe.

As he heads toward Starbucks, alternately fuming and worried, he tries to remember if she had shown signs of being sick. They had eaten tacos earlier. Yes, the tacos. He is sure of it. They had tasted funny to him.

Now, he's inside the Starbucks. Cool air. People were everywhere. They were as busy as hell.

He heads immediately to the bathrooms. His mouth literally drops open when he sees a girl exit the bathroom because it's not his wife. The girl avoids eye contact with him and hurries past. He glances inside the open door. It's empty. He checks the men's rest-room. Empty, too.

I feel his panic. Full-on panic. He dashes out to the lobby, searching, searching. She is nowhere to be found. What the fuck? *What the fuck?*

Now, he's asking employees if they have seen his wife. It's a busy Starbucks. People are coming and going. Workers are making drinks fast, taking orders. Everything is mechanical, rote, all done a hundred times a day, a thousand times a day.

I hear him describe his wife to anyone who will listen. No one remembers seeing her. Wait, one worker does, but she isn't very forthcoming. No, that's not it. She just doesn't remember too much. Yes, she took an order from her. Water only. 'Water?' he asks. 'Are you sure?' 'Yes, sir. Just water. Then she went in there.' She points to the bathrooms.

Henry rushes back to the bathroom. Maybe he missed her. Maybe she is behind the door, or in a stall. Dammit, no stalls. Not behind the damn door. He checks the guys' bathroom again, too. Nothing. Nothing. Nothing.

Now, Henry is outside, rushing back to his truck, in case she has come back, in case he has somehow missed her. But she's not there. Now, he's running around the building, running and run-ning, looking for her. Maybe she had wanted to throw up in an alley? But there's no alley here. Just a big, hot shopping center sitting on the edge of the desert. He stands on a parking lot curb, shielding his eyes from the sun's glare. Nothing. Then stands on his truck's bed, searching.

Nothing.

Now, he's on his cell phone calling the police, weeping, fearing the worst. He's nearly incoherent as he reports her missing.

And then the thoughts repeat.

Over and over.

Chapter Three

"**S**he disappeared," said Henry, speaking into his hands, his voice barely audible, his voice barely human. He was unaware that I had just seen the entire scene in his thoughts. "She just disappeared. And I have no idea where she went or what happened."

I didn't know either, of course. I didn't know all or see all. I was just a woman. Just a mom. Granted, a very freaky woman; and, if you asked my kids, I was a very freaky mom, too.

I said, "You watched her walk into Starbucks?"

He nodded. He held a tissue tightly in his hand. The tissue might have been torn to shreds. "Yes. I watched her in the rearview mirror."

I could have confirmed this by dipping into his thoughts, but I thought I'd had enough of Henry Gleason's thoughts for one day. Hell, for a lifetime. I said, "And you watched her enter?"

"Yes."

"Did you see where she went from there?"

"No. She just, you know, blended with the crowd and I started playing with my phone. You know, wasting time, looking at texts and scores and news and weather."

"*Angry Birds?*"

He gave me a weak grin. "That, too."

"An employee at Starbucks saw her?"

"Yes. She spoke to the police, but she really doesn't remember much."

"Do you have her name?"

"Jasmine."

"Last name?"

He shook his head. "The police will have it, but I can't imagine there are too many Jasmines working at that Starbucks."

I nodded. They would. "Anyone else at Starbucks see your wife?"

"No one."

"What about customers?"

He shook his head. "By the time I went looking for her, anyone who might have seen her was long gone."

"Did you ask around?"

"I did. Like a crazy man. No one had seen her. This isn't your typical Starbucks, you know. People were coming and going, not staying long. There weren't, you know, those hipster geeks in there with their laptops. This Starbucks straddles Corona with Yorba Linda."

I nodded. I knew the area, of course. It was actually a rather great divide, many miles of empty, although beautiful, land, with one lush county segueing into another, harsher, drier, hotter county. The Starbucks wouldn't be your typical hangout for moms and students and guys with square glasses and thick, mangy beards.

No, this Starbucks was a stopover, a place to get coffee while waiting out traffic. Or to use the bathroom. This Starbucks was an outpost. An outlier. Other than the occasional morning commuter who hit up this Starbucks, employees would rarely, if ever, see the same customer twice.

"So, no one else remembered her?"

"No."

"Just the one employee?"

He nodded, said nothing. His aura was crackling with blue energy, split occasionally with streaks of yellow. I wasn't sensing any deception on his part. I felt that I could trust his memory, and I felt that I could trust him, too, although I didn't like the part about him considering hurting her.

"Did you ever hurt your wife?" I asked.

"I told you, she just disappeared—"

"That wasn't my question. Did you ever hit your wife? Hurt her in any way?"

"No, never."

"Did you fight often?"

"What's often? We had your typical fights, I guess."

Despite my desire to stay out of his thoughts, I dipped in quick enough to see him yelling at her—"going off" on her, as he called it. Yeah, he fought like a crazy man. His face twisted. And, no, he didn't hit her. At least, not in the memories I saw. But he was verbally abusive.

"So, what happened next?" I asked, easing back out of his mind again, to my great relief.

"I called the police. Reported her missing."

The police had come out. Had interviewed him and the workers. A massive search had been conducted. The search had lasted for days, and I even remembered it. Whether or not she had been found hadn't made the news. Or, if it had, I was too knee-deep in my own issues to have noticed.

After three days, the search had been called off. There were no leads, nothing to indicate that his wife had ever left the Starbucks. There was video surveillance of her going in, but none of her leaving. A true mystery.

"I didn't kill her, Ms. Moon."

I knew that he didn't kill her. But there was always the slim possibility that his memory had been replaced with a false memory, one so powerful that even his own mind believed it. But I doubted that. Then again, he could have been delusional, of course. Mentally ill. But I doubted that, too. His aura was normal enough. Those with mental health issues had very erratic, scattered auras. Distorted auras that flashed with many colors. His pulsed blue and yellow, and mostly blue. Blue was the color of trust. At least, according to my own experience.

Not to mention, I had seen his memories. Hell, I had lived through them. And then, there was the minor issue that his wife was never seen leaving Starbucks.

"My wife needs help, Ms. Moon. Something has happened to her. Something very, very bad, and the police aren't doing a damn thing about it."

"Nothing?"

"Nothing. The detective on the case, last I heard, was dead."

"Dead? How?"

"I have no clue. They won't tell me anything, other than they're working on it."

"Are you a suspect?"

"They say only that I'm a person of interest. That all husbands are when wives go missing."

True enough. And as I contemplated his words, I checked the time on my cell. Ah, hell. I was going to be late again. *Damn.*

"Will you help me?" he asked.

"Yes. But first, I need to pick up my kids."

Chapter Four

Principal West was a middle-aged man with whom I once had a run-in when Danny had told me I was not allowed to pick up our kids from school. Today, the principal gave me the eye, but this time, he did not try to prevent me from picking up my kids.

I waved politely, ducked my head a little, and mouthed, "Sorry I'm late" through the minivan windshield. The principal wasn't happy—and probably made a noise that sounded like, "harrumph," although I could only guess at the noise, since my hearing, although enhanced, wasn't magical.

When I came to a full stop, the principal, who always waited with students for their delinquent parents—I was late far, far too often—finally released my kids to me.

Anthony's jeans might have been hanging down a little in a style that I didn't approve of. Anthony slid into the back seat, and immediately went to work on his Game Boy.

Tammy was sporting a frowning face, in a style I definitely didn't approve of. Since it was her week to sit in the front seat, she rode shotgun.

"I'm almost thirteen, Mom. *Thirteen*. I don't need a principal to wait with me for my mother. It's so embarrassing."

"Your face is embarrassing," said Anthony.

I waved to the principal again, who gave me a tight, half-smile and turned his back on me as I pulled out of the parking lot.

Once we were cruising down Rosecrans, I looked at Anthony in the rearview mirror. "Apologize to your sister," I said to him.

"No."

Aghast, I looked in the mirror again. "What?"

"Just playing. Sheesh, can't you take a joke?"

"No, I can't. Now apologize."

"Fine. Sorry, butthead," he said in Tammy's direction.

"Give me your Game Boy."

He did, passing it to me between the seats. I opened the center console and deposited it within, along with untold work-related receipts, boxes of gum and one mostly covered box of cigarettes. I quickly shut the console again.

"He just called me a butthead, Mom."

"No, I didn't."

"You said it and *thought* it."

"I can think anything I want. There's no law about thinking."

"He just mentally flipped me off, Mom!"

Anthony giggled in the back seat. I told Tammy to get out of her brother's head and for Anthony to quit mentally flipping off his sister. He giggled some more, then settled down. Tammy pouted, crossing her arms, making her own *harrumph* noise. At least they were mostly quiet. It was about all I could ask.

About a minute later, Tammy said, "I saw them, Mom."

"Saw what?"

"The cigarettes. Whose are they?"

It would do no good to give Tammy a line, or tell her anything other than the truth, although I'd rarely made it a habit of lying to my kids. Of course, keeping my vampiric nature hidden from them as long as I could was one thing, but that cat had been out of the bag for some time now. Also, Tammy was as telepathic as I was. Perhaps even more so, since she could read other family members' minds, including her little brother's, and he was about to hit puberty. I prayed for her soul.

"We'll talk about it later," I said.

"What are you two talking about?" asked Anthony. Now that he was no longer physically attached to a game console, he had joined the land of the living.

193

"Mommy has a pack of cigarettes in the car," said Tammy.

"I want one!" said Anthony, leaning forward between the two seats.

"No, you don't," I said to him, and then glanced at Tammy. "See what you did?"

"I didn't do anything except tell the truth, Mommy."

"Mommy smokes?" said Anthony, perhaps in a higher voice than was necessary. He looked from me to Tammy. "Seriously?"

"I don't know," said Tammy, holding my gaze. "Why don't you ask her?"

I looked at my daughter some more, then over at Anthony's too-eager face, then sighed and pulled the minivan over to the side of the road, where I parked in front of a beautiful, two-story home that was probably even more beautiful inside. My own neighborhood was about two miles away, and was filled with older homes that looked nothing like the ones that lined this street. My small home was the most that Danny and I could afford, and we had been happy to have it. Truth was, I was still happy to have it…but now I associated much pain with it, too. After all, I had been living at that home when my life had been irrevocably changed, when I had gone from being mortal to immortal, when my days were stolen from me, when my husband had rejected me and cheated on me, where my kids had been taken from me, and where I had cried often and still cried to this day. Of course, there were a lot of good memories in that home, too, but with Danny now gone, those memories were getting harder and harder to access.

Perhaps I should have been delighted that Anthony seemed to be coming out of that dark place he had been in for the past few months. In fact, just hearing him playing with his Game Boy was a major step in the right direction. And hadn't he gone many months without teasing his sister? He had, and I had feared that I had lost my kids forever.

But here they were, teasing each other like old times. Yes, I had missed their teasing and fighting and bickering and…

"Don't say it, Mom," said Tammy giggling, and obviously following my train of thought.

"Say what?"

"Farting. You were going to say you even missed Anthony's farting."

"How could I miss his farting?" I asked. "When it never stops."

They both giggled, and I turned in my seat and hugged them both, which was kind of hard to do in the minivan, but we managed. No words were spoken for a few minutes, but we were all soon crying, Anthony the hardest of all. We did this often, now that their father was gone. My tears, however, weren't for Danny. They were for my kids who had lost their father. Danny, in the end, had dug his own grave.

It didn't have to be this way. Danny could have stood by my side, through thick and thin, and through hell and back. We could have stayed a strong family, an unstoppable family.

Such an idiot, I thought, and hugged my kids tighter.

A moment later, Tammy pulled away and said, "Now, about those cigarettes, Mom…"

Chapter Five

The anticipated one-hour drive from Fullerton to Corona took four hours, due to a tractor-trailer accident that had blocked several lanes.

Luckily, I had peeled off the freeway before I peeled off any faces. Now, with the sun setting, and me at my jittery worst, I finally sat in the Starbucks parking lot and did my best to calm down, to relax, to breathe.

This was always the worst time of the day for me, the time just before the sun set. It was a time when I felt less than human, when I felt weak and vulnerable.

As I waited, I cracked my neck. I drummed my freakishly long fingernails on the steering wheel. I breathed through my nose, in and out, in and out, rapidly. Faster, faster.

Pacing sometimes helped, but not always. I could get out and pace next to the minivan, but then, I would look like the freak that I am. I stayed inside and waited it out.

Breathing.

Drumming.

Fidgeting.

Last week when I had been pacing, I had inexplicably driven a fist through my bedroom door. I'd regretted that. And it had cost me about a hundred bucks' worth of handyman services.

So, I waited in the minivan, now gripping my steering wheel.

It would do me no good to step out now, not with the sun just minutes from setting. Minutes that felt like forever. Minutes that were truly torture for me.

Now, the setting sun was at the point where I could no longer think or focus on anything else. I just needed to power through the next few minutes.

I breathed and ran my fingers through my hair. I was aware of someone sitting in a nearby car watching me. I didn't want them to watch me. I wanted them to go away. Or I would make them go away.

Breathe, Sam. Breathe. Forget them.

Fuck them.

Breathe, Sam.

And with that last thought, I felt a sudden deep calm overcome me. I didn't have to look up to know the sun had set. My weird, immortal, cursed, supernatural body was hyper-aware of the sun. Attuned to the sun.

I took a deep, full, useless, beautiful breath and felt my lungs expand, and as they expanded, I felt myself expand, too. I felt my energy, strength and vitality noticeably increase.

I went from a shell of a human, to something unstoppable.

Just like that.

I stepped out of the minivan and surveyed the Starbucks where, three weeks earlier, a woman had gone missing.

Chapter Six

Unlike some movie vampires, I could go for a few days without eating.

I abhorred the word *feed.* Hell, if anything, what I did was closer to *drinking.* Now, I imagined going an eternity and never really chewing on anything ever again.

It was not my idea of fun, although a brief image of nibbling on Kingsley's fat lower lip did pop into my mind. And I left it there, in my mind. Where it belonged. Hidden and buried.

No, I had nothing against Kingsley. Not even these days. But our time might have come and gone. He had had every chance to be with me, and, in a moment of weakness, had decided that some young floozy was worth more to him than me.

Yeah, it still rankled, and, yeah, I might never truly forgive him for it, even though he had been set up by Ishmael, my one-time guardian angel. Set up to fail.

Still, I happened to believe that his feelings for me should have been stronger than a few minutes with some stranger. But it hadn't been, and to this day, we weren't together because of that.

One strike, I thought, as I stepped into the middle of the mostly empty parking lot, *and you're out.*

Of course, Kingsley had been trying to make up for it ever since, even standing by and mostly keeping his mouth shut as I had dated—and perhaps even loved—another man.

Now that I was single again, Kingsley had respectfully kept his distance, but he'd made it known that he was interested in more. A lot more. That he had gone out of his way, twice, to save me, were feathers in his cap.

We'll see, I thought.

The parking lot was lit with overhanging industrial lamps high up on stanchions, spaced evenly throughout the unusually big lot. Surely, there was more parking here than the Starbucks needed. In fact, I knew this area to be a popular holdover or changeover for people on their way out to, say, Vegas, or down south to San Diego. This was a way station, so to speak, for travelers. Still, why the parking lot was so big was beyond me...until I saw the answer.

And it came in the form of a big, rumbling, diesel smoke-belching recreational vehicle, or RV, pulling into the parking lot from the side road.

As it lumbered toward me, I saw immediately the benefit of the epic space, to accommodate the bigger vacation vehicles, and, undoubtedly, big rigs, too.

Yes, it was a true way station.

The RV parked in due course. A moment later, an elderly couple stepped out, stretched, and headed up to Starbucks. Both smiled and said hello to me. I smiled, too, and turned and watched them go.

That I briefly envisioned pinning them down and feasting, first off the man and then off the woman, should have caused me more alarm than it did.

In fact, the thought seemed perfectly normal.

Uh, oh.

Snap out of it, kiddo, I thought, and heard Kingsley's voice in my head. Or was it Fang's? Maybe a blending of the two.

I focused on the task ahead. The task being, of course, to figure out how a grown woman had disappeared off the face of the earth inside of a Starbucks.

Standing in the center of the parking lot, I turned in a small circle as the sky above grew darker. As it grew darker, the tiny filaments of light that only I could see, appeared, slashing and darting and giving depth and structure to the night. A million fireflies. Hell, tens of millions. Billions. All flashing and forming and reforming.

Early on, the flashing lights had nearly given me seizures. They had taken some getting used to. Now, I knew that each particle of light was, in fact, giving life to the night itself. They formed a sort of staticy laser light show for me and me alone. Now, seeing them was second nature for me. Up close, there was less static. What these light particles were, I didn't know, but I always suspected I was seeing the hidden energy that connected all of us. Humans and vampires alike.

Spirits themselves seemed to be composed of this very energy, as I had watched countless such entities form and reform, disappear and reappear, all using this sort of Universal Energy.

Weird shit, for sure, but welcome to my life.

Now, I searched within the staticy light particles for something that could be dead. Something that could be watching me in return. But I saw nothing. Just the dancing lights that jived and boogied through my vision.

The lack of spiritual activity was significant. It meant that some- one *hadn't* recently passed here. That someone hadn't, in fact, been murdered. This, of course, was just conjecture on my part and was based on my own personal experience with the spirit world. Murdered souls often lingered, sometimes for decades, in the locations of their deaths. I had seen such souls. Hell, I had seen a few today when I was driving along the freeway, standing by the side of the crowded thoroughfare, and forlornly watching the living drive by. These, I knew, had perished there on the freeway, in car accidents, no doubt.

Why the dead lingered, I didn't know, but I had seen my fair share of them. So much so that they were now part of my life. My creepy, creepy life. In my experience, spirits appeared in one of three ways: either as souls visiting the living, as the forgotten dead, lost and haunted, or as a *memory* of itself, neither alive nor dead, repeating itself over and over.

I saw none of that here.

Murder sites also had an effect on the environment. A very obvi- ous effect. At such a location, the swirling light energy was even more chaotic. It would swirl and scatter and explode...reminiscent of an active volcano spewing magma. Often, though, I would see another kind of energy within this disturbance. Spirit energy, too. The murdered victim, in fact. Not always, but often.

There was no such energy here. Instead, the light particles swept through naturally, peacefully, unhindered by the shock of death.

I walked the perimeter of the expansive parking lot, which took a few minutes. The east side consisted of a low shrub wall that bordered the Taco Bell next door. At this hour, Taco Bell had more customers than Starbucks, with a line of cars wending through its drive-thru. I spied surveillance cameras above and around Taco Bell. Anyone heading this way would have been picked up by the Bell's cameras, too. I logged this away for future inquiry.

I continued around the perimeter. The south-facing part of the lot, opposite the driveway into the parking lot, was interesting. There were lots of places where someone could hide here. A strip of land bordered it, with the freeway itself next to it. Trash and weeds crowded for space, all of which I saw clearly, thanks to the bright streaks of light that illuminated the night. I continued standing there, scanning.

Sure, there were lots of places to escape to, once a person actually left the Starbucks cafe. So far, there was no evidence of Lucy Gleason ever leaving, only entering.

I studied the Starbucks from the parking lot, taking it in. It was part of a small strip mall: attached to it was a dry cleaner, and next to that was a Subway. The Taco Bell was in the next parking lot over, separated by a shrub wall.

I spotted two surveillance cameras, one on each side of the building. Starbucks itself had only one entrance inside, with a rear entrance as well. I frowned and studied the scene, biting my lower lip, but not hard enough to draw blood.

Next, I went inside the Starbucks. It was a typical 'Bucks, as Tammy would call it. She was the coffee addict in the family. I was a very different kind of addict. This 'Bucks had all the sleek, post-modern, industrial décor that one came to expect from a Starbucks.

A lot of seating. Open space, with a small hallway that led off to the bathrooms. I examined the women's. Typical: a single room with the toilet in the far corner. A sink. A metal trash can. Nowhere to hide. A quick peek in the men's restroom suggested the same.

I sighed, and then headed out to the lobby. I ordered a venti water, which sounded a lot fancier than it looked. I sat in the far booth and studied the interior, searching for any psychic hits or evidence of foul play.

I got neither.

I hate when that happens.

CHAPTER SEVEN

The three of us were jogging.

A human, a vampire, and a witch. Yes, I know it sounds like the opening to a bad joke: a human, a vampire, and a witch go to a bar. The human orders a glass of wine. The vampire orders a goblet of blood. The witch orders a magic potion. Or something like that.

"Well?" asked Allison.

"Well, what?"

"What's the punchline?"

"I don't know," I said. "I was making it up as I go."

"Oh, God," said Mary Lou, "are you two doing your mind-thingy again?"

"That might be the first time I heard anyone call telepathy a *thingy*," said Allison. For the most part, Allison and my sister, Mary Lou, got along marvelously.

Except...

Except Mary Lou, as the only one of us without any obvious extrasensory abilities, felt like the odd woman out. I suspected she might be a little jealous of my friendship and easy communication with Allison. I reminded my sister that, as of yet, I had no ability to read her mind, which was the case for all of my blood relatives. It was no slight on her, and it didn't mean I loved her any less. My daughter, of course, was a different story; she could read family members' minds, mine included.

Your daughter, thought Allison, telepathically following my train of thought, *is going to be powerful.*

I'm not sure what to think about that, I thought back.

But it's not going to happen for a while still, came Allison's reply.

Oh? Is that a psychic hit? I silently asked my friend, whose own psychic abilities were getting scarily strong.

Scary?

Scary as in unknown.

Nice catch, thought Allison. *And, yes, that is a psychic hit. I do, after all, work for a prestigious Psychic Hotline.*

I grinned. In fact, Allison was one of the few legit psychics who worked at the Hotline, as she called it. Recently, her cases had become...interesting, to say the least.

Only if you consider removing a demon from the world's most haunted house as interesting, she thought.

Oh, I do, I thought. *And you can quit bragging.*

Yes, my friend was growing more and more powerful. And apparently, her head was growing bigger, too.

I heard that, she shot back. *And it's not. I still have nightmares about that night.*

As she thought those words, I saw the image that flashed through her mind, the image of a man killing himself before her, a man who had been demon-possessed himself.

I should have shuddered at watching the image of the knife being drawn across the man's own throat. I should have been horrified by the blood that spilled down like a crimson waterfall. I should have been shocked, revolted and scared. But I was none of that.

I was intrigued.

I was interested.

I was...excited.

You scare me sometimes, Sam, came Allison's words. *I mean, really scare me sometimes.*

I scare myself, too.

"Oh my God," said Mary Lou. "You two are so rude. I'm right here, you know."

"We're not talking about you, Mary Lou," I said.

"Well, then, how about talk *to me*? As in, include me in your conversation. It's seriously rude to *think* behind someone's back. Or whatever. You know what I mean!"

I looked at Allison and she looked at me and we both snorted.

"It's not funny, you guys," said Mary Lou, slowing down. As she slowed down, her massively heaving chest slowed down, too. And so did the bouncing eyeballs of any and all guys that we passed. "It's rude to us immortals."

"Mortals," I corrected, and did all I could to stifle a giggle. I heard Allison giggling in my head. "I'm *immortal*. You're *mortal*."

"Well, whatever. You're still my sister and you're still being rude."

"You're right," I said. "I'm sorry."

"I mean, I've gone through just as much shit as you guys. Maybe more so. I think I deserve, at this point, to be let in on all your secrets."

"*Some* of our secrets," I said. "Trust me, there are some things you don't want to know."

"Well, let me be the judge of that."

I shook my head as we continued to jog. Yes, Mary Lou had had a rough time a few months ago, of that there was no doubt. She'd been kidnapped by Rachel Hanner, a homicidal vampire who happened to be a Fullerton PD homicide cop—a vampire who had been my one-time friend. Although Mary Lou had been threatened, and Fang had held a knife to her throat, she hadn't been hurt. Still, I could only imagine her fear when she'd been attacked and taken hostage. Yes, it had been a bad day for my sister. But that didn't mean she should know every deep, dark secret that I had.

"We'll see," I said, and left it at that.

My sister didn't like that answer, but mercifully, let it go.

Although the sun had set an hour ago, the western sky was still aglow with oranges and yellows and reds. I loved that glow. It meant the damnable sun had finally moved on. It meant the worst part of my day—the part just before the sunset—was finally over. It meant I could relax. It meant I could be all that I'm capable of being. It meant I could be who I was meant to be.

205

A killer.

I shook my head as we jogged. Those words, of course, were not mine. They were *hers*. The demon that possessed me, although *demon* wasn't quite the right word. She had been human once, mortal once. But now, she was so much more.

A highly evolved dark master.

A fancy title, I thought, for a murderous bitch.

Her words appeared in my mind only rarely. But when they did, I always got a jolt, followed by a cold chill. And, trust me, it was damned hard to give a vampire a cold chill. Anyway, I was certain I would never get used to her words in my head.

In fact, I *never* wanted to get used to her words. Hell, I was doing all that I could to eradicate her from my life, forever.

I get the heebie-jeebies, too, Sam, came Allison's own distinct voice in my head. A softer voice, and maybe a little nasal.

Nasal? Now that's just rude.

But true, I thought.

Whatever.

Mary Lou stopped running, although her chest didn't get the memo. It jiggled and settled for a few long seconds afterward. "You two are doing it again." My sister might have sounded exasperated.

You are entirely too focused on your sister's chest, thought Allison.

Quiet, I hissed mentally, *I think we're in trouble. And I'm not focused on her chest. It's just, well, so big. How can you not focus on it?*

"Unbelievable! The two of you are actually *still* doing it while I'm standing here pissed. I'm going home."

"Wait, Mary Lou," I said, grabbing her shoulder. She had turned off the boardwalk and was about to cross some random parking lot. We were at least a mile or so from where our cars were parked. "I'm sorry. Really, I am. Telepathy is just, well, easy. And this one—" I jabbed a finger at Allison "—always seems to be *in* my mind."

"Well, you're always in *my* mind."

I ignored her, although we both knew that wasn't true.

Speak for yourself, she thought.

"Unbelievable," said Mary Lou. "Please tell me you aren't *still* doing it. Please tell me you wouldn't keep disrespecting me like that."

She was about to storm off when I caught her elbow. She yanked her arm free—or tried to—and only succeeded in hurting herself. She yelped and I released her. She now stormed down the board-walk. At least she was going in the right direction. Allison and I watched her go.

"Well," I said, "what a fine mess you got me into."

"She'll be okay," said Allison.

I sighed. My sister could hold a grudge with the best of them... and she was only now coming out of her shell over the traumatic events of a few months ago. No, she hadn't seen my husband get killed, hadn't watched the dagger plunge into his chest, as I had. But she had *heard* him die. She had *heard* him scream out...and she had heard his ragged breathing as the blood from the wound had filled his lungs.

Yeah, she had been traumatized, perhaps even for life. I took in a big lungful of worthless air and watched her go, walking as fast as she could away from me.

I sighed again and grabbed Allison. "Let's catch up to her."

207

Chapter Eight

I was alone in my garage.

Not too long ago, I had broken up with my last boyfriend in this very garage. That something like me could even have something so normal as a "boyfriend" was almost laughable. But I had tried. And I had tried with a mortal, someone who wasn't a bloodsucker.

I swiped open a packet of cow and pig blood with a fingernail that was too long and too sharp to be normal. Concealing my hands was one of the many drags in my life. Drinking from these filthy packets was another.

Yes, a few months ago, my relationship had come to an end when I had finally realized that my boyfriend, Russell, was, in fact, a *love slave*. No, not a sex slave. There's a difference. He was devoted to me unerringly, irrationally, supernaturally. I didn't so much as break up with him as *release* him.

Instantly, the strong, coppery, putrid smell of nearly rancid animal blood wafted up from the open packet. Mercifully, the butchery had delivered a cleaner-than-usual batch of blood, with the last few packets being nearly contaminant-free. In fact, I had almost— almost—enjoyed the packets.

Okay, that might be pushing it. But at least I hadn't gagged.

I wasn't so lucky with this bag. As I looked at the opaque bag, now swollen with blood—like a fat, wingless mosquito—I saw the hair and flotsam. Bits of bone and dirt and muscle and sinew—whatever had been collected as the pigs and cows bled out.

As I watched the particles drift within the bag, I realized something disconcerting. There were, if anything, even *more* particles. Perhaps the other bags had been cleaner, but I doubted it. I had assumed they were cleaner because I hadn't gagged, because I had, in fact, quite enjoyed the bag of filth. No, not as much as I enjoyed drinking from Allison. Drinking from her was…heavenly.

But the past two bags had been quite…tasty.

Uh oh, I thought.

Now, as I raised it before me, careful not to spill the precious contents and watched the constellation of filth rotate slowly, I knew I was in trouble.

Real trouble.

But I didn't care. This was blood, after all. Precious blood.

Delicious blood.

Not as delicious as Allison, but it was good enough.

"Good enough," I whispered, and a small part of me tried to rebel when I licked my lips. "Yes, good enough."

Now, with my children doing homework in the house adjacent to the garage—and, no doubt, sneaking in time on the Xbox One—I tilted the bag of filth to my lips…and drained every last drop. I even tore open the bag and licked it clean.

Lord help me.

CHAPTER NINE

You there, Fang?

It was the same question I asked night after night, for the past three weeks, logging on to my old AIM instant message account. The same account Fang and I had first connected through. The account where I had told a complete stranger all of my secrets. Secrets he had used to eventually find me.

I often wondered if I had *wanted* Fang to find me. If I had, in fact, *purposely* dropped enough clues for him to eventually locate me in my small part of the world.

Fang, at the time, had been my only connection to the supernatural. Although not supernatural himself at that time, he had been my source of all things vampiric. His knowledge had been deep and accurate and I missed our easy word play and mild flirtation. In short, I missed my confidant.

Sometimes, I wanted to believe that he had been stolen from me, but I knew that wasn't the case. He got exactly what he had always wanted: *immortality*. He had simply taken matters into his own hands...and had joined the wrong team.

But what was done was done. Fang had gotten his wish, and a whole lot of people were dead because of it. No, my ex-husband's murder wasn't a direct result, but the turning of Fang had caused a domino effect that was still reverberating in my life to this day.

And, yeah, there was the small matter of those joggers Fang had killed. Those and surely others. Perhaps many others.

I couldn't think about that.

Suddenly depressed, I sat back in my office chair and looked at my cell phone. No texts. No missed calls. Not even a Facebook update. The world was asleep at this hour. The mortal world. My kids were sound asleep. Although Anthony was showing some disturbing vampiric tendencies, one of them, thankfully, was not sleeping during the day.

Thank God.

Sure, I had plenty of work to do. These were, after all, my working hours. I knew that most freaks like me were out partying or hunting or running through graveyards, or whatever the hell it was that vampires did together. I had a car payment due next week, not to mention the taxes on the house were due in two weeks. I didn't have time to run through graveyards. I had to make some money.

I looked at the stack of printouts next to my computer. One of my jobs was to run background checks for various companies. I had, for instance, a deal with the Hyundai dealership down the road. When they got new prospects, they provided me with their job applications, and I checked out their criminal histories.

A stack of names. With addresses, including social security numbers, phone numbers, and all their pertinent contact info. With a little digging, I could find out if, say, they lived alone. A Google Maps search would let me know if, say, they had neighbors nearby or far away, neighbors who might hear them scream, or not.

I drummed my long nails on the stack of prospects, most of whom were probably waiting anxiously to hear if they got the job or not. Not one suspected that an honest-to-God vampire was looking a little deeper into their private lives.

I wondered how they would feel about that.

Would they be nervous? Or scared?

I suspected both. I also suspected they didn't believe in vampires. But they would believe, oh, yes, if I showed up on their doorsteps. Then they would be very, very nervous. No, frightened.

Terrified.

Yesss, good.

211

I knew *she* was speaking to me. The devil bitch that lived inside me. She had been gaining some ground in my mind. What that meant, exactly, I didn't know.

But I felt it.

And, for tonight, I didn't care.

Instead, I thought again of the new hires. The thought of anyone fearing me intrigued me. No, not quite *intrigued* me. *Excited me.*

I swallowed, licked my lips.

I felt my heartbeat pick up a little. It went from beating maybe five times a minute to twenty or thirty. *Yeah, I'm a freak through and through.*

No, Sssamantha. You are a hunter.

Yes, I thought. *A hunter.*

I liked that. I would be a damn good one, too. No, I'd never hunted a living person for the express purpose of killing them, just for killing's sake. Other vampires did this. Not me. Indeed, other vampires explored their true natures.

Not me, though.

Not until now. I needed to do something about that. I needed to hunt the living, to feel their fear, to taste their blood, and to live again. To really, truly live.

I knew it was the demon bitch inside me, encouraging me, influencing me, possessing me…but I didn't care.

Not true, I thought suddenly, shaking my head. *I do care. I care very much.*

Alarmed, I sat up. I had to care. *I had to.* Caring was the only thing that separated me from her. And the demon was a *her,* too. I sensed her repressed femininity. I sensed that she had been enamored with her own good looks, too. She had been beautiful once, I felt. Interestingly, I sensed she might have been a mother once, too, but I could be wrong. Either way, more and more of her was creeping through, bubbling up from the depths. Whether or not she controlled what came through to me, I didn't know. Perhaps the information that came through was random. Perhaps not. Perhaps the information was carefully provided, controlled, designed to do exactly what it was doing to me right now: *breaking me down.*

No, I thought. *No, dammit. No one is breaking me down.*

The bitch inside me didn't often express herself clearly by using complete sentences or stringing together a coherent thought. I suspected she couldn't. I suspected our connection wasn't complete, and so, only parts of her came through. Random, stray thoughts.

More often than not, she came through via feelings. At first, I had always known it was her. At first, her bloodlust thoughts were easily distinguishable from my own. Now, not so much.

Now, her thoughts felt natural, comfortable. Even worse, they felt like my *own* thoughts. This should have scared me. In the least, it should have worried me. But it didn't, not anymore.

She was a powerful entity. I would benefit from her presence in my life. She would benefit, too. She would live again, and I would have untold strength.

"Now, dammit, get the fuck out of my head."

I stood, pacing, fighting her presence, recalling how the entity within Hanner had possessed her completely. Would that happen to me? What would it feel like to have another control my body? To speak for me? To act for me? To think for me?

I paced in the small space behind my desk, careful of power cords. Why I had so many power cords, I didn't know. I spotted a charger for my phone, my iPad, my Kindle and even one for a Nook. I didn't even own a Nook.

I avoided it, along with myriad of other cords that seemed to multiply behind my desk, all of which served some damned purpose.

Except the cords weren't what was really troubling. No, my mind was on *possession.* On, in fact, *losing* my mind. Of having it being stolen by another.

"No!" I said, pacing faster and faster. Now, my foot did get caught in the Nook cord. I kicked it, and it came out. Along with all the other wires in the wall.

Cursing—but thankful I had something to distract me—I went about plugging all the wires back in, praying I got them right. A moment later, when I had successfully turned on my computer again, there was Fang's response, waiting for me in the AOL message chatroom.

Hi, Moon Dance.

CHAPTER TEN

We hadn't spoken in many months, not since Fang had shown up one night, here in my office, when he revealed to me that he had killed many.

Fang had been, of course, compelled to kill by a very old vampire, a vampire who was now dead, thanks to Kingsley. With the old vampire's death, the connection had been severed and Fang had come instantly to my rescue, and for that I would be forever thankful to him. That he had killed many while *not* compelled was cause for much concern.

Now, of course, I was having a hard time remembering why the killing of innocent people had bothered me so much. After all, wasn't killing in a vampire's nature? Yes, it was. To kill and to feed and to grow stronger and stronger...

Yesss. Good, Sam, good.

I shook my head and ran my fingers through my thick hair. It was her, of course.

"Not me," I said, gasping a little. "Go back to hell."

I took a few deep, steadying breaths and looked again at the words on the laptop screen before me, framed around the AOL chat window.

Hi, Moon Dance.

I raised my fingers to the keyboard, and began typing...

———

Hi, Fang.

He didn't immediately reply. I waited a few minutes, my clawed fingers hovering over the keyboard. The image of a gargoyle perched on the ledge of an old building came to mind. For some reason, I smiled.

No, *she* smiled. She liked dark things, disturbing things. Granted, gargoyles were hardly the things of nightmares. No, she was pleased that her thoughts were so quickly coming to the surface. That her thoughts were mingling easily with my own.

I shook my head again, fought off a brief wave of panic, and typed: *You there, Fang?*

A minute passed. My house was so quiet that I could literally hear my kids' heartbeats. Anthony's beat a little slower than Tammy's. Was that because of the vampire blood in him? My heartbeat rate was only a fraction of that of a human's. Had I committed my son to a lifetime of making excuses for who he was, and why he was different? Maybe. But the alternative was far, far worse. Better a lifetime of excuses than no life at all.

Not too long ago, the thing within had tried to escape using another means: procuring all four magical medallions, medallions meant to help vampires battle that which lives within them. At least, that was what the alchemist Librarian had told me, and Archibald Maximus should know, since he had created the medallions in the first place. Like all things in life, there was a loophole, a way for something good to be used for something bad. Turns out, the collecting of all four medallions at once could also release the demons within. On a desolate island in the Pacific Northwest, I had been lured to my destruction. That hadn't quite happened, and my son, who had actually *consumed* one of the medallions in a liquefied form, could live on.

And live on he did, growing faster than other boys his age, stronger than other boys his age, and, if you asked me and his older sister, gassier than other boys his age.

I almost smiled. The thing within me didn't want me to smile. It didn't like innocent jokes. It didn't like humor.

"Well, fuck you," I said, and smiled anyway.

And that was when the AOL chatbox flickered and the status read: "Fang950 is typing."

———

Hello, Moon Dance.

Fang and I used to have a strong telepathic link. So strong that we could often hear each other's thoughts over a great distance. Now, since becoming a fellow creature of the night, that link was broken. He was inaccessible to me, and that was a loss greater to me than I was willing to admit.

You are up late, Fang, I typed.

Or early, he wrote back almost immediately.

I smiled, pleased to see some of his old personality coming through. My last memory of Fang had been troubling at best. He was robotic, lifeless, and, if you asked me, lost.

Now that I had him, I wasn't sure what to say to him. It had been many months since we had last spoken, and many more before that when our relationship was irrevocably changed. After some false starts, I finally wrote: *Still a vampire?*

Or something.

I nodded to myself. Yes, being a vampire wasn't all it was cracked up to be. A *host* was more accurate.

Where you living now?

In L.A.'s Echo Park district.

Still bartending?

I almost, *almost* sensed him laughing, but probably not. He would have laughed at that, but not anymore.

No, Moon Dance.

Okay, I'll bite. No pun intended. What are you doing for work these days?

I don't need to work, Sam.

I nodded to myself, suddenly getting it. *Hanner left you money. Probably a lot of money.*

Something like that.

217

Of course, Hanner wouldn't have had a traditional will, not when she was over a century old. Besides, whoever heard of a vampire having a will? More than likely, Hanner had simply given Fang access to her accumulated wealth. Probably the case with other vampires, with money being passed to each new generation of bloodsuckers. I was probably the only idiot vampire who actually worked. For all I knew, Fang was sitting on top of a pile of gold, stolen and stockpiled by the ageless and undead. No doubt stolen and looted from countless victims. Or, even better, just given to them by compelled victims.

I could do something similar, I knew. I could, with some training, stand outside the local Bank of America, and compel all those who came and went to empty their savings accounts for me. In fact, it would probably be easy to do.

Indeed, the entity within me perked up at this line of thinking. Yes, she and her kind were used to living this way, of manipulating and exploiting and destroying.

I pushed her out of my mind, or as far out as I could.

So, you do nothing, then? I asked him. *Just sitting around and drinking goblets of blood?*

Oh, there is much I do, Sam. Some things I can talk about, some I can't.

You are setting up another blood bank, I wrote. No, I might not be able to read his mind anymore, but I was also a trained investigator who happened to be pretty good at her job.

Yes, Sam, but it's not what you think.

And what am I thinking?

That we are killing people, draining them dry, like Robert Mason did in Fullerton.

And Hanner, I said. *Let's not forget her role.*

Indeed, her role had been to help the murders slip through the cracks, to help the police forget, to hide and manipulate the facts.

Fang was writing something, and then paused. I knew this because the words "Fang950 is typing" had been flashing in the upper corner and then it quit flashing. I really didn't know what he was going to write, but a part of me thought he might have been about to defend Hanner.

He loved her, I suddenly thought. *He loved her and he'd killed her...*
Killed her for me.

I knew that Hanner and Fang had been close. I knew that she had taught him the ins and outs of vampirism, something that had never been taught to me. Hell, it still seemed I was learning something new every day.

Yeah, it stood to reason that the very creature who had turned him, trained him, and fed him in his early days would be the object of his affection.

I got it. I understood it. I was sure it would have happened to anyone.

But that didn't stop me from feeling jealous.

And yeah, I got all of this from a simple hesitation, a simple pregnant pause. It might as well have been pregnant with twins.

Whatever that meant.

Anyway, after his telling hesitation, he started writing again. *The Hanner operation was flawed,* he wrote. *Most of the victims didn't have to die.*

Most? I wrote. *Wouldn't it be more human to say that "none of them needed to die"?*

Yes, of course. I was loose with my speech. Or with my fingertips.

I nearly asked what else he was loose with. It was a damn good thing Fang couldn't read my mind.

Then again, why was I feeling jealous? Fang had, after all, practically thrown himself at me. But our timing had never been right. And then, the dumbass had to get himself turned into a fellow creature of the night. Yes, but the Fang I had developed feelings for wasn't the same Fang I was corresponding with now. At least, I didn't think it was. Who this new Fang was, well, I would just have to wait and see.

So, how are you running things differently? I asked, typing.

It's an underground blood bank. We pay the humans for their blood.

How do you recruit them?

Someone who knows someone. Word gets around in the right places.

Addicts, I wrote. It wasn't a question.

Drugs don't affect our system, Sam. You should know that. And if you didn't, you do now.

I could almost—almost—hear Fang's enthusiasm. Yes, he was finally a creature of the night. The thing he had wanted most in the world. More than even me.

You're recruiting crackheads, I typed.

Not all are addicts, Sam. Some are normal people, everyday people. They give us blood and go home. There's no reason to kill anyone and draw attention to ourselves.

Are you doing it for the money?

No, Sam. I don't need money. Not anymore. But others who are working for us—the humans—yes, they are very much doing it for the money.

You're working with crooks?

In a word, yes.

And this is why I haven't heard from you? I wrote. *Because you were putting together this... operation?*

There was a long pause, and then this: *I had my reasons for being away, Sam. Yes, I was putting together this operation, but mostly...*

He stopped there, so I finished for him: *Mostly, you were mourning her.*

Yes, Sam.

You loved her.

In a way, yes.

More than me?

Not now, Sam. I'm not ready to talk about any of this now. Please.

Fine. Sorry. I collected myself, took in a deep breath and wrote: *So, how, exactly, does this operation work?*

We're more efficient now, he wrote. *And we have a consistent, steady supply of blood.*

Are all of your "suppliers" willing suppliers? I asked.

I'm not going to lie to you, Sam. Not to you, not ever. Some of our sources will never know what happened to them.

These would be your fresh sources?

Yes, Sam, he typed. *Those who provide blood straight from the vein, if you will.*

Where do you find these sources?

Same place, he typed. *They are simply led to a special room...*

Where a vampire is waiting.

Yes.

Who feasts from the victim, and then compels them to forget.

Yes, but those are only rare occasions. Mostly, we collect blood in these facilities. It's win-win, Sam. No bodies, people get paid. Everyone is happy.

I should have been repulsed, disgusted, alarmed, or at least concerned. I was none of these things. I was, if anything, greatly intrigued. And I didn't even think it was *her* who was intrigued. No, the person I was now, the thing I had become, saw the useful practicality in Fang's enterprise.

And, I reasoned, was my arrangement with Allison much different? She permitted me to drink from her, not for monetary gain, but for extra-sensory gain. To increase her sixth sense. We, in effect, used each other. If there was ever a codependent relationship, this was it.

Yes, for vampires to exist, we needed blood. But we didn't need to kill and draw attention to ourselves. Fang had figured out an efficient enterprise. I admired him for it.

Lord help me, I *admired* him.

I have to go now, Sam.

Okay, I wrote. *Talk later?*

Of course. Goodnight, Moon Dance.

Goodnight, Fang.

And with that, he signed out.

CHAPTER ELEVEN

I was back in the City of Corona.

This time, I was at the Corona Police Department. The city, which boasted more than a hundred and fifty thousand people, also had, unfortunately, a thriving homicide department.

Detective Jason Sharp was exactly that: *sharp*. Or, more exact, *angular*. His young face segued into a pointy chin. His cheekbones were to die for. At least, for a woman. His nose was long and arrow-like. He looked a bit like a drawing come to life. He wore a white, long-sleeved shirt buttoned snugly at his throat. His Adam's apple rested directly on top of his collar. It bounced and bobbed seemingly with a will of its own. Next to his Adam's apple was a thick, carotid vein. It pulsed every now and then. But that might have been my imagination.

Detective Sharp was busy bringing up a file on his computer screen. I couldn't see his computer screen, although I could see it glowing in his eyes—eyes that flashed and darted in their sockets like butterflies on crack. If I had to guess, I would say Detective Sharp had some serious A.D.D. going on. My son's eyes darted around like that, scanning everything, seeing everything, absorbing everything, reading everything. I always suspected my son had A.D.D. My son was a gamer. I wondered if Detective Sharp was a closet gamer, too.

I said, "You're new to the case."

"Yes."

"Who was the original detective?"

"Renaldo," he said.

"And where's Renaldo?"

"Parkview Cemetery."

"Dead?"

"Gee," he said, glancing at me. "You must be a real detective."

"I was an agent, too," I said.

"Federal?"

"Yup," I said.

"Sorry if I sounded like an ass."

"Oh, you did."

"It's just that some blowhard private dicks come in here with all sorts of swagger—and don't know shit about what they're talking about. I didn't know you worked for the feds."

"Now you do."

"Now you're on your own?"

"I am."

"Happy?"

"Turns out I like working for myself. I happen to be a helluva boss."

He laughed. "I couldn't do it. I need someone riding my ass all day. Otherwise..."

"Otherwise, you would play HALO all day."

"You sound like you're judging me."

"My son plays HALO," I said.

"It's a good game—"

"My son is ten."

"These are more than just games, they're experiences."

"If you say so," I said. "How did the previous detective die, if you don't mind me asking?"

"A car accident."

"I'm sorry to hear that."

"So am I. He was a good guy. We miss him here."

"When was the accident?"

Detective Sharp shrugged. "Three weeks ago."

I made sympathetic sounds that I didn't really feel. Truth was, these days, I found death a lot less...heartbreaking. I found death. more...interesting. Exciting, even.

No, *she* found death exciting.

Deep breaths, Sam.

"Can you tell me any more than that?" I asked.

He studied me, then nodded. "Broadsided over on Grand Street and Main."

"Broadsided by who?" I asked. And just as the word escaped me, I silently cursed myself, certain it should have been "by whom." Sigh. I might be undead, but that didn't make me a grammarian.

"We don't know."

"Hit and run?"

"Yeah."

"You knew him well?"

"Well enough."

"Any leads?"

"We got some."

"But nothing you're willing to pass along?"

He studied me some more, then shook his head. "No," he said. "Not until I know you better."

"I could help."

"We got enough help."

"Fine," I said. "What do we know about Lucy Gleason?"

"The broad who went missing from Starbucks?"

"Yeah."

"We know she's still missing."

"What else?"

He studied me some more. He wasn't sure if he liked me, which was hard to believe. He already felt like he'd said too much, which wasn't much at all. I knew all of this because I was following his thoughts. He was just about to turn me away, claiming he was busy—he was, but not *that* busy—when I gave him a gentle telepathic nudge, planting the words directly into his mind:

Tell her everything. And get her a glass of water.

He blinked, nodded, and then said, "Follow me. And would you like some water?"

"Why, how kind of you, Detective," I said and followed him out, hiding a grin. I should have felt bad that I was controlling another human being, forcing him to do something against his will.

I should have...but I didn't.

In fact, I liked it a lot. Perhaps too much.

Lord, help me.

Chapter Twelve

I was waiting in another room when Detective Sharp returned with a glass of water and handed it to me.

He stared down at me for a moment, frowning. I peeked into his thoughts and watched him, trying to remember why he had agreed to help me further. He couldn't remember why, but it had seemed like a good idea at the time, and so he ran with it.

"Ready to roll," said Detective Sharp, perhaps a little too excitedly. I might have encouraged him to help me a bit too much. "Come to my side of the desk. Bring your chair. This could take a while."

I did as I was told, although I could probably stand all day, or all week. My legs didn't ache, nor did my muscles grow tired. I think, in fact, that my muscles regenerated and refreshed in the microseconds during use.

Such a freak.

No, came the voice from down deep. *Not a freak.*

When I sat, Detective Sharp said, "Shall we get on with it?"

"On with what?"

"The Starbucks surveillance tape."

———

These days, all surveillance tape can be downloaded as a movie file. I watched Jason rather expertly click through various screens and files until he found the one in question. It read: "Sbucks-MP-Feed1-Open" followed by the date and time.

"Have you gone over the tape?" I asked.

"Not yet."

"When did you get the case?"

"Last week, when Renaldo's case files got redistributed. Been meaning to look it over."

"What were Detective Renaldo's findings?"

"According to his notes—"

"Which you just read."

"Yes, but I'd spoken with him previously regarding the case, too. We all had. We were all confused by her disappearance. We all offered theories. Nothing panned out. Anyway, according to Renaldo, there was nothing on the tapes that seemed to indicate that she had ever left the Starbucks."

"So, she just disappeared," I said. "Poof. Off the face of the earth."

"Seems like it. Trust me, it fucked with Renaldo's head. He took the case to heart, worked on it night and day, up until the day he died."

"You mean the day he was killed."

"Right."

"So, what *is* on the tape?"

"I think it's time to find out."

He clicked on the file, and a window opened. He pressed *play* and I think we both sat forward.

"Too bad we don't have popcorn," he said.

"I wish I could eat popcorn."

"You can't eat popcorn?"

"Long story," I said.

He shrugged, and we both watched the screen.

CHAPTER THIRTEEN

The wide-lens camera had been strategically placed.

Positioned in the parking lot at the side of the building, it provided both a wide shot of the front entrance of Starbucks and a side shot of the back door, too. One camera, both front and back doors. Nice.

A few days ago, Henry Gleason had emailed me the "missing person kit" that I always required for such cases: five recent photos, social security number, cell phone number, driver's license number, contact information for family and friends, and anything else that he thought might prove helpful.

Although I had committed Lucy Gleason's face to memory, I had seen the tape a dozen or more times at this point. Most people in the area had. Corona Police Department had released the tape to the public, asking for leads. According to Detective Renaldo's notes, nothing had panned out. The case had gone cold with his untimely death.

So, what leads they had gathered from those anonymous calls, I didn't know. But I would, soon. I recognized her immediately when she appeared from the bottom of the frame. There she was, moving right to left, toward the Starbucks. Had I possessed a normal pulse, it probably would have quickened right about now, thumping steadily just inside my temple. Instead, there was no physical reaction to seeing her, other than my own excitement level increased.

There she is, I thought, *Lucy Gleason,* "The Disappearing Wife," as the press had dubbed her.

Of course, I had studied the video a dozen more times after taking the case, too. But the video available to me online had been only a fragment of what I was seeing now, which was the complete feed.

We'll call this, I thought, *the extended cut.*

Lucy was a thin woman. She was dressed in tight black yoga pants and pink Converse sneakers. The sneakers glittered. Her age was tough to determine, although I knew she was thirty-eight, which was getting close to my own age, although you would never know it.

The woman on the screen, the "Disappearing Wife," seemed oblivious to the fact that she was about to disappear off the face of the earth. This was evidence for me. It was telling. She didn't seem fearful. Indeed, she even casually looked down at her cell phone at some point.

"Would give my left nut to know what she was looking at on her cell phone," said Detective Sharp.

"Too quick to read a text message," I said.

Sharp nodded. "Renaldo pulled her text records. Nothing around that time. Sent or received."

"Maybe she was looking at the time."

"Yeah, maybe."

"But you don't think so?"

"No," said Sharp. "Looks to me like she was expecting to hear from someone, and didn't. She looks, I dunno, sort of disappointed."

I was impressed with Jason Sharp. The "Disappearing Wife" was wearing sunglasses, and so there wasn't much to work with there, as far as discerning her emotions. But, admittedly, I got a sense that she had been disappointed as well. The way she exhaled slightly. The way she paused slightly in mid-step, as if she thought she had just received a message.

"I agree," I said. "Replay it."

He did, using a dial next to the keyboard. He turned it slightly, and the video went back two or three seconds and started again immediately. Yes, there it was again. She virtually jumped when she reached for her phone. And then I saw why.

"The person coming toward her," I said. "Look."

He replayed the video again. A man, maybe twenty yards away and coming toward her, reached for his own cell phone just as she reached for hers.

"His phone rang," I said. "Or beeped or chirped."

The detective nodded. "She thought it might be hers."

"Right," I said.

"Except, of course, what are the chances his cell phone sounded like her cell phone?"

"Not a very good chance," I said.

"Which means she was jumpy," said the detective. "Reacting to any sound she heard."

"Almost as if she was nervous about something," I said.

Sharp nodded. His pointed nose waved through the air like a maestro's wand. "Or nervous about someone," he said. "Except, where does that get us?"

"Nowhere yet," I said. "But it's a start."

"A start is something."

"I agree. Can I see her text history?" I asked.

I didn't need to prompt the young detective. "Don't see why not. The wife's been missing for nearly a month now, and we've got nothing."

"You've got me," I said.

"A private dick with no di—" He caught himself.

"Good catch," I said.

"Er, sorry."

"Nothing I haven't heard before, Detective," I said. "Wanna keep watching?"

He nodded and rolled the video.

Chapter Fourteen

We watched her cross the parking lot and enter the Starbucks with no fanfare. She didn't speak with anyone and kept her head down. Once inside, through the smoked glass, we lost track of her.

"Interior footage?" I asked.

"Wouldn't that be nice?"

I knew this, of course. Everyone knew this. I nodded.

He added, "They have since installed an interior camera. Too little, too late."

I nodded again, and for the next two hours, we watched my client appear and disappear out of the screen, going inside, searching outside, circling the building. Covering his mouth and calling loudly. He looked like a crazy man. He also looked like a man who had lost his wife.

We backtracked the video, going over it frame by frame, studying everyone coming in and going out. But no one looked like her—or even looked like her in disguise. There was no one unaccountable, either. Meaning, a man with a beard didn't suddenly emerge who hadn't already come in.

Later, the police came, searching the exterior and interior, taking statements, and taking photos.

"Police checked behind the counter, the back room, even the freezer. Everywhere. No one saw her go back there, and they had like seven employees working at the time. *Seven.* What coffee shop has seven fucking employees working at one time?"

"Is this a trick question?"

He ignored me and backtracked again. We both were taking copious notes.

"Husband doesn't come into view until..." Sharp checked his notes. "Until fourteen minutes after she goes in. Almost fifteen. If you ask me, that seems like a reasonable amount of time to come looking for your wife. It doesn't seem, you know, suspicious."

I nodded.

"The police come," he checked the notes again, "thirty-two minutes after she disappears. All normal stuff, if you ask me."

"Normal, except she hasn't been seen since."

We both stared at Henry on the screen, who was now frozen in mid-yell, one hand cupping his mouth, the other shielding his eyes from the sun's glare. The disappearance had happened just after noon.

After a moment, Sharp said, "Husband's been taking some heat."

"Shouldn't be. It's obvious that he's at a loss, too."

"Unless he's in on something? Or unless they're in on something together."

"Magic tricks?" I asked. "Teleporting into alternate dimensions?"

"No one asked for a comedian. In fact, he hired you. You talked to him, face to face. What's your gut say?"

I decided against mentioning the fact that I had dipped inside Henry's memory and therefore, knew he was innocent. Instead, I settled for, "I believe him."

Sharp looked at me, and then gave me a short nod. "I haven't talked to him yet, but I know Renaldo wasn't too hung up on him, although..."

"Although what?"

"There was a history of violence between them."

"Oh?"

"Police were called twice in the last two years. Both times by neighbors. Both times, he was given a warning."

"No arrests?"

"No violence. According to the reports, he never touched her. Just a lot of yelling."

"Doesn't seem like a lead," I said.

"Maybe not," he said. "But it's something."

"Something," I said, "is better than nothing."

"They teach you that in private eye school?"

"No, at the Federal Law Enforcement Training Center."

"Fancy."

I chuckled, and we stared at the monitor some more.

After a moment, Sharp asked, "Any theories yet, based on what you've seen?"

I shrugged. I might be a creature of the night, and have access to some pretty amazing talents, but I didn't know all or see all. I said, "No one suspicious came in after her. No one suspicious came out. No one carrying, say, a large plastic bag came out."

"And no one came out the back, either," he added.

Indeed, the back door had remained closed the entire time. "Any chance we missed it?"

"No way," said Sharp. "I was looking."

I was, too, of course.

"Not to mention," added Sharp, "that Renaldo went over this like a hundred times. No one came out that back door."

"Windows?"

"None. It's a corner space in a shopping center. One front door, one back door. Even the bathrooms are windowless. You ask me, a bathroom should have a fucking window."

Now that we had sat together for a few hours, Detective Sharp let go of his tough-guy act, and some of his personality was coming through.

We were silent some more. Admittedly, nothing was coming to me. No hits, no feelings, no theories, no real impressions. *No, that's not right.* I was getting one impression. And it was a big one. And the more I thought about it, the more I was sure it was right.

I think my excitement might have been obvious. The detective snapped his gaze over to me. "What is it?"

"No theories yet, Detective, but I am sure of one thing."

"And what's that?"

"She's still alive."

He looked at me long and hard. "Yeah, I'm thinking that, too."

CHAPTER FIFTEEN

I was boxing at Jacky's gym.

Except this time, I was working out with another trainer—and a trainer who didn't seem to look too happy about working out with me.

Tough noogies.

Jacky himself working closely with my son, up in the ring. My son had wanted to come tonight. I wasn't sure how wise it was to teach a boy how to fight when he was already stronger than most kids. But I understood what was going on here: Anthony hadn't left my side for the past few months, ever since his father had died. Tammy could take me or leave me. Anthony was a different story. He shadowed me just about everywhere I went.

Tammy handled her father's loss differently. She buried herself in books and schoolwork. She finished novels bigger and fatter than anything I'd ever read, even back in grad school. Books about divergents and tributes, featuring characters called Tris and Katness, or was it Kat and Trissness? I didn't know; either way, both had way cooler names than me.

Despite her independence, sometimes, late at night, I would hear Tammy crying softly in her room. I would then put away my files, turn off my laptop, and slip into her room unannounced. I would crawl into bed and pull her to me and listen to her cry against my shoulder until she would finally go to sleep. More than once, I fell asleep next to her, only to awaken late in the day.

The thing about a mommy who works the night shift and goes to bed at the crack of dawn—or slips into a minor coma, to be more accurate—is that a son or daughter can't, well, crawl into bed with her when they need her.

Anyway, the new trainer was holding up punching mitts, or focus mitts, before me. He held them up as I hit them harder and harder. With each punch, I watched him wince until he finally stepped back and said his hands needed a break.

I didn't doubt it. As he slipped off the mitts, I caught a fragment of his thoughts: he was wondering what drug I was on. Speed, he figured. Maybe bath salts.

With my trainer undoubtedly wishing he never showed up for work today, I sat down and watched my son work with Jacky up in the ring. Jacky was personally working out with my son, showing him proper footwork and striking techniques. Presently, he was holding my son's right arm straight, adjusting his elbow and shoulder height and wrists. I could hear Jacky's thick accent from here, barking orders. I could also see a wicked gleam in the old trainer's eye. With my son, he was liking what he was seeing.

Tammy turned to books, while Anthony turned to me.

As the weeks passed, he grew more and more attached to me. Often, he would slip into my office, nonchalantly, quietly, almost secretly. One moment I would be working, the next, I would look up and he would be there. It was a credit to his own supernatural prowess that he could sneak up on me, perhaps one of the few people who could.

Mostly, he would play on his Gameboy or pretend to read a book. I knew he was pretending because he never actually turned the pages. Sometimes, he would come in and talk, usually about nothing important. He would ramble. Other times, he would come in and sit quietly, staring down at his hands. I asked him if there was anything I could do for him, or help him with, or if he wanted to do something together, and the answer was invariably "no."

That is, until this evening, when I found him sitting in my office, holding a book he didn't bother trying to read. The title was *Beautiful*

Creatures, which might have been a movie, too, although we hadn't seen it. I was pretty sure that was his sister's book.

As I shut down my computer, I asked if he wanted to go to boxing with me and, wonder of wonders, he had perked up immediately. I smiled, relieved that I had finally, *finally* found something that interested him.

Now, I almost regretted it.

Almost.

Then again, maybe my son did need to know how to fight. Maybe being who he is—the strongest kid in his school—would prompt older boys to test him, to prove their own worth, to show that a younger kid wasn't tougher than them.

I hoped my son wouldn't use his growing strength for ill. I hoped I wasn't creating a supervillain here, although that thought nearly made me giggle.

My son had a good heart, and he was a boy hurting and lost, and looking for someone to connect with. For a while, I had been that someone. Boy, had I been. From following me out to the laundry room, to sitting with me in the office.

Now, as I watched my son, something curious was happening: he wasn't looking at me. No, Jacky had his full attention. And, more amazingly, he had Jacky's full attention, too.

I saw something even stranger, something I wasn't prepared for: as they moved together in this boxing dance of theirs, as Anthony delivered slow-motion punches and as Jacky corrected his technique, I saw their two auras do something I had rarely, if ever, seen.

Their auras had somehow connected. Where Anthony's aura ended and Jacky's began, I didn't know. Never had I seen this before. The auras looked, at least to my eyes, to be one big aura.

What the devil?

I sat forward in one of the many plastic chairs that lined the perimeter of the gym and actually rubbed my eyes, but there was no rubbing away this strange display.

Yes, I could see auras. From what I understood, all vampires could see auras. Auras were the energy field that surrounded our bodies. And not just the energy, but, some claimed, our souls themselves, which were too big to be contained by flesh and bones.

I knew Jacky had lost his own son years ago to a drug overdose, and I always suspected that he coached and trained these kids here to fill a void. My suspicions were confirmed with my son. Their connection was tangible. Hell, *spiritual.*

What's happening? I wondered.

I didn't know, but with my own trainer long gone—in fact, I'd seen him slip out the front door with nary a glance back—I suspected that Jacky just might have found himself a new protégé.

And, as Jacky reached over and mussed my son's hair—with Anthony grinning from ear to ear, his first grin in months—I suspected Jacky had found much more.

They both had.

Chapter Sixteen

I was with the Librarian, a man who might not be a man, and a man who might not really exist, at least in this physical world.

Who he was remained a mystery. That he had once been an ordinary human, I had no doubt. How he existed now, I didn't know, although his knowledge of alchemy might explain a lot. What it explained, I didn't know, since I didn't know much about alchemy, other than a book I'd read years ago by Paulo Coelho, a book that, at the time, had been meaningless to me.

"Paulo touched on real truths," said the Librarian.

Although Maximus, aka the Librarian, was immortal, he and I had an open telepathic line of communication. Not so much with other immortals, who were closed off to me. With that said, Max and I generally spoke aloud, rather than communicate telepathically. I liked speaking aloud. Call me old fashioned, but speaking aloud was what *normal* people did. I needed to do what normal people did, as often as possible.

He continued, "Some books you are ready for, some you are not. You were not ready for *The Alchemist*, although it laid the groundwork to open your mind."

"What do you mean?"

"You had not awakened, Sam. You were closed, asleep. Life was as it was expected to be, with little questioning on your end. Now you question much and seek deeper answers."

"And *The Alchemist* helped do that?"

"That, along with your attack many years ago. But not everyone needs to be rendered immortal to awaken. There are many paths to greater truths."

"And why should we seek greater truths?"

"There's no 'shoulds' in this world, Sam. There is only following your heart, your own truths, and explore where they lead you."

"Well, they led me here, to talk to you."

"And so they have. You have a question for me, I see."

"I do. It's about my son."

Max nodded once, long and slow, from behind his "help desk" counter within the Occult Reading Room, itself filled with hundreds, if not thousands, of very old and very strange-looking books, many of which were, if you asked me, downright dangerous.

The Occult Reading Room was a secret room located on the third floor of Cal State Fullerton's epic library, a room that few knew about, and even fewer actually saw. *Secret* may not have been the correct word. There were, after all, actual books in this reading room, books that were even referenced in the library's computer database.

"Although referenced," he said, "few would think to look for them, and fewer still have heard of them."

"But if they have heard of them, and they look for it…"

"Then I am always here."

"Always?"

"A figure of speech. But more or less, yes. You can mostly find me here."

That such a young-looking guy could be so wise was still something I was getting used to. I said, "The emerald medallion was used to give my son back his humanity, correct?"

"Correct."

"But he also retained some of his supernatural traits."

"This appears to be so."

"He seems to have retained all the good supernatural traits," I said. "And none of the bad."

"Again, yes."

The Librarian watched me through eyes that never judged and were always kind. I was reminded of a newborn's eyes, full of wonder and peace and joy. I was not used to such eyes. His were a pleasant change of pace, and if I wasn't careful, I could get lost in those eyes.

I asked, "Then how is the diamond medallion any different?"

"It's not, Sam, although it is obvious now that even I cannot predict the reaction each person will have to the medallions."

The four medallions were, of course, created by the Librarian, relics put into place to help creatures like me combat the things within. That all four of the relics had gravitated toward me was something I didn't yet understand. They surely could have landed in the lap of other creatures of the night. In fact, I knew of one such vampire—an ancient vampire—who had spent quite a long time looking for the emerald medallion.

I gathered my thoughts, thinking them aloud. "The emerald medallion didn't just give my son back his mortality, but enabled him to keep some of his immortal powers, too."

"It appears so, Samantha," said the Librarian. "But we cannot know that it was the medallion that gave him these gifts...or if it was something else."

"What do you mean?"

"I'm not sure what I mean, Sam. Your son's reaction to the medallion was unexpected."

"And you suspect...something else might be involved?"

"In a word, yes."

"And you are just telling me this now?"

"I've only recently deduced this...and I knew you would be back sooner rather than later."

"Should I be concerned?" I asked. "About my son?"

He shook his head and his kind eyes seemed to smile. "No, Sam. But there is something else at play here, something—or perhaps someone—who has helped your son greatly. This something or someone is beyond even my own perception."

"That sounds frightening," I said.

"It doesn't have to be, Sam. Your son, it appears, is in good hands."

"But whose hands?" I asked.

"That, as the old game show hosts used to say, is the million-dollar question. As of now, yes, the emerald medallion behaved very similarly to the diamond medallion, which not only returns your mortality, but also helps you retain all the perks, if you will. That is, all the perks of your choosing."

"My choosing?"

"Yes."

"I could retain…my great strength?"

"Yes, that, and more."

"My psychic ability?"

"Yes."

"More?" I asked.

"Much more, Sam."

I thought about what could be much more…and gasped. "Flying?"

He nodded slowly. "Yes, Sam. You would retain that, as well."

"And all this without the bloodsucking and sleeping during the day?"

"Yes, Sam. No more blood."

"And I could finally see myself in the mirror and have normal nails again?"

"Yes, Sam."

How Fang presently owned the fourth and final medallion was another story—a story I didn't presently know. After all, how he came upon the diamond medallion, why he wore it, and what he even knew about it were all questions whose answers were unknown to me. A part of me wondered if he even knew what he had, if he understood the value of the relic that presently hung around his neck.

Maybe, maybe not. Either way, he and I were going to have a long talk…and soon.

"And what of the dark master within me?" I asked. "Does the diamond medallion eradicate her as well?"

He smiled down on me. "Completely."

"And no such creature resides within my son?"

"No, Sam. The emerald medallion took care of that, as well."

"This is all very weird."

"It's a weird universe, Samantha."

I sighed and continued standing there. I found that I was hugging myself. After a moment, Maximus said, "But you didn't come here today to talk about medallions, did you?"

"No," I said, shaking my head. "My son…" But as soon as I began the sentence, the words got caught in my throat, and emotions poured out of me in tears, and the next thing I knew the Librarian had his arms around my shoulders, pulling me into his shoulder.

After a long moment of this, still unable to speak, the Librarian's thoughts appeared in my head, just inside my ears.

Your son and the boxer remember each other on a soul level.

A soul level?

Many lifetimes ago, they were deeply connected as father and son, as they have been often in many lives, in many places.

But Anthony had a different dad…

In this lifetime, Sam. But the boxer, Jacky, and your son, Anthony, made an agreement to connect again, in this life, if your boy was ever lost or sad or lonely.

I wept harder into the Librarian's shoulder and he squeezed me tighter.

There is deep love between them, Sam. Both need each other.

I nodded, and finally couldn't even form words to think, let alone speak. Instead, I buried myself deeper into the young man's shoulder. A young man who was, in fact, ancient, and wept for my son.

Chapter Seventeen

was back at the 'Bucks, as Tammy called it.

The evening shift would be rolling in soon, which was why I was here now. Jasmine Calcutta, who had, perhaps, the most exotic name I'd ever heard, would be here soon, and she was expecting me. We had planned on meeting fifteen minutes before her shift.

I had just sat down with a venti water on the rocks, when I saw a young girl appear at the entrance, blinking and looking around. She was wearing a green Starbucks apron. I waved to her and she nodded and came over.

"Can I get you a coffee?" I asked.

"Thanks, but I'm a little coffeed out," said Jasmine Calcutta.

"Coffeed out," I said. "The two words that keep Starbucks executives up at night. Well, that and their Sumatra Roast."

She giggled and sat down opposite me. "That was kind of funny."

"My kids don't think I'm funny. They think I'm embarrassing."

She giggled again, and I think we were hitting it off. Hitting it off with a witness is always a good thing. Much better than the alternative. Jasmine Calcutta was maybe twenty-five. Her eyes, I think, were violet, which surprised the hell out of me. The girl with the most exotic name might also have had the most exotic eyes I'd ever seen. Some girls got all the breaks.

"You're a private investigator," she said.

"I am. But you can call me Sam."

"A real private investigator?"

"In the flesh," I said.

"Do you have, like, a license or something?"

"I do."

"Can I, like, see it?"

She wanted to see it out of curiosity's sake, not because she doubted me. I didn't need to be a mind reader to see that. I produced it from my purse and she *oohed* and *ahed* at it for a few seconds before handing it back.

"So cool," she said. "I want to do something like that."

I pointed to my license photo, in which I might have been wearing too much makeup. "You mean take great pictures?"

She giggled again. "No. Be a private detective. A real one, like you."

"Well, here's your chance to watch a real detective at work."

She nodded enthusiastically.

I said, "I need you to do your best to remember everything you can about Lucy Gleason."

"I'll try, but it's kind of getting fuzzier and fuzzier."

"Real detectives don't use words like fuzzier," I said.

"Okay, sorry."

"I'm teasing, Jasmine."

"Oh, right, sorry."

"No need to be sorry," I said. "Just give me your hands."

"My hands?"

"Yes."

"Why?"

"It's a super-secret interview trick I learned."

"Wow, really?"

"Really." I then directed this thought to her: *It feels perfectly normal to give your hands to the nice, if not beautiful, lady and do whatever she asks.*

She cocked her head to one side, and then nodded once.

I'm a monster, I thought. A monster who needed answers. I gestured for her hands and she presented them to me from across the table.

I slipped mine over hers and asked her to close her eyes and think back to the day Lucy disappeared. Luckily, most of the Starbuckians were too absorbed with their laptops and their own self-importance to notice two women holding hands in the coffee shop. Additionally, I had found a table that wasn't in direct line with her fellow co-workers, who might wonder what we were doing.

I didn't want to make a scene, so I held her hands discreetly, just like two friends visiting together, sharing a sweet moment. Or, heck, praying together. Why not?

We weren't two friends and we most certainly weren't praying; instead, I was employing the same technique I had used with Henry Gleason, my client. Except Henry's memory had been fresh and vivid and full of charged emotion, which had heightened his remembrance.

Now, as I held her hands, I asked her to tell me anything that she could remember from that day. She nodded, her eyes still closed.

And just as she opened her mouth to speak, I was inside her mind, completely and thoroughly...

———

"It was just like any other day, you know," she began, and as she spoke those words, images appeared in her thoughts, images I was now privy to, as well. In her mind's eye, I saw a very different scene in Starbucks. Yes, I was reliving these memories right along with her, without her knowing it. It's good to be me.

Sometimes.

Yes, we were in this very same Starbucks but, instead of it being evening, the day was bright, at a time when I would have been just been getting up—a miserable, painful time of day for me. On this day, Jasmine had been working an earlier shift, and she distinctly remembered watching Lucy Gleason come in.

"We were busy, but not Starbucks busy," she said.

"Starbucks is an adjective now?" I asked. "Never mind. It's just a rhetorical question. Continue."

She answered anyway. "Well, we have different levels of busy, at least here. Starbucks busy is our busiest, since it can get crazy in here, especially in the mornings and especially on the weekends."

"So, it wasn't Starbucks busy," I said. "Got it."

The scene continued in her mind, and I continued following it with much interest.

"You have to remember, Sam," she said. "We have thousands and thousands of customers a week. Days go by in a blur. Heck, hours go by in a blur."

"I can imagine," I said. "Starbucks busy."

"Right," she said.

Luckily, she did remember some of that day. She had to, because she had been forced to recall what had happened, especially after being questioned repeatedly by the police. For her, it wasn't just another day. For her, it stood out. Sadly, there were still missing chunks in her memory. That was not unexpected. Some claimed that the subconscious remembers everything a person sees. However, that hadn't been my experience when I'd occasionally plumbed people for their memories. No, I didn't go around doing this often. In fact, very little. But the few people I had done this with, I had seen whole chunks of missing memory. Empty spaces filled with nonsense.

That was what I was seeing here: people coming and going, their faces vague, their bodies amorphous, their orders blurring into the next order. Then Jasmine had a gap filled by other memories, other people, and other places and times. I saw who I suspected was her boyfriend. I saw things I really didn't need to see. Then I saw a woman who was clearly her mother. She smiled often at her. All of these superfluous memories were interwoven with the main thread, which was that day in Starbucks.

That fateful day.

———

Jasmine is working the register. People come and go. Money is exchanged, credit cards are swiped, gift cards are used. The door opens, and Jasmine looks up and greets the customer, as any good Starbucks employee should.

There she is.

"Welcome to Starbucks," I hear Jasmine say.

Lucy Gleason nods and appears to say something, but Jasmine's wandering mind fills in the gap with an image of her boyfriend riding a dirt bike, shirtless.

Now, Lucy Gleason is waiting in line behind two other people.

Here, Jasmine's memory is fuzzy at best. The snatches that she recalls of Lucy waiting in line are brief and chaotic, and that's to be expected. Still, every now and then, Jasmine's eyes land on Lucy…and for good reason. Lucy is chewing her nails nervously, and looking around. In particular, she's looking up.

She's looking for cameras.

Now, Lucy's head snaps around quickly, looking behind her, and this also catches Jasmine's attention.

In a blur, the two people before Lucy come and go, and now it's her turn to order. Lucy steps up.

"What can we make for you?" asks Jasmine.

Lucy doesn't look her in the eye. Instead, she cracks her neck a little, then reaches back and rubs it. Nervous, stressed. "Just a water for now."

"Sure," says Jasmine cheerily enough. "Can I get you anything else?"

The image in Jasmine's memory is briefly replaced by another face, another time, another customer. That Jasmine has remembered this much from a brief encounter with thousands of customers is amazing enough. This other customer fades away, to be replaced again by Lucy, who is now walking away.

Jasmine briefly watches her go, before the image fades away. It was, of course, where Lucy was clearly going that got my attention.

She had been headed to the bathrooms.

I released Jasmine's hands.

"And that's all I remember," she was saying.

"You can open your eyes now," I said, aware that she was still mostly under the command of my voice, which did little for me, but excited the bitch within me.

Jasmine opened her eyes slowly, and seemed to return to the present. She blinked hard, and then, opened her eyes wide.

"Wow, what happened? I felt like I was asleep—"

"You won't make a scene," I said evenly, keeping my voice low. I could have just as easily thought the words, but we were isolated enough, and there was enough ambient noise that I couldn't have been overheard.

She nodded minutely, blinked slowly, and said, "I really don't remember much. She ordered a water, and then went to the bathroom."

"And you never saw her again?"

"No,"

"Never saw her exit?"

Jasmine shook her head. "If she did, I didn't see it. We don't monitor the bathrooms here. There are no keys or anything. People just come and go, and the bathrooms are around the corner, sort of out of my sight from the cash register."

"Did you see her pick up the water?"

She thought hard, and then shook her head. "I don't remember."

"That's okay," I said. "Thank you."

"Sorry I wasn't of much help," she said. She looked at her cell phone. "I have to get to work. My shift starts soon."

I thanked her and watched her go, all too aware that controlling her had been very, very exciting.

Too exciting.

Chapter Eighteen

I sipped on my water and considered what I'd learned.

Jasmine Calcutta's statement lined up perfectly with what she had given the police. After all, like Henry Gleason, I'd witnessed her experience firsthand.

And what had I witnessed?

Lucy had been nervous, that much was certain. She had looked over her shoulder more than once. She had looked for a camera, too. She hadn't ordered an iced mocha, but I knew that, too. She had told Henry she wanted an iced mocha, and had come in and ordered a water. The iced mochas were, in fact, a ruse. Almost immediately, Lucy had gone straight to the restrooms.

Had she actually made it to the restrooms? Did she meet someone, say, in the short hallway?

There was no way to know, since Jasmine's memory stopped just as Lucy entered the short hallway to the restrooms.

I drummed my long, pointed nails on the mostly clean table. My drumming was a tad louder than I'd intended it to be, so I stopped. Damned, big-ass nails. Finally, I got up and headed to the bathrooms. Knowing they may have been Lucy's final destination, I decided to investigate the bathrooms anew, with renewed vigor and interest.

Lucky me.

There was little spirit activity at Starbucks, outside of the occasional grandparent or parent or friend swinging by a loved one to say hi. Murders and suicides tended to result in real hauntings. Although violent acts didn't result in hauntings, they almost indelibly left their imprint on the environment.

But I saw nothing. No chaotic, staticy energy. Nothing. Normal energy. Peaceful energy. Starbucks energy.

Whatever that meant.

One thing was certain: no violent act had been perpetrated here. No one had been killed or raped or beaten here, as far as I could see.

Although this Starbucks was a little older than others, it still had that hip, industrial, modern vibe that people loved so much. That Starbucks feel, if you will.

The hallway was short, lined with wood paneling and photographs of Huntington Beach Pier. There was a broom closet that had, yes, a broom, a mop and a bucket in it, along with a water heater. No room for a female adult, even a small female adult like Lucy Gleason. I shut the broom closet door and moved on.

To my right was the men's restroom. Directly ahead was the women's. I tried the handle to the women's, unlocked. I stepped inside, feeling more excited than I should have about going into a public bathroom.

———

The bathroom light turned on automatically.

I wasn't sure what I was looking for. The bathroom, of course, looked exactly the same as it had last time. But she had come here last, dammit.

Here, in this bathroom. I was sure of it.

I had seen it!

I noted the shining metal trashcan, the low, sleek toilet, a sink, a mirror and a baby-changing station. I unlatched the baby-changing station, opening and closing the plastic tray. It worked as it should. There was nothing hidden behind it, no secret panel.

With that thought in mind, I checked the mirror carefully; it, too, was sealed to the wall. I could pry it loose and give a look behind it, but what good would that do? The sucker had been on the wall for a long time.

I turned in the small circle. Outside of disappearing down into the toilet, I was at a loss.

Stumped.

Confounded.

I hated that.

I sighed, looked at myself in the mirror, and saw mostly nothing. I had added some quick foundation this evening, eyeliner, just enough so that I would show up in most reflections, most mirrors, most security cameras. However, I could see where I had missed some spots. An empty spot was there on my forehead, as if I had a hole in my head.

I held up my hands...and couldn't see them. I pressed them against the cold mirror, and neither a smudge nor a fingerprint remained.

This was, of course, nothing new to me, other than another reminder to how far I had slipped from the realm of normal...to that of the paranormal.

I sighed and considered where the devil Lucy had gone, and decided to head for the men's bathroom next.

Might as well.

Chapter Nineteen

"Someone's in here," called a man's voice when I tried the handle and found it locked.

Feeling awkward, I leaned a shoulder against the wall opposite the door, folded my arms and waited. While I waited, a middle-aged guy stepped into the hallway, whistling to himself. He stopped whistling, looked at me, looked up at the nameplate on the door, and frowned.

"The women's is broken," I said.

He nodded and slid into line next to me.

"Is it going to be bad in there?" I asked.

He was a balding guy with a nice build. He wore a Lakers tank top and basketball shorts. He chuckled and said, "It's hit or miss."

"Literally," I said.

He grinned. "Something like that. But it's Starbucks, so…"

"So, it's Starbucks clean."

"I'm not sure what that means."

"Neither do I." And since I had nothing better to do, I took a shot in the dark, which might not be any different than what was going on in the men's bathroom. "Weird about that girl disappearing here."

"Oh, right. Heard about that."

"Apparently, she was last seen going into the bathroom."

He raised an eyebrow. "Okay, now you're freaking me out."

I laughed. "Sorry."

"I'm just trying to take a piss here."

"Me, too. But girls call it peeing."

"Yeah, right. Sorry. Didn't mean to—"

"Just busting your balls, bub. So, what do you think happened to that girl?"

"I would say the husband did her in."

"Except the husband never came inside, and she was last seen inside."

"Last seen by who?"

I nodded toward the counter. "One of the girls working the cash register."

"I dunno, man."

"Woman."

"Well, either way, it's a fu—freakin' mystery."

"If you were hired to look into it, where would you begin?"

"Why are you asking?"

I showed him my private investigator's license, complete with a face doused in makeup. "That's why I'm asking."

"Oh, shit. You're a private cop?"

"Yup."

"And you're looking into this?"

"Yup."

"You really don't have to use the bathroom, do you?"

"Nope."

The door opened, and he jumped in front of me and turned back. "'Cause I really do gotta go, um, potty. Sorry!"

And he slammed the door in my face.

———

He came out five minutes later, drying his hands, thank God.

"Hey, I cleaned up in there a little for you."

"You are a good man."

"You have no idea."

"I have a ten-year-old boy and was married for nearly a dozen years. Guys miss. Often."

He laughed and motioned for me to follow him. "Come here, I wanna show you something."

"If I had a nickel for every time a guy at Starbucks told me they wanted to show me something in the bathroom…"

"Just come on, smartass. Check this out."

He led me inside. It was an exact replica of the women's restroom, complete with the baby-changing station. There was, however, one noticeable difference: the smell of urine. Also, there were one, two, three instances of graffiti, although minor at that. A pencil drawing of a man's genitalia here, a pen drawing above the toilet that said "Shit here," complete with an arrow. Helpful.

"So, I was cleaning the floor a little—"

"Cleaning the floor?"

"I have OCD, what can I say? Anyway, I was using a bunch of paper towels, pushing them around with my foot—"

"Why?"

"You seem like a classy chick, and I don't want you to think all guys are slobs."

"That's sweet," I said. "I still think all guys are slobs. All guys, except maybe you."

"Better than nothing," he said.

"I might have to marry you."

He held up his left hand. "Someone beat you to it."

"Oh, damn. Then can I hire you to clean my house?"

"You couldn't afford me."

I laughed. He laughed. I said, "So, what did you want to show me?"

"Well, I was mopping under the sink when my toe hit something."

"Hit what?"

"Watch."

He used his foot to reach under the sink and tap on the wall vent. Nothing happened at first. He tapped again, and the vent fell away, hanging in place by a single screw.

"Voila," he said, and pointed.

I saw it, too.

It was an opening behind the wall.

An opening big enough for a very small person.

"Please tell me there's not a dead body in there," I said. Of course, the idea of a dead body in there didn't disturb me at all. If anything, it intrigued me mightily.

"I checked, it's empty."

"Big enough to hold a person?"

"You tell me."

"Give me some room," I said, and dropped down to my knees. "Is the door locked behind us?"

"Let me check." He checked. "Yes."

"Good," I said from under the sink. I felt my excitement rising. At least the floor was semi-clean, thanks to Mr. OCD.

I used my index finger to pry loose the remaining screw holding the vent in place. My nails might look hideous, but they did occasionally serve a purpose. I set the vent aside and peered into the dark opening. Behind me, Mr. Clean was peering over my shoulder, too.

"Seems small," he said.

I studied the dimensions, my voice echoing within the dusty, dark opening. "I could fit."

"I sure as hell couldn't."

"You're also not a missing housewife who is, I think, even smaller than me."

"Except she's not in there."

"Good point," I said. I stood suddenly and shoved Captain Obvious hard against the bathroom wall, somewhere between the sink and the door. I pinned him to the wall.

"Hey, what the fu—"

I said, "You will forget me, the bathroom, and especially the vent. Oh, and you will forget me feeding from you, as well."

"I...okay."

I took his hand, made a slit across the inside of his wrist, and drank deeply from the man, all while he stared down at me in dumbfounded shock. I stared up at him, looking, I'm sure, like the ghoul that I knew I was.

When I had drunk my fill—a bloody latte, if you will—I released his hand.

"Now," I said, wiping the corners of my mouth and licking my own fingers. "You will forget all of this." I looked at his wrist, which was already healing nicely. "Now, go."

And he went, confused, blinking rapidly. At the open door, he looked back at me once, blinked fast, and then was gone.

Now, said a voice in my head, a voice that didn't belong to me. *That wasn't so hard, was it?*

No, I thought. *Not hard at all.*

CHAPTER TWENTY

I was sitting with Detective Sharp at a Carl's Jr., a popular fast food chain here in Southern California. At least, it was popular to flesh-eating mortals, of which there were, apparently, many.

Detective Sharp was looking at me curiously as he worked his way through a hamburger that would have fed my entire family. Or would have fed them back in the day. The burger was called the Six-Dollar Burger. The catch being, of course, was that it was only $3.95. Brilliant advertising. You're getting more than what you're paying for. It also implied that you were getting a restaurant-quality burger without the restaurant price.

"You're expecting me to believe that she hid in a vent in the men's bathroom?" said the detective, after a few minutes of chewing. He had mostly swallowed when he spoke.

"Maybe not the men's bathroom," I said. "The women's has an identical vent under the sink."

He took another healthy bite from his burger. Admittedly, it looked like a six-dollar burger. It also looked delicious. What I wouldn't give to—

"Then go buy one," said Sharp.

Oops. He'd read my mind. I guess the detective and I were getting a little closer. I immediately placed my internal wall around me.

I said, "I dunno. Six bucks seems too much for a burger..."

"They're not really six bucks," said Sharp. "They're like three ninety-five or something. Four bucks."

I shook my head. "Says right there on the sign. Six bucks."

"It's called a six-dollar burger, but it's really four bucks."

"I'm so confused."

"Look, it's not really six—oh, you're fucking with me."

"Ya think?"

"Screw you, Samantha Moon," he said, but laughed.

I said, "Looks good, but I'm on a diet."

"What kind of diet?"

"Liquid diet."

"Suit yourself, but this is damn good."

"I'll remember it for next time. The six-dollar burger that isn't six dollars."

He shook his head, reached for some fries. "So, these vents in the bathrooms…you think a woman could fit in them?"

I nodded. "I know I could, but not comfortably, and I wouldn't want to stay in there long—or at all. But yeah."

"And, is it safe to assume there was no woman in it now, dead or otherwise?"

"It's safe to assume it."

"Any indication that someone had, you know, been in it?"

"Nothing that I could visually confirm. Her fingerprints might be there, though."

"Yours, too, I assume."

I didn't, of course, leave fingerprints behind anymore. To do so implied I had oils on my skin, oils that transferred from my skin to say, metal. No such oils existed in me. No, I hadn't seen any signs of prints, but that was often hard to tell with the naked eye. Even a supernatural naked eye.

I said, "I was careful not to leave any prints behind. My guess, though, is that she would have cleaned it thoroughly."

"Why?"

"To leave no sign. To give the illusion that she truly disappeared."

"Not to mention, she was in a bathroom. She might have had plenty of time to clean up behind her."

"There's that," I said.

"So, what do you want me to do?" he asked.

"You know what to do," I said.

He shook his head. He didn't like it. The idea seemed preposterous to him, but he finally acquiesced. "Fine. I'll send a team over, ASAP. Hell, we've got nothing else to go on." He paused, set down his burger. "Was there any sign of force?"

"No sign of force. No blood that I could see. No scrape marks, no hair, nothing left behind."

"So, you're saying she went in there willingly?"

"That would be my guess," I said.

"This is getting crazier and crazier."

"I do crazy well."

"Well, I don't. I like things neat. I like things explainable. I like things to make sense. This makes no sense."

"Not now," I said. "But it might. Someday."

He sighed and picked up his burger.

I tried not to drool.

Chapter Twenty-one

Kingsley and I were having dinner.

While he ate and I slurped idly at the blood that pooled around my very rare steak, I found myself eyeballing the cute waiter. I wondered what I would say to lure him into the bathroom, since that had worked so well back at the Starbucks. That I still hadn't felt guilty about attacking him should have concerned me, but it didn't.

"You've got that look in your eye, Samantha Moon," said Kingsley. He had just bitten into a healthy bite of steak, and so, I had the pleasure of seeing the half-masticated meat in his mouth. He might be a power attorney during the day, but he was all animal at night. At least, around me. Good thing he couldn't read my thoughts. Most immortals couldn't.

"I imagine I do."

"You don't even hide it now? Tsk-tsk. How far you have fallen."

"Hide who I am?"

He set his fork down and momentarily paused in his chewing. Then he reached for a frosted glass of beer and drained it. Yeah, the man was an animal. Had we been dining in his spacious home, he would have wiped the back of his hand across his mouth. Instead, he used a napkin, and didn't seem happy about it.

"Well, the Samantha I know and love was a fighter. She didn't give into the cravings."

"Well, that Samantha was weak."

"I beg to differ. She was the strongest I'd ever seen. Which is why I loved her…and love her still to this day."

The demon within me recoiled at his words. "You're making me sick." Had I said those words, or had *she?*

"The Samantha that I know and love is a mom, a friend, a damn fine investigator, and, most of all, unshakeable in her belief in the inherent good within herself. Within most of us."

The big oaf was pissing me off now. Royally pissing me off. Who the fuck was he to judge me?

"The Samantha I know would have listened to criticism with an open mind. She wouldn't be fighting herself, even now, from leaping over the table and strangling me in public."

"I hate you," I said.

"No, you don't, Sam. The creature within you hates me. Hates love. Hates all that is good in your life."

"You're not good in my life. You're not good for me at all. You're a fucking cheater."

I had raised my voice. People were staring at us. Kingsley didn't care. He reached across the table and took my hand. Or tried to. Instead, faster than I had any right to move, faster than even he was prepared for, I flipped my fork around, caught it in mid-air, and drove it down through the back of his hand, impaling him and it to the wooden table.

"Go fuck yourself, asshole," I said, and got up and left.

Behind me, someone screamed.

———

We were in his oversized SUV.

I'd been crying for the past twenty minutes while Kingsley wrapped his meaty arms around me and rubbed my shoulders.

Had he been able to read my mind, he would have known what was going on, why I had lashed out, and why I had impaled his hand to the table. Then he could have explained it all to me, because I still didn't know what the hell had happened.

When the waterworks were finally done, and I was reduced to a sniffling mess, I heard a curious sound.

It was chuckling.

Kingsley was laughing to himself, even as he continued rubbing my shoulder—yes, with the very hand that I had stabbed, no less.

"What's so funny?" I asked looking up. We were in the Mulberry Street parking lot, which was part of a bigger chain of parking lots for lots of other local businesses. Many of the cars parked near the restaurant had left quickly over the past twenty minutes.

I suspected I knew why.

"You should have seen the looks on their faces," said Kingsley, and now he was chuckling louder. "One woman—" and now, Kingsley quit rubbing my shoulders, and retracted his hand. He needed his hands because he was now holding his belly. "One woman fainted right there in the restaurant." Now, Kingsley was wheezing, fighting for breath.

Damn it, his booming laughter was infectious. Hell, the whole SUV was shaking. I found myself giggling at first. Mostly, I was laughing at *him*.

"She, literally," he gasped, tears streaming down his face, "toppled right out of her chair—*splat* on the floor."

And now, for the next two minutes or so, Kingsley was laughing so hard that he couldn't speak. Worse, I found myself laughing, as well. Not quite as hard as Kingsley.

"And then, and then she looks up from the floor—" Kingsley didn't sound like Kingsley. He sounded like a wheezing, asthmatic school kid. He tried again. "And then, she looks up from the floor just as I pull the fork out of my hand—and faints again."

And now, I lost it again, completely and totally, gasping and kicking his feet. I got myself under control a lot faster than he did. I said, "That poor lady. Is she okay?"

"Yes," he said, still laughing. "The floor had carpet."

That set him off again, and I waited for him to get some control over himself. "Okay," he said, gasping, gulping air. "I think I'm done. But no guarantees."

I shook my head. "How's your hand?"

"Ah, hell, it's fine. You know that."

"Jesus, it wasn't silver was it?"

"Naw, and even if it was, it wouldn't have done any real harm."

"I'm not sure what got into me. I'm sorry."

"Oh, I know what got in you, Sam. Or what's in you now, more accurately." Kingsley sat back and wiped his eyes. That he filled the seat to overflowing went without saying. "It's in me, too. Or something similar."

"Except yours comes out each month," I said.

"Yes," said Kingsley. "And that seems sufficient for it for now."

"She wants to possess me fully. That's her goal. I know it. I can feel it."

Kingsley nodded, suddenly somber, although his eyes still twinkled in the ambient lights.

"It's usually the way, Sam."

"Then how do vampires fight their own demons?" I asked.

Kingsley looked at me sideways, looked at me long and hard, his thick hair piled up on his beefy shoulders. "Most don't, Sam. Most succumb."

"I didn't want to hear that."

"But some also come to an agreement, I think."

"What type of agreement?" I asked.

"They let the inner demon out, so to speak. But only sometimes."

"They let it control them?"

"Yes. For some, it's the only way to have peace."

"She's not controlling me," I said. "Not ever. This one, this one is different. Powerful. She's looking for a crack. All she needs is a crack. If she finds it...I don't think I'll ever come back."

Kingsley nodded, listening, still breathing hard from his outburst. "Some demons are more powerful than others. Some have other agendas."

"What does that mean?"

"She might have a reason to be inside you, whatever that might be."

"Like she picked me, on purpose?"

"Maybe, Sam. I don't know. But trust your instincts. Don't let her out, fight her."

"I'm trying." I took in some air. "I mean, I have to. I have kids, a career. I have a sister, a family. I can't let this…psychotic bitch… loose. Who knows what the hell would happen?"

"Agreed," he said.

"I have no idea what she is capable of, who she might hurt. I have no idea if I would ever be me again."

"I understand, Sam. Perhaps better than most. I, too, have a fear that I may never return. That I would stay chained to the walls of my own mind."

I shook my head. "Fuck her. She's not going to win. She's not getting out. Ever."

He reached over and gripped my hand tightly. I let him, and we held hands like that in his oversized SUV, an SUV that just might have been tilting slightly to one side—his side. After a long moment, he said, "I think we might need to find a new restaurant."

"I think so, too."

"Do you want to come over tonight?"

"We're friends, remember?"

"Friends can still come over."

"I suspect your intentions are more than friendly."

"My only intention is to hold you tight."

"I need to go," I said, and attempted to pull free, but his big, ogre-like hands anchored mine.

"I still love you, Sam," he said, "and I'm sorry for hurting you."

I worked my hands free.

"I need to go," I said, and left his SUV.

Chapter Twenty-two

We were at Hero's.

No, it wasn't the same without the cute bartender with the shark teeth hanging around his neck, but it was still our hangout. It was also one of the few places where my sister and I got to relax together. Where we could be ourselves. In hushed voices, of course. No kids. No men. No work. Just sisters. That one was mortal and one was immortal was irrelevant. Not here, not in this place. A safe place.

That one sister got *mortal* and *immortal* confused was just, well, plain cute.

Only this time, Mary Lou wasn't saying much. We were sitting in the far corner along the crowded bar, where we usually sat. A post separated us from the person next to us, which was perfect.

"You're still mad," I said. We were both nearly halfway through our first glasses of wine and she still hadn't said much. In fact, I was pretty certain she hadn't said a thing...or looked at me for that matter.

Seeing her now, the way she set her jaw, the way her left knee bounced agitatedly, reminded me our fights when we were young. Mary Lou could hold a grudge with the best of them. It was always, always, my job to break the ice. I either broke it...or I got the jaw and knee business.

"How was your day?" I asked. I didn't want the jaw or knee business. I needed my big sister. *Badly.*

"Fine."

"Anything exciting happen at work?"

"No."

"You're telling me, in that big insurance office of yours, not even one person had a birthday today?"

"No, Sam."

"Well, any meltdowns?" I asked. "Someone's always having a meltdown at your—"

"No, Sam."

"Where did you go for lunch?"

"I didn't eat lunch."

"You should really eat lunch."

"Oh my God, you're driving me crazy."

"That's what sisters do."

"No, they don't. And they especially don't keep secrets from each other."

"Can you trust me when I say that there are some secrets you might want me to keep from you?"

She looked at me, that jawline of her still rippling. If she wasn't careful, she might crack a molar. That she didn't catch that thought was, of course, the source of her irritation. Mary Lou and I had always been close. Best friends throughout our lives. Sometimes, we were closer than other times. But always, always, she was there for me.

Now, of course, she felt left out, and I didn't blame her.

"We weren't keeping secrets from you, Mary Lou."

"Then you were making fun of me, laughing at me behind my back, or inside your heads or whatever."

"We weren't laughing at you, either," I said. At least, I didn't think we were. Truth was, how the heck was I supposed to remember an off-the-cuff telepathic conversation I'd had with Allison?

"Then why do you do it?"

"I guess we did it because we can. It's easy and fast—"

"And rude."

"And rude, yes."

"But you do it anyway, even when it makes other people feel uncomfortable."

"What can I say, Mary Lou? I'm sorry. I'm learning how to be a better freak."

She looked at me, and finally unhinged her jaw, to the great relief of her molars. She instantly looked prettier, and more relaxed. Too bad she couldn't read *that* thought.

"You're not a freak, Sam. Maybe a little inconsiderate, but not a freak."

"Remember, this is still all new to me. I hadn't known there was a telepathic etiquette."

"Well, there is. At least around me."

"Just know that I will always try to include you in the conversation, but there are going to be times when thoughts slip through, thoughts that don't always need to be vocalized."

She set her jaw, looked away. "I'm not sure how I feel about that."

"It's the best I can offer."

She didn't like it; mostly, she didn't like being left out. I scooted my stool closer to hers, and put my arm around her shoulders, similar to what Kingsley had done with me not too long ago.

I said, "I don't know why I am the way I am, or do the things I do. I don't know who makes the rules or why there are, in fact, any rules. But one such rule is that I can't communicate with family members telepathically. You're as family as it gets. It still doesn't mean I don't love you, and it doesn't mean I'm closer with Allison than I am with you. If anything, Allison annoys me to no end."

"She is kind of annoying."

"But she has a big heart," I said. "And, well, there's something special going on with her."

"Dare I ask?"

"Maybe you shouldn't."

"Okay, fine. But I still don't have to like any of this."

"Trust me, I don't like any of it either. For instance, right now I smell chicken wings and fries and beer, and they're driving me crazy."

She looked at me, and then gave me a half smile. "You're still pretending to be a vampire, huh?"

"I make a good vampire," I said.

She studied me for a moment, and then leaned her head toward mine. I did the same, and we touched heads and held hands.

"Yes, you do," she said. "Lord help me, you do."

Chapter Twenty-three

I was flying.

That was something else that I did well. Of course, I had some help in the flying department. I'd recently gone for quite an excursion. In fact, it was a trip that I would never forget, ever. And forever is a very long time for a vampire.

As I flew now, I looked up into the sky, to the crescent moon high above...and smiled. Yes, it had been quite a journey, and I had seen sights that few people would ever see.

Speaking of which, I was eager to try my newfound talent again...a talent that enabled me to go just about anywhere I wanted, at any time.

Boy, did it.

A few minutes prior to my takeoff, as I sat in my minivan overlooking the Pacific Ocean near the Ritz Carlton in Laguna—my favorite launching point, if you will—I had studied pictures of a particular spot on earth, a spot I was certain would be cloaked in the darkness of night...but still accessible to me and only me.

I had never been to this place. In fact, I had never even been to the state.

Then again, I hadn't been to the moon either, and look at how that had turned out.

Pretty damn well, I thought. *Thank you again Talos.*

You're welcome, Sam, came a reply deep within me.

Yet another voice inside my head, I thought. Maybe all the voices were just further proof that I was crazier than a shoeshine in a shitstorm, as my grandpa used to say.

I continued flapping my wings. That such a giant, winged creature had human parents was almost laughable. But I wasn't, of course, the giant winged creature, was I?

Not quite. The creature was, in fact, a real creature who lived in a parallel universe, who used this chance to come to me, to help me, to instruct me.

To fly with me.

Are you ready, Talos, I thought.

For you, Samantha, always.

Now that just might be the sweetest thing a giant, flying bat has ever said to me.

He chuckled lightly.

I grinned inwardly, and brought up the image of the single flame, which I saw clearly in my mind's eye. The flame, which usually held either the image of Talos or me, was presently empty. Now, I summoned the image of a snowy peak located in the far, far north. Alaska to be exact. Mount McKinley, to be even more exact.

As I flew now, as the wind swept over me and I beat my great wings, I focused on the image in the flame, the snow-swept mountain peak...

And felt myself rushing toward it.

Faster and faster...

Chapter Twenty-four

I gasped and opened my eyes.

Wind buffeted me. Cold, powerful wind. So cold that even I felt its chill, although it didn't bother me much. Or, rather, it didn't bother the beast I had become. Its hide was thick and impenetrable.

Not quite, Samantha Moon. I can still be hurt, said the voice deep within me. *You would do well to remember that.*

Point taken, I thought. *Now, can I enjoy my vacation?*

As you wish.

I surveyed the landscape before me. It was a helluva landscape— and, if the creature could smile, it would be doing so now; it couldn't, so I settled for an inward smile instead.

I was high up on a frozen rocky crag. In fact, I wasn't very far from the peak itself, which was about where I had tried to "land," as I'd come to think of this last step. It was true night, and the crescent moon was farther to the south, but there it was, shining down, along with, exactly, one trillion stars, all winking at me, the flirts. I was really here. I was not in Southern California, but in the far north, far away from it all.

In a blink of an eye. I could, it seemed, go just about anywhere, including the moon. I had a thought. *Talos, could I someday return home with you?*

Not yet, Sam. You would need a visual image to hold onto. You need to see clearly where you will "land" as you put it.

But you could help me to see? I asked.

Yes, Sam. Someday.

I nodded, pleased, thrilled. That I was now high upon a forgotten crag in the dead of night, surrounded by wind and snow and the distant howl of something forlorn and forgotten, was exhilarating. I didn't belong up here. I shouldn't have been up here. But here I was. A mother of two. A private investigator, a sister, a daughter. Sitting high atop a frozen piece of rock at the far north of nowhere. Out of sight, out of mind. Alone and happy.

I didn't want to think. I didn't want to feel. I didn't want to worry. I just wanted to exist. I just wanted to *be*.

And so I sat on the rocky overhang, my great talons clinging to the rock edge, even as snow and ice began to form around them.

Ice wasn't much of a match for the great beast I had become. Neither were these extreme conditions. The beast laughed at arctic blasts of frozen air. At least, I think it did. I know I did.

Now, I tucked my wings in tight and sat high upon the world, looking down into swirling mists and billowing gusts.

And I was happy.

Chapter Twenty-five

The wonders of the Internet.

I was deemed an asset by Detective Sharp's bosses and he was given the green light to email me two weeks' worth of surveillance video in heavily encrypted, password-protected files.

A busy homicide detective didn't have time to go through two weeks' worth of surveillance tape. Hell, even a week's worth of surveillance tape, fast-forwarded, is still three or four days of mind-numbing work. Luckily, my mind didn't get numb, and my back didn't hurt, and I could sit still for hours on end without peeing or eating or drinking.

Of course, the good detective with the pointed nose and chin didn't know that.

Still, I was the best candidate for the job, and I threw myself into it as soon as I plugged in the various passwords, and opened the files.

They were separated into days, and they had been provided by Starbucks's own security team, their loss-prevention department. Coffee was serious business, after all.

Of course, this "loss" didn't look good on Starbucks either. I knew they had been cooperative in helping the police, but there was only so much a company could do. Or anyone could do.

Hopefully, I could do a little more.

I got to it, settling in for the night.

The next day, I had made the kids mac n' cheese for dinner. Again. One of my four or five go-to dinners. Tonight would be Anthony's second boxing lesson with Jacky, and it had been all the boy could talk about on the drive to school, when I picked them up, and all through dinner. He had even completely forgotten to torment his sister, which was surely a sign of the impending apocalypse.

It was also a Monday night, which meant, of course, *The Voice.* Tammy ate up the bromance between Adam and Blake. And since Usher reminded me a bit of Russell, my most recent of flames, I tended to be an Usher fan. And a Shakira fan. Just loved her and her accent. With that said, there was no way in hell we were prying Tammy away from that TV. At least, not tonight. Or tomorrow, which were *The Voice* results. Damn Adam and his delicious smile. And Blake with those *ah, shucks* dimples.

Anyway, I had an hour to kill before heading out to Jacky's gym, and I killed it the best way I knew how, by plopping down in front of my computer screen and working my way through the rest of that first day of surveillance, the day Lucy Gleason had gone missing.

I was in my office, with the door closed, but I could still hear Anthony in his room, working on his footwork, breathing through his nose. He was probably quickly mastering all that Jacky had already taught him. I was prepared to watch Jacky's mind get blown tonight.

On the screen before me, the video played and customer after customer came and went. Cars came and went. Starbucks, from all appearances, appeared to be a rather profitable establishment.

As I scanned the many faces in fast-forward, Archibald Maximus's words suddenly came to me again:

"Your son's reaction to the medallion was unexpected."

"And you suspect...something else might be involved?"

"In a word, yes."

These words had been bothering me ever since they were first uttered by the ageless Librarian. What the devil did he mean? Who the hell might also be involved with my son?

I considered Jacky. My son and Jacky clearly had a bond that went beyond time, but I didn't think that was who—or what—the Librarian had been referring to.

I pushed the worry out of my mind as best as I could and went back to the video. Time slipped past, almost as fast as the people on the screen in front of me, who were depositing their hard-earned money into the bank of Starbucks in exchange for slightly burnt coffee and that Starbucks experience.

I had the video going at two times the speed, not so slow as to be real-time, but not so fast as to miss anything suspicious. Yesterday, I had started the video where I had left off with Detective Sharp. Now, it was getting past closing time, and the steady flow of customers dwindled, and then finally stopped. A few minutes later, I watched all the lights turn out. A few of the workers talked in a small huddle in the parking lot, no doubt talking about the strange day in which the lady disappeared and the cops came. And then they were gone and Starbucks was finally, mercifully dark.

"Okay, Mom, time to go!"

Only my son could sneak up on me. How he had managed to open the door without me hearing it, I didn't know. I squeaked and jumped and he grinned from the open office door.

"You have to quit doing that, Anthony."

"Doing what?" he asked, not so innocently.

"Sneaking up on me."

"But I thought you were a vampire with bat ears!" he laughed, and from down the hallway, I heard Tammy laugh, too. Great, now I was the butt of their joke.

"Just knock next time, okay?"

"Okay, sheesh!"

"Don't sheesh me."

"Shee—"

"Anthony, I'm warning you."

"Fine. Let's go already. *Please*."

"Give me a minute. And by give me a minute, I don't mean standing in my doorway and looking at me that way."

"What way?"

"Anthony…"

"Fine."

He turned and left, but only stepped a few feet into the hallway. I could still see his shoulder. "Better?" he said.

I sighed and was just about to pause the video when I saw something interesting.

A light had turned on, from deep within the coffee shop. And, if I had to guess, it had turned on down the hallway, where the bathrooms were.

And then it turned off again.

And all was quiet.

"Mom! Jacky's waiting!"

I rolled my eyes, and shut down my computer, making a mental note to return to this spot in the video.

Chapter Twenty-six

I got a quick workout in, too.

I was fairly certain I didn't need to work out. I was fairly certain that my heightened skills just sort of "kick in" when necessary. Of course, working out made me feel normal. And feeling normal, I knew, was half the battle to fighting the demon within. Feeling human meant keeping the demon at bay for another day.

Now I worked on a punching bag at about half speed. Not too long ago, I watched Captain America in *The Avengers* send a punching bag sailing clear across the gym. Once, I'd knocked the punching bag clear off the chain, sending it tumbling a few feet. But flying across the room? Not so much. I'd leave that for the movies. I threw a final punch, sending the bag swinging, and then grabbed my towel.

I often wondered what Jacky thought of me. He, better than most, knew there was something odd about me. If being freakishly strong was odd.

And it was.

To date, I hadn't gotten very far into his thoughts, nor had I tried. I knew Jacky's own brain was muddled from years of taking hits. Punch drunk, they called it. He had brain damage, of that I knew for sure, and I thought his damage was sufficient enough for me to not gain much access.

It was just as well. Some people could keep their secrets.

Now, as I sat on the floor with my back against the wall, my towel around me, and the punching bag still swinging next to me, I watched the old Irishman work with my son, one on one, in the ring.

278

It was late, and so the gym was mostly empty. I checked the time on my cell. Almost closing time, in fact. Jacky had said that was okay. He was going to work with my son after hours, if it was all right with me. I told him I specialized in after hours. He gave me an odd look and shook his head. I got that a lot.

Now, as I sat and watched my son go over the footwork and hand-work, I marveled again at my boy's skill. He was only ten, but he already moved with the ease and precision of a seasoned fighter. His punches were accurate, fierce, rapid-fire. I saw Jacky wincing here and there as he held up the practice mitts.

As I watched my son, as the minutes slipped past and I was almost lulled into a meditative state by the staccato sound of his punches, all punctuated by Jacky's Irish twang, a twang I never got tired of hear-ing, I saw something out of my peripheral vision, something that existed not quite in this world. It was standing near the gym's now-closed front door.

No, not a ghost. It was something else.

An angel.

It was Ishmael.

Chapter Twenty-seven

As I approached the angel, it all started making sense to me, or some of it. Okay, maybe none of it, but I knew the angel, Ishmael, would have some answers. He'd better.

He saw me coming and glanced over at me. Then again, I suspected he knew I would come, since he had partially revealed himself to me now. He was also one of the few supernatural beings who had access to my thoughts. No surprise there, since he had once been my guardian angel.

At the door, I said to him, under my breath, "Let's talk outside."

I turned the handle and two things happened simultaneously: something snapped loudly, and Jacky was calling to me.

"The door's locked, Sam—ah, bloody hell."

"Oopsie," I said, holding up the broken handle. Yeah, I'd snapped the thing clean off. Old locks and a pissed-off vampire mama didn't go well together. "Sorry."

"You broke it," he said, staring at me from the corner of the ring. A single spotlight shone down on him and my son. Behind them, at the back of the gym, a young kid was mopping the floor. Another was wiping down the equipment. Other than that, the place was empty. That is, if you didn't count the seven-foot angel glowing next to me. And I didn't, since the others didn't seem to be able to see him, including my son. "You broke it," said the retired boxer again, this time with more awe in his voice. "Right off the goddamn door."

"I said 'oopsie.'"

"You're a freak, Sam."

280

"I know."

"And so is your son," he said, but as he said it, he turned and mussed Anthony's hair, and, for the moment, the Irishman forgot about his broken door handle. Anthony grinned from ear to ear, something he did far too little of.

Once outside, I tossed the broken handle aside, and told the seven-foot giant to follow me.

Chapter Twenty-eight

I led him to an alley next to the gym.

"Start talking," I said, turning around, facing him. That I was ordering around my one-time guardian angel was further evidence of my descent into madness. Or further evidence that the world really is bigger and more fantastic than I'd ever dreamed possible.

"You're not mad, Sam."

"Says the seven-foot glowing angel."

"I'm here, Sam, and so are you."

"Fine, whatever. Now tell me what the devil you're doing here. And, yes, I said devil to an angel. Except, of course, we both know what kind of angel you are."

He was, of course, of the *fallen* variety. Recently fallen, for that matter. That he had fallen because of me—or, rather, because of his misguided love for me—was a different story.

"Yes, Sam. I know what you think of me. I know you blame me for everything, but I would like to remind you that your son is in there boxing with Jacky because of what I did."

"Or didn't do," I said.

He didn't respond. My "guardian angel" had permitted me to be attacked on that fateful night eight years ago. He had looked the other way while a very old vampire had sought me out for reasons still unknown to me. Sought me out, hunted me down, take your pick. I knew now that the act wasn't random. And my guardian angel, I suspected, had played a role in it.

"I'm not as devious as you make me seem, Sam. I was aware of the interest in you."

"And you saw an opportunity."

He was beautiful. Too beautiful. Too perfect. Long, silver hair. Shoulders as wide as Kingsley's. A faint, silvery glow surrounding him. When I'd first met him, he had glowed more. His luster was wearing off, the further he dropped.

"I am not evil, Sam."

"Never said you were. But if I had to guess, you've inched a little closer to the dark side since last we spoke."

"There is no dark side, Sam. It is the same side, Sam. We are all from God. We are all one."

"Fine, whatever. Tell me, what the fuck are you doing with my son?"

"I'm protecting him, Sam."

I nearly snorted. "What do you mean?"

"Think back, Sam. Back to when you saved your boy by turning him into something he wasn't, something immortal—"

It hit me suddenly. "He lost his own guardian angel."

"Indeed, Sam."

"But…" I wanted to refute his statement. I wanted to tell him this was all ridiculous. That guardian angels weren't real. That those were fairy tales that mothers told their children to give them comfort at night.

Except.

Except that I was standing next to such a creature. A beautiful creature, at that. And what, exactly, were guardian angels? How did they work? Who assigned them? How did they know when to protect you…and when not to protect you? Obviously, there were a lot of people getting hurt and killed in this world. Were all the guardian angels derelict in their duties?

"All good questions, Sam."

"Either someone starts answering," I said. "Or I'm going to start knocking some heads."

Ishmael gave me a rare smile. His mannerisms and gestures were…off. He was not used to holding a normal conversation. I suspected most of his existence had been spent observing humans, but rarely participating, rarely interacting. The truth was, I didn't know the extent of his abilities. He had told me he could save me from my vampirism. I wondered if that were true. There was so much I didn't know about him.

"You have lots of questions, Samantha. Perhaps we should start small."

"Perhaps you should start by telling me why you're interested in my son."

He didn't answer immediately. Not because he was gathering his thoughts, or trying to determine how much to tell me, or not tell me. No, he didn't answer me immediately because he was staring at me, through me. Deep into me.

So weird, I thought.

Finally, after an uncomfortable silence, he said, "I made an egregious mistake that night, Sam. I could have saved you. I could have directed you to go elsewhere."

"Directed me how?"

"With an impulse, with a call from a friend, with a feeling of uncertainty. I could have done something, anything, to save you from what was coming. From what I knew was waiting for you."

"But you didn't," I said, knowing the answer, of course. Knowing it all too well.

"I knew my bond would be broken with you. My covenant, if you will."

"And so you allowed me to be attacked."

"Yes, Sam. I did it—"

"I know why you did it," I said. "You've told me before. Now I want to know why other guardians for other people sit back and watch their own charges be harmed. Why? I understand you made a choice to allow me to be forever changed. But why are others doing this? Why are others allowing their humans to be harmed? Why, dammit?"

"The reasons, Samantha, are far-reaching and complicated and involve universal laws of attraction and karma, all wrapped around past lives and previous agreements."

"Agreements?"

"Yes, Sam. Believe it or not, there are some who have an agreement to kill another. Just as there are some who have an agreement to love another, or to raise another, or to help another."

"I don't believe it," I said. "I just...no, that's crazy talk."

"Perhaps, Sam. But it's true."

"Fucking nuts, if you ask me."

"I agree. But I did not create the world, Sam, or its rules. I only tried to uphold them."

"And failed miserably," I added.

He gazed at me for a long time. "Yes, Samantha. If you choose to see it that way. Yes, I failed you."

"So, I wasn't supposed to be changed that night? I had no past agreement with this vampire who changed me?"

"No, Samantha. You were to be diverted that night. I was to save you."

"Then fuck you."

He looked pained, which was a rarity for him, too. In fact, any expression of emotion was a rarity for him. Ishmael the Angel was not big on emoting. I didn't think he had much use, in fact, for expressions. Any work he'd done had been from the spiritual realm, the spiritual levels, out of sight and out of mind of mankind.

I wasn't sure where Ishmael ranked in the grand scheme of things. I wasn't sure how he filled his days and nights, where he lived, who he hung out with, or who he watched over. I didn't know if there were, say, angel bars where he knocked back some drinks with friends during their down times. I wasn't sure where in the world he lived. This world, the next world, a world in-between?

"A lot of questions, Samantha Moon," he said, reading my mind. "But just know that I am not very different from you. I am a creature of the same Source, the same God. We all are. I wasn't created to evolve. I was created to help."

"But you didn't help," I said. "At least, not me."

"No, Sam. I also wasn't created to love. Not in human terms. Not in romantic terms. But I do. I love you."

285

I couldn't speak. I didn't know what to say. These days, Ishmael rarely made an appearance, although I would sometimes catch him watching me from afar. That he had turned his attention to my son was news to me. But not surprisingly so. He could exist in a realm beyond even my eyes, so he could literally be anywhere.

And then it hit me like a ton of bricks.

"It's you," I said suddenly. "It's you who is giving my son his great strength."

The angel cocked his head to one side. "Yes, Sam."

"So, his strength is not from some latent…" I couldn't find the right words. I was so flabbergasted, frazzled, all the "f" words.

"The latent effect of the vampirism? No, Sam. Those effects departed the moment he was rendered back into a human. Just as his own guardian angel was released the moment he was turned into a vampire."

"Ah, fuck," I said, and found myself circling in the narrow alley-way. Fullerton isn't a big city, at least, not by big city standards. But it did have a popping downtown, and people were moving past the alley opening. Few saw me, and fewer still would see Ishmael looming over me.

I shook my hands, then ran them through my hair. Then I spun on Ishmael, and shoved him hard against the far wall. He flew back, hitting it with a physical force I wasn't expecting. The old building veritably shook.

"What did you do to my son, goddammit? What the fuck did you do to my son?"

"I gave him the edge he will need, Sam, to exist in this life without help."

"He has help from me—"

"No, Sam. Not even you can be with him at all times. Not like his true guardian angel."

"This is really, really fucked up," I said, and found myself circling the alley, shaking my hands, wanting to simultaneously smash the oversized glow stick's head into the brick wall, but needing to hear him out, too. "So, what have you done to my son? What exactly?"

"I gave him strength, Sam."

"But how?"

"I gave him some of me."

I was feeling physically ill, for the first time in a long time. "Is that why your glow has…"

"Diminished? Yes, Sam. That, and for other reasons."

I knew the other reasons, of course. I said, "So, what's going to happen to my son?"

"He will continue to have great strength, which will only increase, but not excessively so. He will, in essence, be able to take care of himself when needed."

"That's all well and dandy, but strength only goes so far."

"Your son, while not immortal, will live a long life."

"How long?"

"That remains to be seen, but longer than most."

"And what if he's…" Except I couldn't bring myself to finish the thought.

"Wounded or sick? He will heal faster than others, Sam. It will take a lot to mortally wound your son. He should be immune to most disease."

That choked me up, and I was, for the first time, grateful to Ishmael. "Thank you," I said.

He nodded once…and disappeared.

Chapter Twenty-nine

Three days later...

And I was still glued to my computer screen, watching the video feeds, hour after hour, day after day. Sometimes, I watched in real time, sometimes, at 2x the speed. I'd spent most of my free time in here, in front of my computer, and had I been mortal, my back would have been aching, my ass would have been hurt and my eyes would have been crossed.

I was none of these; mostly, I was just bored.

Except...except one thing that kept me coming back for more.

The light.

A soft, muted half-light, it still occasionally turned on in the middle of the night, often at different times and often for varying lengths. Where the light came from, I didn't know. But there it was.

There was no good reason why the light would turn on and off. My guess was, it was a smaller light deeper within the cafe. Perhaps a refrigerator light. Or a freezer light.

Two days ago, I had called the Starbucks manager and asked what type of premise security system they had. She told me she wasn't at liberty to divulge that. I almost tested whether or not I could compel her over the phone line. Instead, I called Detective Sharp and had him ask her the same question, plus a few follow-up questions. Apparently, she was at liberty to tell him. Cops get all the breaks. The Starbucks system was pretty basic. Alarm goes off if anything is broken into. No interior motion detectors. No light on timers.

Detective Sharp next wanted to know what I had found. I told him I would tell him when I knew more. He said that wasn't good enough and started to come down on me. I told him he would be the first to know as soon as I had something concrete. He didn't like it, but most cops didn't like being told what to do by private investigators. I reminded him that we were on the same team. I nearly reminded him that I was kind of cute, but luckily, he changed the subject.

"We didn't find any prints," he said.

"You checked both vents."

"Of course. They're both clean."

"She wiped them," I said. "She had the time to clean up after herself."

"If she was there."

"It's the only thing that makes sense."

"The crime scene guys are still laughing at me," he said.

"You are kind of funny-looking."

"Look, Samantha Moon. I trusted you. You came with some good references. Hell, great references. Sherbet stands by you. And so does this Sanchez guy out of L.A. Still, I don't know you for shit, and now the guys at the station are having a good laugh at me because I had them print a fucking vent under a fucking sink at a fucking Starbucks."

"You sound annoyed."

"Damn straight I'm annoyed. Don't fuck with me, Sam. I'm going out on a fucking limb bringing you in on this, and giving you access—"

"She was in there, Detective. I promise."

"When will you show me what you have?"

"Soon."

"How soon?"

"I don't know."

"Jesus, are you always like this?"

"Sometimes," I said, "and don't call me Jesus."

CHAPTER THIRTY

The kids were asleep.

I had already gone for a late-night jog, sometimes running so fast that I might as well be flying low to the ground, feeling invincible and untouchable.

I took a long shower, as hot as I could make it. One thing about taking showers in the middle of the night was that there was no one waiting in line for it. So, I used up all the hot water…and loved every second of it.

Now, dressed in a robe made of human flesh—kidding, pink terrycloth—I was back in front of my computer, prepared for an all-nighter. Of course, an all-nighter for me was really nothing more than my day job, so to speak.

Now, with my hair still wet, I curled one cold foot under me and sat at my computer, ready to dig in.

I didn't have to dig for very long.

Almost immediately, as I fast-forwarded through the fifth full day of her disappearance, after I had watched, precisely, two million people enter and exit the Starbucks in Corona, I saw something that caught my eye. And not just something.

A woman.

Exiting Starbucks.

No, not a big deal in and of itself. I had seen a million different women leave Starbucks up to this point. No, she was different. I unfurled my leg from under me and sat forward, pausing the video, capturing the woman just as she was stepping off the sidewalk that wrapped around the building.

I checked the time on the video: 1:17 pm.

I rewound the video a few seconds—hell, I'd gotten quite adept at manipulating the video controls, having spent the past three days working them—and watched her step out of the Starbucks again, this time closely watching her.

She was smallish, about the size of Lucy, if I had to guess. And I did have to guess. It was my job to guess...to make an informed guess. The woman on the screen was walking with her head down, and talking into a cell phone. The woman had black hair. Very black hair. Almost too black for her skin tone.

Interesting.

Lucy, of course, had light brown hair. The woman was also wearing different clothing, too. Shorts and a tank top. She carried a medium-sized handbag under her arm.

A different handbag than what Lucy came in with.

Maybe it wasn't her.

The woman paused briefly and actually shaded her eyes, even though she was wearing Jackie-O-type sunglasses. She paused and waved her hand. A red SUV, whose license plate was unreadable, pulled up next to the curb, and the woman with the sunglasses, with the pitch-black hair and pale skin, got into the passenger seat, and shut the door.

The SUV pulled away and was gone.

I frowned at the whole scene, replayed it twice more, and then did what any detective would do. I rewound to the early part of the day and painstaking went through each minute of the video.

And at no time did a dark-haired woman with the big sunglasses actually come into Starbucks.

She only exited.

It was Lucy; I was sure of it.

I could have kissed someone.

Even Kingsley.

Chapter Thirty-one

"So, the broad's alive," said Detective Sharp.

"Yes," I said, "And no one says the word *broad* anymore."

"Too bad. It's a good word. My pops used to say it."

It was midday, and we were in his brightly lit office. A few minutes earlier, gasping and whimpering, I had dashed across the half-empty parking lot, only to push through the heavy glass doors. Once inside, I did all I could to compose myself as quickly as possible, although I might have whimpered a little.

Now, in his too-bright office—and sitting as far away from the direct sunshine as possible—I said, "Let me guess, your father was a cop, too."

"How'd you guess?"

"Because you sound like a cop stuck in the seventies."

"What can I say? I grew up with 'the boys,' as my father used to call his cop friends. They were over all the time."

"No mom?"

"She died young. Just me and my pops."

"He's dead, too?"

"Five years now. Ain't a day goes by that I don't miss him."

"He's here now," I said.

"Say again?"

"Your pops is here now. He's standing behind you. His hand is on your shoulder. You can probably feel a tingle there."

He reached up and made a small movement toward his shoulder, and then pulled up short. "Not cool. Who the hell sent you—"

"Shut up and listen," I said. Mercifully, his office door was closed. I hadn't expected to do a reading today, or to give a message from Spirit. I didn't have a TV show where a camera crew was following me around, waiting eagerly for me to give a stranger a reading. And I sure as hell wasn't from Long Island. But, nonetheless, I could see into the spirit world, and I think spirits took the opportunity, sometimes, to relay a message through me.

Your friendly neighborhood vampire.

I said, "I can see spirits, you big boob. I'm kind of like a medium, only cooler."

"Wait. What—"

"Your dad is here. He's a big guy, bald. At least, that's how he's projecting himself to me right now. He's still holding your shoulder. You should be feeling a serious tingling there right about now. He's telling me, over and over, how proud he is of you."

"If this is a joke…"

"No joke, Detective," I said. In the past, I couldn't hear spirits. These days I could, especially vociferous, loud spirits. His father was such a spirit. I relayed his loving message to his son, and when I was done, Detective Jason Sharp was left sobbing at his desk, a real mess. Spirits have that kind of effect on people.

His father seemed to nod, patted his son again, and faded out slowly.

———

Detective Sharp finally looked up from all his blubbering and said, "That was so unfair."

"I don't make the rules," I said. "And your father wanted to come through."

"He's pushy like that."

"Oh, and he also wanted me to tell you not to be such a dick when you talk to me on the phone."

"Did he really—oh, bullshit. You're messing with me."

"I am."

"I guess I was a bit of a douche on the phone."

"A bit, and I hate that word."

"Sorry. Guy talk."

"If you haven't noticed yet…"

"Yeah, yeah, you're a broad."

"That I am, and like I said, no one says that word anymore."

"Well, I'm bringing it back. Now, can we get back to work?"

We did. I first showed him the various points when the muted light had turned on in the back of Starbucks, then progressed quickly over to the fifth day.

"Now watch."

"I'm watching."

When the woman with the dark hair and big sunglasses appeared on the screen, Sharp said, "Well, I'll be damned."

"That makes two of us."

"What?"

"Never mind," I said. "Any mention in the report of anyone with a red SUV?"

"No," said Sharp.

"What about her phone records?"

"She never used her phone again, neither calls nor texts after she disappeared."

"She's using a throwaway phone, then," I said.

"Would be my guess." He looked at me. "So, if we find the red SUV…"

"We find the broad," I said.

He raised an eyebrow. "Broad?"

I shrugged. "What can I say, I guess it's growing on me."

Chapter Thirty-two

I t was late.

I'd spent the day debating whether or not to tell my client about his wife, and decided now was not the time. I needed more answers. And I would find them, sooner or later.

I'd also spent the day thinking about Kingsley. I didn't often spend my free time thinking about my ex-boyfriend who cheated on me, who had been manipulated to cheat on me. Kingsley had, in fact, proven himself to be a good man this past year, despite the fact that I had been treating him like shit.

He'd come through more than once, saving my ass more than once. Being there for me, through thick and thin.

I recalled his tender words, uttered to me not that long ago, as we sat in his own oversized SUV.

"The big oaf," I mumbled, shaking my head now as I sat in my office, staring down at the notes I'd made. I had a game plan to find Lucy, and it consisted of contacting anyone and everyone that Lucy had ever known. It would be a lot of work. Or, as Tammy would say, a crap-ton of work. Luckily, I was up for a lot of work.

I sighed and thought again of Kingsley and those big amber eyes of his, and that hair—Jesus, all that hair. And then it happened...for the first time in well over a year, I remembered what it had been like to run my fingers through that hair. His hair. His thick, yet soft hair.

It had been heavenly, exciting, intoxicating.

Lord help me.

I drummed my fingers on my desk, listening to the sounds of Anthony's snores, which seemed to be growing louder these days, then double-clicked on my AOL IM icon on my computer screen.

Hi, Fang.

  Good evening, Moon Dance.

  And what are you doing on this fine night? I wrote.

  You might not want to know, Moon Dance.

  A woman?

  Yes.

  Then why the heck are you IM-ing me?

  She's asleep.

  Is she human?

  Yes.

  Are you feeding from her?

  I did, yes.

  Is she a willing donor? I asked.

  Yes.

The demon inside me perked up at this. I perked up, too, but it wasn't because of the demon. At least, I didn't think it was.

  No, I thought, *it's her. She's the catalyst for all of this, remember that.*

  Who's the girl? I asked.

  Do you really want to know, Sam?

  I wouldn't have asked otherwise.

  She's an ex-girlfriend.

I knew, of course, what had happened to an earlier girlfriend of his, hell, the whole world knew. He had drained her dry in his lap while making love to her, back when he was a teenager, back when he didn't truly understand the depths of his depravity.

  Does she know she's a donor? I asked.

  She knows everything about me, Sam. I have no secrets from her.

  So, she's willingly giving herself to you?

  Yes, Sam.

Do you love her?

There was a long pause before I saw him typing again on his computer screen. Amazingly, surprisingly, I didn't feel jealous. Well, not *too* jealous. I wondered if my thoughts of Kingsley had something to with that.

Yes, I think so.

I nodded to myself and sat back and analyzed how I felt about that. Yes, there was some jealousy. I did, after all, have feelings for Fang. There was mostly confusion, though. My feelings for Fang were all over the map. He'd done much to help me in the early days, and, later, to turn my life upside down. His siding with Hanner broke my heart. In the end, he had been compelled to act by a vampire much more powerful than me, and much older, too. Still, Fang had made the decision to go behind my back, to move forward without me. And he was doing just that now, with yet *another* woman.

Yes, I was jealous, but I also felt something else.

I felt liberated.

Seeing him like this. Or, rather, hearing him describe his current situation was a reminder to me of how far we had fallen, how distant we had become. Did he still love me? I think so. Love doesn't just go away. Even a small part of me still loved Danny and missed him. A very, very small part of me, granted.

So, Fang wasn't sure about his feelings with his girlfriend. I'd let him figure that out, in his own way, and in his own time. Truth be known, what I missed most was our sweet connection via the Internet. Via the old-school AOL instant message.

Chatting with him now—even reading words that upset me and concerned me—felt natural. It felt right. It felt like how things should feel. This past year had been one long, crazy-ass ride, and now things were finally, finally as they should be.

I typed: *Well, Fang, I hope you can figure out your feelings for her.*

I'm in no rush, Sam. She gives my life balance, security. She accepts me for who I am, exactly what I am. She doesn't judge. She only loves.

And gives you a fresh supply of blood.

Yes, Sam. There is that, too.

297

We were silent for a long time. His "typing" icon remained silent. Finally, I wrote: *You had the diamond medallion all along.*

You knew about that?

Yes. It looked different than the others, so I wasn't sure what it was.

I wasn't sure what it was either, truth be known.

Where did you get it?

The curiosity museum, he wrote.

Where they displayed your teeth? I wrote, referring to the teeth that now hung around his neck, looking to all the world like miniature elephant tusks. They were teeth that had been extracted from Fang long ago, in an insane asylum. Yeah, Fang was messed up, perhaps more than I might ever really know.

Yes. When I went back for my teeth, after I dispatched the owner, I saw the medallion in his safe.

So, you took it?

Of course.

And had been wearing it ever since.

Yes, Sam.

And you still have it?

No, I'm sorry.

My mouth opened and I think a sound squeaked out.

Fang continued typing: *I didn't know what I had. I didn't know its value. I just knew it was special.*

I nodded suddenly. I wrote: *But Hanner knew.*

Yes. She knew that wearing it would possibly nullify my vampirism.

And you couldn't have that, I wrote.

No, Sam.

So, you removed it?

Yes. I had to. It was the price I had to pay for her to change me. I gave it to her happily.

I nearly called him an idiot. Instead, I took a few deep breaths and sat back...and that was when it hit me.

She's still alive, isn't she?

Maybe. If she figured out how to unlock it. She was having trouble with that part.

But I saw the demon escape her when she died. The diamond medallion removes the demon.

Maybe she struck a deal with the demon within.

To keep it inside?

Yes.

Did you see her use the medallion?

I saw her try.

And then?

And then I was compelled to do what I was told, and I lost all track of the medallion.

I drummed my pointed nails on the keyboard, thinking hard. We had left Hanner down in the cavern, under the Los Angeles River, with the silver dagger still in her. Seemed safest to leave it in her. Yes, she had seemed dead. Very, very dead. But who knew?

You never went back for her? I wrote. *To revive her or help her?*

No, Sam. I've thought about it. But no.

But you loved her.

In a way, yes. But I didn't love what she did to you and your family. That was a deal breaker for me.

I thought about that long after Fang and I said our goodbyes.

Then grabbed my car keys and hit the road.

Chapter Thirty-three

"**N**ever thought I would come back here," said Kingsley.

"That makes two of us," I said.

"Three of us," said Allison.

"Well, I didn't invite either of you," I said.

Allison snorted. "Like we would let you come here alone, Sam!"

"Like totally," said Kingsley.

"Oh, brother," I said.

We were standing outside the familiar pile of rocks that led to the secret cavern entrance under the L.A. River. It was also the middle of the night, a good time for a vampire, a witch and a werewolf to go grave-robbing. Anyway, from all indications, the rocks hadn't been touched or moved since we had been here last, three months ago.

Now, with a cool wind blowing and the sounds of smaller animals moving in the thick underbrush nearby, Allison's words appeared in my mind: *Are we sure we want to do this, Sam?*

I caught the image in her mind...and it was of Danny's grave, which I had helped dig with my own hands, also located here in this strangest of tombs, in the woods not far from downtown Los Angeles, along the east side of Griffith Park. If anything, we were closest to the L.A. Zoo, which just so happened to be the setting to a zombie series Tammy was reading, written by a guy who wrote his own vampire series starring an undead mama not too dissimilar from me. Maybe I should sue the bastard.

Or feast on him.

Anyway, L.A. wasn't all stars, glitz and freeways. This park was proof. It was a park that housed not only the zoo, but the Griffith Park Observatory, the Hollywood Sign, and the Greek Theater. Most of which had found their ways into the movies. No surprise there, since they were just a hop, skip and a jump from Hollywood.

"I'm fine," I said aloud. "Really."

Kingsley snapped his big head around in my direction. "What? Never mind. You two are doing your telepathy thing again."

"You can't read minds?"

"No, Sam. At least, I don't think so."

"If you want," said Allison, "you can practice with me. I'm really, really good at mind reading."

Kingsley raised his eyebrows. "Er, thanks, Allie. I'll keep that in mind."

It was no secret that my new best friend had the hots for my old boyfriend. What my new best friend didn't know—and I'd been doing my damned best to shield these thoughts from her—was that I had been thinking a lot about Kingsley these days.

Perhaps too much.

Definitely more than I should have.

Allison had every right to flirt with Kingsley, although I had made it known that it was technically still weird for me. Still, she had been polite about it, never too overt, and so far, Kingsley hadn't seemed very interested.

I suspected I knew why.

He's still in love with me, I thought, making sure my mind was sealed nice and tight. I had no reason to keep these thoughts from Allison, other than I just wanted to analyze them without prejudice or judgment or outside interference. Mostly, I wanted to understand them...and be sure of how I felt.

I looked again at the hulking man standing beside me. He had one giant boot up on a boulder. The boot wasn't a cowboy boot. It looked Italian, and expensive. It also looked good on him. He was waiting for me. They both were.

Now, of course, was not the time to analyze my feelings about Kingsley.

I nodded. "Let's do this."

Kingsley grinned, reached down with one hand, and ripped free a boulder that was much heavier than he made it look. It crashed to the ground below, making an ungodly loud thud.

He pulled free another, then another, removing them with frightening ease and speed. I almost jumped in to help, but Kingsley needed no help.

In a matter of minutes, there appeared a dark hole.

"Ladies first," he said, and stepped aside.

"Gee, thanks," I said, and led the way down.

Chapter Thirty-four

The tunnel was longer than I remembered it.

I didn't need light, nor did Kingsley, but Allison wasn't so lucky. She was also more than capable of creating her own light, which she did by creating a liquid ball of glowing plasma between her palms. At least, that was what it looked like to my eyes. I watched it grow bigger and bigger, marveling at my friend's newfound witchy talents. Then she released it into the air above us, and it followed ahead of us, a hovering, glowing, seemingly sentient ball of weirdness.

Although not necessary, the light was welcoming. As we walked, I used a trick of my own, and focused my inner eye on our immediate surroundings; in particular, what was waiting ahead of us.

It wasn't much, and the macabre scene was exactly as we'd left it.

"It seems we're alone in here," said Kingsley, and I wondered if he had somehow known I had just mentally scouted ahead.

I nodded. "From what I can see, yes."

He pointed to his ears. "From what I can hear, too."

Ah, yes. Kingsley, of course, had a skill set of his own.

Shortly, we stepped into the first of two massive, underground caverns.

That such a rock formation existed under L.A. was enough for me to question my sanity all over again.

But here it was.

As we stood in it, the memories began flooding back. I'm sure I wasn't the only one. We had all had a traumatic experience in here a few months ago, from my ex-husband Danny being stabbed, to Kingsley in the fight of his life, to Allison keeping two crossbow-wielding guards at bay using more of her considerable magic.

Three freaks, I thought, and strode out into the center of the first of the two caverns.

There, in the far corner, was a pile of withering bones poking through darker robes and nicer shoes. That his head was nowhere near his body was a testament to Kingsley's ferocity.

The death of that vampire had freed Fang from his own compulsion. Fang had immediately acted to stop Hanner, by plunging a silver dagger deep into her heart.

Except, of course, I hadn't been aware that she was wearing the diamond medallion at the time.

"So, what does that mean, exactly?" asked Allison, mostly following my train of thoughts.

"Means she might be alive."

"Alive how?"

"I don't know."

"It's always fun," said Kingsley, striding into the next room, "to catch only half of your conversations."

I didn't immediately follow him through stone archway and into the second cavern; instead, I paused and took a deep breath and prepared myself for what I expected to see.

After all, it was within this second cavern that we had buried my ex-husband, Danny.

After I took a moment, Allison and I entered the second cavern, and I immediately saw the reason why I hadn't seen Danny's spirit since his death. There he was, sitting next to his grave, legs crossed and looking miserable, haunting the crap out of this place. He drifted slightly, bobbing and rising, as if he were sitting on an inner tube in the shallow end of a dark pool.

He looked up as I entered.

Chapter Thirty-five

Danny is a recent spirit.

He'd been killed only months earlier, which meant I could still see a lot of his detail, even though his "light body" was composed of tens of thousands, if not millions, of tiny light particles.

"Guys, give me a minute," I said.

Kingsley looked toward the dirt pile where my ex-husband's corpse was still rotting away. He nodded, understanding. Whether or not he knew that I saw Danny's spirit, I didn't know, but he understood enough and said, "I'll go check on our friend Hanner."

Allison gave me an encouraging smile. She, too, could sometimes see into the spirit world, and I knew she, too, sensed Danny's presence. *Good luck, Sam,* she thought to me.

Thanks, I responded, and headed over to my dead ex-husband, whose spirit was looking miserable.

———

"Hi, Danny," I said, addressing the spirit.

I sat on a rock very near to where he was standing. He watched me silently, his body forming and reforming, pulsing and shimmering. Truly the body electric.

"Have a seat, Danny," I said, and patted the rock next to me. "Let's talk."

He studied me silently, rising and falling ever so slightly, drifting on currents unseen and unfelt by the living. Or even the non-living.

The details of Danny's energetic body were so sharp that I could still see the mortal wound in his chest where the knife had plunged deep. I could also see the belt loops to his jeans, his shoelaces and the collar of his short. I knew, with time, such details would fade away. But for now, they were clear enough.

Unfortunately, his facial expressions were lost to me, although I could see the general outline of what had been a handsome face. I saw his ears, his mussed hair, his straight jawline. I couldn't see his eyes, and that saddened me. Danny had beautiful blue eyes.

Unsure of himself—at least, that was the impression I got—he sat next to me. If I were a new ghost, I would sure as hell be unsure of myself, too. As he sat, some of his light fragments scattered towards me like a bag of marbles that had burst. Unlike marbles, these particles of living energy moved over my right arm and around my wrist and fingers and hand before disappearing. I shivered and the goose bumps bumped.

"I should have checked on you sooner, Danny," I began. "I should have suspected you would still be down here."

He cocked his head slightly.

"I should have known you would be confused and unable to move on."

Now he cocked his head to the other side. I had his attention. I wondered how much he was really hearing, and how much he was actually comprehending.

That was when tears came, and they came hard, as I realized again that the man I had planned my future with and built a family with and had wanted to grow old with, had been forgotten in this shitty, desolate hellhole.

"I was taking care of the kids," I said, doing my best to speak through the tears. "They've been so upset."

I wanted to reach out and take his hand. And just as the thought crossed my mind, Danny did just that: he reached out with his own pulsating, crackling hand...and took my own. And he didn't stop there, he leaned over and gave me the most electrifying hug I'd ever had.

———

This was the first time I had really cried for Danny, and I did it now, in the presence of his confused ghost, at the bottom of a forgotten hole in the ground, in the place of his murder. He continued holding me, and I leaned my head in his direction, although I mostly hit air. Mostly.

"The kids miss you, but they are okay. They are both healing, but it will take time, maybe forever. I was worried about Anthony, but he has found…a new friend."

I purposely didn't mention that this was all because of Danny's idiocy. His desire to destroy me, in the end, had directly led to his death. He had aligned himself with the wrong people, people who used him.

I glanced over at Kingsley and Allison, who were both standing over another form, a form we had not bothered to bury, a form that, because of the contours of the cavern floor, I couldn't quite see.

A form who might not be dead, after all.

I knew Danny was sorry. I also knew that he was doing something that he had never done while living…sensing my thoughts. It took him dying before the idiot and I finally became truly connected.

"You're sorry," I said. "I know. I can feel it."

He nodded once, although the gesture seemed strange to him. He tried it again, liked it, and then nodded again and again.

"Okay, goofball. So you can nod. Big deal."

I might have seen the corners of his mouth rise slightly. Back in the day, before his fear of me and his love for other women, Danny had had a nice sense of humor. It was why I had married him. That, and I wanted his last name.

Now, Danny threw his head back and I saw his shoulders shake. He was laughing, and a scattered remnant of his thought appeared in my thoughts: he'd always suspected that was why I had married him.

I laughed, too, and when we were both done and had settled down, I next felt Danny's sadness.

307

"You miss them," I said.

He nodded his head again, and I saw something next that I didn't think I would ever soon forget: a shiny, fiery tear appeared in the corner of Danny's right eye. It slid down his face, leaving behind a blazing trail of quicksilver. The tear dropped free, and, while falling, exploded into a thousand tiny fragments of light.

"You can visit them, you know," I said. "But you can't visit them if you're stuck in here."

He cocked his head again, his way of telling me he was listening. Danny, who had always been the practical, skeptical lawyer, had found himself ill-equipped in the bewildering world of spirits.

"There's a tunnel, Danny. A tunnel of light. I know you've seen it. It will show itself every now and then. Do not be afraid of it. Go to it. Others will be waiting for you. Others you have loved, grandparents, friends, relatives. They will guide you, Danny. Go to them. Go to the light."

He looked down, and I sensed his fear.

"Do not fear it, Danny. Go to it. Only then will you be able to leave this place...and see your kids again."

He turned and stared at me some more, silently, rising and falling in that realm between worlds, layered over this world.

"I have work to do, Danny."

He nodded and released my hand. But before he did so, he thanked me as best as he could. Through feelings, and a hint of thought.

"We'll get you out of here, Danny boy," I said. "And maybe we'll see you around sometime?"

He might have smiled at that.

Chapter Thirty-six

There she was.

We all stared down at what had once been a very old and very powerful vampire. No, not one of the oldest, but certainly she'd had her fill of human blood over the centuries.

"This medallion…" began Kingsley.

"The diamond medallion," I said.

"Yes, this diamond medallion…it's different than the other medallions, no?"

I nodded and, staring down at a woman I had also once called a friend, I told Kingsley what I knew: the diamond medallion vanquished the demon from within, all while allowing the owner to retain all the vampiric power, with none of the ill side effects. That she was dead, there was no doubt. Her skin had dried around her skull, knuckles and wrists. The skin itself was just months from rotting off completely.

"Would you remain immortal?" asked Kingsley, unaffected by the gruesome sight before us. Truth was, I was unaffected, too. Death wasn't something to fear…but something to embrace.

You're scaring me, Sam, came Allison's words.

I ignored her, and said to Kingsley, "my understanding is, yes. Or something very close to it. With the diamond medallion, you get to pick and choose the gifts you want."

"Sweet deal. Wish I had that," said Kingsley. "How do we know that Hanner didn't use the medallion, and, you know, use up its juice?"

"For one, she's dead. Two, I saw the demon leave her when she was killed."

"So, she hadn't figured out how to use it?"

I stared down at her grinning skull. Her eyes had rotted out. "My guess, is no."

"So, what do we do now, Sam?" asked Allison.

I knelt down and said, "For starters, we check her out."

I tore open her blouse, revealing a bloody, mostly empty bra. The silver tip of the knife protruded exactly where her heart would have been. Fang had been deadly accurate.

Allison made a noise and looked away. I didn't blame her. The scene before us was horrific and macabre, the stuff of nightmares. I loved it. Loved it more than I should have. I stared down at the ghoul before me, intrigued, excited.

Stop, Sam. Just stop, came Allison's voice.

She's weak, said a voice deep, deep within me, too deep for even Allison to hear.

I ignored them both and said, "No medallion."

"So, what next?" asked Kingsley.

I shrugged. "Let's check her pockets."

Her clothes were decidedly looser on her than they had been a few months ago. As I searched her, I wondered where her own soul had gone, and if she had finally reconnected with her dead son. Or, worse, had her soul dissipated into nothingness?

No, I thought, as I moved over to her other side, careful of the knife blade projected through her chest. *I can't accept that. Souls are eternal. Even more so than vampires.*

I knew some believed that a vampire was, in fact, *all soul.* You kill the vampire, you kill the soul, too.

Don't worry about that now, Sam, came Allison's reassuring thoughts. *You're not dying any time soon.*

Thank you, I said, and reached down into Hanner's front pocket. And there it was.

I pulled it out by its leather strap and held it up. It was smaller than the other medallions...and contained only a single diamond rose in the center, which glistened brilliantly in Allison's ball of magical light.

I half expected to hear Fang's voice at this moment. I half expected this to be an elaborate trap. I half expected for other vampires—or even vampire hunters—to descend upon us.

But none of that happened. Real life wasn't the movies, of course. This wasn't an episode of *The Vampire Diaries*. Real life didn't throw every conceivable, nonsensical twist and turn at you.

At least, not this time.

I held up the medallion before me, letting it spin and catch the light.

For the first time in a long time, I felt hope.

Chapter Thirty-seven

I was back in the Occult Reading Room.

Archibald Maximus greeted me, and then asked me to wait while he disappeared into the back rooms. What was back there, I didn't know, and what he did back there, I didn't know that either.

The Occult Reading Room wasn't very big. It was located on the third floor of the main Cal State Fullerton Library. The room itself was found against the far wall, which took some time getting to, since the floor itself was nothing short of epic, with rows upon rows of books as far as the eye could see. Once you reached the far wall, there it was, through a nondescript doorway that existed for some, but not for others. If you needed the room, it was there. If you were *ready* for the room, it was there. If not, then you were shit out of luck.

"Let those with eyes see," said Archibald, as he approached me now down the short hallway behind the help desk, a hallway I had never been down. "Let those with ears hear." He stopped behind the desk and smiled. "Do you understand, Sam?"

"I do," I said. "And I think someone is a little full of himself."

The Librarian threw his head back and laughed. "It does sound a bit pretentious, doesn't it? But it's a truth, Sam. A universal truth, in fact." He motioned to the array of books shelved neatly throughout the room. "Most of this information would be lost on those not ready."

"It would be lost on me," I said. "Yet, I'm here."

"You are further along than you might know, Sam."

"Further along in what?"

"To understand the mystery of it all."

"And you understand?" I asked.

"No, Sam. But that is the goal, is it not?"

"If you say so. I just want to be a good person, a good mom. I don't want to kill or be intrigued by death. It's not me. It's *her*."

"Understandable, Sam. I think you will get there. But, yes, you are not my typical seeker."

"And who is your typical seeker?"

"An initiate well-versed in the occult, well-versed in mastering himself inside and outside, and mastering those around him as well."

"And then, they come to you for what?"

"Their final training, if you will."

"Pardon my French, but who the fuck *are* you?"

"It's not French, Sam. And I have been many people, throughout time and space."

"Anyone I would know?"

"I doubt it, Sam."

"But you are an alchemist," I said.

"I am that, and much more."

"Lucky you," I said. I drummed my fingers on the desk, thinking. "I've heard of Hermes. And Thoth. Actually, I've heard of the *Book of Thoth*. I couldn't tell you what it is, or what's in it, but I've heard of it, somewhere."

"Many people have, although few understand it."

"Oh, God, please tell me you didn't write it. And if you did, can I get it on my Kindle?"

He smiled. "Hermes was my teacher, Sam. Hermes Trismegistus, to be exact. The Thrice Great."

"Okay, now you're just making up words."

"Master Hermes would have smiled at your flippancy, and perhaps added a joke of his own. He had a great sense of humor."

"Had? So, he's dead now?"

"He's moved on."

"Of course," I said. "No one dies anymore. So, who was he?"

"The father of alchemy, and my teacher."

"You sound like you miss him."

"Every day, Sam."

"You knew him for a long time," I said, sensing the depth of their relationship.

"Centuries."

I think I hit upon a nerve, and he changed the subject. "You have brought something with you?"

"Would be more impressive," I said, "if you couldn't read my mind." I slipped my hand inside my sweater pocket and removed the smooth, dense object. I placed it before him on the help desk. "This look familiar?"

"It does."

"I took it from the corpse of a vampire."

"Sounds like the beginning of a novel."

"Or the end," I said.

He motioned toward it. "May I?"

"Be my guest. You created the damn thing."

He smiled and picked up the glittering relic, turned it over in his hand, and rubbed his thumb across the back. *Did he just activate it?* I wondered.

"A smudge," he said, grinning.

He continued turning it and polishing it, almost affectionately.

"Yes, affectionately, Sam. It took many, many decades to perfect this very relic."

"And yet, you let it collect dust in a curiosity museum for God knows how long—"

"Thirteen years. And I'm not God, although we are all aspects of God."

I opened my mouth to speak, closed it again.

"I'm always aware of my creations, Sam. I am deeply connected to them, you see."

"Actually, I don't see, but I'll take your word for it. I still don't understand how you could let something so valuable out of your sight."

"Never out of my inner sight, Sam."

"Enough with the doublespeak, Max," I said. "You know what I mean."

"I do, and there comes a time when every parent must release his children into the world. You will discover this soon enough."

"I'd prefer to not think about it."

He smiled. "You are equipping your children marvelously, Sam."

"And you know this, how?"

"Your children are always at the forefront of your mind, Samantha. I do not have to plumb very deep to see what a remarkable job you are doing, under the circumstances. A mother's love is a beautiful thing."

"Let's stop right there on a high note, before you start creeping me out."

"Agreed," he said. "Back to the medallion. It needed to find its way into the world—"

"Yes, yes, like children. I got that. But why?"

"Don't you know, Sam?"

"Know what?"

"So that it could find *you*. On its own."

I looked at him; he looked at me. Somewhere behind me, a student walked past the Occult Reading Room without missing a step. *Let those with eyes see,* and all that jibber-jabber.

"You could have just given it to me, you know," I said. "And saved yourself a lot of time."

"And what fun would that have been?" His eyes might have twinkled. "But that's not the way it works, Sam. I did not know it was for you, for starters. Not until I met you. Not until you started gathering the other medallions."

"Then you're not surprised that I have this one, too?"

"No, Sam. I would have been surprised if your one-time friend Detective Hanner had figured out how to unlock it."

"But she couldn't?"

"No. But she tried valiantly."

"I take it there's more to it than just wearing it?"

"A tad more."

I drummed my freakishly long nails on his help desk, a desk that looked like any other help desk at any other library. The room looked normal, too. Only the oversized, ancient-looking books that filled the nearby shelves looked anything but normal. They looked dark, felt dark and *were* dark. Some darker than others.

"Why me?" I asked suddenly. "Why am I the one finding all these medallions? Why do you help me? I'm just me, no one. Just a mom who got attacked a long time ago."

As I spoke, I couldn't help but notice the Librarian's demeanor softening. He set the medallion down on the desk, near my drumming fingers. He inhaled and, for the first time ever, I saw the young man who wasn't young express real emotions. And the emotion was heartbreak.

I looked at the medallion, and then, looked him in the eyes. No, I couldn't read his mind, but I sensed there was something big going on here.

Sensed it from deep within me.

Sensed it from *her*, in fact. The demon within.

A cold shiver ran up and down my spine. "The demon inside me..." I began, but I was unable to find the words. Not with Archibald looking at me like that, with so much emotion that it was breaking my heart for reasons I didn't know.

"She wasn't always a demon," he finished. "She was my mother once."

Chapter Thirty-eight

Maximus let me have these moments to work out what I had just heard, except I wasn't doing a very good job of it.

"I think I need to sit," I said.

I found one of the plush reading chairs that were scattered throughout the room. Of course, I'd never actually seen anyone reading in the chairs, but that was par for the course. I wasn't sure who the Librarian's other clients were, or initiates, as he put it. Truthfully, I didn't want to know, either.

I sat; he took the chair across from me.

"Just two normal people sitting at the library," I said, "although I'm probably talking a little loudly."

"No one can hear you, Sam."

"Of course not. Why should they?"

"Sam, you're upset."

"Wouldn't you be?"

"I can see how I wasn't forthright—"

"How long have you known that the bi—the thing inside me was your mother?"

"You can say bitch, Samantha. My mother is very much one, and far worse, truth be told."

"So, now the truth is being told?"

"Sam, remember that part where I said let those with ears hear—"

"Well, I have ears, and you damn well could have told me sooner."

"I didn't know, Sam, not until you arrived with the diamond medallion. Then I knew for sure—"

"But you suspected all along?"

"I did, yes. The medallions would seek her out. I would know if it was her only if—and only if—all four medallions were returned back to me."

"By the same person," I said.

"Yes."

"You could have told me…"

"No, Sam. I could not. It would have affected the outcome. I needed to know, and I needed to know organically."

His words made sense, although, for me, one demon was the same as any other. Mother or not, I wanted her out. But even that thought was so…fantastical that I was having trouble wrapping my brain around it. I said as much, although I knew that Maximus was closely following my every thought.

He answered with, "Every highly evolved dark master started as a human, Sam. And every alchemist, too. Your angel friend is the exception. He was never human."

"You know about him, huh?"

"I'm afraid I do, but he is for another discussion at another time."

"Fine," I said. "Let's get back to your mother."

"She came from a long line of mystics, which shouldn't come as a surprise."

"Right," I said. "Seeing how you turned out."

He nodded. He was sitting forward now in the chair, elbows on his knees. He looked like any other college student. He was handsome, youngish, and clean shaven of the previous pointy beard he had once worn. The deep intelligence and kindness in his eyes gave him away. I noticed that at various times when I had previously seen him, his eyes appeared bright blue, or violet, or even bright green. Today, they were bright blue again and I chalked it up to some mysterious alchemy of his old soul. He was clearly not like other students. Or like anyone else, for that matter.

"My mother was seduced by the darkness, to put it lightly. She wasn't, shall we say, very disciplined."

"She looked for shortcuts," I said.

318

He nodded. "Very good."

"What year are we talking about?"

"Fourteen thirty-two. Over six and a half centuries ago."

"Gee, you don't look a day over two hundred."

He cracked a smile. "There are far older in the world, Sam. I'm a relative newbie to all of this."

"Did you just say 'newbie'?"

"I did, and I'm proud of it. It's a good word."

I wanted to laugh at the insanity of it all, but that would have only added to the insanity. I kept my emotions in check and said, "So, your mother took shortcuts."

"They all took shortcuts, Sam. They sought immortality quickly, without the necessary work."

"And you put in the necessary work?"

"I did."

"With Hermes?"

"Yes. Myself and others."

"Other alchemists?"

"Yes, there are many out there like me."

"Many?"

"Okay, a few."

"So, your mother and others like her, they sought a shortcut to immortality?"

He nodded. "And their shortcut was a very dark and wicked one. They hurt a lot of people. They hurt themselves, too."

"They hurt you?"

"Yes, Sam. I was witness to many horrible acts. It is why I sought another purpose."

"To stop her."

"To stop *them*. But I needed help."

"Hermes?" I said.

"Yes, Sam. The greatest of us all. The master's master, as he is referred to."

"Sounds kind of badass."

"The baddest of all asses."

Okay, now I did snort. "So, what did Hermes do?"

"He removed them, Sam."

"All of them?"

"Yes. And it wasn't easy. There were battles and wars, often fought outside of history books. My mother and others like her—that is, those who mastered the dark arts—put up a tremendous battle. We lost some good people, and so did they. But in the end..."

"Good triumphed," I said.

"In a word, yes."

"And how long did that last?"

"Perhaps a half century."

I did the math, and saw the date in my mind. "That would be the end of the fourteen hundreds."

"Correct, Sam."

"Don't say it," I said, suddenly gasping.

"Yes, Sam. There was a warlord king in those days. A powerful and wicked young man who delighted in killing others. Who delighted in impaling them and watching them bleed."

"Don't say it," I said again.

"Yes, Sam. Dracula was the first of your kind."

"Damn, you said it."

Chapter Thirty-nine

"**I**s Dracula still alive today?"

"Yes, Sam."

"And the old vampire, Dominique, the one who Kingsley killed in the cavern—"

"Was one of the first to be turned by Dracula."

"Am I dreaming?" I asked.

"No, Sam."

"That's exactly what I would expect someone in my dream to say."

"I assure you, Samantha. This is all very real, and it's happening now."

"Fine," I said, sitting back. "Continue."

And continue he did. The dark masters had found a way to circumvent Hermes' spell that had cast them from this world. And the way back in was through *possession*.

"Okay, that part I know," I said, "but where does your mother fit into all of this?"

"She was one of the greatest of her kind."

"Dark masters?"

"Yes," said Maximus. "I watched her kill many and destroy many lives. I watched her torture and maim and wreak havoc. I watched her drink blood from the very old and the very young."

"Was she a vampire then?"

"There were no vampires then."

"Okay, now that's just sick."

"That was Mother."

"No wonder you have issues."

He smiled sadly, and continued, "She was unusually powerful. Unusually proficient in the darker arts. She didn't have to go this route, you know. She could have done goodness in the world."

"Maybe your mother was a good, old-fashioned psychopath."

"I suspect so."

"Lucky me," I said.

"Quite the opposite, Sam. Lucky her."

"What does that mean?"

"I suspect she is benefiting by being a part of your life, Sam."

"I don't understand."

"She is with you constantly, seeing through your eyes, experiencing life through you."

"Yeah, so? She's a parasite."

"You are her first host, Sam."

"Do you have any idea how creepy that sounds?"

"I imagine, but hear me out. She has been waiting for the right person for many centuries."

"And I'm the right person?"

"Yes."

"Why?"

"I'll explain that in a moment."

"How about if you explain it now?"

"Very well, Sam. You are particularly attractive to her because of your bloodline."

"What about my bloodline?" I had a very bad feeling about this.

He held up his hand. "No, Sam. You are not my distant relative, but you are a distant relative to someone else."

"Oh, God. Please don't say Dracula."

"Not Dracula, Sam."

"Then who—" Then it hit me. "Hermes."

"Yes, Sam. The greatest alchemist who'd ever lived had a child."

I thought back to the time in the cavern. Hanner had said my sister would do just as well. They were prepared to kill me and infect her with the same demon who lived in me, his mother. And my sister would have come from the same bloodline, of course.

"Now that you know, Sam, perhaps you can understand why your own powers seem to be growing so quickly. Combine your lineage with my mother's power…and you have the potential to be unstoppable."

"I don't want to be unstoppable. I just want to be me."

"I know, Sam."

"So, what do I do?" I asked. "Remove her?"

"You could."

I ran my fingers through my hair. "Then what would stop her from going after my sister? Or my daughter?"

"Good points, Sam."

"What does she want with me, anyway?"

"Only an offspring of Hermes can unseal the doorway between worlds."

"Okay, now I know I'm on the set of *The Vampire Diaries*." I looked around. "Where's Damon? Hell, I'll even take Stefan."

"This is not a film set, Sam. I'm sorry."

I sat back, exhaled. "Let me guess: if she can possess me completely, she could potentially return all the banned dark masters?"

"Yes, Sam."

"Well, fuck." I stood and paced along the carpeted area before the reading chairs. Maximus sat back, fingers steepled under his chin, watching me. "I almost…" and I couldn't believe I was about to say this, "I almost think I *shouldn't* release her. That I should keep her caged in me. That I should keep fighting her."

He said nothing, watching me carefully.

I continued pacing. "I am doing a good job of fighting her. But…but she's gaining ground. I can feel her inching closer to the surface."

"You can fight her, Sam."

"Fight her how?"

"You won't believe me if I say it."

I stopped in front of him. "Try me."

"You fight her with love."

Chapter Forty

"She's laughing," I said.

"I imagine she is. My mother rarely, if ever, used words like *love*."

"She's calling you worthless, a disappointment. Should I stop?"

Maximus shook his bowed head. I couldn't see his expression, but from what I could tell, this was nothing he hadn't heard before. "Better to let it out, Sam, than to keep her vitriol bottled up inside you."

"She says you're an embarrassment. She's telling me that you are my enemy, to not listen to you, to fight you. To kill you."

"Nice chatting with you, too, Ma," he said.

The demon inside—his mother—was filling my thoughts with her anger, her rage. They bubbled up from down deep. I sensed I could have stopped them. Demanded that she back off. I sensed she would have to listen, too. That she *had* to listen. But I spoke her words anyway.

"She wants to make a deal with me. If I give her a few minutes a day, or a week, she will back off, leave me alone."

"I caution you against it—"

"She tells me I will have peace again, if I give her a chance to make an occasional appearance."

"Sam, please…"

"She tells me that it won't hurt, and that she won't hurt any of my loved ones."

"Sam…"

"She's telling me that she and I, together, could start something new, something great. We could stand up to you, and to the world, and create our own destiny."

"Sam, I beg you…"

"Well, don't worry. I told her to go fuck herself and crawl back under the rock she came from."

The Librarian, who was leaning forward on his elbows and staring at me with enough intensity to power a Prius, exhaled audibly. "Thank you, Sam."

"I'm not sure what's going on, or how she intends to use me, or what she intends to do with me once she has me, but one thing I do know: she's pure evil."

"That's my ma."

"So, what's this business about beating her with love?"

"It's happening already."

"What's happening now?"

"You. You are effecting change just by being who you are. She is forced to see love, to see good, and she hates it. It's why she is pushing to get out. Your life is affecting her."

"My life is chaotic," I said. "My life is filled with my kids fighting and Anthony's skid marks. And not necessarily in that order."

He smiled. "Perhaps, Sam. But it's also filled with love. You loving your kids. You sacrificing for your kids. You loving and caring for your friends and family. She cannot help but to feel it as well. And this is a new experience for her. The more you love, the more your spirit shines, and the more she is affected."

"And then what?" I said.

"And then, I don't know."

"You expect her to change?"

"Love has that effect on people. It's been known to happen. Love and hate are but two ends of the same pole. Extreme ends, granted. But each day you love is another day she is being exposed to such influences."

"And another day that she rebels," I said.

"Indeed, Sam. I did not say it would be easy."

325

"So, I'm a big experiment."

"You don't have to be, Sam."

"No," I said. "Except, if I let her loose with the diamond medallion, she might go after my family next. To conveniently arrange for one of them to be attacked, too."

"I would not put it past her."

"So, I'm stuck with her."

"That is up to you, Sam."

A horrible thought just occurred to me. "What's to stop other dark masters—not necessarily your mother—from attacking my daughter and sister, since we are all descendants of Hermes, as you say."

"It's a good question. My mother was clearly one of the strongest, greatest of her kind. It could only be her, or someone like her, who could perform the necessary magicks to bring down the veil."

"So, how many are like her?"

"Only a small handful, Sam. Three or four at most. And these are currently in residence with other hosts."

"You mean they're currently vampires."

"And werewolves, too."

"Demons and vampires and werewolves, oh my!" I said.

I paused next to the diamond medallion, picked it up and turned it over in my hand. It caught the surrounding light, and returned it a thousand times. Pure gold and the clearest diamonds will do that. "I need to get a drink," I said.

"I bet. I could use a stiff one myself."

"Stiff one? Yeah, you are an old-timer," I said.

"Well, Sam. What would you like to do with the medallion?"

"I want you to hold onto it," I said. "For now. I might someday come back for it and take my chances."

"Fair enough." I handed it over to him and he took it from me. He stood and slipped it into his pants pocket, and went around the help desk, where I was used to seeing him.

"I guess I'm doomed to drink blood for all eternity," I said. "And stay out of the light of the sun."

The Librarian snapped his fingers. "About that. I've been a busy boy back here." He motioned to the hallway behind him.

"I take it those aren't just offices back there."

"Far from it."

"A lab?" I asked. I had an image of frothy test tubes and beakers and Bunsen burners.

He grinned. "Something like that. Hold on."

I held onto the desk, shaking my head over the craziness of it all. I checked the time on my cell. *Shit! I was late picking up the kids again.* Damn the Librarian and his crazy hours. I sent Tammy a quick text and told them to wait for me, and that I was on my way. Her text came back just as the Librarian returned. Her text read: *Get a grip, Mom!*

Never had truer words been spoken. Or texted.

"Is texted a word?" I asked.

"It is now," he said, and stepped behind the help desk again. He held out two fists. "Pick a hand."

"A game?" I asked.

"Games are good for the soul. Pick one."

I picked the right. He turned his fist over and opened it. There. Sitting in the center of his palm, was one of the prettiest gold rings I'd ever seen. Embedded within it was a blue sapphire that sparkled, amazingly, as bright or brighter than the diamond medallion.

"Beautiful!" I said. "Is that for me?"

"Yes, Sam. Put it on."

I did, on my right index finger. It fit perfectly. "Don't look so smug," I told him. "You got my ring size from my mind."

He looked satisfied anyway. "Pick again."

"More games?" I asked.

His eyes twinkled for an answer.

I touched his left fist, and he opened it, revealing another ring, with a slightly different design. This one contained an opal. I said, "What are these?" And then it hit me. "They're from the earlier medallions."

"Indeed, Sam."

"But...I destroyed them."

"In a way, yes, but I managed to rebuild them. Remember, I am the one who created them." He pointed to the first ring. "The sapphire ring will enable you to exist comfortably in the sunlight. You experienced that before, when you wore it as a medallion. Remember, you are still not at full strength in the sunlight, but at least you will not suffer. The opal ring will allow you to—"

I couldn't contain myself. "To eat!" I screamed "And to drink!"

"And to be merry. Yes, Sam."

"Holy shit! I could kiss you." And I did just that, planting a kiss on his cheek. "But you warned against having all four medallions together. That a dark master could use them to release one of his kind."

"Indeed, Sam. As you can see, these aren't medallions. That error has now been fixed."

"I could kiss you again," I said. "And again and again."

And I did so, again and again. Showering the young man who wasn't really young with kisses on his cheeks and forehead.

Chapter Forty-one

I t had been a week, and I was waiting.

The downside of working as a private investigator from one's home was that all sorts of sketchy types could turn up. Which was why I rarely gave away my home address to anyone I hadn't screened first. Without a published address, I was hard to find. That was a good thing...unless you *wanted* to be found.

And this time, I very much wanted to be found.

Which was why I was using another detective's office. Mr. Jim Knighthorse was a piece of work, and his office was riddled with bullet holes, bloodstains and dog hair, but he let me borrow it for the week, and for that, I was grateful.

Presently, he was on a road trip to Sedona, following up clues to his own case, one that involved a child actor who might or might not be dead. Private eyes are like that. We follow the clues to wherever they may take us. Sometimes they take us to dark places. Other times, they take us to Sedona. At least, he got to write-off a trip.

Anyway, using Knighthorse's office as a launching point, I followed up with anyone and everyone who might know Lucy Gleason. I visited her parents, her friends, her co-workers. I let them all know that I was looking for her. I gave them all newly printed cards that had Knighthorse's office address on them.

I did this throughout the week, for hours on end, running people down as they went to work, came home from work, at lunchtime, in their offices. I harassed anyone who knew Lucy, focusing on her family, although I never did come across her sister. I also never came across the red SUV, but that was okay. I had gotten the word out—and there was no evidence that I was going to let up, either.

Now, I knew, it was just a matter of time.

My new rings worked marvelously. I could just kiss the Librarian again, and I just might. I wore one on each index finger, and with them, I was able to work most of the days while my sister watched over my kids. Additionally, I woke up easily and dreamed deeply. But best of all. Best of all...

Was the food.

Oh, God, the food...

———

It had taken me two days to work up the courage to eat and in the end, I had just suggested takeout for my first meal.

"Are you nervous?" asked Kingsley on that second day. We were both staring down at a plate full of rich gnocchi from my favorite Italian restaurant—that is, back when I could have Italian food—Geno's in the City of Orange.

"A little," I said. "I mean, what if the ring doesn't work?"

"Then I expect to see you running to the bathroom. That is, if this shithole has a bathroom."

"It's outside," I said, motioning through Knighthorse's now-open pebbled-glass door. "And down the hallway."

"Classy," said Kingsley. "Well, are you going to try it or not?"

"Give me a minute."

"It's getting cold, Sam," said Kingsley, grinning. "And it looks awfully good, whatever it is. Guh-noshi."

"Gnocchi," I said, pronouncing it correctly. "And they're potatoes."

"And why again did you pick potatoes over meat for your first meal?"

"Because...they'll go down a little easier. My stomach hasn't had to digest anything other than blood in nearly a decade. Well, blood, wine and water."

"Sounds like a Christian band," said Kingsley. "Blood, Wine and Water."

"Will you just zip it?" I said. "This is serious business. You do realize that this will be the first time I will have eaten anything—"

"Yes, Sam. The first time since the last time you sneaked some Oreos a few years ago and subsequently vomited them within seconds."

"No one likes a know-it-all," I said. "And this is a momentous occasion for me."

"And you're sharing it with me," said Kingsley. "Should I be touched?"

"You should be quiet," I said, but gave him a half-smile.

He made a gesture of zipping his lips closed, locking them, and tossing away the key.

"Okay," I said. "Here goes."

Kingsley watched me with great interest and some amusement as I lifted a forkful of the still-steaming gnocchi—which Kingsley had thoughtfully brought to me on his lunch break—up from the plate and toward my lips. That it smelled heavenly went without saying. My mouth watered. A very human reaction.

"Here goes," I said.

"You said that."

"Right."

And in it went, slowly. I wrapped my lips around the fork hesitantly, cautiously, then used my teeth to scrape the gnocchi clean off. Butter, olive oil and garlic exploded in my mouth. I had wondered if my taste buds would even work. But they did—and then some. More so than I was prepared for.

"Oh, my God."

"That good, huh?"

"Mmm. Holy shit."

"Jesus, Sam. You're gonna turn me on."

But I wasn't listening to him. I was doing all I could to not dive headfirst into the greasy to-go box. Still, I waited. After all, it had only been a few seconds since that first bite. I forced myself to set aside the fork...and waited.

"What are you doing?" asked Kingsley.

"I'm waiting."

He nodded, getting it. "Oh, right. Barf city. Fingers crossed."

"Fingers and toes."

A minute went by. And then another.

"We in the clear?" asked Kingsley. "Should I run for the exit?"

"I don't know."

"Any pain?"

"No pain," I said.

"Feel like vomiting?"

"Only when I see your face."

He reached for the to-go box. "Take that back, or I'm taking back the food."

"You want another fork in your hand?"

"Sam…"

"Fine. Your face doesn't make me want to vomit. there's a small chance that you are still kind of cute. A very small chance."

"Better," he said, and retracted his hand. "I think."

A minute later, while Kingsley feasted on a boxful of riblets, I ate my second bite of gnocchi…and loved every chew. It didn't take me long to finish that box…and I was already hungry for more.

———

That had been three days ago, and I have been eating heartily ever since. Eating anything and everything. Thank the good Lord, I wasn't gaining any weight. At least, not yet.

Now, a week after canvassing the area—often with a full stomach—I finally hit pay dirt.

Pay dirt in this case was the sound of a car pulling up outside of Knighthorse's office. I pushed aside the Cinnabon I had been devouring and closed my eyes, casting my mind out, and saw her emerge from a blue compact car. Dark hair, big glasses. It was her, minus the wig. She had dyed her hair.

I licked my sticky fingers clean and shot Detective Sharp a quick text: *She's here.*

Detective Sharp knew where I was, of course, although he hadn't been too keen on the plan. Next, still using the iPhone, I swiped over to the audio app and pressed "record."

Oh, the wonders of technology.

CHAPTER FORTY-TWO

I waited patiently behind the desk.

A moment later, the door opened and a woman stepped inside. It was Lucy Gleason, and I was excited, although I didn't show it.

"Samantha Moon?" she asked.

"You got her," I said cheerfully.

"May I come in?"

"You may."

She did so, closing the door behind her. A small woman, even smaller than myself. She was cute, too, until you remembered she had hid out in a women's bathroom for five days.

She looked at me from just inside the door. I sat behind Knighthorse's leather-tooled desk. It didn't fit the ambiance of the bullet-riddled room, which was covered in pictures of Knighthorse himself, depicting him back in his college football days.

Lucy had big, round, baleful eyes, complete with half-moon shaped dark bags hanging underneath. "I assume you know who I am," she said.

"Have a seat, Lucy."

She did, picking the middle of three client chairs. I wondered when and if Knighthorse ever had three clients in here at one time. *Ever the optimist,* I suspected he would say.

"You did it," she said.

"I did."

"You flushed me out."

"I can see that."

"I had to come see you just so you would leave my family and friends alone."

"How many knew of your disappearance?"

"Only one, my sister...and one friend."

"Who drove the red SUV?"

"My sister."

"Whose red SUV is it?"

"Her co-worker's. She borrowed it for the day. Told them she was picking something up."

"Boy, did she."

"Yes," said Lucy.

Dammit, I liked her. She had a calmness to her that I admired. A tranquility that I not only craved, but seemed elusive. At least to me. But she had it, except I doubted that she'd always had it.

She has it now, I thought. *Now that she is free.*

"Why did you do it?" I asked. "Why Starbucks? Why at that moment and time?"

She looked over at my cell phone, which wasn't doing a very good job of hiding itself behind the lamp. "I assume you're recording this."

"You assume correctly."

She nodded. I was tempted to dip into her thoughts, but her aura was bright blue, which was the color I associated with honesty. Green would have been a different story. So, I waited, knowing I was going to at least hear some semblance of truth.

"I've wanted leave Henry for some time."

"Most people do just that...leave," I said. "Most don't hide in a Starbucks's bathroom."

"I chose the location very carefully," she said.

"Not a coffee fan?"

"You would think, but no. This Starbucks is unique in that it only has one main opening, no drive-thru, nor any open windows."

I said, "And this was important to you, why?"

She shook her head. "You tell me, Samantha Moon. You've already figured out so much. Obviously, you sat through five days of tape."

335

"Mostly on fast forward," I said.

"And yet, you spotted me leaving."

"I have good eyes."

"Remarkable eyes," she added.

"Don't try to butter me up, missy. You're still in hot water. And why do I suddenly sound like Dick Tracy?"

She laughed lightly at that. A high, refined laugh.

I laughed, too, not so high, and not so refined, and had I known her a little better, I might have thrown in a snort.

When we were done laughing, I considered her reasons for disappearing in this particular setting. I could cheat, of course, and dip into her mind. Except I didn't feel like cheating. I did the next best thing: I puzzled it out aloud.

"For some reason, you chose a location with only one entrance and one rear exit. A location with no other obvious security cameras, except the one perched high in the parking lot."

"Keep going."

"Most important, you must have somehow come across the vent under the bathroom sink. Maybe you dropped your eyeliner—or a paper towel. You looked down and saw the vent partially open. You pulled it all the way open, and saw that, wonder of wonders, you could fit inside. At that point, you checked yourself in for some serious therapy."

"Very funny, Ms. Moon. Continue."

"Continuing. Now that you found a possible location to stage your disappearance, you would have come back and staked out the parking lot, perhaps under disguise and out of sight of the camera. Inside, you already noticed there were no cameras, which is what you would have wanted. You didn't want to be recorded entering the premises."

"Keep going, Ms. Moon. You're doing wonderfully."

I tapped my fingernails on the desk. Until I remembered that my nails looked like something out of a Frankenstein movie. I retracted my hands. Ever the freak. I said, "You wanted the exterior camera to document your disappearance. To prove you went in."

"Very good."

I bit my lip, thinking hard. "But you wanted to create the illusion of truly disappearing, which is why you waited five long days, thinking that was surely long enough for any normal person to quit watching the video feeds...and to give up looking for you."

"Or so I thought," said Lucy. "Which implies that you, my good lady, may not be normal."

"You have no idea," I said, and left it at that. "Moving on. Your disappearance, then, was well documented. Your reappearance, not so much. And it took some luck on my part to even notice you. Admittedly, at that point, I was close to giving up looking."

"Your perseverance is admirable," she said.

"Again, quit trying to get on my good side."

"I'm only stating the facts, Ms. Moon. Continue, if you will. This is fun."

"Your disappearance baffled everyone, including the police and the public at large. The police opened up a missing person's case, although not a homicide case, because no body was found, and no one, really, had any clue what happened to you."

"Keep going, Sam. You're close."

I felt it, too. This time, I tapped my nails on the desk's drawer, near my leg, and out of sight of her eyes. "There were no suspects because no crime appeared to have been committed. Even your husband—and husbands are usually the first suspects—wasn't really considered a suspect. At least, not after the initial questioning and viewing of the tape. Once your disappearance had been established, your husband was no longer deemed a suspect." I shook my head. "I'm sorry, that's all I've got."

"You circled it, Samantha. You got so close. I'll fill in the blanks." She sat forward, collected herself. "I love my husband. But I'm not in love with him. My husband is also abusive."

"Physically?"

"Sometimes. But mostly, verbally and psychologically."

"Hold on," I said, and now I did scan her thoughts, her memories. There he was, yelling at her. There he was, holding her against a wall by the throat. There he was, threatening her. There he was, weeping over his poor judgment and begging her to take him back.

"Did he ever hurt you?" I asked.

"Not really; he just scared me."

"I think I understand now," I said.

"Enlighten me," she said, sitting back.

"You wanted out, but you wanted to punish him, too."

"Very good, Sam."

"You wanted him to always wonder what happened to you, to perhaps never find a moment's rest again."

"Very, very good, Sam."

"And in the process, you could start a new life somewhere. Start over. I take it you had no kids."

"None, and not a lot of family either."

"Just your sister," I said. "Who knew about the plot."

"Yes, the *plot*. I like that."

"And had you just walked away, hopped on a plane somewhere and started over…"

"My husband, more than likely, would have been arrested for murdering me. There were enough phone calls to the police to warrant that."

"You could have just divorced him."

"He threatened to come after me, to never let me go. To make my life a living hell."

"But you loved him."

"Enough to not want to see him rot in jail."

"But not enough to not traumatize him."

"I lived with similar trauma for many years. He was due. He loves me. I know that. But he is not a good man."

I looked at her and suddenly appreciated the depth of her cunning. "So, you disappeared in such a way—a documented way—that your husband wouldn't be a suspect. A true disappearance."

"Yes."

"And he would always wonder, perhaps until the day he died, what happened to you."

338

A long, slow smile spread over her face. "Yes, Sam. Oh, yes."

"And you would be free to start over."

"That was the plan."

"All while your husband suffered and drove himself mad."

"It would serve him right."

I drummed my fingers on the edge of drawer. "You are a devious woman, Lucy Gleason."

"I've had many years to cook up my escape, Ms. Moon."

"I assume you have fake passports, fake identities."

"You name it," she said, "and I have it."

"So, you can truly start over somewhere."

"Yes, at least, that was the dream."

"There is, of course, the small matter of the dead homicide investigator," I said. "Detective Renaldo."

"Yes, I heard, from my sister, that he had passed. You think I had anything to do with that?"

I scanned her thoughts, scanned them deeply and completely, and saw that she hadn't. Saw, in fact, that she would never commit such a heinous act. I felt her horror at just the thought of it. His death had been a true hit and run. Maybe I would throw in a freebie for the Corona Police Department and run down Renaldo's killer. *Maybe, we'll see.*

"No," I said, finally. "I don't think that at all."

"So, what do we do now?"

"*We* don't do anything," I said. "*You,* on the other hand, would do well to disappear. I hear Borneo is nice this time of year."

"Your tape…"

"Will be erased."

"Would you mind if I watched you erase it? Sorry, but I've been on the run for a few weeks now, and I'm a little, ah, paranoid."

"*No problemo,*" I said, busting out my Spanish. I showed her my phone, and then had her watch as I erased the latest audio recording, *her* audio recording.

"Thank you, Samantha Moon," she said. She reached over the desk and shook my hand, flinching only slightly at my ice-cold touch. Then she nodded, thanked me again, and left.

I watched her leave, and then waited for Detective Sharp to come all the way over from Corona, before I gave him the bad news that it had been a case of mistaken identity.

Oh, and there was also the matter of wiping his memory clean of me finding her on the tape...and anyone else in his department he might have told.

I smiled at that...

And so did the demon inside me.

Chapter Forty-three

"**A**re you alone?" I asked.

I was sitting with my back against a brick wall. I held my phone loosely against my ear. I had to, because I was dripping sweat. I had gone for a long jog, and had done a lot of hard thinking while I ran.

My jog had led me to here, many miles from my home.

"I've been alone for a long time now, Sam," said the deep voice on the other end. A voice that was deeper than most men, which made sense, since his lung capacity was much bigger, too. Much bigger by a lot.

"You mean from the parade of young, nubile women coming and going in and out of your house at all hours of the night and day?"

"Jesus, Sam. It was never like that. Well, maybe for a few years, but never like what you just described."

"A full decade is more than a few years."

"Not when you're something like me," said Kingsley, who always hated talking about who we really were on the phone.

"And me," I said.

"Two freaks," he said.

"That's my line," I said, and watched a moth flutter around the outdoor light. Now, two moths. They looked a tad confused. I wondered if they thought they were circling the sun.

"I miss you, Sam," he said, and I heard his voice break. "I've missed you ever since my stupid mistake."

"Stupid, stupid mistake," I said.

"I've missed you every day, of every hour, and I have been empty ever since."

"You've dated..."

"I've *tried* to date. Nothing's worked out. Truth was, I didn't want anything to work out. I wanted you back. I want you back now."

"Why?"

"Because you're my girl, Samantha Moon."

"Am I now?"

"Yes. I felt it from the moment I first laid eyes on you."

"The moment you first laid eyes on me, I was a married woman."

"And I was respectful," he said. "I waited. And when we did start dating, I knew you weren't in a good place. I sensed you were skittish, hurt, and not ready for anything too deep or too fast. I kept my distance, and let you find your way to me. And then, you did. And I was so happy."

I didn't say anything. I didn't have to. We both knew what had happened next.

And, for the first time, I let his mistake go...and I forgave him. Maybe not completely, but enough to move on.

"So, what do we do now?" I asked.

And for an answer, the front door swung open, and Kingsley stared down at me from high above, his shaggy hair almost covering his face entirely. He was still holding his phone to his ear.

"Stay with me," he said. "Tonight. One night is all I ask."

He reached down, and I looked long and hard at his thick paw... then took his hand. He lifted me to my feet effortlessly...and pulled me into his arms. I went willingly enough.

"One night," I said, lifting my face.

"One night is all I need," he said, lowering his face to mine, and he kissed me harder than he'd ever kissed me before.

And he kissed me like that all night long...and well into morning.

The End

MOON DRAGON

VAMPIRE FOR HIRE #10

DEDICATION

To Abraham.

ACKNOWLEDGMENT

A special thank you to the beautiful and talented, Diane Arkenstone.

MOON DRAGON

"Here be dragons."
The Lenox Globe, circa 1510

"It is a rare vampire who can transform himself
into something greater. It is an even rarer vampire who can control the demon within."
Diary of the Undead

Chapter One

Last night, *Sixty Minutes* ran a segment on Judge Judy, which I made a point to record.

Now, with a pile of clean laundry in front of me and a pair of Anthony's briefs momentarily forgotten over one shoulder—a pair I had dubbed "The Forever Stain"—I sat, transfixed, for the entire segment.

I watched Judge Judy's rise from a small New Jersey Family Appellate Court judge to one of the highest-paid TV personalities today. *The* highest-paid part surprised me. Then again, I think she deserves every penny. After all, she is a role model for many, and the voice of reason to all. Anyway, the segment showed a softer side of the judge, and I appreciated seeing that. I like her softer side. She is a mother and grandmother. Someday, I hope to be a grandmother, too.

That I would be the world's youngest-looking grandmother was another story. That my granddaughters or grandsons would, within a few decades, look older than me, was...well, the same story. That I might never meet them was too heartbreaking to consider. Perhaps I would be introduced as a long-lost aunt or something.

I sighed when the segment was over. The judge has a beautiful life, a challenging job, and grandkids everywhere. She has aged gracefully, seemingly stronger now than ever.

Myself, I have been a vampire now for nine years. I had been turned in my late twenties. Twenty-eight, in fact. I still looked twenty-eight, perhaps even younger. Perhaps closer to twenty-five or twenty-six. I should be on the cusp of looking like I was forty. Instead, I look like I am a few years out of grad school.

I might look young. I might have the strength of ten women. I might even occasionally turn into a giant vampire bat. But raising two kids—one of whom was a teenager and the other was damn close—seriously took a superhuman effort. How mortals did it, I would never know.

I sighed heavily when I turned off the TV, briefly jealous of the life Judge Judy had created, and wondering how the hell my life was going to turn out, knowing I would have to cross that bridge when I got there.

My doorbell rang.

I looked at the time on my cell. My potential client was early.

I glanced at the laundry piles scattered over the couch and recliner and shrugged. That's what my potential client got for being early. Still, I quickly shoved the briefs under the biggest pile. No one deserved to see The Forever Stain. Even early clients. Hell, even my worst enemies. Truly cruel and unusual punishment.

I had long since ditched my annoying habit of reaching up for my sunglasses every time I opened the front door, or checking my exposed skin for sunblock. Indeed, those habits had been eradicated in this past year. A year I had spent "living in the light," as Allison liked to put it. *Allison is annoying too, but I love her.*

Now, I confidently opened the front door and ushered in a woman I knew. A woman I loathed. A woman I nearly slammed the front door on, or tripped as she came in. Or blindsided and tackled her to the floor where I wanted to give her the world's biggest noogie and wedgie and then drag her over to my bathroom toilet for a "swirlie," as the kids used to call it back when I was in high school.

But I didn't.

I had been preparing myself all day to see Nancy Pearson. Or, as she liked to be called in a former life, Sugar Pearson.

She was, of course, the woman my murdered ex-husband had cheated on me with while we were married. She had called earlier today and requested to see me. I had nearly told her to go to hell. In fact, I was fairly certain I had thought it loud enough for her to hear it, because she had said, "Excuse me" at one point.

Anyway, she needed help and thought I was the right woman for the job.

Oh, joy.

So, being the sucker that I am—or, as Kingsley puts it, the bleeding heart that I am—I allowed the woman into my home, the woman who'd helped to destroy my marriage. I led her down the hall and into my office.

I settled behind my desk, and she did the same in front of my desk, in one of the three client chairs.

"So," I said, noticing my heartbeat had picked up its pace, which, for me, was saying something. I also noted that my inner alarm system was ringing slightly just inside my ear. "Talk."

She nodded, took in some air and tried to look me in the eye, gave up, and finally looked away. "I'm fairly certain—no, scratch that—I'm most definitely certain, that my ex-boyfriend is a serial killer."

Chapter Two

Her aura glowed a light blue.

She was telling the truth, and yet my warning system was still chiming slightly. I've learned to listen to this warning system. The problem was, well, it wasn't precise. I didn't know exactly *why* it was ringing, only that something about this woman presented a threat to me.

I thought about that when I said, "Why not go to the police?"

"I can't prove anything."

"Then how do you know?"

The girl with the stage name of "Sugar," but whose real name was Nancy Pearson, was having a hard time sitting still. She crossed and recrossed her legs in, let's admit it, a fabulous display of dexterity. I could see how someone as feeble-minded as Danny would get seduced by such athleticism. She had probably worked the stripper stage impressively. None of which made me like her any better. Now, her high-heeled foot jiggled and bounced hyperactively. She looked like a woman with a secret, or someone who had to pee, or...

"Do you mind if I smoke?"

"I do."

"Seriously?" she said.

"Seriously," I said.

"Please?"

"No."

"Pretty please?"

"Okay."

"Really?"

"No."

"You're mean."

"You have no idea. Now talk."

She took out her packet of cigarettes anyway, opened it, removed a slightly bent one, stuck it between her teeth, and said, "Then let me at least pretend."

"Pretend all you want."

She did just that, sucking on the end of it like a real pro. She even exhaled. She did this again and I tried not to laugh.

"It's not funny," she said.

"I tried not to laugh."

"Well, you didn't do a very good job of it."

I waited as she inhaled again on her unlit cigarette, exhaled some nonexistent smoke. Her foot bounced at the end of her ankle like a fish dangling from a line. Then, she actually asked for an ashtray.

"There are no ashes," I pointed out reasonably.

"Please," she said. "It helps."

I sighed and rooted around a bottom drawer and found something Anthony had made back in arts and crafts when he was in first grade. I use the words "arts and crafts" liberally. Whatever it was—a hand or a butt cheek—I set it in front of her. She shrugged and proceeded to tap off some invisible ashes.

Our last encounter was a memorable one. Sugar had tried to stop me as I approached my then-husband's office. Tried being the operative word. I might have hit her hard enough to break her nose. And I might have enjoyed it way too much.

"I said sorry about that," said Sugar. She had picked up on my thoughts and assumed, like most people did, that I had spoken. I had not. And, yes, earlier on the phone, she had apologized again about sleeping with Danny.

"So you said."

"I mean, you aren't still mad about that, are you? That was, like, years ago."

"Two and a half years ago. And, yes, I'm still mad."

355

"Well, I'm sorry. If it wasn't me, it would have been any of the other girls. Your husband was, like, into all of us."

"Good to know."

"Besides, I haven't seen him in, like, over a year. Have you?"

"On and off," I said, referring to his ghost who appeared occasionally in my home. I usually found him in the kid's rooms, standing over them as they slept. Sugar didn't need to know that Danny had been murdered by a vampire who had been out to get me, too. Or that Danny had aligned with the wrong team...and had gotten himself killed. Which is why I blocked those thoughts.

She said, "Okay, well, tell him I miss him."

And I saw it there, on her face, and heard it in her voice. She truly had feelings for him. Sadly, I didn't miss him so much. Rarely, in fact. Perhaps only once or twice, tops. Not like the kids, who still mourn for their daddy. At least someone had loved Danny before he died, because it sure as hell wasn't me.

"I'll tell him," I said, and my voice might have softened a bit, dammit. Yeah, I have a bleeding heart for sure. "Now, why do you think your ex-boyfriend is a serial killer?"

She picked up the unlit cigarette and held it loosely between her fingers. "Because he told me."

Chapter Three

"And why would he do that?" I asked.

Yes, she looked ridiculous with the unlit cigarette hanging from her lips. Admittedly, I admired her commitment to her habit, unhealthy as it was. I decided not to let her know that, I, too, smoked from time to time, but never in the house. Usually in the car or on long stakeouts. Even if cancerous cells did develop in my lungs, the vampire in me eradicated them instantly.

There were benefits to being what I was. And these days, now that I could go into the sun and eat and drink and be merry, the benefits far outweighed the risks.

"He talks in his sleep," said Nancy.

"And this was recently?"

"Yes."

The word *slut* might have slipped through my mind, although I wasn't one to judge. I'd had two relationships since my divorce from Danny, and three, if you counted my mental relationship with Fang, which I kinda did.

"You don't like me very much, do you?" asked Nancy. Oops, the "slut" part might have slipped out. Might have.

"No," I said. "Not really."

"You're probably wondering why I came to you and not, say, another detective."

"The thought occurred to me."

Yes, I could probe her mind for the answers I wanted. The thing was, I didn't *want* to probe her mind. I didn't *want* to dip down into her thoughts and see what made this woman tick. I also didn't want to stumble across any memories of her and Danny. At present, such memories were probably brewing on the surface...all of their lies and deception and sneaking around and not-very-good-sneaking around.

"Danny talked, too," she said, looking away.

"Not in his sleep," I said.

"No, never in his sleep. I guess we both know that." She laughed at that and kicked her leg a little; we were just two girls sharing memories of the same man in bed. A man she had taken from me, although he went willingly enough. Actually, I imagined him running from me. Turned out his instincts were partly true. Had Danny and I continued to sleep together, he would have been bonded to me as a sort of sex slave, as had been the case with Russell. I shuddered at the thought.

"Danny would tell me things," she said, sucking ridiculously at the end of the unlit cigarette and blowing out her pretend smoke. I wondered if she was even aware that the fag wasn't lit. *Yes, I'm channeling my inner Brit.*

"What things?" I asked. My eyes might have narrowed suspiciously.

She took the cigarette out of her mouth and looked at it, wrinkling her nose. Then looked me directly in the eye. "He said you're a vampire."

"Did he now?"

She nodded vigorously. "And he was scared of you. Like, irrationally scared of you."

"Because I was a vampire?"

"That's what he said."

"And did you believe him?"

"I really, really want to light this cigarette," she said.

Suddenly, I wanted one, too. I stood and said, "Follow me."

Chapter Four

We were in my back yard, smoking.

We sat side by side on the broken cement stairs that led from the kitchen down into my back yard. Despite being broken, the stairs sported a coat of gray paint. That had been Danny's answer to all of our home improvement needs: paint the crap out of it.

One of us was smoking because she had an addiction. The other was smoking because she still had a need to feel normal. There was a chance I was the latter. Of course, the entity inside me wanted nothing to do with normal.

The entity inside me could go to hell.

"I'm sorry for what I did," said Nancy, aka Sugar.

I inhaled, peering through the smoke rising before me, obscuring the neon Pep Boys' sign that itself rose above my backyard fence. Yes, I shared a backyard fence with the Pep Boys' parking lot. Handy for when I needed an emergency fuel filter. Danny did get one thing right: he got us a big back yard, which had proved to be kinda fun, back when we were a real family.

We're still a family, I thought, *just minus the Danny part.*

Of course, Danny still came around, just minus the body part. In fact, he came around more in death than he did when alive. Funny how being dead made him a more attentive father. Better late than never.

"Did you say something?" asked Nancy.

Oops. Sometimes, despite my best efforts, my thoughts leaked out, especially when I was bonding with someone.

Oh, bloody hell, I thought. *Please don't tell me I'm bonding with her.*

"I'm not that bad," said Nancy, inhaling and looking around. "And who are you talking to?"

"Sorry," I said, inhaling deeply on my own cig. "I do that sometimes."

"Do what?"

"Think out loud."

She giggled. "So do I!"

Great.

I sighed and looked at her and exhaled a plume of smoke in her direction. I had been tempted to do so in her face, but realized the longer I was with her, the more my hate for her was quickly ebbing. Above, a seagull squawked. I was fifteen miles from the sea. This time, I kept my thoughts purposely open.

"Maybe it's lost," said Nancy. "Wait a second...your lips didn't move."

"No."

"But I heard you..."

"Oh?"

She thought about that. "Actually, I heard you directly in my head. Just inside my ear."

"How cool is that?"

"I...I'm not sure it's cool. How come you aren't blinking?"

"I don't need to blink," I said.

"Oh, Jesus."

"He might have blinked," I said. "But then again, I'm not an historian."

"Then it's true," said Nancy.

"That I'm not an expert on Jesus."

She slapped my arm, a gesture that surprised both of us. "Oh, shit," she said. "Sorry."

"It's okay."

"You really are a vampire."

"I'm something that has vampiric traits," I said. The suggestion always rankled me, although, to be honest, few people suggested it. "What, exactly, I am is open to interpretation."

"You're not going to, like, kill me, are you?"

"Only if you sleep with my next husband."

"I'm really sorry about that."

I nodded toward my house. "You didn't sound sorry earlier."

"I guess I was feeling a bit defensive...and didn't think about your feelings." She made a small face at the word *feelings*. Speaking of feelings, I had a strong feeling that Nancy didn't much like talking about her own.

"And how do you think I feel?" I asked.

She scrunched up her face at the question, as if she'd bitten into a sour grape. "Well, it's like...I can feel how you felt. It's weird."

"Go on."

"You felt abandoned. Alone. Jealous. Scared. Heartbroken. And I..."

"And you what?"

"And I contributed to a lot of that."

We were silent some more, each sucking and puffing and sitting closer than I ever thought I would sit next to my ex-husband's mistress.

After a moment, she said, "It's no secret that I was a stripper. And when Danny showed an interest in me...I mean, he was a lawyer, for Christ's sake."

"You couldn't help yourself," I said.

She shrugged and I sensed her getting defensive, so I mentally pushed her to continue. If anything, hearing her side helped me to heal a little. Helped me understand a little more, too. Danny was a shit, but I had been in love with him and his actions back then had been a dagger to the heart. Mercifully, not a silver dagger.

"I had a rough life," she went on. "I'd been turning tricks since I was fifteen, after I left home."

Despite my best efforts to shield myself from her own memories, I saw them now, flashing through her mind, each more disturbing than the next. She had been abused by her parents and grandparents. Her memories made me want to never let my kids leave the house again.

"How did a hooker..." My voice trailed off.

"Go on, you can say it."

"Fine. How did a former hooker end up as Danny's legal secretary?"

"I have a funny how-we-met story." She paused. "I had a car wreck when I was hit by a drunk driver on the way home from the strip club. I had to be cut out of my car with the Jaws of Life and Danny was there when they took me to the hospital."

"Let me guess. He wanted to take your case on contingency."

"Yeah, how did you know?"

"Lucky guess. Did someone rich hit your car?"

She nodded. "I was hit by a local politician who desperately wanted to settle out of court. Danny told me that during the case, I couldn't work as a dancer, since we were claiming disability, so he gave me a little job as his legal secretary at one-tenth of what I made before, you know, to show that I had lost earning power." She paused. "Danny got me a nice out-of-court settlement and he used his part of the proceeds to buy out the strip club where I worked because I told him it was a gold mine. I used my part of the settlement to get a little condo in Beverly Hills. I went back to dancing at the club he now owned and the rest is history."

Now the pieces were coming together about why Danny had left lawyering to own a strip club. I tried not to let my eyebrows go up. "And you and Danny got pretty close, I guess," I said, not bothering to hide my irritation.

She shrugged. "Danny seemed like he liked me. And he told me he was getting a divorce from you, and that you were this horrible person. He made me not like you in return. And then…"

"And then he told you about me being a vampire."

"Yeah."

"What did you think about that?"

She looked at me long and steady before she replied, "Let's just say that I wasn't as weirded out by it as you might think."

What I saw next in her mind made me gasp. I snapped my head around and stared at her. "Your ex-boyfriend…"

"Is not so different from you, Sam…"

CHAPTER FIVE

Allison and I were at a place called Alicia's in Brea.

Besides being a typical sit-down café, Alicia's specialized in, of all adorable things, making to-go picnic lunches, complete with wicker baskets, silverware and checkered tablecloths. A picnic with Kingsley sounded like fun, now that I no longer shrank away from the light of day like a monster in a 1930s' horror movie. Maybe we could go to Tri-City Lake. Spread out a blanket in the shade. Lots of wine. And lots of canoodling—

"Canoodling?" said Allison. "Are you sure you aren't, say, a hundred and five?"

"A hundred and five?"

"It was the first number that popped into my head."

"Oddly specific."

Allison shrugged and bit into her smoked roast beef and raspberry jelly sandwich on, of course, a slender baguette. And because I regularly fed on her—which not only enhanced my strength but also increased her own witchy powers—Allison and I also had the closest of all telepathic links.

She seemed to revel in that. Me, not so much. Luckily, she and I had become best friends—and yes, to my extreme annoyance, she even used the word "besties." Anyway, Allison had proven herself as a good and loyal friend, and a steady source of blood. Yeah, our relationship was...unorthodox. But we both benefited. Symbiosis at its best.

Except for the "bestie" part, of course. In fact, I might be the only bloodsucker on earth who has a bestie.

My life, I thought.

"Quit bitching," said Allison between bites. "You should be so lucky. I happen to come in handy."

The next thought that crossed my mind, I regretted, but there it was, and she picked up on it instantly.

"And I am not needy, Samantha Moon. I have a full, rich life, of which you should be honored to be a part."

"Oh, brother."

"Well, you should."

"Fine," I said, picking up my own sandwich. "I'm honored as hell."

"Don't patronize me…"

It went on like this throughout the next five minutes, all while I ate the first half of my sandwich. It had been over a year since I had been given the gift of food and sunlight, thanks to two special rings, one on each hand. The rings had done much to give me back my life. Eating lunch in the light of day with my friend was a gift beyond measure.

"Okay, that's more like it," said Allison, beaming.

"Happy?" I said.

"Oh, yes," she said. "Now tell me about Nancy Home Wrecker."

"Nancy Pearson," I said. "And she's not that bad."

"Not that bad? Didn't she steal your husband and ruin your life?"

"A lot of things contributed to ruining my life. And he was on his way out anyway."

"That's a lame excuse, Sam."

"Well, the guy is dead, and what happened can't be changed… and, well, it turns out she's not that bad."

Allison, who always got a bit jealous over my other friends, set her fork down. "I thought you were going to tell me about her sadistic ex-boyfriend, not that she *wasn't that bad.*"

She rattled on like this for the next few minutes, all while I consumed the second half of my sandwich. When Allison was done ranting and raving, and when I had convinced her that no one would be replacing her "bestie" status anytime soon—which seemed to mollify her—I told her what I'd learned about Nancy's ex-boyfriend.

"A werewolf?" said Allison, perhaps a little too loudly.

I shushed her. "Yes."

"Have you talked to Kingsley about him?"

"I will soon," I said. "He had a lunch meeting today."

"So, I was your second choice?" asked Allison.

"You're in rare needy form today," I said.

"I'm not nee—" She paused. "Okay, maybe a little. What can I say? You either love me or leave me."

"I love you," I said. "For now."

She stuck out her tongue at me as the waitress came by and cleared our table. I enjoyed everything about going out to eat. I treasured the small moments, even the waitress clearing the table, asking if I wanted a refill on my iced tea. I just loved it all. I loved the chatter of women from a nearby table; they were insurance adjusters from the nearby Mercury Insurance office. One of them kept glancing at me, a tall redhead who reminded me of Nicole Kidman. Some people sense I am different; some people have enhanced psychic abilities. They may not understand why I am different, but they feel it, and give me strange looks. Like the redhead just now. I smiled at her. She blushed and gave me a half-smile and busied herself with her salad.

When the waitress was gone, Allison leaned over the table said, "So he's a bad werewolf?"

"A bad doggy?"

She giggled. "Yes."

"You could say that," I said.

In fact, Nancy had said more than that. Apparently, her ex-boyfriend did more than transform each full moon. He killed, too.

"Killed, how?" she asked, reading my thoughts.

"In a cabin in the woods."

"We have woods here?"

"Arrowhead, ding dong," I said.

"Oh, right, and don't be mean."

I sighed, and continued. "Apparently, he…preps for his turnings."

"Preps, how?"

"With bodies."

"Live bodies?"

"Yes."

"But how…"

"Hikers mostly. Kidnapped, drugged, locked up in his cabin's basement. Where he, in turn, locks himself up each full moon."

"And then what?" asked Allison, eyes wide. "Wait, I don't wanna—"

"He feasts on them, of course."

"…know," she finished, turning a little green.

The waitress came by with our bill. I thought paying was the least I could do, since Allison suddenly looked traumatized. Hearing about a werewolf exploring his true nature—his powerful nature—and feasting on weakling humans, didn't quite haunt me the same way it did Allison. I also knew this was the demon inside me. Or, rather, her influence on me. Or was it? These days, I wasn't quite sure. This should have concerned me more than it did.

"Well, it concerns me, Sam," she said. "And thanks for lunch. I think."

"Oh, cheer up," I said.

"You sound oddly perky for someone who just told me that a local werewolf has a kill room up in Arrowhead."

"Not perky…intrigued."

"Okay, that might be even worse. And he confessed to all of this while asleep?"

"Apparently so."

"What are you going to do next?"

I looked at the time on my cell. "Meet with Kingsley. You know, my *first* choice." I winked as we stood.

"I hate you, Samantha Moon."

"No, you don't."

"You're right, I don't...but don't be surprised if you push me away someday into the arms of another bestie."

"One can hope," I said, and nudged her with my elbow as we left the café.

The red-haired girl watched me the whole way.

CHAPTER SIX

I was in Kingsley's office, waiting.

These days, Kingsley employs male receptionists and secretaries. I might have had something to do with that. Kingsley, a known playboy, didn't need the temptation. Did I trust him these days? Mostly. Did he need a blond bimbo leaning over his desk with her cleavage showing, looking to move up in the world of paralegals? Hell, no.

I knew he loved me, and I seriously doubted he would do anything to screw this up again. Then again...

"Once a cheater, always a cheater," or so my sister liked to tell me.

Except I knew that Kingsley was looking for something more, something real, and something with another immortal. Truth was, my own choices were quite limited, since I tended to turn mortals into love slaves. Not a bad idea in theory, but in practice, it was miserable. Try getting through your day when another is literally waiting on you hand and foot, and mostly underfoot.

Yesss, came a voice deep within me.

Of course, *she* would approve. For all I knew, she was instrumental in creating the love slave bond-thing. Which made sense, since she wanted to enslave me, too. To control me completely and totally.

I continued walking through Kingsley's spacious office. The hairy oaf was still into his moons. Everywhere I looked was another full moon. In fact, he had some new additions since the last time I'd been here. The moon globe was new, as was the moon mouse pad and, yes, there was an actual moon rock fragment sitting inside a

368

glass case next to his wet bar. A single spotlight shone down on the rock, which itself was encased in a domed glass. How the man had acquired it, I didn't know. Could you buy moon rocks on eBay?

I was leaning down, peering at it closely, when I heard the door whisper open, and felt a presence enter the room. A very big presence. "It's from the Apollo 14 mission," said a deep voice from behind me, so deep that I seemingly felt it in my own chest. Hell, if I listened close enough, I would have probably heard the glass case rattle. "It's also highly illegal to own it."

"I should turn you in, counselor," I said, turning.

I hadn't even made a complete turn when the big guy pounced, faster than he had any right to pounce, defying physics and, no doubt, straining his expensive suit to the limit. He was on me before I knew it, turning me all the way around, his mouth covering mine, his hair hanging down all over me. To say that he smothered me would be an understatement. To say that I didn't love it would be a lie.

It took all my willpower to push him off me, which I did. He didn't go willingly.

"Down boy," I said, using nearly all my strength to pry the big lug nut off me.

He pushed back his mane of thick hair. He propped a hand on the wall above me and leaned down. I could have been in the shadow of a giant sequoia. "To what do I owe this unexpected visit?"

I stepped under his arm, ducking, although I didn't need to duck. I adjusted my shirt and hair, both of which had been thoroughly groped and mauled and pulled by his giant man-hands.

"I had the strong need to be felt up," I said.

"Really?" He moved toward me again, clearly moved by my romantic words.

"No, ding-a-ling." I held him back at arm's length. The thing about dating a known playboy and an alpha male is, well, they have a high testosterone level, and they know how to get what they want. And they're used to getting what they want. The trick is to make them earn it. Work for it. Beg for it.

369

But now, of course, wasn't the time or place for any of that, as much as I liked to see Kingsley beg. I asked, "Do you know a man named Gunther Kessler?"

He blinked...and seemed to deflate a little, which wasn't a bad thing, under the circumstances. Kingsley all hopped-up on testosterone and adrenaline tended not to be the best conversationalist.

He sighed and crossed his arms and sat on the corner of his over-sized desk. I might have thought he was compensating with such a huge desk...but I knew better. The man wasn't compensating. He was just huge, and growing steadily at the same time. Yes, the big oaf was only getting oafier as the years went on. How big he would eventually get remained to be seen.

"No, why?" he asked.

Unlike Allison and most mortals, I didn't have a telepathic link with Kingsley and other immortals. That wasn't quite true. I did have a telepathic link to the Librarian, who was immortal via alchemical means.

Anyway, Kingsley couldn't read my mind, nor I his, which was probably a good thing.

"He's a werewolf," I said. "I think."

Kingsley raised an eyebrow—an eyebrow that was one or two tweezings away from being a unibrow. "I don't know all the were-wolves in the area. Some, but not all."

"How many *are* in the area?" I asked.

"A few dozen of us, but this is also Southern California."

"Werewolf mecca of the universe?" I said.

"No, but a highly populated part of the country, although you will generally find more werewolves up north."

"Where it's cooler," I said.

"We do tend to be on the plus size," he said. "So, what about this guy?" Kingsley crossed his arms over a massive chest.

Did I detect a hint of jealousy?

"He's a killer," I said. "I think."

"What do you mean?"

I told him what I knew about Gunther. About talking in his sleep. About the cabin in the mountains. About the killing room. About the feeding.

Kingsley stared at me while I spoke. In fact, I was fairly certain he didn't blink either.

Just a couple of freaks.

The difference being, of course, his eyes glowed amber. What color mine glowed, I hadn't a clue, since I hadn't seen them in nine years. My sister had told me that my eyes had turned a darkish brown, almost black. They had once been blue. I sighed at that all over again.

When I was finished, Kingsley pushed off the desk and walked over to the wet bar, where he poured himself a finger or two of Crystal Skull vodka, which seemed fitting under the circumstances.

"Some werewolves hunger for fresh blood," he said. "Or live food."

"You don't," I said, and it was a memory I would rather forget. The one time Kingsley had escaped his own "safe room," which was deep under his estate home, he had gone straight to a local cemetery...and dug up a freshly buried body. That he had consumed it was something that should have been a dealbreaker for me. Luckily, Kingsley didn't have much control over himself when he was in his changeling state.

Still...so gross. *And I kiss that mouth.*

"No, Sam. I don't hunger for fresh blood. But many do. In fact, we're very nearly divided down the middle."

"Half prefer corpses, half prefer the living."

He winced a little. "Right."

We both knew what the wince meant...and we both let it go. I doubted Kingsley was proud of his actions. Then again, he had very little control of his actions, either, although he had ended up in my hotel room...and had restrained himself from attacking me. *Somehow.*

I said, "Well, there's a chance he's killed many."

371

"I don't doubt it, Sam. Not all werewolves are responsible, Sam. Nor are all vampires. Some kill. Some love to kill. But, like you and me, many of us take precautions against our true natures."

My precaution was feeding regularly from Allison—and, if desperate enough, from the packs of cow and pig blood in my refrigerator in the garage. Kingsley had a holding cell beneath his house. A safe room.

I said, "Well, he's taking precautions, too. Except he's locking up hikers with him."

Food, although I couldn't bring myself to say it.

The entity within me was enjoying this conversation very much. I felt her rise up through my consciousness so that she wouldn't miss a word. *Crazy bitch.*

"Some people are killers before they turn, Sam," said Kingsley. "And some of us give in to the darkness within us."

"And feed the demons within us," I said.

"Right. It takes willpower and fortitude to stay true to ourselves."

"Tell me about it," I said, and sighed.

As he drank, I considered having a finger or two of vodka myself, but I had to pick up the kids soon, and, although alcohol had no effect on me, it wouldn't be a good thing picking up the kids with vodka breath. The principal already didn't like me as it was.

Instead, I folded my arms over my own chest and drummed my pointed fingernails along my upper arm. "He's going to have to be stopped."

"I agree," said Kingsley. "Let me ask around, see what I can find out on the guy."

"Thank you."

"And Sam?"

"Yes?"

He sighed loudly. "Please be careful."

I stood on my tippy-toes and ruffled his thick mane of hair…and planted a big kiss on his thick lips.

"Always," I said, and left.

Chapter Seven

It was late.

Although I now existed nicely in the sun, I had gotten used to my late-night hours. My vampire hours. Turns out, working late and private investigations sort of go hand-in-hand. Plus, the night time just...suited me. I felt comfortable under the cloak of darkness...and exposed and vulnerable in daylight. After all, I was just a vigorous hand-washing away from losing my precious amethyst ring down, say, a sink drain, and then where would I be? Back to working the night shift, permanently. And shrieking in the light of day like the pathetic monster I am.

Now, making a mental note to use minimum amounts of soap—I relaxed in the back seat of my minivan and kept a watchful eye on Gunther Kessler's two-story home.

The lights had been out when I pulled up thirty minutes ago. There was a Dodge Charger parked out front. The home was a turn-of-the-century wooden deal, with a wraparound porch and lots of shutters. A half-dozen wide cement stairs led up to the front door. Very typical for Old Town Orange, an area I loved.

It was past midnight and the kids were asleep. These days, I often left them alone. Tammy was thirteen and Anthony was eleven going on twenty. Meaning, he didn't look anything like your typical eleven-year-old. After my son had lost his own guardian angel—long story—Ishmael, my ex-guardian angel, had imbued Anthony with all sorts of angelic powers, some of which had caused my boy to grow a bit taller than your average eleven-year-old. And to become far stronger than your average eleven-year-old, too. Hell, far stronger than even your average adult male.

Anyway, now my son acted as his own guardian angel, meaning, he could take care of himself and then some.

Of course, I'm pretty sure Ishmael did all of this to get on my good side, to sort of make up for his negligence in protecting me, back when I was first turned nine years ago.

Truth was, his gesture to help my son did go far. I appreciated it. My life was weird enough without having to worry that my son no longer had his guardian angel.

Now, he didn't need a guardian angel. Now, my son was a hell of a force to be reckoned with.

And he was only eleven.

Sweet mama.

Now, I was on a quiet street in downtown Orange, near the offices of a private investigator friend of mine, Mercedes Cruz. Mercedes, or Mercy, was a different kind of strange altogether. She was, I was certain, a witch. Of course, she and I didn't discuss such matters. Nor did we discuss that I was a vampire, although I always suspected she knew. Witches are like that. What we did discuss was our kids, our work, our mutual friends, all while eyeing each other suspiciously. Anyway, I knew she was doing good work here in Orange, protecting the legal—and illegal—immigrants from those who would take advantage of them. Like I said, good work.

Whether she knew of any local werewolves or not, I didn't know.

Then again, I wasn't certain Gunther was a werewolf. I had only the word of my dead ex-husband's mistress. And even then, he'd only been talking in his sleep.

"What am I doing here?" I said.

Easy. Nancy had caught me in a lull. No pending cases, and certainly no paying cases. And, no, she hadn't offered to pay me either. Still, try as I might to hate her, I just couldn't. Truth was, with Danny now dead, most of my anger had died, too. As she'd said, if it hadn't been her, it would have been another girl at Danny's strip club.

I know how to pick 'em.

Earlier, I had run Gunther Kessler's name through my various databases. Outside of his downtown Orange home, there was nothing to suggest he even owned a home in Arrowhead, where Nancy claimed he had a "killing room." A place where he turned from human to werewolf on each full moon. And where, apparently, he feasted on the living.

I drummed my pointed fingernails on my steering wheel.

The demoness within me was highly interested in this line of thinking. I could feel her following along, mostly approving of what she was hearing. She enjoyed death and destruction. She enjoyed feasting on the weak. She knew that fear made people less powerful, and her more powerful.

Yesss, came the single word.

For the most part, I'd been able to contain her in a small section of my mind, but she often figured a way out, slipping back into my consciousness like smoke under a doorway. These days, I didn't mind when she slipped through. Other than being a psychopath hell-bent on taking over the world, I found her company...less and less annoying.

Shaking my head over the insanity of it all, I continued to watch Gunther Kessler's home, all the way up through the morning.

Interestingly, not one but two cars sporting big, furry mustaches on their grills drove past me on the street. One was odd enough... but two?

I nearly Googled "cars with furry mustaches" when Gunther's front door opened and he stepped outside. I knew it was him because Nancy had emailed me pictures of him. Not to mention I had done a Google search on him and found his Facebook page. Yes, even werewolves had Facebook pages.

If he was a werewolf.

Anyway, he was dressed in a suit and tie, with his long hair gleaming wet. A medium-sized man, he headed straight to his Dodge Charger parked in the driveway. He clicked it open, got in, and backed out.

When he was halfway down the street, I forgot about the cars with mustaches and eased away from the curb to follow him.

———

I didn't follow him for long.

After a brief stop at a Starbucks—where I longed to follow him inside but somehow restrained myself—he soon pulled into the parking lot of American Title in Orange, off Main Street, about a mile away from where Kingsley worked. *Here be monsters.*

I stopped along a curb and watched him park near the front of the building. Assigned parking, surely. He got out, went around to his trunk and removed his laptop bag. Then he headed through some smoky glass doors, through which he disappeared.

Other than the longish hair, he didn't look like much of a werewolf. Kingsley, I could believe. This guy? I didn't know.

But I would find out.

I pulled away from the curb and hit up the very same Starbucks frequented by Gunther earlier, and ordered myself a venti mocha with extra mocha and extra whipped cream. I also ordered a bagel with extra cream cheese. Go big, or go home, as Anthony would say.

Long ago, I had arranged for a neighbor to take my kids to school, since, back then, I tended to be comatose in the morning. I saw no need to change the schedule. After all, during cases like this one, I might find myself working all night and well into the morning.

Or at Starbucks.

CHAPTER EIGHT

We were in the kitchen, us girls.

My sister, Mary Lou, myself and my daughter. It was later that same day, Thursday, which also happened to be our *Vampire Diaries* night. That's right, as if my life wasn't crazy enough, I also watched fictional vampires on TV...and loved every minute of it.

Not only did I love the show, I studied it. I seriously think that someone on staff was a vampire. They get so much right. Not everything, granted, but enough that I have learned much, well, about myself.

Now we were making spaghetti with spicy sausages, which happened to be Anthony's favorite, too. On Thursdays, he mostly made himself scarce, although I often caught him keeping an eye on the TV. I think he was a closet *Diaries* fan, although he wouldn't admit it. Had the show been called something like *The Vampire Scrolls*, he would have been all over it. *Boys.*

Now the three of us girls were in my kitchen, each with a job to do, although Tammy's job seemed to devolve into leaning against the counter and drinking her grape juice, while watching us with a smirk on her face. Mary Lou and I were drinking wine from goblets. Would a vampire drink wine from anything less?

"Oh, brother," said Tammy, rolling her eyes. She sipped some more of her drink.

"Oh, brother what?" I asked. I was chopping cucumbers for the salad. Mary Lou had been in the middle of telling me another work story. There was a slight chance I might have zoned out. Slight.

"I'm pretty sure not *all* vampires drink from goblets, Mom. And since when did you start calling yourself a *vampire*, anyway? I thought you hated that word."

I stopped chopping and looked at my daughter. She knew better than to read my mind when her aunt was around. Or read my mind, period. We had talked about it. Ad nauseam.

"Are you freakin' kidding me?" said Mary Lou, turning on me.

"Mary Lou…" I began.

"No, Sam. It's bad enough that you and Allison go around reading each other's minds, but now you and your daughter, too?"

I set my knife down and glared at my daughter. *You're in trouble, Missy,* I thought. Then to Mary Lou, I said, "It's not like that…"

"Oh, and what's it not like, Sam? Not to mention I'm pretty darn certain that you just, you know, *thought* something to your daughter."

"Yes, but—"

"But what? I thought you couldn't read family members' minds, Sam."

"I can't, but—"

"I thought we had an agreement, Samantha. No more leaving me out."

I took hold of her shoulders before she could work herself into a full-fledged tizzy. Behind me, Tammy giggled. I would deal with her later. "I can't read your mind, Louie. And I can't read my daughter's mind, either. But she can read mine. And she can read yours. Unless you learn how to block her out."

"I can even read Kingsley's," said Tammy. "He doesn't know it, but I can."

I hadn't thought of that before. My daughter, being the super mind reader that she was, could potentially read *anyone's* mind, mortal or immortal.

"Of course, Mommy."

We'll, talk about this later, young lady, I thought.

Meanwhile, Mary Lou didn't like being held in place by me, but tough shit. She had started this little tirade and I wasn't letting her go until she calmed down. Luckily, my words were finally sinking in.

"Tammy can read my mind?"

"Yes," I said.

Mary Lou looked from me to my daughter. Then, for some damn reason, my goofball sister actually smiled. "Really?"

"Yes, really," I said. "And this makes you happy, why?"

"Because I don't feel left out now! I feel, you know, like part of the gang."

"Of course you're part of the gang, Mary Lou, and I think you've had enough wine for tonight."

"But I just got started…"

"You've had a rough day," I said, and began steering her out of the kitchen and into the living room. "Just sit down and relax. We'll take it from here."

She called back over her shoulder. "What am I thinking now, Tammy?"

"Aunt Louie!" giggled Tammy.

I didn't have to be a mind reader to know where this was going. "Let me guess," I said, steering her toward the couch. "Damon."

They both giggled as I deposited my sister in front of the TV. Once back in the kitchen, I again didn't need to be a mind reader to know that my daughter was acting a little strange. I needed only to be a mother. I snatched her "grape juice" out of her hand and sniffed it.

Uh-oh.

CHAPTER NINE

It was after *The Vampire Diaries.*

Truth was, I didn't much enjoy the show this week. Sure, Damon looked sexy. Even Stefan had his moments. The others in the cast were electrifying and gory and funny. The plotline was convoluted but ingenious, and all in all, a great addition to the series.

Except, of course, I was having trouble concentrating on it.

Now with my sister mostly sober and gone home, and still giddy that she wasn't being left out of the cool group, I sat with my daughter in her bedroom.

Anthony had gone home with my sister, as well. I didn't want him to overhear us. Turned out, his hearing was getting better and better, too. Too good for my comfort. The kid was turning into Captain America.

Or Captain Skidmarks.

"That's funny, Mom."

"Don't try to get on my good side," I said. "And yes, that was kind of funny."

She giggled. I was fairly certain the alcohol hadn't worn off yet. It had, after all, only been an hour or so. "What have I told you about reading my thoughts?"

"I'm not supposed to. But sometimes, I can't help it."

I knew the feeling. I said, "I know you can't help it, honey. And sometimes, I can't help it either. But I want you to do your best to not listen in on adult conversations."

"I'm sorry."

"And don't listen in on your brother's thoughts, either."

"Gross. I learned my lesson about him, Mommy. Do you know that sometimes all he thinks about, for like ten straight minutes, is boobies?"

My son, of course, was eleven going on an apparently early puberty. I said, "I could have gone my whole life without knowing that."

"Well, now we both know it," and she giggled some more and, despite myself, I giggled, too. "Why do boys like boobies so much, Mommy?"

I opened my mouth to answer. "Honestly? I haven't the faintest idea."

She found that funny, too, and laughed harder...until she saw the serious look on my face.

"Uh-oh," she said.

"Uh-oh is right, young lady."

"You're mad, aren't you?"

"Says the girl who can read my mind."

"What does that mean?"

"It means you know darn well that I'm mad."

"It was just a little wine," she said. "And it was so good. No wonder you and Auntie love it so much!"

Uh-oh.

"Honey, wine is for adults. You know that."

"Well, I'm thirteen. I'm a teenager. I'm in middle school. Half the kids in my school drink beer."

"Half?"

"Well, some. And Angie Harmon's mom lets her drink at home, on special occasions."

I rubbed my face. I might have moaned.

"And I figured tonight was a special occasion!"

Now, I was massaging my temples.

"And it's not like I'm out drinking with friends on some street corner."

Now I definitely moaned.

"I drank responsibly, Mom."

I hugged my knees and started rocking on her bed. Rocking and moaning and wishing my sweet, innocent little girl wasn't saying words like "drinking responsibly."

"It's not that bad, Mom. Just a little wine. Sheesh, get over it—"

That's when I'd had enough. I quit playing the victim and took in a lot of unnecessary air, mostly to clear my mind and to calm myself down, and said, "I will not get over it, young lady. I will get right on top of it. In fact, I will get right inside it."

"Gross."

"If I *ever* see or hear of you drinking again, you are going to be in a lot of trouble."

"I'm a teenager—"

"You are thirteen and far too young to be drinking."

"But Angie and almost everyone at school—"

"I don't care about Angie and almost everyone at your school. I care about you. My daughter. Who's far too young to handle alcohol—"

"But I drank responsibly!"

"If I hear you say, 'I drank responsibly' again, I'm going to home-school you for the rest of your life."

"You can't do that."

"I can do anything I want."

"Then I will tell everyone you're a vampire! And a killer!"

My mouth fell open. It stayed open for a long, long time.

"I'm sorry, Mommy. I would never do that. Ever."

"You think I'm a killer?" I finally asked.

Tammy looked away, tears forming in the corners of her eyes. "I...I don't know, Mommy."

"You've seen me kill," I thought. "In my memory."

"Yes. You've done it a few times."

"You shouldn't be in there, baby. Ever."

She nodded, which shook free the tears.

I said, "Mommy had to...do what she had to do."

She kept on shaking her head.

"Baby, I'm sorry you had to see that."

"It's okay, Mommy. They were bad men."

I mentally ran through the horrors of the past few years. *Jesus*, I thought.

I took in some air. "You need to stay out of Mommy's thoughts, baby. Okay?"

"Okay."

"Do you promise?"

"I'll try." She paused, and what she said next had me laughing harder than it should have. "Now do you see why I was driven to drink?"

When I was done laughing into my hands, tears streaming down my cheeks—and I wasn't entirely sure if some of those tears weren't real tears—I grabbed her feet and proceeded to tickle them until she promised to never drink again.

Ever.

CHAPTER TEN

The Occult Reading Room wasn't empty.

A man was doing just that: reading in a chair in the far corner, very near the darkest, creepiest of the books. The books that seemed to possess a dark intelligence. The books that seemed, in fact, to be alive.

I heard their whisperings now as the man read. The whisperings sounded more excited than usual. In fact, they hardly seemed to notice me at all. They were, in fact, focused on the man reading.

"You hear them, too, right? The books?" I asked the Librarian, whose real name was Archibald Maximus. He was Max to me sometimes. Or even Archie. Other than my daughter, Max was the only other entity alive who seemed capable of reading my thoughts. He also seemed to have all the answers, which is why I came around. That he was easy on the eyes had nothing to do with it at all. I swear.

"Yes, Sam. I hear them. In fact, I hear all of them."

"All of them?"

"They each speak, Sam. Some louder than others."

"But...how?"

He looked at me, then at a book stacked on a nearby counter, and said, "As you know, these aren't your average books. These books have been imbued with intent, some even written in blood."

"So, you're saying they're...haunted?"

"Not quite, Sam. But energy is attracted to them. Sometimes dark energy, but usually, just an *aspect* of that energy."

"Not the entire entity."

"Right, Sam. Just like not all of you is contained within your physical vessel."

"An aspect of me?"

"An idea of you, Sam. Your soul. Your real soul lies in the energetic world, observing all of this with interest."

"So, who am I, then?"

"Think of yourself as a representative of who you really are."

"Are you trying to hurt my brain?"

He laughed. "Some of this is not easy to understand. Much of it was never really meant to be understood, except by those who seek answers or…"

"By those of us who are forced to find answers."

"Yes, Sam. For most of the world, the search for spiritual truth is a personal journey of their choosing. For you, your spiritual journey was thrust on you."

"And by thrust," I said, "you mean forced upon me, when I was attacked and turned into what I am now."

"Your attack has left you seeking bigger answers, and has exposed you to the world of spirit. And often, the underbelly of the world of spirit. For there is darkness out there, Sam. Great darkness. Powerful darkness, as you are well aware."

"I *am* the darkness," I said.

He shook his head. "They might have made a very, very big mistake coming after you, Sam. They might have unleashed their own undoing."

"I'm just a mom…"

"With a powerful bloodline."

"Lucky me," I said.

"Perhaps unlucky for them. They have taken a chance by making you one of their own."

"Because they need me…"

"Yes, Sam. But the person they most need…is the very person who can destroy them."

"You do realize that I'll be picking up my kids in thirty minutes, right? I won't be destroying anyone anytime soon."

He laughed. "Let's consider it a process."

"Fine," I said. "Back to the books. Are you saying they're possessed?"

"In a way, yes."

"Well, they're possessed enough to beckon me."

"I imagine they do, Sam."

"Why?"

"Because the energy within some of them recognize the thing that is within you."

"That thing being your mother," I corrected.

"*Was* my mother," he said. "She hasn't been my mother for a very long time."

I thought I detected a note.

"There is no note, Sam."

I wasn't so sure about that. I said, "Do you miss her?"

"It's hard to miss a monster."

Another note, whether he wanted to admit it or not. "Do you still love her?"

"Fine," he said. "Yes, I love the memory of her, back when I was young, back when there was some semblance of good within her. Back before she was lured…"

"Don't say it…"

"To the dark side."

"You said it," I said, and grinned.

He did, too, then sighed heavily. "Melodramatic, I know. But true. She was different back in the day. She was a real mother."

"What turned her?"

"That's a story best told another day, Sam."

"Fine," I said. "But I want to know. After all, your mother is very much a part of me now."

He looked at me long and hard. "I know."

"She wants me to let her out. She wants to talk to you. She wants to apologize for all that she's done—"

"You can't let her out, Sam. Ever. Remember that. The moment she gets out, you will no longer be able to control her. *Ever.*"

"What...what do you mean?" I asked, gasping slightly. His mother's presence was strong in me, stronger than I had ever felt before. Pulsing at my temples. My head literally felt like it might explode.

"Think of it like a neural pathway. Once established, she will always be able to access it again and again."

I took a deep breath, and, using all my willpower, pushed her back down, back into the mental box I envisioned her trapped inside. I even threw up another mental wall or two, sealing her in.

Once done, I opened my eyes, blinking hard. Even the muted light within the Occult Reading Room seemed too bright. I shied from it, turning my head. As I did so, I noticed the man who had been reading was gone. I blinked, sure I was seeing things...but there was no one there.

"You okay, Sam?"

"Your mom's a bitch."

"Tell me about it."

"She...she almost got out," I said. "I almost let her, just to release the pressure."

He nodded and released my hand. "Maybe it was a bad idea bringing her around me."

I didn't know what to say to that, but I did push back my black hair. My forehead was sweating. My temples still throbbed.

"You're right, of course," he said after a moment. "I'm not just keeping an eye on her."

I waited. My head still hurt, reminding me what a headache felt like, since I hadn't had one in nearly nine years.

"She's pivotal for stopping all of this," said Maximus.

"All of what?"

"The infusion of dark masters into our world."

"In the form of vampires and werewolves," I said.

"Yes," he said. "And others."

"What others?"

"There's more under the sun, or moon, than just vampires and werewolves, Sam. The dark masters take many forms."

"Like the soul-jumping demon," I said, remembering my memorable vacation on a small island in the Pacific Northwest.

"Right," he said. "But that's not important now."

"Sure," I said, still rubbing my head, and looking over at the now-empty reading chair. "Why worry about all sorts of monsters roaming our streets?"

"There are not as many as you might think, Sam."

"Seems that way."

"As they say, like attracts like. The dark masters gravitate toward each other."

"Sounds like a party," I said.

"A dead man's party."

"Good one, Max. So, what's this about your mother being pivotal to stopping all this craziness?"

"She and one other," said the Librarian.

"Dracula," I said, remembering our conversation from last year. Dracula, who was the first vampire.

The Librarian nodded. "Indeed. The son of the dragon."

I knew my history, limited as it was. *Dracul*, of course, meant House of the Dragon. Dracula meant, in turn, son of the dragon.

"Very good, Sam," he said, picking up my thoughts. "There's something I haven't told you yet."

"That doesn't sound promising," I said.

He pressed his lips together and looked at me, then looked away, then looked at me again.

And then it hit me. "Oh, no," I said.

"Oh yes," he said.

"You're not going to tell me..."

He nodded. "They were in love, Sam. At least, I think it was love. For all I know, it could have been a convenient bonding. A convenient union of dark masters."

"Wait, are you telling me..."

"Yes, Sam. The entity that's within Dracula is and forever will be, in love with my mother."

"Ah, shit," I said.

"Ah, shit, is right."

CHAPTER ELEVEN

I met Sheriff Stanley at a coffee shop in a small mountain town called Crestline, gateway into the San Bernardino Mountains.

The coffee shop had probably been any number of shops over its lifetime. The building was old and nestled under a Mexican restaurant that sported, I noted on a chalkboard near the wooden stairs leading up to it, wine-a-ritas.

"First off," I said to the sheriff, after he shook my hand and I sat opposite him, "what's a wine-a-rita?"

"A margarita made with wine," he said. Sheriff Stanley was a young guy who sported an old-school mustache.

I understood quickly enough. "They lost their liquor license."

"Hard liquor."

"Are the wine-a-ritas any good?"

"I tried it once."

"And?"

"I think I vomited a little in the back of my mouth. But then," he shrugged and rubbed his mustache, "I dunno, they kind of grow on you. I guess they're not the worst thing in the world. Still, kinda makes my stomach turn a little just thinking about them."

"Let me get you a coffee," I said.

"Black," he said. "Blacker than black."

"Says the guy who ordered a wine-a-rita."

"I don't know you well enough for you to bust my chops."

I shrugged. "Never stopped me before."

I slid out of the booth and ordered our coffees.

Sweet nectar of the gods, I thought.

The gift of coffee might have been the greatest gift that Maximus—and his rings—could have given me. After eight years of not having the stuff, now, I couldn't get enough of it, especially since the caffeine didn't have any effect. Nor did alcohol. My body neutralized both equally.

Luckily, my addiction for coffee went beyond the caffeine high. It was the taste. The aroma. The experience. Coffee made me feel human. And humanity is what I needed most if I wanted to keep the thing inside me at bay.

"Should I, uh, leave you alone with your coffee?" asked Sheriff Stanley.

"Now, who's busting whose balls?"

"Hey, I'm not the one moaning and groaning over my coffee."

"You would," I said, "if you had the day I had."

"Look, Miss—"

"Ms."

"What the fuck is the difference?"

"*Miss* implies a woman who's never been married. *Ms.* is an indefinite title for a woman whose marital status is unknown."

"Well, you ain't wearing a wedding ring. Just those other rings."

I set the coffee mug down. "*Ms.* is also an appropriate title for a divorcee, which I happen to be."

He wanted to say something smart-alecky, or rude, or show me how tough he was since he now regretted owning up to drinking the wine-a-rita. He opened his mouth and I was prepared for more bluster. After all, I was used to such bluster, having spent much of my professional life working in the male-dominated field of law enforcement. Instead, he closed it again and sort of rebooted.

"Sorry about the divorced part," he said. "I'm going through that right now. It really sucks."

"I'm sorry to hear that," I said.

He nodded, sighed.

"Any kids involved?"

He shook his head. "Elise and I were talking about having kids, until…"

"Until what?"

"Never mind," he said. "I don't know you well enough to burden you."

I nodded and dipped into his mind and—right there at the forefront of his thoughts—I saw him opening the door to his bedroom and seeing his wife with another man. Then the scene looped again. And again.

"She cheated on you," I said.

Sheriff Stanley was a young guy, maybe thirty-two. I caught a glimpse of something else in his thoughts. Something he had dreamed about often. I saw three kids running. I saw him playing with them, a sort of game of hide-and-seek. Two girls and a boy. Now, he was rolling in the grass with them. A golden retriever bounded between them, licking indiscriminately. Someone had seen one too many episodes of *Full House*. Kids were fun, but maybe not that fun. Scratch that. Anthony was a hoot. And so was Tammy, in her way. It's just that…well, it's just that it's not all fun and games.

Anyway, I could have laughed at his innocent, almost naïve approach to having a family. In fact, I might have if I didn't feel his overwhelming sense of loss. He wanted a family, and he had thought it would be with the woman he'd caught cheating.

He nodded. "That obvious?"

I held his gaze and felt his loss and heard him crying inside. He didn't know I could hear the sobs that echoed through his memories. "Lucky guess," I said softly, and reached out and patted his hand.

His aura sort of reached out to me. That man needed a hug in a bad way, but then, it recoiled and he pulled back his hand. "I don't really wanna talk about it, you know?"

"I know," I said.

After a moment, he said, "Did your old man cheat on you, too?"

"He did," I said.

"Pretty shitty thing to do to someone who loves you, huh?"

"About as shitty as it gets," I said. That, and trying to kill them, too, which was what Danny had tried to do in the end, with the help of a vampire named Hanner.

I saw something else in his mind. I saw his wife apologizing over and over. I saw her weeping, begging. I saw her phone calls and the texts. Her appearing at his work, at the apartment he had moved into.

"Who was the guy?" I asked.

"Her old boyfriend. A friend of mine, too. We go back to high school, all of us."

"Are they together now?"

"No," he said quickly, and looked very uncomfortable talking to me. "Elise said it was a mistake."

Relax, I thought.

He nodded and took a deep breath, cracked his neck, and sank a little deeper into his seat. We could have been two friends lounging on a couch, playing X-Box in our basketball shorts.

Not that relaxed, I thought.

He nodded and sat up a little, unaware that I was prompting him with my suggestions.

"Why did she do it?" I asked, and added telepathically: *It's okay to talk to me, I'm a friend.*

He looked at me, cocked his head slightly, nodded. He really didn't want to talk about it. In fact, I was fairly certain, outside of a few close guy friends and family, he hadn't talk about it at all.

"We were fighting. I left in a huff. I said something stupid."

"How stupid?"

"I told her I should never have married her. That it was a mistake, and that I might go look up an old girlfriend."

"That's a whole lot of stupid in a row," I said.

"Tell me about it," he said. "So then, Elise calls her ex-boyfriend."

"And the rest is history," I said.

He nodded.

"And now, you won't forgive her?" I asked.

"Did you forgive your old man?"

I shook my head. "He didn't give me a chance. He moved on. But I have forgiven someone else…and it's not easy."

"My mom says once a cheater, always a cheater."

"Maybe," I said. "Or maybe not. No one knows the future. People make mistakes. People learn from their mistakes."

He shrugged, still uncomfortable despite my mental prompting. As we sat there, and as I considered what to say to him, if anything, three entities materialized in the booth behind him. Small entities, although they were too fuzzy to make out any real details.

Kids, I realized. Unborn kids. Which was a first to me. I had seen the spirits of the departed…but never the not-yet-born. Until now.

"You wanted to build a family with her."

"Yes."

"Her and only her," I said.

"Elise was my everything," he said. "I screwed it all up. And she sure as hell didn't help."

Now the smallish spirits slipped over the booth and pushed up next to him. One sat on his lap, except he didn't know it, of course. I watched in amazement as another crawled up onto his shoulder and the third, the girl, curled under his arm. He shivered.

"Do you still love her?" I asked after a moment.

"Yeah," he said. He looked away, fighting the tears, jaw quivering. "I don't know why I'm telling you all of this."

"Maybe I'm easy to talk to."

"Maybe."

It's okay to cry, I told him.

And he did now, but not very hard. It wouldn't be very becoming for the town sheriff to weep loudly at the little coffee shop. But the tears flowed anyway, silently; he didn't bother to wipe them away.

"Yeah, I love her, but I can't…" He cried a little harder now, and this time, he did reach up to wipe his cheeks and eyes. "I can't forgive her, Ms. Moon. I can't. I don't know how to. I just don't… know how…"

One or two people looked over at us. I telepathically told those one or two people to mind their own business. They did, turning their backs to us.

I considered what to do, even as the spirits swarmed around the grief-stricken man. *Their future father.* One even tried to wipe the tears from his face, and I knew what I had to do.

———

Give me your hands, I told him.

He blinked rapidly, eyelashes beaded with tears, then held out both of his hands. Thick, calloused hands.

Look at me. Good. Now, can you hear me?

"Yes."

Speak to me only in your mind.

Like this?

Yes. Good.

I slipped deeper into his consciousness, and pushed through the pain and confusion and loss and hurt, deeper than I had any right to be.

There, buried under the jealousy and grief was something bright and glowing and spinning slightly. I knew what this was from my experience with Russell, my boyfriend from two years ago, the man who had inadvertently become my love slave. Of course, finding Russell's higher self or soul had been a lot harder, for it had been buried deep, deep beneath the curse that was, well, me.

Sheriff Stanley was only a few layers down, although his grief was real and, if left unchecked, it would be lifelong. Grief like this would, I assumed, give him issues for the rest of his life, from distrust of other women to never feeling secure and loved and worthy.

And so, I spoke to him directly, to this higher aspect of himself. I told him to find the courage to let it all go, to find the courage to forgive her and to accept the responsibility of his own actions. I reminded him that he had a family to build with her, and with my words, I flamed his love for her back to life. The love was real, and it was deep, and it was easy to flame to life.

Most important, I told him to forget he ever met me. When I was done, when I slipped back out of his mind and found myself sitting across from him again, I released his hands and sat back.

He blinked, blinked again, then said, "I have to go."

"Figured you did," I said, and grinned.

He stopped as he was getting out of the booth. "Wait, who are you?"

I waved him away. "I'm not really here, remember?"

"Oh, right."

And then, he was gone, dashing through the coffee shop to, I assumed, his wife. The three staticy, small entities trailed after him. They were holding hands and skipping.

CHAPTER TWELVE

I was at the park ranger station just outside Arrowhead.

This time, I made it a point to get to the point. My last meeting had gone precisely nowhere, although I might have helped to salvage a relationship. And helped to build a family.

Both of which, I knew, pissed off the demoness within me, which was exactly why I had done it. Well, *one* of the reasons. What can I say? I happen to be a romantic at heart.

Ranger Ted sat behind a dented, metallic desk. A coffee mug was warming in an electric coaster that might have been the coolest thing I'd ever seen. Ranger Ted was graying and thin and didn't look very intimidating. Then again, I didn't think his job required him to look very intimidating. I think I could have taken him, vampire or not. The aggressive, competitive side of me was relatively new. I suspected it was *her* bleeding into my personality.

Oh, joy.

At the moment, Ranger Ted was looking through a thick blue folder, which was sub-divided further with little plastic tabs. When he was done flipping through the folder, he looked up at me.

"Nineteen missing," he said, "since 2010. And twelve missing from 2000 to 2010."

"So, nineteen in the last four years," I said. "And twelve in the ten prior to that."

He frowned, not liking the sound of that. "Yup."

"It went from just over one a year to almost five a year."

He nodded and looked pained. "Troubling as hell, I know."

"Any theories?"

He blew some air out, then shrugged. "The mountains are as popular as ever. More hikers means more disappearances."

"Quadruple the hikers?"

"I thought you said five times," he said.

"Caught me," I said. "I couldn't think of the word for increasing fivefold."

"Quintuple," he said.

"Yeah," I said. "That word."

The ranger almost grinned. In fact, he might have if the missing hiker stats weren't still depressing him. "I'm not sure how I know it, myself. I guess there are benefits to getting old. You come across enough shit over the years, and some of it even manages to stick."

I nodded and felt a sudden surge of relief. Relief knowing that I would never age, never wrinkle, never grow old. Ideally, my memory stayed as sharp as ever, even while I accumulated more and more knowledge. Not a bad deal.

I said, "Are the disappearances centralized anywhere on the mountain?"

"Well, the San Bernardinos are a chain of a dozen mountains. But I would say the bulk of the disappearances are along the popular hiking trails near Arrowhead."

"Who oversees the searches?"

"The San Bernardino County Sheriff. We provide support and aid."

I nodded. "Have any of these hikers ever been found?"

"'Bout fifteen years ago, we found a college professor who'd gone missing for about three days. Found him in a cave, half dehydrated."

"But none in the last fifteen years?"

He shook his head sadly. "I guess we don't have a good track record up here."

I said nothing, and looked again at the topographical map hanging on the wall behind him. It was looking more and more like the missing hikers would never be found.

Especially with a hungry werewolf prowling the woods.

CHAPTER THIRTEEN

It was nearly dusk.

I hiked alone along a sometimes winding trail, although mostly it meandered through ponderosa pine, cedar, black oak, white oak and dogwoods. I knew this because I had read the posters that lined the park ranger's office. I was a little sketchy on which were the black and white oaks, but other than that, I was fairly proud of myself for picking out the different trees. Granted, none were as big as the pines in the Pacific Northwest, but that was to be expected. This was—according to the chart—a transiticonifer forest, which meant little to me, although it probably got botanists all hot and bothered.

I picked up my pace, although the forest was getting darker by the minute. Luckily for me, light particles danced and swarmed before my eyes, lighting my way, enough through the darkest of nights…or along a darkening forest trail.

Not quite light particles, I thought, as I picked up my pace even more. *God particles, maybe. Spirit energy, definitely.*

Tree trunks flowed past me. Ferns and smaller bushes swept by. I picked up speed, hitting the trail hard and fast. I could have been on a rollercoaster. Up and down and around tight corners and through mud puddles, up steep slopes and down sharply angled trails that led down into ravines.

Faster, I ran. And faster.

I adjusted my footwork on the fly, supernaturally fast. I should have broken my ankle a hundred times over. Instead, I sidestepped small holes, rocks and tree roots. I pumped my arms and laughed and could have sworn that there were times that my feet didn't even touch the ground. I could have been flying through the forest.

I knew I was grinning from ear to ear as I ran, but I didn't care. No one could see me. I was in the deep, dark woods, which was only getting darker by the minute, although it was becoming more alive to me, alive with flashing light.

Critters scattered in my wake. I surprised two deer on the trail. I moved between them, smelling their musky coats, and hearing them dash off after I was dozens of yards past them. I could have grabbed one. I could have broken its neck. I could have feasted on it. And then what? I would have been covered in deer blood. But it would have been...exciting, invigorating, thrilling.

I pushed past the feeling and continued running. As much as I enjoyed fresh blood, I was enjoying this night run even more.

I found a trail that seemed to lead up, and up I went, higher and higher into the mountains, hurdling logs and boulders and running up a trail I was certain few humans had ever used. A game trail, surely. High above, the quarter moon appeared within a thick stand of Douglas firs.

How far had I run? Two or three miles? Five? Ten? I didn't know, but I knew I was lost as hell...and I didn't care.

Up I went, higher and higher, and, if possible, my speed seemed to only increase.

At one point, I finally did hit a hidden tree root, and I tumbled head over ass, skidding on my face. I got up, spitting out dirt and twigs and laughing. Nothing broken. I wasn't even scratched. I dusted myself off, then started running again, zigzagging up the trail, knowing I was nothing more than a blur to anything watching me, and feeling like I was on the ride of my life.

No wonder I was grinning like a fool, all the way up past the treeline, and over loose rocks and boulders until finally, finally I stood at the top of Old Greyback, the highest peak in the San Bernardinos. At 12,000 feet I finally stopped and looked down upon Southern California far, far below.

I wasn't even out of breath.

I found a cluster of boulders and climbed to the top and sat there and relived my mad dash up the mountain. It had been exhilarating, thrilling—and it had all been possible, courtesy of the demon within.

No, I didn't hate her. She had, in fact, shown me a side of life that few would ever see.

Of course, I knew now that I hadn't been randomly picked, that my bloodline reached all the way to the greatest alchemist of all time, Hermes Trismegistus.

Yes, my bloodline was desirable.

For what, I didn't exactly know, although some of it had to do with helping the dark masters back into this world. Directly. And not through hosts like myself.

Directly and permanently.

I pulled up my legs and wrapped my arms around my knees. There was a hole in my pants. My running shoes were kinda ruined, too, I saw. I didn't think Asics had something like me in mind when they field-tested their products. I flicked a hanging piece of the rubber sole. I needed new shoes anyway.

The wind was strong up here, and infused with a mix of desert and mountain scents. After all, one side of the mountain sloped down into Joshua Tree, one of the more epic of Southern California's deserts, which just so happened to be the name of my favorite U2 album. Yes, I'm showing my age.

Then again, a hundred years from now, with music coming and going and my kids long since dead, I would still have a fondness for 80s' and 90s' alternative rock.

Suddenly depressed, I considered my case. Which was the reason why I'd come up here in the first place.

That something was stalking these woods, I had no doubt. There had been no witnesses, and no evidence of foul play. The bodies had never been found. Something or someone had either consumed them completely, or had been damn good at hiding the evidence. I figured, it was probably a little bit of both.

A gust of hot wind blasted me, whipping my hair into a frenzy. I let my hair flap and felt the wind on my neck and skin, relishing the feeling. I figured the thing inside was relishing the feeling, too. Through me. Sensing the physical world again through me.

So, we both sat there on the rock, enjoying the night breeze, as the nocturnal creatures came out, although not as many this high up, above the treeline with little vegetation. Still, I heard the scurrying, the scratching, the vocalizing. It was late fall and I should have been cold. I wasn't.

Of course, I had a good bead on who was stalking the hikers up here. Nancy wasn't lying to me. She believed what she was telling me. Whether or not her ex-boyfriend was killing the hikers—or that he was, in fact, a werewolf—remained to be seen.

I closed my eyes and felt the wind ripple my clothing and rock me gently. I rested my hands on my knees and let my mind slip away, far away from here. Where it went, I didn't know, but there on the mountaintop, far from anyone and anything, I found a rare moment of peace.

And I treasured it.

Then, when I was back, I opened my eyes, took a deep and useless breath, and then did what any other lost girl would do on a mountaintop.

I stripped off all my clothing and used a much-honed technique of wrapping my clothes, including my shoes, inside my shirt and tying it all together with the legs of my jeans. Just add a stick through it, and I could have been a hobo.

Then I summoned the single flame and saw the giant creature I would soon become.

A moment later, in a process that was painless, unlike in the movies, I was very much not just another lost girl. I was something monstrous and far too scary for this world.

Using a clawed foot, I hooked my makeshift traveling satchel, gathered myself there on the rocky outcropping, and then launched high into the sky…

And spread my wings wide.

Now, I thought, as I caught a hot gust of wind and sailed out over a dark valley, *Where did I park my car…?*

Chapter Fourteen

We were in bed.

It was past midnight, and the evening had been invigorating. Thanks to my little tirade last year—a tirade which involved the impaling of Kingsley's hand with a fork—we had been forced to look for a new hangout. We had found it by way of The Cellar restaurant in downtown Fullerton. More accurately, *under* downtown Fullerton, as the name was indeed fitting. It was also underneath the offices of our local congressman, which, I think, might have been cooler than it really was.

The Cellar was more our style. Dark, gloomy, isolated. I probably still couldn't get away with impaling Kingsley, but at least we could probably sneak back in.

Afterward, we had walked around downtown Fullerton, holding hands, looking in windows, avoiding drunks and rowdy college students, often one and the same. It was, after all, a Friday night and nearby Fullerton College was in full swing. Harbor Boulevard was lined with white lights, in a sort of year-round Christmas décor. We walked past Jacky's gym, which was presently dark, other than a small, muted glow in the back offices. Maybe Jacky was going over the books.

Spirit activity was everywhere. Downtown Fullerton was particularly old for Southern California. Lots of activity here over the years, lots of death and crime, too. Lots of heart attacks and car accidents and muggings. In fact, one such accident kept replaying itself, over and over, on a nearby street corner. Two cars coming together in an explosion of light. Over and over. I watched three spirits separate from the wreckage and stand together, looking down and looking confused.

Kingsley saw the spirits, too, but rarely let them get to him, and never did he feel a need to help the truly lost souls. Early on, I had. I wanted to go to each one, and urge them to move on. To the light, and all of that. But I have since come to realize that I can't help them all.

And the truth is…

Well, the truth is, I am caring less and less these days about whether they move on or not. Their plight is not my plight. I have my own issues. Yes, I know some of the uncaring was coming from *her* within me. Then again, it was because of her that I could even see the damn spirits in the first place.

After our stroll—and after Kingsley had tossed aside a young punk who had pinned a girl to a wall and had been talking to her a little too aggressively—we had made our way back to his place.

Once there, and once Franklin had taken our coats, we somehow, magically, ended up in his bedroom. From there, the clothing was optional…and mostly optional.

Thirty minutes later, the big oaf lifted himself off me. Damn good thing I didn't have to breathe. Afterward, we had gotten a midnight snack and eaten it over his kitchen counter. I was wearing his long shirt. He was wearing no shirt. While we talked, I might have giggled one too many times, because Franklin had appeared in the doorway, looking none too pleased. Then again, he rarely looked pleased to see me. Of course, he also sported a scar that literally wrapped around his neck. A scar that implied, well, that he'd lost his head at some point.

Someday, I would get Kingsley to open up about Franklin.

Anyway, we both apologized to the patchwork butler. Franklin sneered, turned his head, and loped away. That one leg seemed longer than the other or that one ear was actually a different skin tone than the other, was disturbing.

Now, back up in his room, I lay next to Kingsley, with one hand propping up my head and the other veritably buried in his chest hair.

"I get that you are a werewolf," I started. "I also get that you change each full moon. I even get that you play host to your own highly evolved dark master, as do I. What I don't get is why you are so damn hairy."

"It goes back to what I said a while back, Sam."

"That you continue to grow."

"With each transformation, I'm just that much bigger. That much closer to the beast within."

"And that much hairier?"

"In short, yes," he said. "Will that be a problem?"

I didn't have to think about it. "It won't be a problem for me," I said. "But I can't vouch for your shower drains."

"One of Franklin's many jobs is maintaining the household plumbing. Let's just say, I keep him busy."

"Eww."

He laughed and pulled me into him. I don't think I could have resisted him if I tried. Instead, I went willingly, and found my face buried somewhere between his shoulder and neck...a good place to be.

"You are too much," he said.

"I'd like to think so."

We were quiet some more. I heard Kingsley's late-night snack rumbling in his belly—his had been a roast beef sandwich, mine had been sherbet ice cream. After a moment, I said, "When you had sex with mortals in the past, did they, you know, fall under your spell, too?"

"The way the boxer did with you?"

"Yes, and he has a name."

"Any man who had sex with you ceases to have a name. They are no-names, at that point."

"Fine. Yes, the boxer."

"No. Not that I know of. That particular spell might be Samantha Moon-centric."

"Meaning?"

"Meaning, it's particular to the entity within you."

404

That gave me pause for thought. As I paused and as I thought, I discovered that I was making curlicues in Kingsley's chest hair. He didn't seem to mind. I said, "So, you're saying that not all vampires have the same powers?"

He shook his granite-like head slowly. I think the whole damn bed shook with it. "Nor do all werewolves. We all have similar traits, true. All werewolves change at the full moon. But not all werewolves, for instance, can change at will."

"Like you can," I said.

He nodded. "But not all talents are gifts, Sam. The entity within me craves the dead."

"You mean corpses," I said.

"Yes, Sam. The fucking sick bastard literally gets off on it."

"Jesus."

"Jesus is right," said Kingsley. "Which brings up a point. Some vampires can see themselves in mirrors, others can't."

"I can't," I said.

"I know. Some vampires can turn into mice, into fog, others can climb sheer walls."

"You know a lot about vampires for being a wolfie."

"We are not that dissimilar, Sam. We're all possessed by the same dark forces."

"I love when you sweet talk me," I said.

"There's more," he said, taking in a lot of air and propping his free hand under his head. I almost felt sorry for his hand...and pillow. "Some vampires prefer living humans. Some prefer dead."

"Mine prefers the living," I said. "Of course, she can prefer all she wants. She gets what she gets."

"And that brings up another point. In the end, we all have some semblance of free will. For instance, I can cage the creature within me, thus depriving him of fresh corpses. And quit shuddering every time I say that."

I shuddered again.

"Jesus, Sam. We are grown adults here, dealing with the same shit."

"Sorry," I said, patting his meaty chest. "I'll do my best to get used to the thought of you chowing down on the dead."

He rolled his eyes, which I saw clearly enough in the dark.

"None of us asked for this," he said.

"Some did," I thought.

"Fang?"

"Right."

Kingsley nodded. "Someday, he will wish that he hadn't. You still talk to him?"

I nodded. "Yeah."

"How often?"

"Regularly."

"How often is regularly?"

"Almost every day," I said.

"Oh, brother. Should I be worried?"

"No. We're friends again."

"Like old times?"

"Almost," I said. Fang had sort of gone off the deep end in the months following his transformation. In fact, his hedonistic lifestyle could have been lifted from the pages of every Anne Rice novel ever, with a little Poppy Z. Brite added in for good measure. He had lovers coming and going. He feasted on whoever and whatever he wanted. He stole, he robbed, he worked with real criminals.

It took him about a year to get it out of his system. And he had, thank God. He still ran a blood ring, but he'd ditched most of his loser business associates. Now, he mostly operated it alone and, as far as I could tell, he mostly didn't kill anyone.

The good news was, he was back to living alone, with only the occasional girlfriend showing up. What I didn't tell Kingsley was, of course, that I suspected Fang had cleaned up his life...for me.

Fang also understood that I was in a relationship with Kingsley, and had mostly kept his distance, only occasionally dropping hints that he might want more.

"Well, that's good," said the werewolf in bed next to me. "Because I will rip his head off if he makes a move on you."

406

"You mean that metaphorically, right?"

Kingsley grunted.

I laughed nervously and patted his chest. The truth was, I wanted to be right here, in Kingsley's arms—and nestled in that warm nook between his shoulder and jaw.

Shortly, I was asleep…and I dreamed of nothing.

Which wasn't necessarily a bad thing.

Chapter Fifteen

It was the strangest popping sound. Like hundreds of soap bubbles bursting at once. I was just turning to see what the hell it was when I heard, "Your son is very skilled."

I gasped, mostly because no one had been standing next to me just a few seconds ago. I was certain of it. Somehow, I managed to calmly turn and look at whoever was standing next to me, whoever had managed to sneak up on even me, which, I was certain, was virtually impossible to do.

"It's you," I said.

"It is me, yes," said the man I instantly recognized. "Is this section of the mat taken?"

"No," I said before realizing that I probably should have said yes. Not that it mattered. Any man who could sneak up on me—and the Librarian, too, for that matter—was going to talk to me whether I wanted to or not.

The man nodded and I almost—almost—sensed that he could read my mind. He was dressed a little too nicely for a boxing gym. Hell, a little too nice for Fullerton, in general. His black suit was immaculate, if not a little dated. His thick black hair was slicked back with some sort of oiled wax—Brylcreem maybe—and combed perfectly. Although his clothing and hairstyle seemed a little dated, there was nothing old-fashioned about the brightness in his eyes. They flashed over me quickly and appreciatively, and he made a show of sitting down by unbuttoning his jacket and flipping up the longish tails as he sat. I had a mental image of a maestro taking a lunch break.

As he sat, I caught sight of his claw-like fingernails. I also sensed the impenetrable wall around his thoughts and a distinct lack of an aura.

He was a vampire, and, I suspected, a very old one.

He sat smoothly, in one fluid motion, his narrow limbs coming to sharp points. In fact, he didn't use his hands at all. He dropped down, legs folding under him neatly, like a collapsible picnic table. If I didn't know any better, I would have said he glided down.

Meanwhile, in front of me, my son danced in the ring with Jacky. Granted, Jacky wasn't doing much dancing these days, but he kept pace with my son, using the punching mitts, urging my son to keep his hands up. My son, for his part, seemed to revel in the workout. Heck, he even seemed to enjoy Jacky's good-natured verbal abuse. Once, after a flurry of devastating punches, he reached over and ruffled the Irishman's gray hair, to the old man's surprise and, I believe, delight. This got a swift condemnation from Jacky, but they did pause, and I caught the two of them laughing in the corner of the ring a moment later.

"Your son has phenomenal control and power," said the man sitting next to me. He had an accent that I couldn't quite place. Then again, I'd always been crappy with accents.

"Long story," I said.

"I would like to hear it someday," said the man.

I shot him a look. And the more I looked, the more I could see the fire blazing just behind his pupil. It was, I was certain, the brightest fire I'd seen yet. What that meant, I didn't know. But there it was, a single flame leaping and crackling and snapping. I should have found it distracting, except I found it to be the exact opposite.

I found it hypnotic.

So, I shifted my gaze to his long, slender nose. I had to. I felt myself...slipping into his own flames. So strange. I said, "You assume I'll see you again or that I'll want to talk to you."

"Perhaps I was loose with my speech."

I forced myself to look at my son. My warning bells had been ringing steadily, although not very loudly. There was danger here...

409

but not immediate. I said, without looking at him, "You also presume that I care about what you like."

"And you don't?"

"I could give a fuck about what you like."

He threw back his head and laughed loudly. Except...except no one looked at him. No one but me.

"I can see why Elizabeth was keen on you, Samantha Moon. You remind me so much of her. In fact, you look quite a bit like her."

I glanced at him. "Elizabeth?"

"Don't you know?" he asked, raising a single narrow eyebrow. His sharp elbows rested lightly on his equally sharp knees.

"Know what?"

"Ah, I see her son hasn't yet shared her name with you."

The flames inside his pupil danced and wavered and sputtered as if a wind were rattling around inside his skull.

"That's her name..."

"Indeed," said the man.

"Her name is Elizabeth..." I heard myself say. Hearing her name had a strange effect on me. It...humanized her. I wasn't sure I wanted her humanized. I preferred to think of her as a demon. It was bad enough that I thought her son was kind of cute.

"And a fine name it is."

The entity within me responded to her name, and came rushing to the surface of my thoughts, but I shut a mental lid on her before she got too far, or could take too much control.

"And who are you?" I asked.

But the man next to me seemed to guess what I was about to ask, for he was already standing and giving me a small bow. He tipped a non-existent hat, and said, in a rolling, sing-song voice, "Wladislaus Dragwlya, at your service."

Coming from him, coupled with his strange accent, the "W" sounded like a "V" to my ears.

In fact, I was certain he had said... *Vladislaus Dracula.*

CHAPTER SIXTEEN

I caught myself rocking a little and breathing hard, although there was no damn good reason why I was breathing hard. It was a reaction, I knew. A reaction to yet the further absurdness that was my life. That had been my life for the past nine years.

While I breathed and rocked and tried to process, the man continued to watch me sideways, sitting completely still. The fire behind his pupils seemed almost palpable, to radiate real heat. But I knew that was not true. Vampires were cold, were they not?

My son took a short breather, although he barely seemed to breathe hard. Jacky, however, staggered away from the heavy bag. The poor guy literally didn't know what had hit him. First me, then my son. He must have thought we were the freakiest of freaks.

Not the freakiest, I thought. *In fact, the original freak was sitting next to me now.*

Dracula.

I forcibly calmed myself. After all, had I not met other vampires? Hell, I had encountered werewolves, angels and body-hopping demons. Wasn't he just another...

No, he wasn't.

He was fucking Dracula and, according to the Librarian, the original vampire. The first vampire. The oldest vampire.

Jesus...

"You seem upset, Samantha Moon."

"Wouldn't you be?" I said. "If, you know, you just met you. Okay, that sounded lame."

411

He threw back his head and laughed easily. "Yes," he finally said when the laughter subsided. "I suppose I would be upset, too, if, you know, I had just met me."

For the first time in a long time, I felt embarrassed, although my face didn't burn with embarrassment. To do so would have implied that I radiated some degree of heat, which I didn't. Not like the creature next to me.

Confused, I shut my mouth and might have rocked a little. We lapsed into silence, although the thoughts in my head weren't so silent. And the demon bitch inside me wasn't helping either. She was clamoring to get out. It was all I could do to stamp her back down and throw up a mental wall, which was harder to do than it sounds, especially when you've got something living in you...and that something desperately wants out. Months ago, I had learned that I didn't like communicating with her directly. Despite what the Librarian had told me last year, love didn't seem to be working. She only seemed to be getting angrier or more desperate. Then again, maybe she was getting angrier and more desperate because of love. Either way, she had made my life a living nightmare.

"Why are you here?" I asked.

"Isn't it obvious?"

"You want to take boxing lessons?"

He laughed again, the sound coming from him surprisingly easily. I would never have guessed that Dracula had such a good sense of humor, other than, say, laughing maniacally as he watched those being impaled before him: men, women and children. Indeed, Dracula had been a monster before he became a monster.

"Not quite, Samantha, although I see your friend Jacky is quite gifted."

I was disturbed by his knowledge of my name and Jacky's. He undoubtedly knew my son's name, too. He'd been following me, for how long, I didn't know.

"So, why are you here?"

"I thought it was time to make my presence known."

"And I care, why?"

He didn't laugh at my abruptness this time. Instead, his eyes narrowed and I caught a brief glimpse of the monster he was. Something flashed behind his eyes, something that did not approve of being talked to in such a way. I could give a fuck about what he approved and didn't approve, Dracula or not.

"Because we are connected, Samantha Moon."

"I beg to differ."

"You can feel her reaching out to me, can't you?"

"Not you," I said. "The thing within you."

"Myself and the thing within me...are very much the same, Samantha, as we have been for many centuries. Call it an equal partnership."

"I call it creepy as hell."

"Perhapsss..."

I shivered at that. Indeed, I was sensing that Dracula and the demon within were interchangeable, coming and going at will, one rising to the surface, while the other stepped back, almost instantly. Perhaps they existed side-by-side, if that was possible.

"What do you want from me?" I asked.

"You know what we want, Sssamantha."

"Yeah, well, you ain't getting her. So, you can both go to hell."

The man, known as Vlad Tepes, who had killed tens of thousands of the innocent back in the day, whose name was synonymous with evil, smiled at me slowly. "Do not be so quick to dismiss us, Sssamantha. We can offer you much."

"You have nothing I want—"

His movement was instant, certainly faster than I could react. One moment his hands were folded in his lap, and the next, he was holding my own hand, gripping it tightly. I tried to rise, but he held me in place.

"Do you feel that, Sam?"

"Let go, asshole, or this is going to get ugly."

"Do you feel my warmth, Sam? Do you? This could be yours again. This, and so much more."

"Let me fucking go."

"No one can see me, Sam. They think you are talking to yourself."

I stopped struggling and looked around. Indeed, others in the gym were staring at me, including my son and Jacky, who had stopped their recent round of workouts.

"I don't understand," I said under my breath.

"I will explain everything to you, Samantha. This and so much more. Every secret. Everything."

"Let go," I said, "or I will tear your fucking throat out."

Vlad Tepes held my gaze, and released my hand. "Consider my words."

"Go to hell."

"I'll be back," he said.

He smiled, stood, and walked away, exiting the gym and heading out into the night.

Chapter Seventeen

"It looks closed, Ma," said Anthony.

He was right, of course. In fact, the whole damn campus looked closed. No surprise there, since it was Friday night, the only night the school's epic library closed early.

I might have growled under my breath. The Librarian and his damn inconvenient hours. Where he went when the library was closed, I hadn't a clue. But I was going to find him and talk to him, dammit.

A handful of students milled about, some alone, some walking with friends, others standing around and making plans for the weekend. Some lights were on in some of the buildings, but for the most part, the place was closed for business.

Anthony and I stood at the library's front entrance, whose automatic doors normally whispered open. There was no whispering now. Inside, through the smoke glass, the place was dark and empty, save for a dim light hanging over the help desk inside.

"So, Jacky thinks I'll be ready soon..." continued Anthony. My boy had been talking non-stop since we'd left his practice session with Jacky.

"Uh-huh," I said and led him around to the side of the massive structure. Anthony trotted along, pretty much oblivious to his surroundings, so wrapped up was he in his story.

"But he says I gotta keep practicing my footwork."

And to show me what he meant—or just to get some extra reps in—he did just that. His sneakered feet moved rapidly over the wet grass, crossing and scissoring. As they moved, my son moved his shoulders, too, dodging an invisible assailant, moving faster than he had any right to move.

No, I thought, *he has every right.*

He was, after all, now acting as his own guardian angel.

Craziness, I thought. *All of this.*

We were now standing under a floodlight next to the library, where no mom and son belong. So, before anyone spotted us, I grabbed hold of his juking and jiving shoulders—which was no easy feat—and led my son out of the light and over into the shadows.

"Fly like a butterfly, sting like a bee!" he said, still moving his feet this way and that.

"I'm going to sting your butt like a bee if you don't keep it down," I said, whispering.

"But Mom…"

"Don't 'but Mom' me," I said. "We're going to break into the library and I don't want any backtalk."

"But…wait, did you say we're going to break into the library?"

"I did," I said, then knelt down and turned around. I motioned to my back. "Climb on, kiddo."

"But I'm almost as big as you."

"Anthony…"

"Fine, but if I break your back, then that's on you, not me."

As he climbed on, I considered leaving him here in the shadows…but then shook my head sharply. Hell, no. Meeting the King Creep had freaked me out completely and totally…and I needed more answers, and I needed them now.

"Hang on," I said, standing.

And with my son's long legs dangling down on either side of me, I took hold of the drainpipe and started climbing.

Rapidly.

Chapter Eighteen

Twenty seconds later, we slipped in through a third-story window that had been left cracked open. I cracked it all the way open. There was no fire escape or ledge, and whoever had left it open hadn't expected someone to climb three stories up a drainpipe. With her son hanging off her back, no less.

"This is cool, Mom!" said Anthony, when he slid off and found his feet.

"*Shh!*"

"Oh, right. Sorry."

We found ourselves in an administrator's office, complete with a blinking monitor and a glow-in-the-dark keyboard and mouse and a small, gurgling fountain that was presently running. Wasteful.

"Come on," I whispered.

The office led to a hallway, lined with many doors. The halogen lighting above was off. The floor was polished vinyl squares. I led the way down the hallway toward an "Exit" sign hanging over another door.

I already knew that my son hadn't inherited my night vision, which was, apparently, primarily a vampire and werewolf trait. The angel had only bestowed upon him great strength, agility and quickness.

Good enough, I thought.

I paused at the door at the far end of the hallway and pressed my ear against it. Nothing. I was fairly certain the door would lead to the main library on the third floor. I turned the knob and cracked the door open a smidgen…

I heard a door bang open, followed by the sounds of running feet. Many running feet. Security guards approached, and from the sounds of it, at least three of them. So much for sneaking in.

I turned to my son. "Do *not* tell your sister about this."

"Oh, I won't."

"Or your auntie."

"My friends?"

"No," I said. "This stays between me and you."

"Fine," he said, and flashed me a giddy smile.

"Are you ready to run?" I asked, as the voices and pounding footsteps got closer.

"Yes!"

And run we did, exploding out of the doorway and hanging a quick right down a side corridor, where we ran along the west wall. The Occult Reading Room was on the south wall.

"This way!" someone shouted behind us.

"Faster," I said to my son, and we kicked into a whole other gear. Bookshelves swept past us in a blur. I looked back once and saw my son keeping up with me virtually step for step, although I was pulling away. I slowed down and let him catch up. Then we made a quick left. The Occult Reading Room was about halfway down the south corridor.

A bobbing flashlight was directly ahead. Someone was running toward us. I reached back and took my son's hand.

Unlike the movies, I didn't just appear somewhere when I ran. I actually had to cover some ground. I had to pass through time and space. There was no movie magic here. Just my son, me, and a security guard, all converging at or around the Occult Reading Room.

We were too far away for him to see us, although I'm sure he heard our pounding footsteps. Our furiously pounding footsteps. The guy probably didn't know what was coming at him.

"Hang on," I said to my son.

As we rapidly approached the security guard, who dropped his flashlight and held up what appeared to be a Taser gun, I hung a hard right through a narrow doorway, pulling my son with me.

The security guard screamed. So did my son.

I didn't blame either of them.

———

Worst mom ever, I thought.

"It's okay," I said, hugging my son. "We're safe."

"But he's right—"

"He can't see us. This is a secret room."

"Secret?"

"Yes."

"Like magic?"

"Exactly like magic," I said.

Outside, through windows that only my son and I could see, we watched the confused security guard sweep his light over the wall. Each time, my son ducked, until he started getting the picture that the guard couldn't see us.

Still the worst mom ever, I thought.

More security guards appeared, each sweeping their light over the area while the first guard did his damnedest to explain what had happened.

"They went through here," he said, and now he sounded like he was doubting himself. He should doubt himself. To all the world, "there" was just a blank wall.

"They went through *where?*" asked another guard.

The first guy pointed his light right at us. My son's previous reaction was to duck, but this time, he held firm, standing his ground. "Right here. Through this wall."

All the flashlights hit the wall at once.

"It's a wall, Mick—"

"I swear to God—"

This went on for another half minute, until one of them got the bright idea that there was a chance that we went left instead of right. And so, they dashed off down a side corridor, flashlights bobbing and pounding footsteps receding.

I felt the presence behind us before he spoke. "You certainly know how to make an entrance, Samantha Moon."

CHAPTER NINETEEN

I got my son settled in one of the reading chairs, where he was doing just that: reading.

No, he wasn't brushing up on his dark magic or even studying for his potions finals with Severus Snape. No, he was using the Kindle app on my iPhone to plow through *The Hunger Games* trilogy, reading like there was no tomorrow. And, according to *The Hunger Games*, tomorrow looked bleak indeed.

Anyway, I'd admonished him to not touch anything, under any circumstances. He had agreed with a wave of his hand, face aglow in the phone's back light. What chance did I have to compete with Katniss Everdeen?

At the Help Desk, Maximus, who was wearing a tee-shirt and sweats, said, "You are annoyed at me."

"Pissed would be a better word. You didn't warn me that Dracula himself would come looking for me someday."

"And if I had, what would that have accomplished, other than to make you nervous? To make you jump at the slightest shadow? There was and is no way to prevent him from seeking you."

"Well, he did, and he found me, and it freaked me the fuck out."

"I imagine so. Would you mind if I relived the experience, Sam?"

"Relive away," I said. "But I'm still pissed at you."

Maximus sighed and came over to my side of the help desk...and then helped himself to my memories. By helping, I meant he placed his hands on my head and asked me to relax and to go back to when I first saw the Count, as I was now affectionately referring to him.

Anyway, I did go back to when the creepy bastard first appeared in the gym. I then relived the conversation as best as I could remember. A few minutes later, Max pulled away.

The alchemist blinked rapidly, then made his way back to his side of the Help Desk. "He can appear and disappear."

"You can say that again," I said.

"And yet, when he was here in the Reading Room, I didn't see him. And when he laughed loudly in the boxing ring...no one turned to look."

"What are you getting at?" I asked.

"I don't actually know," he said. "But he seems to have the ability to project himself where he wants. Then again, you are the only one who seems to see him."

"Yay," I said. "So, what does that mean?"

"I think," said the Alchemist. "I think he can project an aspect of himself, seen only by you. Or, if not just by you, perhaps others of his kind."

"You mean vampires?"

"Yes."

"But am I seeing him, or a part of him?"

"I don't know," said Maximus, "but this adds a new wrinkle to stopping him."

"So, you're saying this bastard can literally appear to me anywhere, at any time of the day."

"So it appears."

That thought alone made me want to run to the diamond medallion, which would, according to Max, remove the entity from within me. Except the entity within me wanted to attach herself to my bloodline. And a female bloodline at that. Leaving my sister—and even my daughter—the next in line for them to attack. I had a thought.

"Couldn't you just make other diamond medallions?" I asked, knowing the alchemist was more than likely following my thoughts anyway. "One for myself, and for my sister and daughter?"

"You would risk having your sister attacked? Or your daughter? And what if neither of them were able to control my mother? What if she took hold of them early on, possessed them fully, and fled to parts unknown?"

I shuddered at the thought. He was right, of course. The best way to manage—or control—his mother was, for now, through me.

Again, *yay.*

"It's easy to see the bad, Sam. I know that. Having something dark and angry living inside you cannot be fun. But try to see the good in this, if possible. I think, perhaps, that is your only saving grace."

"She doesn't want me to see the good," I said.

"Of course not. Seeing the good keeps her at bay. Seeing the good empowers you and disempowers her. Seeing the good, in effect, keeps her locked up, where she belongs. Remember always that letting her out, even for a moment, would be far, far worse."

"How bad?" I asked.

"Madness, perhaps. Or worse."

"Worse than madness?"

The Librarian shrugged, and I considered again the man known as Vlad Tepes, which, I now knew meant Vlad the Impaler. Had he gone mad...or was he already mad? He didn't seem mad. He seemed keen...aware. He seemed, above all, stable and in control of himself. That was, of course, until the entity had spoken through him.

"There's no knowing their relationship," said the Librarian, following my trail of thoughts easily enough. "And there's no knowing the extent of Cornelius' possession of Vlad, either."

"It has a name?"

"Yes, Sam. Just as my mother has a name."

At the sound of it, the entity within me—Elizabeth—perked up noticeably. I had a mental image of her fighting against her restraints. She could fight all she wanted.

Max went on, "I've sometimes wondered if Cornelius had bitten off more than he could chew."

"What do you mean?" I asked.

"Vlad might have been a bigger psychopath than even Cornelius. That Vlad might have, in fact, been on the road to mastery himself."

"But I thought all the dark masters had been banned," I said. "Run out of Dodge, so to speak. By your mentor, Hermes."

"And so they had, but it is possible some had slipped through our fingers. Or, in the case of Dracula, someone who was close to being one, but not quite there."

"And how would he, Dracula, know of this Occult Reading Room?" I asked. "I thought only those who needed the room—or were ready for it—could find it?"

"A good question, Sam," said Maximus. "My guess? He's been following you for quite some time...and saw you slip in here often enough. Such hidden rooms—magical rooms, as you explained to your son—would not be unfamiliar to Cornelius, the entity within Dracula."

"And he followed me how?"

"Dracula is a shape-shifter with the best of them, Sam. He is purported to turn into fog when convenient."

"And mice," I added, recalling my teen years reading Stoker.

"Exactly."

I chewed on that for a moment. Chewed a lot. Didn't like it. Wanted to spit it the hell out. Where was a spittoon when you needed one? I said, "So, you're telling me you're not sure who is controlling whom."

"Exactly, Sam. Cornelius was and is a force to be reckoned with, second only to my mother. But Vlad..."

"Vlad is a whole other kind of crazy."

"Exactly. One the most fierce—and feared—rulers the world has ever known."

"They make for interesting bedfellows," I said, and was fairly certain that was the first time I had ever said the word "bedfellows."

"Indeed, Sam. Potentially, they are unstoppable."

"Unstoppable from what?" I asked.

"Whatever it is they want. Which, in this case, is to open the veil between worlds."

"Um, what?"

"The veil," he said. "Between worlds."

"Oh, right," I said. "That veil. Silly me. And this is a veil that Hermes himself created."

"Created and sealed," he said.

"And I happen to be a descendent of Hermes," I said.

"Yes."

"And where is he now?" I asked. "Seems like we could use him again."

"Hermes is gone," said Max, and I suspected we had hit upon a sore spot for him. *He misses him,* I thought. Maximus held my gaze for a moment, then looked away.

"Gone where?" I asked.

"I don't really know, Sam. There are other worlds out there. Other people who need help. You have experienced these other worlds with the creature known as Talos, who lives in such alternate worlds."

"You're making my head spin," I said.

"Sorry, Sam. But such highly evolved masters as Hermes Trismegistus aren't long for our world. They're needed elsewhere."

"To fight other dark masters."

"Indeed, Sam. But he would never use words such as 'fight.' He saw it as maintaining balance."

"So, he would go to worlds that were out of balance?"

"Something like that."

"And our world is balanced now?"

"It had been, Sam. For the past five hundred years."

"And now?" I asked.

"Now," said Archibald Maximus, "I don't know. But Hermes did not leave us without hope."

"Oh?"

"He left behind his bloodline. A very powerful bloodline. I think you see where I'm going with this."

"I do," I said. "And I think you might see me curl up in the fetal position any moment now."

He laughed lightly. "You are more powerful than you know, Sam. And you are not alone. Not ever."

I was just about to tell him a fat lot of good that did me, when my son screamed bloody murder.

Chapter Twenty

What I saw shouldn't have surprised me.

A thick book lay open on the floor, black smoke billowing up from its yellowed pages. My son was shrinking away in fear...and screaming for his mom.

I dashed through the reading room, nearly flying, and swept my son up into my arms and watched in amazement as the swirling, twisting smoke morphed into a monstrous, undulating, amorphous snake. Now it wove throughout the room, just above our heads. It moved and slithered and my son whimpered in my arms, burying his face into my shoulders.

I didn't blame him. I found myself ducking from the flying, circling serpent, a serpent that seemed to only grow bigger and bigger, expanding exponentially. It also took on mass, shifting from something smoky and ill-defined, to sprouting actual scales and fangs, and two black eyes...and a flicking tongue.

Now I heard it, too. A harsh whisper, a sound that seemed to fill the room, or perhaps just my head.

"Yesss, yesss, yesss..."

Bigger it grew, until, I suspected, it was going to bust out of this very room. I found myself ducking with each passing, with each flicking of its forked tongue. My hair billowed in its slipstream.

Amazingly, Max stepped *through* it. As he did so, its slithering, coiling body exploded, then reformed again in the air above us. The young alchemist raised his hands and whispered words I could not understand—hell, words that I did not want to understand.

The flying serpent circled faster and faster. Its tongue flicked. It undulated and grew. Its black eyes were watching me, watching everything. Now its huge jaws opened wide and it struck at the alchemist's head. I was ready to spring into action, but he didn't need me. Indeed, he waved off the attack with a swipe of his hand, and the snake's head momentarily exploded into smoke, and then reformed itself. Bigger than ever.

"Yesss, yesss, yesss…"

Now, Max was no longer mumbling. Indeed, he spoke loudly and rapidly and with commanding authority. I still couldn't make out the words. I still didn't want to make out the words.

But something was happening. The snake was slowing down. It was also shrinking. The wind in the room was decreasing, too.

"Nooo…" it hissed. *"Nooo…"*

A moment later, I watched the rapidly-diminishing creature return to smoke vapor…and reverse back into the book from whence it came. Its anguished cries disappeared with it.

When it was gone, the ancient book slammed shut on its own.

Chapter Twenty-one

It was much later.

Too late for a mom to be talking to her son about demons, black magic and cursed grimoires. But here I was, doing exactly that. Not to mention, my son wouldn't let me leave his side, which was why I was now lying in bed next to him, running my fingers through his hair. Periodically, he would convulse and shake so violently that his teeth would rattle.

Each time he did so, I hated myself more and more.

We'd been lying like this for the past two hours. I kept waiting for Anthony to drift to sleep, but he hadn't yet. Every so often, he let out a pitiful, cat-like mew that broke my heart into a thousand pieces. My son had been reduced to a frightened, shivering newborn kitten, and it had been all my fault. Not to mention, he kept apologizing, over and over, which he did again now.

"I'm so sorry, Mommy," he said into his pillow, and the words came out hoarse and barely discernible.

"It's not your fault, baby."

"But I let it out, Mommy. It was all my fault."

Again, I told him it wasn't and patted him and quietly wiped tears from my cheeks with my free hand. It was all I could do to not cry in front of my son. I knew that it was important to be strong for him now. He needed to know that his mother could protect him... from anything.

"Mommy," he asked after a few minutes, "what *was* that thing?"

I knew exactly what it was. The Librarian had filled me in, and now I considered just how much to tell my boy. I decided not too much.

"It was something that can't hurt you, baby. Not now. Not ever."

"It asked me for help."

He had told me this a dozen times before, but I let him get it out again, if he needed to.

"I didn't know what it was. I know you told me not to touch any-thing, and not to listen to anything, but I…"

"I know, baby."

"I guess I wasn't expecting something to ask me for help…and it was coming from a book."

"I know—"

"A book, Mom. Do you know how crazy that is?"

"About as crazy as it gets."

"You were so busy talking to Max, and he was holding your head like you had a headache or something, and all I did was open the book…" His voice trailed off and he whimpered again.

I knew what happened next, of course. The voice had asked him to repeat a word or two. And my son had…and that had been all the demon needed.

At the time, I had been worried that something else might have happened, that somehow, my son had gotten possessed, but the Librarian had waved it off, insisting the demon was back where it belonged, sealed within the book. Still, I had him check out my son, although I wasn't sure what we were looking for. Max had given my son a clean bill of health—or, rather, a clean bill of *possession-free* health.

Another hour of whimpering and patting and mewing later, my son finally turned to me and said, "I'll be okay now, Mommy. You can go to bed now. Or go to work. Or whatever it is you do all night."

I smiled and kissed him on his warm forehead.

Two hours later, after finishing up some work in my office and clearing out my email—I always wondered what people thought about getting emails from me at 3:28 in the morning—I found myself standing in the open doorway of my son's bedroom, watching him sleep, relieved all over again that all seemed to be well.

That had been close, and scary as hell, even for me.

I was about to turn away—about to get some shuteye of my own—when my son rolled over onto his side...

And looked directly at me.

Except, he wasn't looking.

He was staring.

I blinked, sure I was seeing things—and when I opened them again, his eyes were closed and he was sleeping soundly.

Rattled—and apparently still shaken from the night's events—I headed off to bed.

Chapter Twenty-two

I couldn't sleep.

And since dawn was still a few hours away, I stripped down in the shadows of my backyard orange tree, and transformed into something giant and alien and most definitely out of this world.

For those unlucky few, they would have seen a giant, hulking creature leap from the shadows of my back yard…and straight up into the sky, flapping its huge, leathery wings hard.

Now, I followed the coastline, which was always my favorite route. The cresting waves foamed and glowed under the quarter moon. The full moon was just under a week or so away.

When the werewolves play.

Well, some of them, at least. According to Kingsley, most werewolves tended to stay indoors and locked down, which made sense, since there really weren't a lot of "vicious wild animal attacks" reported in Southern California.

There were, of course, dozens and dozens of missing persons in California…and just about everywhere else, too.

Kingsley called tonight and, in much coded language, had let me know that little was known about Gunther Kessler in the werewolf community. Kingsley suggested, in even more coded language (he never liked talking about this stuff over the phone), that many of his wolfie friends had been somewhat guarded when he approached them about Gunther. This confused Kingsley. He'd never known his friends to be guarded. He didn't know what to make of it, and neither did I, although he told me again, for the umpteenth time, to be careful.

I flapped lazily, continuously.

I could have been a giant manta ray, sailing through the heavens. What I was, exactly, was not clear. I knew a creature from another world was summoned to be exchanged with my own body. A sort of parallel universe swap. I knew that my own body would be resting comfortably—and, hopefully, safely—in this other world. Presently, I did not have access to my human body, wherever it was. At least, I hadn't figured out how to have access to it yet. Talos, on the other hand, *did* have access to his body here on Earth, a body he permitted me to take over completely.

Could I die in his world? I didn't know. Could Talos die in our world? It was hard to say. I knew Talos could kill in our world, as we had done together on that remote Washington island, years ago.

It was, of course, enough to make my head spin.

We are together, and we are separate, Samantha Moon, came a deep voice inside me. And not just inside my head. It seemed to surround me, fill me. *Your world is not used to the concept of duality. Or, rather unwilling to accept it.*

Well, hello, Talos, I thought. *Fancy meeting you here.*

An earth idiom, I assume.

You assume correctly, I thought.

Your inability to understand duality is expected.

Because of the physical world we live in, I thought.

Indeed. Time and space render such concepts difficult to comprehend.

I thought: *Well, few of us—outside of our most advanced mystics—will ever fully wrap our brains around the idea that we can be in two places at once.*

And yet you are, in fact, in two places at once, Samantha Moon. I would even argue three.

You're referring to my higher self, I thought.

Indeed, Sam. The higher self or soul or the spark of the divine or whatever you choose to call it, that which is truly you exists elsewhere.

Where?

Beyond the physical, in what some would call the energetic realms.

Is that where you're from?

433

Close, Sam. My world is a hybrid world.

And what the devil does that mean?

Both physical and spiritual exist side by side. We have long since mastered how to be in two places at once, and sometimes three or four places.

Now my head really hurts.

Careful, thought Talos, *it's my head, too. The truth is, your world is a hybrid world, too, although your kind is slanted primarily toward the physical. But at any time, humanity could make the leap to embrace the spiritual.*

Well, don't expect that any time soon.

You might be surprised, Sam. There is greater good going on in your earth than is presently being reported.

You would think, I thought, *from the news we see that war is just around every corner.*

And is it? Is that your experience?

No, I thought. *But it's the experience of others—*

Not the vast majority of others, Sam. The truth is, a slight shift is occurring in your world as we speak. A shift toward peace.

Not if the thing within me has any say in it.

Oh, there will be a few who will fight the shift to their last breath…but their days are numbered. But do not think of this as a war, Sam. Remember what you were once told: defeat the enemy with love.

And how do you know what I was once told?

Because I am you, too, Sam. We are one in this moment.

And you have access to my memories?

In a way, yes.

And I have access to yours?

If you so choose.

I'm not sure I can handle your memories, I thought. *I kinda have a lot to juggle on my end.*

So it seems.

What is a demon? I suddenly asked.

A lost entity, one that has been lost for so long that it chooses to never, ever find itself.

Were they good once?

It's hard to say, Sam. They are from God, so, of course they were once good.

Because we're all one and all that jazz?

Exactly. But not all entities evolve. Some choose to do the opposite.

To devolve?

Something like that. But if you ask me, I secretly suspect such entities are fulfilling a role for God.

So, they were created on purpose?

Perhaps, perhaps not. I do not know. I am only postulating an hypothesis.

And since when did giant flying vampire bats postulate hypotheses?

I might be the first.

I laughed, then thought: *Perhaps they were created to be a foil?*

Or to show us darkness.

Because without darkness...

You cannot see the light, finished Talos. *But make no mistake, Samantha. Demons are real. They are powerful. And they are everywhere.*

Gee, thanks for that pick-me-up.

There was a long silence as I continued up the coast, now flying high above Santa Barbara. I would have to circle back soon, but not yet. In the far, far distance, I caught sight of something else. A shadow moving through the heavens. A shadow in the shape of a...

No, I thought. *That can't be.*

But it was, I certain of it.

It was a dragon.

Chapter Twenty-three

We were in my minivan.

I'd forgotten that this evening was "ghouls' night out" as Allison liked to call it. I'd compromised with her and now here we were on a stakeout together...and she wouldn't stop talking.

"Stakeouts," I said, "are generally done in silence."

"That was a rude thing to say, Sam. Besides, tonight was ghouls' night out—"

"Will you quit saying that?"

She continued, without missing a beat, "—and you know damn well I look forward to this night all week. Besides, it's also been a week since, you know."

Yes, I knew well. It had been a week since I'd last fed from her wrist and I could feel the effects. A little lethargic. A little less than what I knew I could be. True, I'd drunk my fill of cow and pig blood from my supply in the garage, but it wasn't the same. That was equivalent to living on McDonald's. Eventually it wore you down and sapped your energy. Sadly, normal food didn't help. At all. I could eat ten scones from Starbucks and still feel depleted. I needed blood, and I needed it about every other day.

Yeah, a true ghoul, I thought.

I heard that, came Allison's thought.

"You caught me," I said. "And we'll take care of that later."

That being, of course, me drinking from her wrist, usually from the same old scar. Luckily for her, she healed almost instantly as soon as I pulled away from her. Vampire saliva had that effect.

We were sitting in the front seat of my minivan, parked in the same spot down the road, in front of a house that mostly appeared empty, which was why I had chosen it.

"Is he always this busy?" asked Allison.

"Not so far," I said.

Indeed, we saw the silhouette of a man—Gunther, no doubt—flashing back and forth behind the glass of his front door. We saw lights turn on and off. At one point, we heard him in the garage.

"So, what do you think he's up to?"

"Hard to know," I said.

"The full moon is in, what, three nights?"

"Two," I said. "Sunday night."

"Why don't we, you know, confront him? Before he hurts someone else?"

"And make him tell me what I need to know?"

"Well…" she thought about that. "Yeah, I guess."

"If he's a werewolf—and it's looking more and more like he is—then he'll be as strong or stronger than me. Besides, if I confront him, he could go into hiding, or disappear altogether."

"So, you're waiting to flush him out, or catch him in the act."

"Something like that."

"To think there are actually these *things* running around at full moons, hungry for people."

"Most aren't running around at full moons. Most are responsible. Most don't want to get caught. Most lead fairly normal lives and want to continue leading them."

"Like Kingsley," she said.

"Right."

"And maybe this guy, too."

"Maybe," I said.

"So, you're saying that they practice safe transforming?"

Sometimes Allison, despite her neediness and clinginess, made me laugh, which I did now. "Responsible transforming, yes."

"I can see the public service announcement now," said Allison and adopted a mock announcer voice: "Transform safely and comfortably in a padlocked cell deep beneath your home..."

"The More You Know..." I said.

Now, we were both snickering, although I really didn't feel like snickering. Not after seeing what I had seen last night: Vlad Tepes, the escaped demon, and my son staring at me, although that last one could have been my imagination. Still, the laughter felt good, and it might have been my first laughter in the last 24 hours.

When we were done, we both smiled at an old lady walking her labradoodle past our parked minivan. She gave us a good, hard look, and I waved to her and smiled. So did Allison. The old lady didn't smile back.

"She's going to be trouble," said Allison.

"Probably," I said.

"Then why don't you do your vampire-mind-trick on her? Or whatever you call it."

"I don't call it anything. Besides, I already called the Orange Police Department days ago. They know I'm in the area doing surveillance."

"Gee, you private dicks think of everything."

I was about to comment when I saw it again: a car sporting a mustache attached to its grill, driving slowly by.

"You see that?" I asked, pointing.

"What? The car with the mustache?"

"Yeah, that. What's the deal with that?"

"I don't know, but I feel like I've seen those before."

"I have, too. In fact, three of them on this very street."

"Three different cars?"

I nodded and thought about that and nearly Googled it again when Allison suddenly turned and faced me. My friend was quite lovely. Dark hair, almond-shaped eyes, caramel skin. She reached out and took my cold hand. I flinched involuntarily, as I always do when people touch me.

"There's something about this case that you're keeping from me, Sam. Something buried so deep that I can't quite see it."

"You don't get to know all my secrets," I snapped, pulling my hand free.

Allison, to her credit, didn't take offense. She also knew that I could get pretty damn moody sometimes. She got it. She also knew when my snapping wasn't about her. Of course, having a mostly open telepathic connection helped, too.

So, instead of being hurt or snapping back, she blinked and calmly said, "Nor do I want to, Sam, but I can feel the conflict within you. It's bubbling up to your surface, then sinks down again. I've felt it ever since you took on this case."

I drummed my fingers on the steering wheel. I almost wished Gunther would make an appearance, just so I wouldn't have to answer Allison's question.

"That bad, huh?" asked Allison.

"I'm afraid so," I said, and let the full extent of my misgivings percolate to the surface of my thoughts.

"Just know that I'm here for you," she said. "And I don't mean that in a needy way."

"Yes, you do."

"Bitch," said Allison.

Had we been guys, I might have socked her in the arm. But we were girls so, I winked at her and blew her a kiss and she shook her head, then grew somber again. "So, what gives about this case?"

I drummed my nails on the steering wheel...and decided to come clean. "I'm just having a hard time caring," I said.

"Caring about what?"

"About catching Gunther Kessler."

"But...but you have to care, Sam."

"Why?" I asked. "Why do I have to care?"

"Didn't you take, like, an oath to care?"

"To protect and serve?"

"Yes, that."

"No. That's the police."

"But if you don't care, then you are falling into their trap, playing right into their hands."

I drummed my fingers on the steering wheel, fighting a feeling inside me...or, rather, trying to understand my *lack* of feeling. My lack of caring for the missing hikers.

It's her, I thought.

No, it's me.

I gripped the steering wheel more tightly. The conversation was making me feel uncomfortable. I suddenly needed some air, although air is not what I needed, ever. I rolled down the window and got a breeze going. The day was warm, and the street was mostly quiet. The old lady with her labradoodle was gone. For now.

I had a sudden, exciting image of breaking the old lady's neck, twisting her head so hard that she died right there in my hands, while I feasted from her spasming corpse.

"Holy shit, Sam. Please tell me you didn't just think that."

"She's asking for it."

"No, she's not, Sam. She's a concerned citizen, wondering why two women are parked on the street for hours on end."

I felt the anger rise in me. I felt a strong need to lash out at Allison for being such a stupid bitch. It took all I had to not say something horrible...and to not do something horrible either. I held my hands in my lap, interlocking my fingers, putting myself under house arrest. I rocked back and forth, releasing some of the energy.

A moment later, when I had calmed down, I heard Allison audibly exhale, too. She sensed correctly that the worst had passed. For both of us. Allison was, after all, a powerful, albeit new, witch. There was no telling what she would have done to me in return.

"That was scary, Sam."

I shook my head, looking down and rocking, rocking.

"But I think what's scariest of all is that I..." she paused, tried again. "Is that I know that was all you."

She was right, of course. The entity within me—Elizabeth—was still firmly caged in my mind. This last little outburst had been me. *All me.*

440

After a moment, Allison looked at me. There was sweat on her forehead. "What does it mean?"

"I don't know," I said.

"And you really don't care about the missing hikers?"

"I'm trying to," I said, then paused and looked away. "But some people deserve to die."

"I think I need to go, Sam."

I nodded. "I think you should, too."

CHAPTER TWENTY-FOUR

*G*ood evening, Moon Dance.

When you say it that way, Fang, I wrote in my little IM window, *I always hear Bela Lugosi's Dracula.*

Maybe that's how I'd intended it to sound, Sam. What's on your mind?

My fingers briefly hovered over the keyboard before I typed: *How can I keep doing my job…if I no longer care?*

Care about what?

If people die?

His answer came a half minute later: *I'm not sure what to say to that, Moon Dance.*

But surely you agree, I wrote. *We are the same, you and I. We are hunters, are we not?*

We are, Sam. But we can decide who to hunt and what to hunt and when to hunt. Or to not hunt at all. You have a viable source of blood from a willing donor.

I shook my head there on my couch, although he couldn't see me shake it. The lights were out and, although it wasn't quite twilight yet, the room was dark enough. The sun had set about an hour ago and I was feeling…hungry. Allison had left before my feeding, and my body was letting me know it. My stomach never growled, nor did I feel hungry, as I remembered it back when I was mortal. No, this was different. This was a physical need. I suspected this is what a heroin addict felt—an overwhelming desire to satisfy the deepest yearning. To the point where rational thought went out the window.

I missed my feeding today, I wrote. *I think I was scaring her.*

You're scaring me, Sam. You have the cow and pig blood packets.

Fuck the packets.

I'm coming over. I have my own packets. Human blood. Are you home?

Yes.

Sit tight.

He logged off.

Except I didn't sit tight, whatever the hell that means. I closed my laptop and stood and paced my small room and wished like hell my living room was bigger so I could pace in longer steps. I didn't have to live this way. I could have more money. I could take the money I needed from those who had it. I could then take their lives, too. I could take and take and take, and nothing could stop me, not ever.

I paced the small room and shook my hands, then ran my fingers through my hair. I was hungry. *Starving.* I shouldn't have let her leave without first feeding from her. I had cow and pig blood in the garage, mixed with all sorts of filthy pollutants.

I deserved better than that.

I paused at my big living room window. It looked out from my end of the cul-de-sac, all the way down the street, itself lined with houses on either side. Most had big trees out front. Lots of cars were parked out front, too. It was evening. My kids were with my sister. I had begged her to take them. I wasn't feeling like myself...I'd told her. She had looked oddly at me when I had dropped them off.

Now, along the street, I saw some kids playing. A sort of chasing game as they weaved in and out of parked cars. Reckless. Careless. Shitty parenting. I watched the kids some more. Laughing and now playing a game of tag. Refreshing, actually. Still, why would you let your kids play outside when there were predators out there? Predators watching them, even now. Predators who would snatch their kids away.

Stupid fucking parents.

I paced in front of the window. I wondered what those same parents would think if they knew an honest-to-god vampire lived on their very street. Something that drank blood and stayed up at night and watched their children play.

I shook my head, rubbed my eyes and paced some more…and then, I saw it. The thing I had been hoping to see. It was exactly what I needed, but hadn't known, until now.

It was a tomcat, walking along the wall that separated my front yard from my neighbor's front yard.

Before I could think, before I could plan, I was out my front door, pouncing faster than I ever thought I could, and certainly faster than the cat had expected.

It was a short time later when I heard the familiar voice behind me. "Ah, shit, Sam."

I pushed the remains of the cat away, tossing aside a leg that I had been sucking the marrow out of.

"Aaron," I said, using Fang's assumed name. He was, after all, officially on the run and wanted for murder. "Fancy meeting you here."

CHAPTER TWENTY-FIVE

Fang spent the next half hour cleaning me up, and cleaning my place up, too.

He deposited what was left of the cat in a heavy trash bag, along with my clothes, which he had made me strip out of in the bathroom and pass through to him. I noted that he averted his eyes.

Rather chivalrous of him.

I also noted that I was still ravenously hungry. The cat hadn't been nearly enough, although it had, for now, satisfied my need to kill something.

My *overwhelming* need to kill something.

And when I had killed it, when I had held its broken body in my hands and tore into it with my mouth, I knew something inside of me had died...and might stay dead forever.

My humanity.

This was, I was certain, the first time I had killed something that didn't deserve to die, something that hadn't done anything to me. Something that was, in fact, innocent. The cat was not only dead... but I had torn it to shreds, even going so far as breaking apart its bones to get to the good stuff inside.

"This is not like you, Moon Dance," said Fang from my living room, where he was presently wiping up the bloody mess from the wood floor.

I was dressed in a bathrobe. The now-bloody rag he was using intrigued me. "I suppose not," I said, and sat down on one end of the couch and watched him.

"You always had so much self-control."

"I was weak then."

"No," said Fang. "You were yourself."

"Well, this is me now. Get used to it. Did you bring the blood?"

"It's in the refrigerator."

He had barely finished the sentence when I was moving, flashing across the room—and probably flashing him, too. I didn't care if I flashed him. I only cared about the blood.

Human blood.

From Fang's own blood bank.

And there it was, in a white paper bag. Heavy bag, too, full of life, full of my sweet addiction.

I pulled out the first clear packet. Fang had used plastic medical bags to store his blood, all very official looking. I bit through the corner, spitting out the plastic, and drank deeply from it. I noted immediately—all over again—the difference between human and animal blood.

So different, I thought. *So perfect. And so right for me. Clearly, the entity within me preferred human blood.*

No, I thought, *I preferred it.*

I started on the second.

"Easy, Tiger," said Fang.

I opened my eyes. Yeah, I think they might have rolled back into my head. Like a shark. No, like a predator. Fang was leaning a shoulder against the kitchen doorway, watching me with an expression of bewilderment, amusement and concern.

Pick an expression, asshole, I thought.

And as I drank, I sensed myself slipping a little further away. A little further offshore, so to speak. The tide of hate and anger and hunger was pulling me further out to sea.

"Penny for your thoughts," said Fang, which was almost funny, since the man had once read my thoughts with ease. Now, no more, being a fellow creature of the night.

I dropped the second bag on my kitchen floor, the remnants of which splattered over my bare feet and up onto the base of my refrigerator. Blood had also spilled onto my robe in my haste to suck down the packages.

I started on the third bag when it occurred to me that I'd killed my neighbor's cat, Tinker Bell.

It hadn't been a stray tomcat. It hadn't been wild. In fact, I had chewed through its collar in my haste to get to its neck, even spitting out the little jingle bell it wore. Something inside me had dehumanized it, so to speak. Had rendered it into nothing but a stray, when, in fact, it had been something: a loving house pet.

But what if, instead of Tinker Bell, one of my elderly neighbors had walked past? Would I have rendered one of them into nothing as well? Would I have convinced myself they were homeless? Or meth addicts? Or something beneath me? Would they, even now, be wrapped in a trash bag, rendered into shreds?

Or what if my kids had been home? Would I have dehumanized them, too? Would they even now be as dead as Tinker Bell?

The thought scared the unholy shit out of me, and I dropped to my knees and buried my face in my hands, and as I wept, I heard a voice not very deep inside my head—my own voice, in fact—whisper: "Pathetic."

Chapter Twenty-six

"Rough day, Moon Dance?"

"Shut up," I said, and tried to laugh but failed miserably. It sounded halfway between a cough and a sob.

We were sitting on my bed, with the shades pulled down, and drinking ice water. I couldn't stand the thought of more blood. I'd had my fill for tonight. For many nights.

"It's safe to say that you just saw me at my worst."

"Well, if that's your worst, Moon Dance, then I think we're going to be okay."

"No," I said. "You don't understand. Well, maybe you would understand. Actually, you would understand better than most."

"You're rambling, Sam."

"That's me," I said. "Ramblin' Sam."

"And what is it you think I don't understand?"

"It might have been only a cat—oh, God, Tinker Bell—but I seriously lost *all* control of myself."

"It was only a cat—not to say that Tinker Bell wasn't an awesome cat. So, try to relax. Deep breaths. You didn't kill anyone, right?"

I nodded, perhaps with a little less conviction than he wanted.

"Right?" he asked.

"Right," I said. "I didn't kill anyone. I swear."

"Pinky swear?"

"Yes, dammit. Just the cat, and I feel terrible enough as it is."

"Terrible is good, Sam."

"What do you mean?"

I had my down pillow laid over my lap. Fang was sitting opposite me, legs crossed as well. He was as tall as Kingsley, certainly, but not as big, not by a long shot. No one was. Perhaps ever. I doubted Kingsley could sit cross-legged on a bed to save his life. Having tree trunks for legs had that effect.

Speaking of Kingsley, I knew he would not be happy to know that Fang and I were currently sharing my bed. Of course, we were both sitting on my bed, and one of us was currently doubting her sanity, but guys tended to overlook such minor details. I had no reason to hide it from Kingsley, and I would tell him later, and he would just have to get over it. For now, Fang was the only vampire I knew, and certainly the only one I trusted.

"It's good that you feel terrible, Sam. We need you to feel terrible. That terrible part is your humanity."

"But it didn't feel terrible in the moment. It felt right. Damn right."

"I have no doubt, Sam."

Fang rested his elbows easily on his knees. He was a good-looking guy. Straight nose. Bright eyes. His pale complexion went without saying. Earlier in his transformation, he had gone to a dark place, and had stayed there for a while. During so, my relationship with Kingsley had blossomed all over again, and Fang and I had lost touch for many months. Our rebuilding was slow. A few emails. A few texts, and then the IM-ing started again. Officially, we were the last two people on earth to still instant message.

Anyway, I was glad he had pulled himself out of it. Mostly, I was glad to have my Fang back in my life again. Our relationship seemed to have evolved into a true friendship, which was what I needed. He seemed to be mostly okay with it.

Now, he studied me long and hard, and I knew he was wishing like crazy that he could dip into my thoughts again. He was my first, so to speak. My first telepathic link. And, as with all firsts, he held a special place in my heart.

449

"I think, Moon Dance, that the key here is to never allow yourself to get to that place again."

"What place?"

"That place of darkness. Hear me out. The Librarian told you that the key to defeat the thing within you—"

"And within you, too, I might add."

He nodded. "Yes, but so far, the thing within me has stayed buried deep, as had been the case with you."

He was right. Elizabeth had lain dormant for many years, only recently making an appearance...and making my life a living nightmare in the process.

Fang went on: "Anyway, the Librarian had told you that the key to defeating her was with love."

"He did, yes. Maybe he's the original hippie."

"Or maybe he knows what he's talking about," said Fang. "What if the love he's referring to is...love for *yourself*."

"I'm not following."

"Exactly," said Fang. "You have spent so long hating yourself for what you are. Hating yourself for what you have become. Hating the thing within you. Hating your predicament. Hating Danny. Hating anything that has come up against you—"

"And my nails."

I held up my hands. "I hate my nails."

"Right, your nails. Anyway, my point is this: your own self-hatred has awakened the beast within you. Literally. That is why, I think, she has made such a strong showing. You have created an environment within yourself for her to flourish."

"Hating myself is kinda my thing."

"I know, Sam. But you didn't do anything wrong. You don't deserve this. You deserve love. Self-love."

His words hung in the air, and I did my best to absorb them. Truthfully, the concept of loving myself seemed...foreign. Which shouldn't be the case. Not for me, not for anyone.

"Self-love," I said again, and for some reason, I giggled.

"Not that kind of self-love, Samantha Moon! But surely *that* wouldn't hurt either."

And, yeah, we both laughed...and, yeah, I'm pretty sure I would be keeping this last exchange from Kingsley. The big oaf didn't need to know everything, dammit. Of course, the poor guy was currently in lockdown mode at his residence. I was never, ever permitted to see him the day before the full moon or the day after. Which was fine by me. At this time of the month, he tended to be grumpy as hell anyway.

"You said something about never letting myself get to this point again. What did you mean by that?"

"You will need to be diligent in your feeding, Samantha. Get yourself on a regular schedule. Go back to the cow and pig blood, as filthy as it is."

"Wait, why?"

"Hear me out. It's filthy and disgusting, yes, but the key here is that you did not *crave* that blood. You did not hunger for it. You consumed it only to stay alive. However, you only awakened the beast within when you began consuming human blood on a regular basis."

"*She* prefers human blood," I said, nodding.

"Then don't give her what she wants."

"Don't feed the beast, you mean?"

"Right."

"But I need blood—"

"Of course you do. We both do. Our bodies have been forever altered by the entities within. But we don't need *human* blood. You don't need human blood. Cow and pig blood satisfy your cravings."

"But I'm not as strong—"

"Perhaps not. Or perhaps that's a false belief she's given you."

"I may not be able to go back—"

"You can, Sam. You have to. Or next time I come here..."

He didn't have to finish. We both knew what he meant. The next time he came here, he might not see a dead cat...but a dead person.

He said, "The key is love."

451

"And cow blood."

"Yes, Sam."

"So, how do you love yourself when you've hated yourself for so long?"

Fang reached over and took both my hands. He held my gaze for a long, long time, then finally shook his head. "Only you can answer that, Sam. But I think you might be better at it than you give yourself credit for."

CHAPTER TWENTY-SEVEN

Fang was gone, and I was restless.

After much pacing and running my fingers through my hair, I decided it was time that I got real answers, and it was time that I started caring that real people might be getting killed in the worst way imaginable: being eaten alive.

Jesus.

With my kids now staying over with my sister—God bless her—I grabbed my car keys and hit the road.

I was parked in front of Gunther's house.

It was the middle of night, with dawn still hours away. The street was quiet and Gunther's two-story home looked empty. I shouldn't have left his house this evening. I should have stayed here, watching it, then followed him. But I had let my hunger get the best of me, and now, he was gone. I was sure of it. After all, tomorrow was the full moon, and there was a very good chance Gunther was, even now, looking for his next victim.

Up in the San Bernardino Mountains, perhaps along a hiking trail.

Or, more likely, he was setting up on a carefully chosen trail. Come morning, he would wait for the perfect victim. He was fairly indiscriminate. Men and women alike...although he leaned toward women.

No, this wasn't a paying gig. I had no dog in this fight. And up until now, the idea of something hunting humans in the woods didn't seem entirely horrible.

It had seemed right. Natural.

The strong shall live, and all of that.

But now that my hunger had been satiated, and now that I had begun the process of removing the hate and anger from my thoughts...something interesting was happening.

Something Fang had predicted, that smart little bugger.

I started caring. I started feeling like my old self. I started realizing that killing the innocent wasn't right, no matter what, and if I could do something about it, then dammit, I would.

A simple shift in focus had been all that was needed.

A shift from hate to love.

"Self-love," I whispered and laughed lightly.

I needed to do something, and that something was to find his damn cabin in the woods. A cabin that was, I suspected, off the grid or owned by someone else. Or even owned by one of his victims.

So, I closed my eyes and projected my mind out.

A neat trick and one that every investigator should be so lucky to have the ability to do. Anyway, as my consciousness expanded, I focused on the house before me, and soon, I was pushing through the front door. My projected mind now stood in his foyer. From there, I scanned the house. Empty. Lights out, except for a single lamp near the camelback couch. The view before me flickered and wavered, like a TV going on the fritz. I was stretching my mental scanning abilities to the limit. I pushed on down the hallway, scanning into each room. The downstairs was empty. Back in the living room, I noticed a camera sitting on his mantel, pointed at the front door. It was the only such camera I saw. I also saw a home security system that seemed pretty elaborate. Motion detectors in all the living room corners.

I headed upstairs and confirmed the same, then took a quick peek in the garage. The Challenger was still here.

Someone picked him up, I realized, and returned to my body.

I stepped out of my minivan...and slipped into the shadows around Gunther's home, searching for a way in. I ignored the downstairs windows; most would be wired. I continued around the house, reaching over and opening a side gate. No dog, but I knew that. I scanned the upper stories.

There, high up, was a circular vent that would lead, I assumed, into the attic. I would take my chances.

I leaped up onto the stone fence separating his property from his neighbor's. Now the neighbor might have a dog...but it turned out they didn't. Either way, I wasn't on the fence for long. From there, I gathered myself and sprang as high as I could. Turns out I can spring with the best of them. A moment later, I landed smoothly on the roof.

I dashed along the crest of the roof and leaped onto the second-story tiles. A moment later, using brute force, I had the attic vent off.

Once inside, I began removing my clothing.

All in a night's work.

Chapter Twenty-eight

I was naked. In someone else's house.

Lucky for me, without clothing, the camera and motion sensors wouldn't pick me up. Still, I was naked. In someone else's house.

Feeling more than self-conscious, I headed down his stairs, careful not to touch anything. I might be undead and a supernatural badass, but I still left fingerprints.

The house was large, but not exceptionally so. I didn't see a basement entrance outside, nor did I expect there to be. Few homes in Southern California had basements. Anyway, the first floor consisted of a large living room with a black lacquer Steinway piano in one corner. The fireplace with its mantel and camera. The mantel had a few candles on it, which I thought was overkill. The living room was immaculate. Freshly vacuumed. Furniture polished. Magazines spread neatly over the coffee table. I looked but didn't see a copy of *The Werewolf Times* or *Furry Illustrated*.

I did see, however, an abundance of moon paraphernalia. What was the deal with that anyway? Okay, I get that their lives revolve around the damn thing, but did they also need to collect moon crap, too?

Apparently so.

Kingsley's office was adorned with the stuff, and so was Gunther's home. A full moon painting above the black leather camelback couch. A crescent moon painting over the piano. A supermoon photograph over the fireplace. Moon statues inside an inset glass display case. The statues ranged from the very elegant to the surreal to the

absurd. A Dali-like moon, made of clay, in mid-dissolve, was seemingly spilling onto the glass shelf. Actually, I kinda liked that one.

I moved on.

The kitchen was behind the living room, around a central set
of stairs that led to the upstairs bedrooms. The kitchen was modern
and industrial and looked like it had never been used. There was,
yes, a moon potholder hanging from a hook near the refrigerator.
Moon magnets on the fridge. I was beginning to hate the moon.
Which was sad, considering my cool last name.

So far, I hadn't set off any alarms.

I headed upstairs and into the master bedroom. Freshly cleaned
and freshly vacuumed. Yes, Gunther had been busy tonight. Maybe
he preferred coming home to a clean house after his monthly killings. Call it a quirk.

As I stood in his bedroom, hands on hips and leaving nothing
to the imagination, I noted a distinct lack of *new* spirit energy. Sure,
there were a couple of older energies, so old that they were barely
recognizable as human. They ignored me completely, which most
older energy did. No one had died here recently, I was certain of
it. Gunther Kessler wasn't shitting where he eats, as the saying goes.

That's what the kill cabin was for.

I noted the motion detectors were reserved for downstairs, so I freely
rummaged through drawers and closets upstairs. I checked pockets and
inside shoes and behind dressers. I checked under his bed and under
his mattress. I lifted paintings and flipped through books. No tell-tale
receipts. No photographs. Other than being a closet E.L. James fan, he'd
left no clues that I could discern. I next checked the guest room. Nothing.

I left the guest bedroom and headed down the short hall to his
office, where I hoped to hit pay dirt. No such luck. Or dirt. The com-
puters were password protected, and I barely remembered my own
passwords. His filing cabinet would have been my best bet, except he
didn't have one.

As I stood there in his office, naked as the day I was born, feeling
foolish and oddly liberated, I realized I only took Nancy Pearson's
word for it that Gunther was a killer.

The truth was, outside of a ridiculous amount of moon paraphernalia, I wasn't even entirely sure the man was a werewolf. Even Kingsley hadn't known him. And Kingsley's wolfie friends weren't talking either.

Maybe Gunther had gone on a short trip. Maybe a taxi had picked him up. Or the airport shuttle. Or maybe he was hunting his next victim even now, in the woods, all while I stood naked in his house like an idiot.

I shouldn't have left the surveillance of his house.

But I had. I had let my hunger get the best of me.

It didn't have to be that way. I could have satiated it with a packet of animal blood. A cooler in the van, maybe. Fill it with a few emergency packets. I had convinced myself that I wanted—no, needed—human blood. Perhaps Fang was right. Perhaps that was a false belief. Perhaps giving *her* human blood only made her stronger, and me—the real me—weaker.

Most of all, she fed off my own self-hatred.

"No more," I thought.

Now, as I stood there in his office, hands on hips and thinking hard, I was certain of one thing: someone had picked him up. Whether it was a taxi or a shuttle or a fellow creature of the night, I didn't know.

But if I could figure out who picked him up...then I would find Gunther and his kill cabin in the woods.

CHAPTER TWENTY-NINE

The call came the next morning.

These days, I tended to sleep lighter. Before, it would take a lot more than a phone call at 10 a.m. to wake me up. Especially after the night I'd had.

The phone number was restricted, which didn't surprise me. At least not on today, of all days.

The full moon.

It was all I could do to sound coherent, when I clicked on the call. "Moon Investigations," I said. At least, I think I said it.

"Rough night, Samantha?"

"Who's this?"

"Ranger Ted with the California State Parks."

It took a moment for that information to sink in. I was still lying on my side in bed, with my pillow mostly over my head.

"Got a minute?"

I sat up and yawned. "Sure, what's going on?"

"We have another hiker missing."

"Shit."

"You can say that again. You mentioned you met Sheriff Stanley the other day, right?"

"I did," I said, and nearly added that I'd helped save his marriage, but decided that might come off as unprofessional and a little egocentric...and a little off-topic. "Is he overseeing the case?"

"You could say that," said Ranger Ted. "It's his wife, Elise, who's missing."

"No," I said, and might have shouted it and sat a little straighter. "No, no, no."

I had seen the unborn children. I had felt his love for this woman. I had helped save the marriage, off-topic or not.

"Exactly. This isn't good, Sam. Not good at all. People know the two of them have been fighting. People even know that she cheated on him. We live in a small town. People talk. Speaking of which, there's already whispers that there might be foul play."

"Foul play, how?"

"Sheriff Stanley has a temper. He's been reprimanded in the past."

"No way," I said. "He would never have touched his wife. Not like that."

"And you know this how?"

"Just trust me on that."

"I wish I could, Sam. Either way, this doesn't look good for him, and it's looking worse and worse for her."

"When did she go missing?"

"This morning. She went on an early hike. At daybreak. She's usually home for breakfast at 7:30 at the latest."

I checked the time again. 10:10 a.m. "She's been missing for a little over two and a half hours," I said. "That's hardly a reason—"

"You don't understand, Sam. This is a small community. She told her husband she would be back in an hour. The word is out that Elise Stanley is missing. If someone had seen her, they would have reported her. I don't have a good feeling about this, Sam."

Neither did I. Try as I might to play devil's advocate, I knew full well that there might very well be a missing hiker today. Damn well. After all, Gunther was gone and tonight was the full moon.

"We have all available manpower on the case. We've even called in some boys from San Diego and Los Angeles counties. It's a sheriff's wife, after all. One of our own, in a way. Anyway, I thought you should have a heads up, since you were just here asking about missing hikers."

"Thank you," I said, and we clicked off. For the next few minutes, I thought about Sheriff Stanley and his three unborn children.

I got dressed, grabbed my keys, and hit the road.

Chapter Thirty

"Master Kingsley is terribly indisposed—"

"I'm terribly sorry to hear that," I said, and pushed past the tall butler and into the house.

He caught up behind me. Not hard for him to do with those long legs of his. His mismatched long legs, I might add. "Master Kingsley has given me strict orders—"

"I'm sure he did."

I was through Kingsley's big house and in his kitchen, and over to a nondescript side door that led, I knew, to his basement of horrors.

"I'm afraid I can't let you go down there—"

He had tried to bar the door down into the basement. Tried being the operative word here. I pulled it open, even while he had pressed it shut. I sensed that Franklin wasn't using all of his great strength. I also sensed that, despite perhaps not liking me very much—for reasons I still didn't understand—he would never use all of his strength against me. I sensed his restraint. Smart man.

Now, as I headed down the narrow flight of stone stairs, I might as well have been a half a world away, heading down into the dungeon of a forgotten castle along a mist-shrouded hillside. Dracula's castle.

"Master Kingsley will not be happy," said Franklin, following behind.

"Master Kingsley can bite me."

"No truer words have been spoken, I'm afraid."

I was about to reply when I paused in mid-step. I paused because something deep and rumbling seemed to emanate up through the stone steps themselves. Hell penetrated through the surrounding walls and ceiling.

"What the devil was that?"

"Again, no truer words have been spoken."

On that ominous note, I continued down the dimly lit stairs. As I neared the landing, a hand fell onto my shoulder. "Madam, please. Kingsley will not want you to see him like this. Please stop."

I stopped in mid-step and looked back. Franklin's pale face hovered in the darkness. Gone was his usual look of distaste for me. Why the man didn't like me, I may never know.

"Has he turned?" I asked.

Franklin shook his head. As he did so, I could see the scars that stitched his right ear on. The stitching wasn't done with very much care. "It's still early, but the process has begun."

"Because it's a full moon somewhere," I said.

"Perhaps. You must turn back. I must insist on this."

"I know you're just doing your job, but so am I."

Strange energy flitted in the hallway below. Small, amorphous energy. Animal energy, I realized. Lots of it. The place might as well have been a slaughterhouse.

Lots of killing in here, I thought.

I had a vague idea what I was in for. I had, in fact, seen Kingsley completely transformed a few years ago. It was then that I had been introduced to the entity within him…and the realization that something was, in fact, in me as well.

"Please, *Sam*," said Franklin, and it was, I was certain, the first time he had used my first name. "I beg you. This will not be pretty."

"I'm not here for pretty," I said. "I'm here for help."

And with that, I turned my back on Franklin and continued down.

Chapter Thirty-one

I found myself in a narrow corridor, with a stone wall to the left, and a long metal wall to my right. I could have been walking along the hull of a great battleship. Halogen lighting flickered overhead, giving the impression of torchlight. You'd think Kingsley, with all of his bucks, would dish out some of it for better lighting.

Somewhere, water dripped.

And since we weren't anywhere near a Scottish loch, or under a medieval moat, I could only assume that Kingsley's sprinkler system was on the fritz.

No, I had never been down here before. But not for a lack of trying. Kingsley had been firm about keeping me away. Even to the point of being kind of a dick.

I heard Franklin stop behind me, felt him watching me, felt his disapproval, his concern.

I continued forward.

Before me, set into the steel wall, was a heavy-looking metal door that looked like it belonged on the space shuttle. As I walked, I heard...something on the other side of the metal wall. Breathing, perhaps.

As I continued, something thudded loudly on the other side of the wall, so loudly that the ground beneath me shook. I stopped and swallowed. Maybe this wasn't a good idea. Maybe I really didn't want to see Kingsley like this.

No, I thought. I had to talk with him...and now. A talk he and I had never had before, but it was time.

Another thud from the other side of the wall. This one louder, sounding as if something meaty and big had been slammed against the wall. There was only one thing meaty and big on the other side of that wall. That thing happened to be Orange County's most prominent defense attorney...

And my boyfriend.

Still another thunderous slam, and now, the wall next to me shook as well. Dust sifted down from above, and the light flickered, went out briefly, and then flickered back on again. I continued down the cement corridor.

The closer I got to the metal door, the more I could smell it: death.

Putrid death, too.

Something that been dead for many, many days. Perhaps even a week.

I looked back and saw Franklin staring out at me from the shadows of the stairway. I was beginning to understand why they had tried so hard to keep me away...

The entity within me perked up at the smell, but I had been doing a pretty damned good job of keeping her locked up, so I wrapped a few more mental iron bars around the cage I imagined her in.

A few years ago, I would have gagged at the smell of death. Now, not so much. Now, I was intrigued by it. What had died? How had it died? Perhaps I could never truly go back to who I had been. Perhaps I'd done too many things, seen too many things.

Still, I tried to find a neutral feeling about the smell. In fact, I tried to not have any feeling about the smell at all. My new goal these days was to not give the entity within me any hope. Or any escape.

With each step I took, the pounding on the other side of the wall seemed to keep pace with me, but as I reached the door, the sound stopped altogether, and a deathly silence followed.

More nervous than I thought I would be, I stood just to the side of the door. There was a small, square opening in the door, no bigger than a small fist. Certainly not big enough for Kingsley to reach through. Most important, I could see that the door itself was at least six inches thick.

Jesus.

Now, from the other side of the door, I heard the breathing. Deep and ragged. Something was just off to the side of the door, listening to me. That something was, of course, Kingsley.

At least, I hoped it was.

I held my breath; after all, the putrid stench was pouring through the opening in the door. Muted light came through, too. The light was high up, casting a squarish light on the floor before me.

"Kingsley," I said hesitantly. "It's Sam—"

A face suddenly appeared in the small opening. A very hairy and sweating face...wild and contorted and in obvious pain. I squeaked and took a step back.

"Sam!" Kingsley gasped, pressing his face into the square opening. "What...what are you doing here?"

Now that I saw him like this—desperate, wild, angry, shocked, and in mid-transformation—I wanted to *un*see it. I also wanted to *un*smell what I was smelling. Maybe this was a bad idea.

But it wasn't. I needed him. I needed help.

"I...I have to speak to you—"

"Leave, Sam!" he growled, and turned away from the square, I could see him pacing through the opening, passing back and forth behind it. God, he looked massive, the few glimpses I saw.

"I'm sorry, Kingsley, but I can't."

"I'm warning you, Sam..."

He wasn't himself. I could see that. Or, rather, he was tapping into a very, very angry and primal and hate-filled part of him.

The demon, I thought. *It's the demon coming through.*

I powered on, "How do I stop a werewolf?"

I knew all the stories. I'd heard all the rumors. The truth was, I really didn't know. It wasn't a question I'd ever needed to ask Kingsley. I suspected Fang would know the answer. But I didn't feed into rumors or legends. I needed to know facts, and I needed to stop Gunther tonight.

"Why, Sam?" he growled, pacing behind the small opening, each footfall shaking the ground beneath me. If I had to guess, I would guess that he was easily a foot taller, and maybe another hundred pounds heavier.

And he would only get bigger.

And stronger.

"Gunther has another hiker. A woman this time. A woman I know, well, kind of, long story—"

"Enough!" he roared, and I shrank back. And it took a godawful lot to get me to shrink back. But never, never had I heard such force and powerful volume from a human.

Because he isn't human, I thought. *At least, not now.*

I knew Kingsley could transform into a wolf—as in an actual wolf—at will. Few werewolves had this ability to shapeshift. But on the night of the full moon, he didn't turn into a wolf. No, he turned into a hulking, hybrid monster. A true wolfman.

We were still hours from dusk and already he'd changed so much. I knew his transformation was a slow, painful process for him. Unlike the wolf that he could conjure quickly—which, I suspected, was closer to what I did with the winged Talos—his monthly transformation into a hulking beast was nearly unbearable for him. After all, this was when the entity within made a full appearance and, while doing so, apparently delighted in torturing Kingsley along the way.

"I don't care about the hiker, Sam..." His voice rattled, rumbled, like an idling Harley.

"You do, Kingsley," I said. I almost said 'Wolfie,' which was my term of endearment for him, although he didn't much like it... unless, of course, we were in his bedroom.

He yanked his head away from the square opening and stretched his neck to and fro, and I saw what was happening. His neck was getting bigger. Muscle mass was appearing before my eyes. Muscle mass and fur. He grunted and might have whimpered.

"Leave, Sam. Leave, goddammit."

This wasn't the Kingsley I knew. The man I knew was attentive and playful, even if a little stubborn. This creature, stalking behind the door, was only a semblance of the man I now loved. The immortal I loved.

"Kingsley, please—"

He growled as he paced behind the door. I could only see flashes of him behind the small window. The flashes that I saw were horrific at best. With each passing minute, I would lose more and more of him. I doggedly asked my question.

"How do I stop a werewolf, Kingsley?"

I saw him shaking his head as he paced. "Too strong," he was saying, mumbling. "Too strong, even for you."

I wasn't so sure about that, but I wasn't going to argue the point.

Kingsley went on: "Kill and destroy and feed, and will fight to the death once engaged."

"Then tell me how to defeat him, Kingsley."

"Don't do it, Sam. Wait...for me."

"He has to be stopped. Tonight."

He didn't like my answer and pulled away angrily. His heavy footfalls seemed heavier than just a few minutes earlier. His great head and beefy shoulders appeared and disappeared through the square opening.

Now, I pressed my face into the square opening. "Tell me, Kingsley. Tell me what you know."

I sensed his hesitation. After all, once I knew how to defeat a werewolf, I would know how to defeat him, too. A small, protective side of him was keeping that information from me. Or not. But that was my guess.

Suddenly, Kingsley's thick, sweating, panting face appeared just inches from mine. I saw the fangs pushing through his gums, which bled profusely. It was only noon and he was suffering so much. I had no idea he went through such a prolonged, hellish transformation. And he still had many hours to go. How many hours, exactly, I didn't know. When did a werewolf turn into a full-blown werewolf? At sunset? At dusk? At midnight? At the first sign of the full moon? I didn't know exactly. But looking at Kingsley now, it looked like the transformation wasn't very far away.

And I still had to find Gunther.

Shit...

"We are not so different, Sam," he said, gasping. Blood bubbled between his lips. "The same silver that kills you, kills me."

"A silver dagger—"

"No, Sam. You'll never get close enough with a dagger. He'll be too fast, too powerful. You've never seen anything like this, Sam."

"Then what?"

"A silver bullet."

"But where..."

"Franklin..." he gasped. "Franklin has them. Just in case..."

He held my gaze, although his bloodshot eyes wavered. I got his meaning: just in case he ever got out and needed to be put down. Of course, he had gotten out a few years ago. Where was Franklin then? A question for another time.

"Go, Sam! Leave me be!"

With that, he slammed his huge hands against the door, and kept slamming them until I gulped and skittered off down the hallway, back to where Franklin was still waiting in the shadows. The thick, metal wall vibrated. More dust and dirt sifted down.

———

Upstairs in the oversized kitchen, as Franklin locked the door that led down into the cellar, I said, "That smell..."

"A deer carcass," said Franklin, turning to look down at me as he pocketed the key. "I hunted it last week."

I nodded, sickened and relieved...relieved that it wasn't a human corpse. Sickened that I kiss that mouth of his. "And it's been rotting down here ever since, I presume."

"You presume correctly. Master Kingsley prefers them...putrid. The more putrid, the better."

I felt my stomach turn, which in itself was a good sign for me. It meant that I was keeping the bitch at bay. The crazy, crazy bitch. Far below, the earth shook violently, as did the kitchen walls around us.

"When will Kingsley fully turn?"

"At sundown, of course," said Franklin. "Like all true creatures of the night."

I almost asked what kind of creature he was...except I thought I just might know. Not so much a creature as a *creation*.

I had six hours, at most. Five, if I wanted to play it safe.

"I need those silver bullets, Franklin."

He looked at me long and hard, then nodded. "This way, Ms. Moon."

Chapter Thirty-two

I was sitting in my minivan, along Kingsley's crushed-shell driveway, weeping.

To think that my boyfriend would be feasting on something dead and rotting...in just a few hours...was a little upsetting.

I shouldn't have seen him. Perhaps Franklin would have told me how to stop a werewolf. Or perhaps not. His loyalty to Kingsley ran deep...and for reasons I didn't quite understand. Yes, I had suspected it would be silver. The same silver that removed the entity from me would remove it from him, too.

Except, I would have gone into the fight with a silver dagger, and I might not have returned. Yes, I had known a werewolf would be powerful...but I hadn't quite grasped just how powerful. The silver bullet was the key, of course.

And not getting too close.

I looked at the Smith & Wesson .357 Magnum sitting on the seat next to me, chambered with the six silver bullets.

It would take a helluva shot. Especially at a charging werewolf.

I was risking my life, I knew. I was risking everything that I held dear. I was risking, most of all, being a mother to my children. No, I didn't think a werewolf needed to use silver to kill me. Ripping me from limb to limb, and then devouring me, would probably do the job, too.

I looked at Kingsley's sprawling estate before me. I was certain I could hear his roars from here, and feel a slight rumbling beneath

471

me. He was angry. He was turning. What happened to him each month wasn't very fair either.

I wiped my eyes and considered my next move. I had to find Gunther, of course. He was up there, in the woods, changing throughout the day, much like Kingsley was. And nearby was a woman. A live woman. Waiting to be consumed by him, no doubt watching his transformation in complete and utter horror.

Some preferred them dead and rotted, others preferred them fresh and alive. I was happy to see that I remained repulsed by both notions.

I drummed my fingernails on the steering wheel, knowing my time was slipping through, well, these very fingers.

On a whim, I pulled out my cell phone and typed in "cars and mustaches."

What came up next was very intriguing.

Very, very intriguing.

CHAPTER THIRTY-THREE

I was back in the city of Orange, parked this time in Gunther's driveway.

He wouldn't be using it anytime soon. After all, I had no doubt he was in the midst of a full-blown transformation. And in the company of one woman—the wife of my new friend, Sheriff Stanley—who was, no doubt, witnessing all of it. Then again, if this script played out, she would be doing far more than witnessing. She would be an unwilling participant.

So, I did what any normal investigator would do under the circumstances: I downloaded an app to my iPhone, the Lyft app to be precise. An app that was, in fact, pure genius.

According to the website, with a simple touch of a button, the Lyft driver closest in proximity to me (thanks to my phone's GPS) would get pinged that I needed a ride. The app also connected our Facebook pages, apparently for safety reasons. My Facebook page sported an outdated picture of me from nine years ago, back when I was camera-friendly. Luckily, I didn't look much different now.

Which wasn't a good thing, I suspected. Soon, I would be getting to the point where my friends and colleagues were clearly looking older than me...by nearly a decade.

Worry about that later, I thought, when the app had finished downloading.

I was almost giddy with excitement.

When the app opened, I pressed the "pick me up" button and waited. While I waited, I sweated. The day was sweltering. I might be immortal but I got hot—and sweated—with the best of them. Which is why I had the A/C running in the minivan while I waited.

A moment later, my phone chirped.

A driver had locked onto me and was en route. Okay, now I was definitely giddy. In fact, there he was on Facebook. A youngish-looking Latino with a round face and wide-set eyes. I scanned Paulo's profile because I had nothing better to do. Married. A writer on the side. I checked out the links to his books, too. A vampire series, of all things. A witch series, too. And something about gods in Los Angeles.

"This should be interesting," I said.

According to the app, he was only two minutes away. I looked at the time on my cell: 1:38. According to my weather app, sunset was at 6:19 p.m.

I did some serviceable math. I had five-and-a-half hours before a woman would be consumed alive by a real werewolf.

And, yeah, I cared, dammit. I cared a lot. I had met her husband. I had met her unborn kids. They needed her, dammit. They needed her alive. They had a family to build. Not to mention, I had given Sheriff Stanley some of my best marital advice. I didn't want to see that advice go down the drain.

Not funny, I know. But try as I might, my new morbid sense of humor didn't seem to be going anywhere.

"Choose your battles," I said to myself.

After all, a morbid sense of humor I could live with. Not giving a shit about death—and feasting on my neighbor's cat because I couldn't control myself—wasn't something I could live with.

Quite frankly, I was better than that. I lived to fight the bad guys. I lived to protect the innocent. I was not a bad guy myself. I was one of the good ones, dammit, and I was going to do everything I could think of to ensure just that.

That I stayed as good as possible.

Further down the block, a white Toyota Prius turned onto the street. As it approached, I could see the driver through the windshield, sort of leaning forward, forearms wrapped around the steering wheel, scanning. Yup, it was the same guy in the Facebook page—Paulo, the vampire/witch/demigod writer. Most telling was the furry mustache attached to the front grill of the Prius. My Lyft ride had appeared.

I stepped out of my minivan, waving. He frowned, thick eyebrows bunching up, then pulled into the driveway, next to my minivan. He jumped out, smiling, but also looking confused as hell.

"I'm sorry," he said, talking fast, eyes scanning somewhat wildly. He either had a serious case of A.D.D., or something else was going on. "But I'm a little confused. You need a ride, right?"

"Maybe. Mostly, I need some information."

"Okay, now I'm a lot confused." Paulo gave me an easy laugh, although his eyes never stopped scanning.

A.D.D., I thought. *And bad.*

"First," I said, "why are you confused?"

"Because I usually pick up Gunther at this address."

"Only Gunther?"

"Yes. What's going on here? Do you need a ride or—"

I stepped forward and reached out to his mind. Holy sweet hell, that was a scrambled, nearly incoherent mind. I reached deeper, through the chaotic miasma of thought streams, and found his core and told him to relax and to answer my questions, and that I was a friend.

He nodded, and for the first time, his eyes settled down, and settled on me. He exhaled. I suspected this was the first break his mind had had in years. Decades, perhaps.

"First question," I said. "Why do so many Lyft cars come down this street?"

"It's because Gunther tips so well. Usually $200."

"But I thought the app summoned drivers, not the other way around."

He nodded, smiling easily. He was good-looking, in a round-faced, wide-eyed sort of way. "It does work that way, in theory. But some Lyft drivers will game the system. After all, the system pings the closest driver, so we'll sometimes patrol areas where known big tippers live or work, hoping to get pinged. With Gunther, we know we can make an easy $200, especially when it starts getting close to the full moon."

I blinked. "What do you know about the full moon?"

The driver shrugged, still looking at me, eyelids dropping a little. Now that his rapidly-running mind had shut off, he was getting sleepy.

"We Lyft drivers sort of figured it out, since he'd been doing this for so long."

"Doing what for so long?"

"Grabbing a lift up to Big Bear. Turns out, it's every full moon."

"Has he told you why he leaves every full moon?"

"He told me he's an amateur astronomer. That he has a cabin in the woods where he has a telescope."

My heart thumped once, twice, loudly, excitedly.

"And why does he tip so much?"

Here, the Latino driver paused and fought against my control, but I silently encouraged him to continue and he finally nodded. "He pays us to keep quiet about the location."

"Have you seen the cabin?"

"No, but I drop him off at the same spot every time."

"Why don't you take him to the cabin?"

"I dunno. I just do what he says."

"Did you take him this last time?"

"No, but I kinda hoped I hadn't missed him."

"Which was why you were patrolling nearby," I said.

"Right."

"When do you usually take him up to the cabin?"

"Usually two days before, sometimes three."

"Will you take me to the cabin, too?"

His eyes flicked over me and he smiled. "Of course, Samantha Moon."

"And after you take me to the woods, I want you to forget we had this conversation."

He gave me an easy smile. "I'll do my best."

And with that, I slipped into the front passenger seat of the Prius and we were off.

Chapter Thirty-four

I checked the time: just past 2 p.m.

Sunset was in four hours, and it was a two-hour drive up to Big Bear, which was higher and further back than Arrowhead. I thought about that as we drove, then nodded. Yes, Gunther kidnapped them in Arrowhead...and then brought them back to Big Bear.

He has a vehicle up there, I thought.

Why he left his car in Orange County, I didn't know. I suspected it was an attempt to cover his tracks. Of course, the Lyft drivers themselves might start getting suspicious. I had a thought.

"Are you aware of any Lyft drivers disappearing?"

Paulo was still feeling the effects of my earlier mental prompting, and so he answered easily enough. "Two of them over the past few months, actually. Both were found killed in their cars. Both in Orange County. There's a running joke that being a Lyft driver in Orange is the new most dangerous job."

I nodded. The bastard was covering his tracks there, too.

As my own Lyft ride commenced, he drove through Orange and headed for the 22 Freeway. I imagined Gunther standing on, say, a boulder, overlooking a popular—or perhaps not-so-popular—hiking trail, and hunting his next target.

Perhaps he used a tranquilizer gun. Or perhaps he used a real gun, and shot them in, say, the foot. Or perhaps he ambushed them or trapped them or lured them into his car.

I didn't know, and it wasn't important how he found them. Since none had survived, I might never know. What mattered was stopping him from preying on the innocent. From killing tonight.

And ever again.

My own entity, of course, would prefer me to kill and maim and torture and to control. And, if I gave her half a chance, she would possess me fully and do it for me.

It did take some fortitude to take on these entities, to fight against them…and to not give in.

Had Kingsley given in? Was he weak by allowing the thing within him to feast on the rotted deer carcass? Maybe, maybe not. I didn't know just how far Kingsley had let the entity out. Maybe they had come to some agreement: if Kingsley feeds it what it most wants, perhaps it lets him live a normal enough life. Not feasting on a human corpse was, perhaps, Kingsley drawing the line. *Maybe.*

I didn't know, but what I did know was this: there would be no agreement between myself and Elizabeth, the woman inside me, the woman who fueled me, the highly evolved dark master…and perhaps the highest evolved of them all.

No compromise. No getting out, ever.

The bitch picked the wrong person.

Moving on. Admittedly, I was nervous as hell to confront Gunther, even if he was half the size of Kingsley. Either way, he was going to be trouble. Perhaps more trouble than I was ready for. I patted my purse next to me, which concealed the Smith & Wesson. This gave me some comfort. Not much, but enough.

I considered calling Allison for backup. She might be needy as hell sometimes—even dingy—but man, oh man, was that girl a force to be reckoned with.

Still, I thought, chewing my lip as we eased onto the freeway, there was no way in hell I was going to expose her to the ferociousness of a werewolf. No, she was out. Fang could be of help—a lot of help. I pulled out my phone and clicked on the messenger and nearly sent him a text.

No, I thought. He would be weak all the way up to sundown. Truth was, I was weak, too, although not as weak as before, back when I didn't own the ring. I was operating, I suspected, at about eighty percent, which wasn't that bad. The problem being, of course, when I got to full strength at sundown, Gunther would be fully turned, too. And he would be at full strength, as well.

And a full-blown werewolf.

Another thing: I was feeling a tad guilty about my time with Fang the other night. Yes, he had talked me down and given me the world's best advice on how to beat the thing within me, but I was still feeling some guilt about us in my bedroom, holding hands.

I would tell Kingsley about it. He would understand. I hoped.

With all of that settled in my mind, I planned to get to Big Bear well before Gunther turned. Of course, I still had to find his kill cabin, which I highly doubted doubled as an observatory, as purported.

So, I settled back for the two-hour drive, mentally going through how I would face a partially-turned werewolf, when my phone rang.

Restricted number. These days, that was never a good sign.

"Moon Investigations," I said.

"Sam, it's Sherbet."

"Do you always refer to yourself by your last name, Detective?"

"Almost always. We have your daughter."

I sat up. "What do you mean?"

"We found her in the park, drunk as a skunk. You need to come get her."

Chapter Thirty-Five

I had Paulo alter our course and we headed out to Fullerton along the 57 Freeway.

Now, with the Lyft driver waiting for me outside—I might have compelled him to wait for me, I didn't, after all, want to lose him—I found my daughter in Sherbet's office, sitting before his desk with her head buried in her arms, as a female officer stroked her hair. Sherbet himself sat back in his desk and didn't look too happy. Then again, I couldn't remember the last time Detective Sherbet looked too happy.

"We found her in Hillcrest Park, drinking with her buddies."

"Who found her?"

"One of our boys. We got a report of some kids drinking and smoking and making general asses of themselves. Turned out to be true. The others scattered like frightened fish. This one tried to scatter. Turned out she was too drunk to scatter, and instead, fell flat on her face. Don't worry, she's okay. Just a few scrapes."

Tammy moaned, her face still buried in her arms.

I thanked the female officer, who gave Tammy a final pat, and gave me a consoling smile, then got up and left. I had a distinct impression that the officer had been there before, with her own kids.

I took the seat next to my daughter, except I very much didn't feel like stroking her head. It was all I could do to not chew her ass out. I took a few deep breaths.

Easy, Sam, came Sherbet's telepathic words.

I'm too pissed off to be easy about anything, I shot back, *and she can hear you, so be careful.*

He nodded, then said aloud, "Should have figured."

"Is she still drunk?" I asked.

"My guess: yes. We probably should have had her checked out at St. Jude's." He shrugged. "She didn't look sick and responded well enough."

"Can you leave us alone?" I asked him.

"You do realize that I'm a busy homicide investigator, right? And the *busy* part isn't necessarily a good thing."

Please, I thought to him.

He sighed and his cop mustache fluttered a little. Then he hefted his thickish body from behind the desk and made his way toward the door.

"Thickish?" he said.

"You know what I meant," I said.

He might have sighed again, and then left us alone, shutting his office door behind him.

Chapter Thirty-six

I checked the time...2:30. Less than four hours.

"Less than four hours for what, Mom?" asked Tammy, her face still buried in her arms.

"Never mind that," I said, and threw up a mental wall about all things wolfish.

"You're hiding something, Mo—"

"Never mind what I'm hiding, young lady. Do you care to explain yourself?"

"No. And quit shouting. My head..."

The stench of beer wafted from her as well as the blood from the scrapes on her face. Like a shark, I can smell fresh blood within a few dozen feet. Not always a good thing, especially in a room full of women.

"Gross, Mom," said Tammy, obviously following my thoughts.

"Don't change the subject, young lady."

"Hey, you're the one talking about—"

"Never mind that, Tamara Moon," I said, using her full name, which meant that I meant business.

Instead, she giggled. "Relax, Mom. Sheesh. Everyone drinks a little—"

I moved her chair around to face me, dragging it easily with one hand over the carpet. Tammy, whose head had been propped up on the desk, pitched forward, "Hey!"

"Don't 'hey' me, and look at me when I'm talking to you."

She did, and for the first time, I saw her bloodshot eyes and puffy lower lip. I stood and paced in Sherbet's office, glancing at the clock overhead. 2:45. I didn't have time for this...and yet, I had to make the time.

"How long have you been drinking?"

She shrugged. "A few months now."

"Where do you get the alcohol?"

"Friends. Friends of friends. Mostly we steal it from—"

I spun around and nearly yanked her to her feet...at a police station, no less. Inside a clear glass office, no less. Sherbet, who was talking on his cell phone in a nearby cubicle, raised a hand and lowered it, motioning for me to calm down. Good advice.

"Relax, Mom. Sheesh. We didn't steal from stores. Just from parents, mostly."

"Have you stolen from me?"

She looked away, "Maybe a bottle..."

"Tammy!"

"...or two," she finished.

I sat again and ran my fingers through my hair and knew I was making a scene. I had to calm down about this. Then again, I'd never faced anything like this before—whatever *this* was. Teenage rebellion? Jesus, she was *barely* a teen. If this was a taste of what I was in for...well, I was in trouble.

"Relax, Mom—"

"You tell me to relax again, and so help me God, I will bend you over my knee right here—"

"No, you won't. You would never embarrass Sherbet like that... and risk going to jail, even though I don't think any jail could hold you."

"Don't talk back to me, young lady. And don't tell me what I will and won't do."

"Okay, sorry, geez."

"And don't 'geez' me."

"Okay, I won't geez you," she said, and broke into a grin, and for some damn reason, I broke into a grin, too. She knew she had me, and she knew how to push, too. "Who would ever want to *geez* you anyway."

I laughed, and said, "Okay, stop. Now I'm looking really bad."

"It's no big deal, Mom. Everyone does it, and I like to do it. It's fun to drink. I know why Auntie and you like to drink now, and all the adults in all of the commercials. It makes sense—"

"Just stop," I said, holding my head and resuming my pacing. I looked at the time: 2:52. "How do you feel?"

"Buzzed."

To hear my little girl tell me she felt "buzzed" was enough to drive *me* to drink. "We're going to talk about this later. Get your stuff, let's go."

And we went, this time detouring toward my sister's house in Placentia, which was next door to Fullerton. My sister was gonna be thrilled to see us. I texted her brief details and she texted back her confirmation to bring Tammy. Gotta love Mary Lou. She was my right-hand woman.

Meanwhile, my daughter slept it off, while Paulo, our Lyft driver, drove steadily, sometimes casting sideways glances my way, and in the rearview mirror at my daughter snoozing in the back seat.

We dropped off Tammy with a stern Mary Lou and then continued toward the original destination.

I checked the time: an hour wasted.

Chapter Thirty-seven

"This is it," said Paulo.

"This is where you drop off Gunther?"

"Yup."

"Every time?"

"Yup."

"And is this where the others drop him off, too?"

"I wouldn't know that."

I briefly scanned Paulo's thoughts and took a look at his aura. He was telling the truth. We were parked on a side road that had ended as soon as it began. Massive cement blocks, connected with thick cables, barred the way further. The drive had been speedy enough. We had, in fact, made decent time. I checked my cell.

5:20.

I had just over an hour to find his cabin, find him, stop him, and save Elise Stanley.

All in a day's work, I thought, then turned to my driver. I commanded him to forget me, forget our conversation and forget about this tip. He would, I knew, still get paid for his efforts, even if he didn't remember his efforts. My account would be charged for the trip, so he would at least get something out of this, even if it was a big hole in his memory.

When he was gone, I found myself alone at the end of the blockaded street.

We had very much gone off the beaten path. Indeed, we had taken at least a half-dozen roads to get to this one. In fact, the two roads before this road had both been dirt, including this one.

Few, if anyone, would have known about this spot.

I checked the sun, and knew instinctively it was about an hour before it set. The day was still warm, but I was wearing jeans and a gray tank top. I let some air in the tank top, and kind of wished I could let some air in the jeans, too, but decided that would be unseemly, even for me.

Additionally, I was not at full strength, but neither was I shrinking away from the sun. I felt, in fact, pretty damn good. In about an hour, I would feel pretty damn great.

I doubted Gunther—or Kingsley—would feel pretty damn great in an hour. I suspected they sort of lost their minds for a while, or shrank so far into the background that they might as well have been frightened children hiding in a closet from their abusive parents.

The air was infused with pine and juniper, scents I love. A small wind moved some of the branches overhead, where birds tweeted continuously, apparently unaware of the 140-character limit.

I wasn't what you would call an outdoorsman or a master tracker, but I could see footprints in the dirt with the best of them. And I saw them now. Boot prints. Men's boots. How old, I didn't know, but my guess was within the past few days.

I didn't see another print, and certainly not a female's. Which suggested that this was only Gunther's Lyft drop-off point. From here, he hiked. To where, I didn't know. But to another vehicle, I suspected. And, of course, to a kill cabin.

With the sun now slipping behind the massive evergreens, I stepped over the cable barring the dirt road...and followed the prints.

At some point, I started jogging lightly, easily.

Not too much further, the footprints ended in a field of grass and I lost his trail. I looked for any telltale signs of beaten-down grass or a trail that might have picked up elsewhere. I didn't find it.

The wind was blowing stronger now, flattening the grass. I spied the full moon above, creeping up from the distant horizon. It was getting darker, and I was losing hope, until I realized I had, of course, an ace up my sleeve.

Speaking of sleeves, I disrobed, bundled up my clothing, and summoned the single flame.

Chapter Thirty-eight

I was flying.

I also wasn't too worried about being caught. After all, I was in a very remote part of the mountains, and the day was losing light rapidly, too rapidly for my taste.

Was there really a woman being held against her will, waiting to be feasted on? Even now, was she perhaps watching a man stalk and pace before her, slowly shape-changing throughout the day, and now, undoubtedly, much faster?

Hard to believe…but it was all adding up.

I didn't need to know that I was down to the last twenty minutes. Hell, from up here and above the trees, I could see the sun slipping away to the west.

My clothing hung in a bundle below me on my talons, all stuffed into my purse, along with the gun and silver bullets.

I ranged far and wide, buffeted by wind, sometimes sailing, sometimes flapping hard. All while I searched with eyes that were a lot better than my own. From up here, I saw trash on the ground. I even saw mice scurrying. I saw rabbits and lizards, all while flying hundreds of feet above.

Still, I was losing hope.

Maybe Sheriff Stanley's wife had been found. Maybe Elise really was missing in a traditional sort of way. Why did I jump to the conclusion that she had, in fact, gone missing for nefarious reasons?

The clues were all there. A missing hiker. The full moon. A werewolf on the run. It was all leading me to here. To where, exactly, I didn't know, and soon, it wouldn't matter. In about fifteen minutes, the werewolves of California would be fully transitioned and, from what I knew, out of their minds with blood lust. In fifteen minutes, all of this would be a moot point, unless I saw some sign of Gunther's kill cabin.

And when the sun had gotten to the ten-minute mark, I saw something flash in a valley far below, a valley very nearly hidden beneath a canopy of trees. A flickering flame. I circled it, trying to get a bead on it, but it was mostly hidden at the bottom of two sheer rock walls.

And that's when someone screamed.

I tucked in my great, leathery wings, and dove.

Chapter Thirty-nine

The canopy was too thick for my wingspan.

I alighted, instead, on an overhanging rock that afforded me a view into the narrow valley—and what I saw couldn't have been more strange.

There wasn't just one fire, but many. Most were attached to poles and scattered between the sheer cliff walls. There, to my left and what would be south, was a small cabin. Perhaps the kill cabin, perhaps not. I didn't know.

Most interesting was the massive gate that sealed off entry into the valley—itself about as long as a football field. If I had to guess, the iron gate was a few dozen feet tall. The canyon walls that rose up starkly to the east and west were nearly sheer, difficult to climb, even for the most experienced mountaineer, and probably for a werewolf, too.

Most disturbing were the many, many men who now roamed at the bottom of the valley. All were naked, and all were very, very close to fully transforming into werewolves. I counted eight of them. Unfortunately, my weapon only carried six shots. And there, milling with the others, was Gunther. He, too, was nearly fully transformed. I didn't recognize the others, but I was willing to bet Kingsley would have.

I thought I'd just discovered the source of their reluctance to speak with Kingsley. After all, a good representation of the werewolves of Southern California were here in this valley. My guess was, these were werewolves who preferred to consume live prey, unlike Kingsley who preferred the taste of the rotting and dead.

My eyes caught something else. There, staked to a pole in the center of the valley, was the object of the eight circling, partially-turned werewolves: a woman I could only guess was Elise. Her eyes were closed and she was weeping nearly uncontrollably. I didn't blame her. After all, in a few minutes, she would be dead.

Behind me, out of sight, the sun was nearly set. I had, at best, five minutes.

The valley appeared to open beneath the thick forest canopy, as many of the trees grew straight out from the sheer rock walls. Perhaps there would be room to fly below, I didn't know. But there was no way I was breaking through that tree canopy, not with this wingspan. No, from here, I would have to go at it alone as a human.

I closed my eyes, saw the image of my Samantha Moon self standing in the center of the flame, and a moment later, I was squatting there on the rocks, naked. But I wasn't naked for long. One thing was for damn certain: I wasn't going to fight eight werewolves naked. I dressed in seconds.

Now standing on the rock outcropping, fully clothed and holding the Smith & Wesson .357 Magnum in my right hand, I considered my options. The partially-turned werewolves were much too far for me to squeeze off an accurate shot. Not to mention they were pacing and jumping and clawing the ground and their faces and each other.

They could smell me, too. Already, some of them were sniffing the air, and looking around wildly. The sun was just a minute or so from setting, and I knew what I had to do.

I closed my eyes...and saw the single flame...

CHAPTER FORTY

A hot wind blasted over me as I focused on the single flame.

Last year, Talos had taught me that even I could go to the moon, using the single flame as a portal. After all, if I could summon him from another dimension, and summon me out of this world and into his, then why I couldn't I summon myself elsewhere? And so I had, and I had frolicked on the moon, no doubt giving one or two unlucky astronomers a heart attack.

Later, I had tested teleporting on earth, and teleported my giant bat self to a snow-covered peak far, far away from here, high in the Alaskan mountains. In fact, I had gone there a few more times, sitting there on an unknown ledge, unseen by human eyes, unexplored, too, no doubt, as I could not imagine any man making his way up there.

But this…this was different. I had never tried to teleport in my human form. In fact, I had never even considered it possible. That is, until I'd seen Dracula himself do it…and he seemed to indicate that I could do it, too.

We'll see, I thought.

The flame was empty for now, flickering there in the forefront of my thoughts…waiting for me to give it a command. Waiting and flickering.

The growling from below intensified. The poor girl had been reduced to whimpering. Why shouldn't she? Here be monsters. Eight of them, in fact. Nine, if you counted me.

Within the flame, I imagined my landing spot, a spot just before the woman chained to the pole. I saw the spot clearly in the flame... and felt myself rush toward it.

When I opened my eyes again, I looked up into the startled face of a weeping woman. Her mouth opened into a scream, and then she did just that: Screamed bloody murder over and over again.

I stood and turned and pointed my weapon at the first creature charging toward me.

Chapter Forty-one

My plan wasn't to fight all of them.

Not now, not here. Not like this. And not with only six silver bullets. With eight circling werewolves, the odds weren't in my favor.

No, the plan was to grab her and get the hell out of Dodge.

Or out of this valley of death.

The sun, I knew, was just a few seconds from setting. I knew this as I always knew this, just as the creatures before me knew this, too. We were all slaves to the sun, who was the enemy of the darkness within us. As such, I was always, always aware of its movement through the sky, whether I could see it or not.

All of them were damn close to changing. Most seemed like they were in excruciating pain.

Except for the one charging me now. Although not fully transformed, he seemed to have the most wits about him. Lucky for me, he'd spotted me almost as soon as I'd appeared.

I had hoped that the precious few seconds I had left of the sunlight could be used to untie the girl and teleport our asses out of here.

Instead, I found myself drawing a bead on the creature charging, the half-man, half were-beast, who ran at me with surprising speed. I could only imagine just how fast they would be once fully transformed.

But these thoughts were fleeting and mostly drowned out by the creature's growl and the woman screaming behind me, as I leveled the gun and aimed for his heart.

And pulled the trigger.

———

The shot was true.

The racing man clutched his chest and lurched forward. His momentum sent him tumbling over the ground. He gasped once, twice, and then lay still. Then, before our very eyes, he transformed back into a naked, middle-aged man. I couldn't see his face, and that was just as well. A very dark and oily shadow rose up from him, swirling, and then the wind seem to catch hold of it, and dispersed it into oblivion. But I knew it wasn't gone. Not entirely. It would wait for another victim, and start its accursed life all over again. It was the way of the dark masters.

I wondered what they thought of a fellow dark master killing their own. That is, until I didn't care what they thought.

I moved around the still-screaming girl and told her to stop screaming. In fact, I quickly reached into her mind to calm her down. Her screaming was making it hard for me to think, and attracting more of the semi-werewolves.

Not that it mattered. Just as I reached out with a pointed index finger, I felt it happen. From one second to the next, I was a different person...and so were the creatures now bounding toward me. They were very, very much different.

The sun had set.

Just like that.

I swiped clean through her ropes and had just reached for her hand, when something powerful hit me from the side...and sent me hurtling head over ass into the grass.

———

I spun to my back and lifted the gun, just as the creature was in mid-leap, its massive, clawed hands reaching for me, its oversized mouth gaping open. The creature was nearly as big as the creature Kingsley had turned into. Nearly, but not quite.

As it flew through the air, I had a clear shot at its chest, and I took it, simultaneously firing and rolling to my right.

The ground shook with the thudding weight of the beast, who gasped and clawed the earth, and then lay still. As he transformed back into a naked man, I was already up and moving, scrambling back to the now-freed woman.

Chapter Forty-two

Six werewolves, all of different sizes and shapes.

Which one had been Gunther, I didn't know, nor did it matter. Not any more.

Six werewolves, four bullets.

The problem was: I couldn't seem to focus long enough on the single flame. I needed a sense of peace around me. Some quiet. The ability to focus.

I could do none of that now as I held the girl's hand and pointed at the circling, hulking, massive creatures that could have just as easily been giant apes or Sasquatches.

For the first time in a long time, I knew I was in a bad situation. There was a chance I could outrun them, although I doubted that. There might even be a chance I could scale this sheer rock wall, or climb the massive gate. But I suspected the werewolves were faster than me.

All of those scenarios involved leaving Elise behind.

And I wasn't going to do that, not now.

I needed to focus to bring forth the single flame, and I couldn't. Not at this moment, and not with these creatures coming closer and closer. They were fearsome, even to me. Each standing well over seven feet tall, some as tall as eight feet. Their heads were huge, as big as a lion's. Their shoulders and arms were thick enough to drag a car behind them. Thick tufts of hair covered each, especially over their chests.

"What's happening?" the girl asked, and just as she asked it, another werewolf charged, one of the smaller ones. I fired and hit him in the neck, and still, he came. I fired again, and hit him just below the heart. Not a direct hit. I fired again and again, until I finally got the fucker in the heart.

He pitched forward, skidding on his face, and when he transformed back to human, I saw that it was Gunther.

Except now, I was out of bullets and we were out of time. To make matters worse, the remaining five werewolves charged at once.

———

They moved fast.

Faster than I could probably run, and certainly faster than I could pull Elise along. There was going to be blood, and it wasn't looking good for either of us.

I had just decided to target the werewolves' eyes—they might be immortal, but they needed to see—when I heard the familiar popping sound.

The man I knew to be Dracula—a man who wasn't really a man, but something else entirely, the first vampire, in fact—appeared before me, brandishing a silver dagger.

Before the closest werewolf could react, Vlad Tepes plunged the blade deep into its chest. As the werewolf pitched forward, Dracula disappeared again with a pop.

The remaining four werewolves appeared confused, although hard to tell through all the fur and the general rage in their eyes. They did, however, pause, and I used that chance to pull Elise away, deeper into the valley.

Behind me, I heard another pop, and turned in time to see Dracula appear behind another werewolf, and drive the silver dagger into its heart from behind.

As it dropped dead, Dracula disappeared again.

Three left, and one of them was gaining on us rapidly, its long stride covering the ground much faster than I could pull Elise along. So, I stopped and did the only rational thing a five-foot, three-inch mother of two would do.

I ran at it as fast as I could, my legs whooshing the air as I built up speed.

Somewhere behind me, I heard another pop as another werewolf howled and thudded to the ground, courtesy of Dracula's blade. Two were left, but I only saw the shaggy beast directly before me. I leaped off my feet, just as it did the same.

Chapter Forty-three

Its huge, fur-covered hand caught my fist in mid-strike.

Never had I encountered something so powerful...and this were-wolf wasn't even close to being as big as Kingsley was. Its grip was unreal, and its sheer force brought immediate tears to my eyes. It crushed down on my hand, and I felt the bones breaking. It lifted me off the ground and studied me curiously.

I whimpered through the pain and fought his grip to no avail. It brought me closer and I thought that it might look at me more closely, or even smell me, but its mouth opened instead. It was going to take the mother of all bites out of me.

His jaws came at me quickly, rushing at me—and I reverted back to my original plan.

I drove my two fingers deep into his eyes. Hell, I drove them all the way through his eyes and to the back of his skull. The creature howled in pain and tossed me to the side and as it dug its palms into its face, turning in circles, Dracula appeared before him...and drove his dagger deep into his chest. The creature dropped his hands, then dropped to his knees, and pitched forward. A moment later, it reverted back to a middle-aged man with love handles.

This time Vlad didn't disappear, and for good reason. The were-wolves were dead, as evidenced by the eight naked men with wounds to their chests. Apparently, Dracula had killed the last while I had been dangling like a fish on a line.

"Are you okay, Samantha Moon?" he asked.

"Yes," I said. "I think."

He wiped the blade in the tall grass, then sheathed it and came over to me, examining my hand. "Nothing that won't heal itself in a few hours. Did he bite you?"

"No, I don't think so."

"Good. Werewolf bites are nasty. They take months to heal, and leave a mark." He pushed up the sleeve of his blood-splattered bowling shirt. Numerous half-moon bite scars criss-crossed his flesh. Apparently, this wasn't Vlad's first rodeo.

We were silent, and I digested what I had just witnessed, had been a part of. Behind me, Elise wept quietly but steadily. The smell of blood was strong in the air. The demoness within me had broken out of my mental cell block, especially at the sight of the Count. I let her be, not wanting to deal with her for now.

She had not approved of the fight. I could tell that immediately. She had not approved of me saving the girl or taking on the were-wolves. She had been legitimately concerned for my safety, if only because she didn't want to lose such a valuable host.

Gee, thanks, I thought. *Now keep quiet.*

The blood did not appeal to me. It smelled…tainted somehow. Strange, undesirable.

Vlad must have seen me sniffing and wrinkling my nose. He shook his head. "Stay away from werewolf blood. Their blood, like ours, is mixed with alchemical magic. Some would say dark magic. It would do more harm than good."

Good to know, I thought. Which ruled out me sucking on Kingsley's neck any time soon.

"You killed them," I said.

"You killed them, too, Samantha."

"But I thought…I thought they were your, I dunno, allies."

"Low-level entities tend to favor werewolves, Sam."

"What does that mean?"

"It means, not all are as highly evolved as the entities within us. It means, some of these werewolves were barely journeymen in the dark arts. In fact, it's safe to say that any werewolf who prefers feed-ing from the living is not very evolved, and they are often a problem.

Your werewolf friend, on the other hand, is one of the oldest and most evolved of the lycans."

"He prefers to feed on the dead," I said.

"And so it is with others like him."

"Other evolved werewolves?"

"Right. But there is another reason why I came to your aid, Samantha Moon."

"Because you enjoy killing?"

"Perhaps. Or maybe I fancy you."

"Did Dracula just say he fancies me?"

"He did," said Vlad Tepes. "And now, apparently, he speaks in the third person."

For some reason, I laughed. I never knew Dracula would have a sense of humor...or be heroic. Although his heroism wasn't for altruistic reasons. There was a reason for his noble act...and it was because, well, he *fancied* me.

Unbelievable.

"And, of course, the entity within me more than fancies the entity within you. They were great lovers once, Samantha. They have been lost without each other, until now."

"Well, that's not my problem, and I know where you're going with this...and it's never going to happen. *Ever.*"

Dracula smiled and nodded once. "Nor would I push you to do something that you don't want to do. But perhaps, someday, I can convince you otherwise."

"Don't hold your breath," I said, although that took on a completely different meaning to creatures who didn't breathe.

The Impaler surveyed the surroundings and spied the weeping woman. "You did all of this to save her?"

"Yes."

"You would have died, Samantha Moon."

"Maybe," I said.

He shrugged once and looked again at the woman. I saw a brief flicker of hunger appear in his eyes.

"Don't even fucking think about it," I said.

503

"I would never take your spoils—"

"She's not my spoils. She's a living, breathing woman that I have every intention of returning safely to her husband."

"Very well, Samantha Moon. Then perhaps this is where I should leave you—"

"Wait!" I said.

He looked at me, tilting his head slightly. He waited.

I said, "How do you keep finding me?"

"Don't you know, Sam?"

"Know what?"

"The entity within me is deeply connected to the entity within you. I can always find you. Always. Just as you can always find me."

"So that was you," I said. "In the sky...the dragon."

He winked...and disappeared.

With a pop.

Chapter Forty-four

I wasn't sure this would work, but I tried it anyway. I figured if I could teleport—or apparate—with my clothes on and holding a weapon, I figured I could do the same with Elise.

So, I had her hold me tight around the wrist, then summoned the single flame, and finally envisioned the main highway into town, where there was a sign welcoming tourists. I envisioned the spot just behind the sign.

The pop came again...and it worked much better than I had hoped. When I opened my eyes again, Elise was still holding me tightly, and now we were standing in the shadows of the sign, just a few hundred feet from the town of Arrowhead.

Next, I slipped inside Elise's mind and removed all her memories of the night. I replaced them with a suggestion that she had been lost for the better part of this day. I told her to count to ten before opening her eyes again, and to head straight into town. I told her to give her marriage another chance and reminded her that her husband loved her deeply.

And then, I was out of her mind and, shortly, amazingly, I teleported myself back inside my minivan, in Gunther's driveway, not entirely sure I hadn't dreamed all of this.

I started the van and drove home.

———

I headed straight to my sister's and gathered up my kids.

I bought two Hot N' Ready pizzas at Little Caesar's on the way home. One for Anthony and one for Tammy and myself.

Once home, I told them they could watch whatever they wanted, just so long as we watched it together. They looked at me funny. Then again, they usually did.

Tammy's hangover was mostly gone, and if I ever thought the words "Tammy's hangover" again, I was going to cry.

In fact, I did cry. With my kids on either side of me, both munching on pizza and with the latest Teenage Mutant Ninja Turtles movie on Netflix, I cried quietly, holding both of their hands, and not releasing them.

Tammy looked at me at some point, obviously wondering what had gotten into her mother, then her eyes widened in horror at what she must have seen in my thoughts. I shook my head slightly and motioned toward the TV.

She set her pizza slice down and curled up next to me, holding my hand tightly.

We would deal with her drinking later. But we would deal with it with love. All the love I have…and then some.

The End

ABOUT THE AUTHOR

J.R. Rain is an ex-private investigator who now writes full-time in the Pacific Northwest. He lives in a small house on a small island with his small dog, Sadie, who has more energy than than the late Robin Williams. Please visit him www.jrrain.com.

CPSIA information can be obtained
at www.ICGtesting.com
Printed in the USA
BVHW032144190219
540702BV00001B/43/P

9 781512 043716